Wager
WITH A
SIREN

SOFIE DARLING

OLIVERHEBERBOOKS

The Race of the Century

The thrill! The pulse-pounding exhilaration!

Hark ye!

Attend, one and all! The most anticipated and electrifying Thoroughbred contest of this century -Nay, **of all time!**

Only and Exclusively this Season's Winners of The 2,000 Guineas, The 1,000 Guineas, The Oaks, The Derby, and The St. Leger shall vie for the prize of

£10,000

To Claim the Mantle of Greatest Champion

SATURDAY 21ST OF SEPTEMBER

IN THE YEAR OF OUR LORD 1822

EPSOM DOWNS

CHAPTER ONE

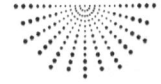

LONDON, MAY 1822

*T*attersall's on a Monday was a necessity for any gentleman of the turf with an eye toward maintaining his competitive edge.

Lord Julian Batchelor, Fifth Marquess of Ormonde was no exception—and as he stood nearly head and shoulders above the excitable fray, he had a view of it all.

Of course, it wasn't only gentlemen who filled the auction hall for the dispersal sale of the late Earl of Dutton's famed stable. Here was a gathering of military men, and there stood a gaggle of raucous lordlings. That man could've been a duke, and the man shoulder-to-shoulder with him a jockey. Of course, tulips, swells, and dandies abounded, too—men who knew not a jot about horseflesh, but followed the scent of a fashionable gathering like hounds to the hunt. And scattered throughout were the stable lads, grooms, and tidy helpers who served to shuttle the proceedings along, efficiently leading one horse in and another out as the auction moved forward.

From his place at the edge of the crowd, Julian noted the gray hunter, Belladonna, being led into the hall. With her strong walk and gentle demeanor, the bidding would be fierce for the two-year-old filly, but Julian held a slight edge over the others, for he possessed a power unmatched by any gentleman here.

He was liked by everyone—without exception.

He'd happened upon this power early—likely when he was still in leading strings, for he couldn't remember back to a time when he wasn't in possession of it. Perhaps it was to do with the clarity of his blue eyes or the boyish amiability of his smile, but people generally took one look at him and liked him.

As a result, people wanted to see him win. A prized horse could incite a riot of emotion. Duels had been fought. But when Julian prevailed and won the horse of his choosing—as he usually did—it wasn't held against him. In fact, people were usually only too happy for him.

"Now, gentlemen, here we have a special filly for your consideration," came the auctioneer's *rat-a-tat* voice.

All eyes landed on the gray hunter, and a buzz heightened the air. "A right beauty she is," said the young viscount to one side of Julian.

The young earl to his other side leaned forward. "Too bad you lost your Scottish estate in that card game last week and no longer need a hunter."

The viscount groused and grumbled and scuffed his feet against cobblestones, but didn't deny it. The loss of an estate during a night of gaming was a common affliction amongst a certain fast set of the *haut ton*, most of whom also shared a penchant for quality horseflesh.

"Can we start the bidding at one hundred pounds?" boomed the auctioneer.

A high opening bid, to be sure, but one that suited Julian as competitors would be few. He lifted a finger and made eye contact with the auctioneer. The man nodded and the bidding was off to a flying start as another three lords entered the fray, including the Duke of Richmond, a tough competitor both on and off the turf, as the bidding quickly flew up to £200.

Soon, it was only Julian and Richmond, the lively crowd quieting to a muted roar as a duke and a marquess battled it out, revealing the bottomless depths of their renowned coffers. *£300... £400...£500...* They weren't even bothering to meet the eye of the auctioneer, but only each other's as they drove up the price of the filly, both focused on victory—but each in a different manner.

Richmond revealed his intensity and determination in the scowl on his face and the tension of his shoulders.

Not Julian.

Though he held as much intensity and determination within him, his exterior revealed none of it. His eyes remained bright and open and his lopsided smile amiable.

The familiar light sheen of competitive sweat pinpricked his skin as the bidding raced up to £850. After a slight hesitation, Richmond chose not to lift his finger. Instead, he gave a shake of his head and lifted one corner of his mouth, which was as big of a smile as one was ever to get from the duke. Those gathered released their collective breath and sent up a buoyant cheer.

Such was the power of being well liked.

"A grand show, old chap," came a congratulation from Julian's left.

"Just a bit of luck," he demurred, modest as befitted a winner. No one liked a chap who flashed his win about.

Another lord sidled up to him. "Let me know when you want that filly covered. I have a stallion who wouldn't mind getting in there," he said with a wag of his eyebrows.

"Ah," said Julian, noncommittal. He had no intention of taking up that offer. He made informed and calculated decisions regarding breeding in his stables.

"Couldn't you have let Richmond take the win?" groused the young viscount.

"Why should I have done that?" asked Julian, though he had his suspicions.

A shuffle of sheepish feet. "It's just that Chudleigh and I had a little side wager going."

"And you bet Richmond would prevail," Julian finished for him without taking offense, his feet already on the move to arrange payment for his new filly and get on with his Monday.

For all his amiability and well-liked status, the truth was Julian didn't count any of these lords as friends. A friend was someone who knew not only his light self—his sun-kissed exterior the world saw and gravitated toward—but also the self that skulked within the murk of interior depths.

Julian's truer self.

The self only a select few knew.

"Ormonde," said a lord in passing.

"Billingsley," Julian returned, mildly, without a flinch, even as the fine hairs of his neck prickled to a stand.

Ormonde.

Julian's name to the world these last three years.

A name that wasn't supposed to have been his for another thirty.

Ormonde.

Each time the name was lightly tossed his way, two figures flashed through his mind in the split of the second it took to blink.

Clarissa...Father.

Her wasting death...his quick suicide.

Although those two events occurred twenty years apart, they were bound together.

And that left Julian as *Ormonde*—the marquessate he'd inherited upon Father's death.

Linked in life...linked in death...linked by blood...linked forever.

But in moments like this—when he was in public and getting on with his day—a flash was all it was. No one would've noticed the flicker that passed behind his eyes at the name—*his* name—*Ormonde*.

On Mondays, Tattersall's was only the first stop of his day. Now, he was off to White's Club, where he would peruse the betting books to see what wagers had been recorded this week. Lord Byron was always a popular subject. Once it had been speculation about his next mistress; now it was whether he would remain in Italy or return to England or go somewhere altogether different. One never knew with Byron.

But it was the sillier and more outlandish wagers that Julian enjoyed most. Once, on an ordinary rainy day, a lord had bet one hundred pounds as to which raindrop would reach the bottom of the club's famed bow window first. Over at Brooks's, Lord Cholmondeley bet Lord Derby £500 that he would one day tup a woman in a hot-air balloon one thousand yards up in the sky.

As yet, that wager was still outstanding.

Julian was just tucking into a light repast of tea, cold meats, a chunk of Stilton, and a dense slice of bread, when a matched pair of young bucks—upon reaching his thirtieth year, he'd stopped being able to tell them apart—lowered themselves into the leather armchairs opposite, their eyes bright with possibility.

"My lords," he said by way of greeting.

The bolder of the two shifted forward. "I say, Ormonde—"

Julian didn't flinch—as ever.

"—are you filling in the numbers at Almack's tomorrow evening?"

"I'll need to consult my diary," he said, crossing his fingers that it was full.

A bachelor marquess had certain responsibilities. That he frequent Tattersall's and gentlemen's clubs, even the occasional gaming hell. That he accept invitations to exclusive soirées and attend balls where he would dance with, at least, three young ladies. That he help fill out the numbers for supper parties.

Julian accepted these duties as part of the life of a gentleman.

Except he had a line—one he would never cross.

Those young ladies with whom he flirted at a ball or soirée... he never committed more than an evening's flirtation to them. His heart remained solely an organ useful for the pumping of blood through arteries—and his hand remained determinedly devoid of a wedding ring.

As he was thirty years old, it hadn't been remarked upon. A gentleman of thirty years yet had wild oats to sow. However, by the time he reached his thirty-fifth...fortieth...fiftieth years, the excuses would've become stale. Society would begin to view him askance and wonder what had gone amiss with the Marquess of Ormonde. Some with long memories might connect him with his utterly debauched wastrel of a father. But when they looked at Julian and saw the opposite sort of man, society wouldn't understand that Julian's debauched wastrel of a father, actually, had *everything* to do with it.

Or rather it was the blood of Julian's debauched wastrel of a father flowing through his veins.

Such tendencies ran in the blood, and Julian wouldn't carry it forward.

The family line stopped with him.

Now, the other lordling shifted forward. "Is it your Filthy Habit running the Derby in two weeks' time?"

Julian nodded. "He is."

"Same horse that took second place at the Two Thousand Guineas?" asked the first lordling.

"One and the same."

The two lordlings exchanged glances that set Julian's teeth on edge before the bolder of the two asked, "Was he injured recently?"

A groove dug into Julian's forehead. "No."

Julian didn't like the direction of this conversation. Racing ran rife with injuries to horses—be they accidental or deliberate. Did they know something he didn't yet?

"Why do you ask?" he asked, slowly.

"The odds for Filthy Habit are ten to one at the Derby."

Ten to one?

"You must've got the wrong horse."

The lordling shook his head. Too definite for Julian's liking. "That's what I thought at first," continued the increasingly irritating man, oblivious to the storm brewing inside Julian. "But, no, it's Filthy Habit."

"Where did you see these odds?"

"At the Subscription Room at Tattersall's today."

Blast. Julian knew he should've popped his head in before he left.

"But that's not where the lousy odds for Filthy Habit originated," chimed the other lordling.

"How do you mean?"

Most betting ran through the Ring at Tattersall's, as it was the Jockey Club's only chance of exercising a modicum of control over the corruption inherent in the sport of horse racing—not that they found much success.

"It started at The Archangel last week," chimed a third lordling, who had joined their group without Julian noticing. Truly, they were indistinguishable from one another.

"Since Gabriel Siren—"

"That'll be the recently minted Seventh Duke of Acaster to you," cut in a cheeky fourth lordling to a round of guffaws.

"Well, since Acaster became involved in the Race of the Century, The Archangel has been making odds on the season."

Annoyance struck through Julian, though his exterior air of affability remained solidly in place. He even laughed, as if it were no matter of importance—as was expected of him. Why should such trivialities concern the Marquess of Ormonde?

A fifth lordling laughed along with him. "So, you reckon Filthy Habit will take the Derby?"

Julian bit back the reflexive *yes* perched on the tip of his tongue. It was early in the racing season, but Filthy Habit was a goer. He would win—it wasn't a matter of *if*, but *when*—and the Derby was where Filthy Habit would claim his first. The Derby track was the perfect distance for the Thoroughbred to hit his stride.

But Julian didn't like to tempt Fate, so he gave a noncommittal shrug. "Let's see how the day goes."

Though it didn't matter in the general scheme that The Archangel was giving the Thoroughbred lousy odds, it was the principle.

Filthy Habit should have odds closer to two-to-one.

Lordling upon lordling continued to gather around, and the conversation moved along—but Julian didn't. In fact, an idea began to solidify into resolve within him. Tomorrow, he would pay a visit to The Archangel and have a chat with their oddsmaker.

He pulled a gold pocket watch from his waistcoat. *Half-past noon.*

He unfurled his long form and came to his feet. Time to leave for his next Monday appointment, if he was to make it by one o'clock. "Gentlemen," he said, "I must be getting on."

Within minutes, he was pulling his carriage door shut and relaxing back against leather squabs, taking in the city as it rolled past his window. He was on his way to a different side of London —the side well away from the prying eyes of the *ton*.

As a marquess, he had access to every bit of London's myriad offerings—from the highest echelons to the lowest dregs. Whatever tickled his fancy on any given day. Not that he was a capricious lord—but he could be if he chose, and that was rather the point.

If a man could relate himself to a city in an interior sense, he related to London thusly. There were the external trappings that everyone liked. Impressive squares, like St. James's and Grosvenor...parks, like Hyde and Regents...cathedrals, like Westminster and St. Paul's...For those in Julian's social set, that could be all London was, if they chose to leave the exterior façade undisturbed.

But another side of London lurked in the shadowy spaces just beyond—places of honest work, dishonest work, poverty, and vice. Places that, in fact, constituted the majority of London. Here, Julian related to the city at its core, for it reflected his own duality, as well. An exterior self—the one everyone gravitated toward—and an interior self...The larger part of him that if ever exposed to the light would send everyone fleeing in the opposite direction.

And so it was that his coachman knew to take him out of the pretty, ordered environs of Mayfair and across Town toward Cheapside, a respectable enough neighborhood with St. Paul's Cathedral looming in the near distance and the goldsmiths plying their wares, but not a place where anyone would expect to find the Marquess of Ormonde.

Which was why he'd chosen this area for his two Monday afternoon appointments.

The carriage rolled to a stop, and he jumped to the cobbles. "I can make my way for the rest of the day," he called up.

The coachmen nodded and flapped the reins to urge the horses on, having expected as much.

Surrounded by environs that had grown familiar over the last year, Julian entered Brewster's Boxing Salon, housed in a nondescript building with gray paint flaking off its moldings and steam clouding its few windows. It was the smell that always hit him first. *Sweat*, humid and ripe, and the specific aroma of male musk—the sort that came from exertion mixed with fear.

A year ago, after a dull afternoon spent politely humoring two ancient old lords, one Tory and the other Whig, as they battled it out over whose vision best suited the future of England, Julian accompanied a group of young bucks to Gentleman Jackson's boxing salon for a lark. Just to see what all the fuss was about.

9

Julian wasn't a violent man, so he'd never understood the sport's appeal.

Until he'd stepped into the ring with Gentleman Jackson himself and took a bare-knuckle punch to the face.

And he was hooked.

Since, Julian had been getting punched in the face once a week. Not at Gentleman Jackson's. He didn't like the idea of boxing at a fashionable salon, so he'd arranged with one Mr. Brewster to have his salon cleared out for one hour on Monday afternoons—for a pretty penny, of course.

But everything exacted a price, didn't it?

It was simply a question of how one chose to pay.

In Julian's experience, money was the simplest and cheapest form of payment man or universe could exact.

He made his way through a warren of narrowing dark corridors to a small room set aside for dressing. He stripped down to trousers, even removing his boots and socks. Then it was a barefoot walk down another corridor which opened into a large open room, a ring for boxing marked out in the center. Brewster stood in the middle, his meaty hands clenching and unclenching in anticipation of the bout to come. "Ready?"

Julian gave a curt nod. "Aye."

That was the full extent of their greetings. In the ring, Julian didn't have to be amiable or liked. In fact, it was better to be neither, for boxing stripped a man down to elemental parts. The mind and all its busyness could slip away for this blessed hour in the ring—his favorite hour of the week.

The hour that offered him oblivion and relief.

He held up his hands and went light on his feet in a side-to-side hopping shuffle, as Brewster had taught him. The men came within punching distance but didn't start brawling straight away. Instead, Julian delivered light jabs to work the muscles and get them ready for the bout to come. This went on for about ten minutes, long enough to get the blood pumping and the anticipation building. An elemental stirring began to take over, where he became one with his body in a way he never experienced outside the ring.

"Let's go," said Brewster.

Julian circled his head around, cracked his knuckles, and nodded.

And so it began—two men locked in battle, each intent on pounding the daylights out of the other. If his lordly peers saw him now, they would place bets and cheer him on, but also, they would wonder about the Marquess of Ormonde. His focus and intensity...his *drive*. For when Julian was in the ring, gone was the marquess they knew.

After their first few bouts, Brewster called Julian a natural boxer, and he couldn't help feeling the truth of those words. He didn't mind getting punched in the face or meting out the same to a skilled opponent. The rules were clear. Besides, Julian was a sizeable man. He could take the punishment. Brewster, too, was a big man, so Julian felt no qualms about giving it.

But this hour in the ring was more than punishment.

It was a cleansing.

In boxing, there were the big, showy hooks to the face—the ones that produced bloodied noses and cracked jaws. But there were others, too. The jabs delivered to the body. One had to move close to dispatch them—the relentless ones that wore an opponent down. The ones that made him vulnerable to those big, showy blows.

For that was the thing about boxing, it was almost like chess. One had to think three moves ahead and march with bold intent into the plan. Sometimes it worked; others it didn't. But once one committed, one didn't back down.

And yet...

No matter how he tried every Monday, the impurities running through his blood wouldn't be pounded out.

*Debauchery...vice...morosity...*They yet flowed through him—and ever would.

He understood this at a cellular level.

But during the Monday bouts and for a few sweet hours afterward, he experienced the absence of those impurities, for—*blessedly*—he felt nothing at all.

Only one other act made him feel so—his next Monday appointment.

The hour flown by, Brewster lowered fists that had delivered quite the pummeling this afternoon. Perhaps he, too, needed to exorcise some demons of his own. Julian's jaw would be smarting for a few days.

"Until next Monday?" asked Brewster, unwinding linen wraps from his hands.

"Aye," Julian tossed over his shoulder, his feet already on the move.

And there was the extent of their interaction, aside from the pouch of coin Julian never failed to leave in the dressing room.

Now, he was off to his next Monday afternoon appointment, only a few streets over. After he'd taken up boxing at Brewster's, he'd purchased the townhouse for its walking-distance proximity to the salon.

He turned off Cheapside Street and onto Basing Lane, then again at Little Thomas Street, to a nondescript black door. He turned his key in the lock and turned it again once inside. In the second-floor bathing room, he found the tub already filled with steaming hot water.

For the second time today, he undressed. But now to the skin —and with more deliberation, his body bruised, but more alive than it would feel until next Monday's pummeling. Before lowering into the tub, he knotted his unfashionably long hair on top of his head. Then, gradually, he slipped into the water, relaxing his head back, eyes closed, heat penetrating through skin to muscle and on to bone, his mind still blessedly blank.

The water had begun to cool when he heard the downstairs door open on quiet hinges and click shut. Soft footsteps crept up the stairs and turned directly into the bedroom.

Careful not to anger bruised muscles, Julian shifted forward in the tub. The time had arrived for this second Monday afternoon appointment.

He stood and toweled himself dry before shrugging on a dressing robe. Feet bare, he padded into the next room. On the bed, she sat, fully dressed, awaiting instructions.

With a simple nod of greeting, he stopped before a locked cabinet, key in hand. There were many such locked cabinets in his life. He opened the door, and a quick scan revealed the small mahogany box he sought.

He turned to find her watching him, her bottom lip between her teeth, a saucy light in her brown eyes. "Do you have a new toy for me today, my lord?" she asked.

Julian opened the box and pulled a long, cylindrical object from its blue velvet seat. "I thought we would revisit an old favorite."

Her eyes went dark with anticipation and no small amount of desire.

Debauched blood running riot through his veins, he said, "Undress."

Who was he to think he could ever escape it?

CHAPTER TWO

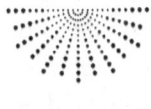

NEXT DAY

*J*ulian had awakened at seven o'clock in the morning with the single-minded intention that The Archangel would be his first stop of the day.

The more he thought about the odds on Filthy Habit, the more he was bothered.

Why were the odds so poor?

Filthy Habit was an elite Thoroughbred who had placed second in the Two Thousand Guineas. Not some sway-backed nag slogging through Wednesday afternoon races in Yorkshire.

However, The Archangel was a gaming hell. It wouldn't be open at seven in the morning—or seven in the evening, for that matter. The business of a hell was conducted in the deep indigo of night until dawn's first rays straggled into the sky to announce the arrival of day.

So, he'd taken his new hunter Belladonna for a ride in Hyde Park so they could become acquainted before he had her walked to his family seat and racing estate in Suffolk—Nonsuch Castle.

Which was how Julian found himself entering the unhallowed walls of The Archangel at two in the morning.

As gaming hells went, The Archangel was a sophisticated one. Its exterior plain and tastefully in keeping with the row of Mayfair townhouses to either side. In striking contrast, rich woods from exotic locales and sparkling crystal chandeliers imbued the interior with a lavish, comfortable opulence. One could almost forget this was a gaming hell at all—if not for all the gaming tables and half-foxed lords shambling about.

But the gaming tables couldn't be denied—neither could the aristocrats gathered for a spin of the Roulette wheel or a toss of the Hazard dice. Lords congregated with the communal intent of making merry. After all, they'd paid their dues the prior evening by attending musicales featuring tone-deaf sisters or supper parties thrown by one's in-laws who'd always harbored the not-so-secret belief that their only daughter could've married a duke, if she'd only set her mind to it.

With the time gone well past midnight, the wives lay tucked away in bed for the night.

The night was for the husbands.

They'd earned it.

However, if one peered more closely at those aristocratic faces, it wasn't joy or genuine delight one found behind their smiles, but rather a hollowness—even desperation. Those lords assembled around gaming tables weren't men making merry. They were men wretchedly attempting to stave off the soul-crushing boredom of their lives, because no one had ever taught them how to create a point to their existence...how to find a meaning in life.

To ask, *what was it all for?*

And strive to find an answer.

Nay.

It was better to pass out dead-drunk than to lie in bed awake, stone-sober, alone with such wonderings.

Julian stopped himself there.

He wasn't here to muse about the meaning of life—that was for his own stone-sober self in the dark dead of night.

He was here to talk about a horse.

A topic less fraught with the question of one's own existence, to be sure.

As he made his way through The Archangel, greeting one and all as he went, it was the same faces as ever, whether at Tattersall's, White's, or Newmarket on race day.

Always the same faces.

'Twas a small, predictable world occupied by the *ton*.

He appreciated the predictable part—after all, hadn't humans been trying to create certainty in the world since the beginning of time?—but the small part could grow dull.

As he cut across the central aisle separating the Hazard from the Roulette tables, he kept an eye out for The Archangel's owner, Gabriel Siren.

Except the man wasn't Gabriel Siren anymore. He was the lost Seventh Duke of Acaster, recently found. The news had spread through society like wildfire.

Julian stepped into the card room. A quick scan revealed no Siren there, either. He found a quiet corner, propped a shoulder against the wall, and waited. A few minutes later, a server appeared with a silver tray bearing a tumbler of whiskey.

"From the Earl of Clifton," intoned the man.

Julian lifted the tumbler off the tray and smiled at the earl, who toasted him silently from across the room. Julian brought the whiskey to his mouth...

And didn't drink.

As ever, he only gave the appearance.

With what ran below his surface—the propensities and proclivities bred into him—he knew that if he stumbled a little and fell, it wouldn't be a small tumble.

It would be a complete and total dive into the sea of iniquity.

No half measures for the Marquesses of Ormonde.

Sure, he'd be able to hold his head above water, just as his father had. But one could only tread water for so many days... months...years.

The sea would eventually claim its due.

As it had done with his father.

He should vacate The Archangel and leave the matter of Filthy Habit's odds be. So his racehorse wasn't getting the respect he deserved off the course. What did it matter? Filthy Habit would hit his stride at the Derby.

He should simply sit back and let it happen.

But the principle of the matter had him between its teeth.

He couldn't let it go.

A woman entered the card room—*strode* through.

Julian knew her—knew *of* her, more accurately, for they'd never crossed paths. She was the only woman allowed within the masculine confines of The Archangel.

Tessa Siren.

Nay.

Lady Tessa Calthorp—sister of the recently elevated Seventh Duke of Acaster.

Of course, Julian had taken note of her on the odd night he'd visited, even if all she ever offered of her presence was a flash. Lady Tessa was not only a woman on the move, but a decidedly unconventional one, if her mode of dress offered a clue to her inner workings.

The bottom half of her was standard enough with its modest black bombazine skirt. But it was the top half that arrested the eye and surely made more than a few brows, both masculine and feminine, crinkle with bemusement. She wore a white linen shirt, white silk cravat, and lilac watered-silk waistcoat that would strike a chord of envy through the heart of the *ton's* most discriminating dandy.

But the woman—*Lady*—herself didn't exude a fussy air.

Rather, she kept her head down and eyes averted, discreetly and efficiently dashing from card table to card table to confer quietly with the dealers. She listened and nodded, all the while writing notes in the small book she carried with her. Then it was on to the next dealer, a quick conference, and she was gone from the room, her presence hardly noted.

But Julian was left with a furrow trenched into his brow.

Lady Tessa was a beauty—a fact the strawberry-blonde hair tightly knotted at the base of her neck and stern, mannish mode of dress couldn't obscure. In fact, all it did was incite various wonderings in the male mind: How far down her back would those strawberry-blonde tresses fall, unbound? What curves hid beneath layers of mannish clothes?

Wonderings she likely thought she was preventing, rather than provoking.

Oh, how little the feminine mind understood of the masculine.

Julian tucked those wonderings away. He didn't allow himself such wonderings about women in general—and ladies in particular. A discreet, well-chosen mistress on Monday and Thursday afternoons was where he focused such energies, a solution to his nature that provided the needed outlet and served him well.

Right.

Best he find Acaster, sort out the odds for Filthy Habit, and see his way out of The Archangel.

And leave all wonderings regarding the provoking Lady Tessa within these four walls.

* * *

TESSA HAD HAD BETTER NIGHTS.

In life, in the general sense—and at The Archangel, more specifically.

Take the bellicose aristocrat currently staring her down.

Well, he would be staring her down if it weren't for her height.

Anyway, his eyes were flashing with the *utter and complete indignity*—his words—of having a woman—*a woman!*—handle a problem of masculine honor for him.

"I would speak with the duke," he demanded, frigidly.

The duke.

Improbably, her brother.

Oh, she'd known Gabriel was her brother all her life.

It was the duke part that had come as a surprise.

A week ago, they'd been informed that the late Sixth Duke of Acaster had not only been their long-lost, paternal great-uncle, but had also died without legitimate issue, leaving Gabriel—*unbelievably*—the Seventh Duke of Acaster.

Which, equally improbably and unbelievably, made her *Lady* Tessa Calthorp...No longer Miss Tessa Siren.

Her...a lady.

Life never had proceeded in a straight line for her and her siblings, but that twist couldn't have been anticipated.

Tessa waited, and, at last, the lord heaved a long-suffering sigh. He would have to settle for her...*a woman*. "Five markers are missing," he repeated, as if she hadn't heard him the first time. "That's five hundred pounds."

Tessa shook her head. Here, she stood on firm ground. "Only in the context of this game."

Her logic found no purchase, for the lord repeated, *"Five hundred pounds."*

Apparently, she wasn't only a woman, but a simpleton, too.

She tried again. "But only because that's the value assigned the markers in *this* game. You could move to another game at another table, and the markers could be worth five pounds."

"But they're *my* markers."

Tessa understood this man was an aristocrat...a lord...the

core of The Archangel's business...But, oh, how she longed to call him a dull-witted dunderhead.

A temptation she would resist, of course, but, oh, how it cost her a bit of her soul to keep that truth inside. Still..."If you would care to clarify for my simple woman's mind, exactly what reason would our card dealer possibly have to steal your markers?" She really, truly tried to keep the sarcasm from her voice.

Really, truly, she did.

And no doubt failed.

"Well...well...," blustered the lord, growing increasingly red-faced. "They're mother-of-pearl."

Tessa saw no way out of this without a concession. "Of course, it would be The Archangel's pleasure to provide you with a new set of markers."

A canny light entered the lord's eyes. "They're one of a kind."

One of a kind, Tessa's sweet arse..."Then we shall find another one-of-a-kind set of markers—"

With a greasy, smug expression on his face, the lord lifted his tumbler of whiskey and stopped the words in Tessa's mouth. There, where the tumbler rested only seconds ago, lay the five markers. Unbeknownst to him, he'd been using them as a coaster. His eyes lifted and met hers.

She wouldn't gloat...she wouldn't gloat...

"I take it this business has reached a satisfactory conclusion?" she said in a voice well-versed in keeping clear of all emotion.

If the lord felt at all chastened, he didn't show it. Instead, he grunted and tossed two markers into the pot for the new hand just starting.

Tessa turned on her heel. Oh, the vicissitudes of the life of a gaming hell owner—if only she could call such dealings a rarity.

Dull-witted dunderheads abounded in this world, that was a fact.

As she neared the staircase to head to the second-floor gallery, Monsieur Ricard, The Archangel's doorman and general man-about-the-club, met her at the foot of the stairs. "A lord wants to speak with you."

"I just finished with him."

A wry smile formed at the corner of Ricard's mouth. "A different lord."

Tessa sighed. "They're all lords, aren't they?"

Ricard nodded. "They are."

"Which one, then?"

"The Marquess of Ormonde."

Tessa's eyebrows lifted. "Not just any lord, but a marquess. And he wishes to speak with *me*?"

Of course, she'd noted the marquess on a few occasions. She made it a point to connect the faces with the names of all their patrons. She'd even noticed him in the card room tonight. With his height and breadth and general air of golden-lord-of-the-*ton*, he was a hard man to miss.

"Actually, he asked to speak with the duke."

Of course.

Which was how Tessa preferred it.

"Did you tell him Gabriel will be gone for the next few days tending…"

She was stumped. What was it dukes did, anyway? She'd only ever seen them toss Hazard dice or play lousy hands of Macao.

"I did," said Ricard. "Then he asked to see our oddsmaker."

"Is that so?" Tessa's curiosity couldn't help perking to life—and that was her mind made up. "I'll deal with him."

Relief shone in Ricard's eyes. One—even one built as solid as a medieval castle wall, like Ricard—wouldn't be keen to tell a marquess to go about his business.

"Is he still in the card room?"

Ricard nodded, and that was Tessa off to talk sense into yet another dunderheaded lord tonight. Was it a full moon?

Oddsmaker.

The word piqued Tessa's interest.

Whatever business the Marquess of Ormonde had with The Archangel, it would be related to the horses. She knew it in her bones, even as she slightly resented it.

It was Gabriel who had gotten them mixed up in horse racing and now the Race of the Century business. For her part, she'd advised against entangling The Archangel with anything related to horse racing. But he'd insisted it was a safe investment. A *diversity of interests* was how he liked to put it.

A bloomin' headache was how she liked to put it.

With its corruption and general danger, best to leave the Sport of Kings to others.

Tessa entered the card room—or rather sidled into it, head down, eyes casting about to ensure all was well. She never stepped into a room in a manner that made her an object of attention. She was here for business. That was all.

Well, now, she was here for the Marquess of Ormonde.

And there he was, propped against the same wall where she'd last seen him a quarter of an hour ago. The man was impossible to miss. At a glance, she'd known him to be tall and, well, massive. But now that she was actually looking at him straight on, he was even more so *everything* in all areas. *More tall...more massive...more handsome...*His long sun-streaked hair tucked behind his ears. His smile *more*, too. He had the sort of smile that likely made every recipient of it feel that all was right with the world if such a man was smiling at them—even if he did have the look of a Viking, for ancient Dane blood surely flowed through his veins.

His gaze shifted, and their eyes met—and held.

His eyes...the open blue of a summer afternoon sky...

It was only when Tessa's step faltered that she realized she'd forgotten to release her breath. His head cocked subtly, and his amiable expression shifted into one inscrutable.

And she understood why.

He was trying to read her just as she was trying to read him.

Then her sense of purpose returned, and she jutted her chin, indicating he follow her into the study. It was The Archangel's quietest room with several groupings of overstuffed leather armchairs where lords could sit and peruse the paper or converse in private groups.

Tessa took a seat in one such armchair and Ormonde lowered himself into the chair opposite.

"How may I help you, Lord Ormonde?" she asked, her demeanor all brusque impatience.

His amiable smile didn't falter. "I'm here to speak with The Archangel's oddsmaker."

Tessa spread her hands wide. She and Gabriel didn't advertise the fact, but they were equal partners. "Again, how may I help you?"

A bemused line formed between Ormonde's eyebrows. "*You* are going to help me?"

Tessa decided she would take no insult. Men simply never saw her coming. "Perhaps. Once you state your purpose."

Actually, in truth, she was irritated. She had a night to get on with.

The marquess shifted in his chair and crossed an ankle over a thigh. A rather *thick* thigh, one couldn't help noticing. "The Archangel keeps giving my Thoroughbred Filthy Habit poor odds, which is influencing the other legs to give him poor odds."

This was about the odds on a horse? Spoiled lords and their horses...

Truly.

"If you're a betting man, Lord Ormonde," she began, determined to be diplomatic, "that would only work in your favor if he wins."

"I don't gamble."

The statement emerged with such finality that Tessa felt her brow furrow. What was the point of racing horses if one didn't gamble? Wasn't that the *entire* point of it? She supposed, in theory, some were in it purely for the sport. But she'd only encountered that possibility in theory—not in practice.

"It's the principle," he continued.

"*Principle?*" This marquess kept following one confounding statement with another. "I wasn't aware principle played a role in horse racing."

Her words almost returned his smile to its place. *Almost.* He was still trying to work her out. "Filthy Habit is going to win this season."

"Is that so?"

"What are you basing your doubts on? The Archangel didn't start bookmaking until this season."

"A valid point," she conceded. "But I'm not one to commit to an enterprise blindly. I did my research, and—" Oh, he wasn't going to like the next words out of her mouth. "I'm basing my doubts on *you.*" Into the stunned silence that followed, she added, "My lord."

Ormonde's eyebrows looked as if they might fly off his forehead, even as his summer-blue eyes went thunderous. "*Me?* You and I have never met."

Tessa suppressed the sigh that wanted release. "When my brother decided to take on this Race of the Century enterprise"—she almost said *nonsense*—"I studied the racing calendars from the last five years."

"Industrious of you."

Was he patronizing her?

She couldn't abide patronizing men. Except in this case, it only made it easier to say…"And I noticed some patterns."

"Which were?"

"Of the winning stables and the losing stables."

He didn't blink. "My stables don't lose."

"But they don't win, either, do they?" She settled back in her chair and shrugged. "They place or show, but *never* win."

The evidence was indisputable.

The marquess went still, a stunned air of incredulity radiating about him.

A petty part of her wanted to dig in a bit more—to tweak the nose of this golden lord. "You are content not to win," she said with the vocal equivalent of a shrug.

"I'm not out there running on two feet, you know. It's the horses."

"But *you* are the owner."

"Indisputable fact."

"It's down to you to put the fire in the belly. But you don't seem to have that."

She was all but calling him an insipid lord.

Objectively, this was no way to be speaking to a peer of the realm. She might've been getting carried away.

"You don't know me or anything about me."

She shook her head. "There, you're wrong. It's all laid out on the turf and writ in the racing calendars, plain as day. You're complacent, Lord Ormonde. So, your bosom friend Rakesley wins all, and Ormonde takes second or third. Complacency doesn't win races."

Again, she shrugged. His jaw clenched and released, irritation clear. Fortunately, as a woman who had been operating a gaming hell these last few years, she was accustomed to spoiled, irritated lords who hadn't gotten their way.

"Will that be all?" she asked.

The loudest silence she'd ever heard expanded between them.

"I have one of the best stables in England."

"Scotland, Ireland, and Wales, too, undoubtedly."

Oh, she was piling it on, wasn't she?

And she must stop.

She wasn't a cruel person. She was simply annoyed with spoiled lords presently and this spoiled lord was bearing the brunt of all that irritation.

Which wasn't quite fair.

As she stood, her gaze caught on a shadow on his jaw.

Except it wasn't a shadow..."Is that a bruise?" she asked without thinking.

A trace of opaque emotion passed behind his eyes. He settled back into his chair and closed in on himself.

Tessa suddenly felt conscious of herself in a way she never had in all her five and twenty years.

"If that will be all, Lady Tessa," rumbled from the depths of his chest.

He didn't stand.

And he should have—as a gentleman.

The fact only just registered in Tessa's mind.

She'd been dismissed.

Somehow, a shift of power had occurred—and she hadn't the faintest idea how he'd done it.

Behind his summer-blue eyes and lopsided smile, this spoiled, golden lord of the *ton* contained hidden depths...*calculation*.

Equal parts intrigued and annoyed, she pivoted and strode from the room.

Just as she began to ascend the staircase to make her way to the second-floor office, Ricard, again, intercepted her. "Can we have a private word?"

Oh, what now?

Still, whatever Ricard had to say would provide a welcome respite from her desire to stew and mull over her puzzling interaction with the Marquess of Ormonde.

She didn't like that he contained hidden depths—and had a bone to pick with her.

She'd only taken a few steps before she stopped and turned to Ricard, who, though two steps below her, was nearly at eye level. "Let's shorten the odds on Ormonde's Filthy Habit to five-to-one." She hesitated. "Make that three-to-one."

Perhaps that would appease the man.

Ricard nodded. "Wise move."

It wasn't wisdom guiding the move, but rather a feeling whirling through her gut like a dervish. That fire she'd said the marquess lacked…Well, she wasn't so sure she hadn't seen a spark of it a few minutes ago.

And the thing about sparks was all it took was a single gust of wind to light it into a roaring conflagration.

A result best avoided with the Marquess of Ormonde, to be sure.

Upstairs, she opened the office door and let Ricard enter before closing the door behind them. Strictly speaking, she was a lady now, and it wasn't proper for her to be alone in a room with a man. But others had foisted that title upon her, and she had absolutely no intention of leading the life of a lady.

She'd rather deal with spoiled aristocrats as a gaming hell owner than as a lady any day of the week.

She propped a hip onto the solid oak desk and crossed her arms over her chest. "What warrants a private word?"

"Jagger paid us a visit."

A different sort of tension entered Tessa's body. "When?"

"While you were engaged with Lord Ormonde."

Blaze Jagger.

This was Gabriel's doing.

When he'd involved them in the Race of the Century, he'd insisted they cut the Ring and its blacklegs out of the betting post on race day.

Which wasn't going down well—at all.

Tessa had known it was only a matter of time before blacklegs began stirring trouble. Blaze Jagger was a young upstart on the rise in London's underworld dealings, his fingers in multiple enterprises of the criminal variety. He had a reputation to prove and build.

Tessa understood there were few people more dangerous in this world than young men with something to prove—and nothing to lose.

Now, he'd made the first move, and they would have to deal with the rogue.

More accurately, *she* would have to deal with him. Gabriel was now all tangled up in this duke business. It would be down to her to solve this.

"And his purpose here?"

"He asked to join the club."

Tessa let that unexpected morsel of information settle for a long moment. *"Join* The Archangel?" She needed to be clear.

"I sent him packing."

A bad idea—a *very* bad idea. Tessa could feel it in her bones. "If he comes back, let him join."

Ricard cocked an ear, as if he couldn't have heard her correctly. "Pardon?"

"You heard me."

"He will lower The Archangel's reputation."

"Sometimes, it's best to keep one's enemies close."

Ricard snorted and shook his head. "As you please."

Tessa knew Jagger wouldn't return.

Well, that wasn't precisely true.

He would return.

But next time, he wouldn't be asking politely. He had something to prove on the London streets. With The Archangel cutting him out of the betting post for the Race of the Century, they were endangering both his money and his reputation. His rivals would be watching to see if he let it stand.

How easily this could turn into a turf war.

She hoped there was time yet to avoid it.

* * *

As THE SUN began transforming the horizon from gray to gold, Tessa crept across the threshold of the Knightsbridge townhouse she shared with her three siblings—Gabriel, Saskia, and Viveca—careful to keep quiet and not disturb their sleep.

Though for not much longer, she suspected.

It was this duke nonsense that had been thrust upon them. Gabriel would, of course, take up residence at some dukely residence, and since by the letter of the law he was Saskia and Viveca's guardian, they would surely follow.

But not Tessa.

That wasn't her life—or the life she wanted to lead.

But she saw the wisdom in Saskia and Viveca joining Gabriel and becoming ladies, for they led entirely different lives from hers and Gabriel's—which was very much by design. They had absolutely no involvement with The Archangel. Even if the Archangel was London's most exclusive gaming hell that catered only to aristocrats, it was still a gaming hell—a den of iniquity and vice…an institution of London's underworld.

Tessa was under no illusions about that.

Saskia and Viveca were intelligent and innocent and they would have the best of whatever sort of lives they chose. Tessa was determined it would be so.

Which was what nagged at her about this Race of the Century and Blaze Jagger business. By dabbling in horse racing, Gabriel was only looking at pennies and pounds and disregarding the larger picture, which revealed the world of horse racing to be a dicey proposition full of dangerous characters.

And Gabriel had centered them dead in the sights of one of London's most notorious blacklegs.

It couldn't stand.

If Jagger came after The Archangel, Tessa would handle it.

Saskia and Viveca would be protected.

Tessa crawled into bed, dawn fully risen.

Not that she would know it.

The first change she'd made when they'd moved into the

Sloane Street townhouse was to have all her bedroom windows fitted with special interior shutters that blocked the daylight.

As exhausted eyes drifted shut, her last waking thought, however, wasn't of family or criminals.

But of a spoiled lord with summer-blue eyes.

A lord who wasn't quite who he presented himself to be.

A lord who might intrigue her.

Irritating, that.

CHAPTER THREE

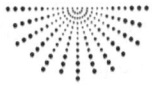

A WEEK LATER

*T*essa stepped out of Fortnum & Mason and onto Piccadilly cobbles, a ridiculous sense of triumph coursing through her.

She'd managed to procure the last two pounds of jasmine tea that would grace the town of London for three months, at least, depending on shipping schedules from the Far East.

*Tea...*her one indulgence in life.

She adored the stuff. The way it made one sit down for the time it took to drink a cup or pot, depending on her mood. Otherwise, she didn't stop in her day. It was all *go...go...go...*one quick decision to be made after another.

Tea forced one to sit and consider—and enjoy.

And this London day was a rare lovely one—the cloudless sky above, the air sun-warmed, yet crisp. Even so, one was hard pressed to enjoy the pleasant day as Piccadilly was one of London's busiest thoroughfares with all manner of folk. Impatient Londoners who kept their heads down as they trudged from one errand to the next. Folks traveling through, their heads up as they attempted to gather a sense of their surroundings and pick a direction. And that was only those on foot. Horse carts trundled along, pulling all manner of loads from chickens to potatoes, even dirt...Hackney coaches with their fares...The odd dandy in his cabriolet, broad smile on his face, not a care in the world.

Tessa tended to duck her head down and keep her reticule tight against her body to ward off pickpockets, as she kept her feet moving.

Today, however, just before she did so, she spotted something unusual up the block—a familiar form. A male form that she wouldn't have given a second glance a week ago, but now caused her gaze to stick—tall and broad, golden-brown hair tucked behind his ears and falling in loose waves below his shoulders.

A man who'd tipped his hat to no fewer than three other gentlemen in the ten seconds Tessa had spent observing him.

The Marquess of Ormonde.

After their encounter a week ago, she'd mostly put the man out of her mind. A spoiled aristocrat who didn't like not getting what he wanted was no concern of hers.

Even so, she couldn't deny that a small part of her reveled in having thwarted the man. Lords should be thwarted every so often. A good thwarting was medicine for the soul, and she was only too pleased to have delivered it.

She snorted.

Aristocrats.

Except he hadn't been the only aristocrat involved in that conversation.

Apparently, she was one, too.

Though it had been two weeks since the news was delivered, it still hadn't entirely sunk in and found purchase within her.

Lady Tessa.

The great-granddaughter of one duke and the sister of another.

Still, a feeling of unease regarding the Marquess of Ormonde crept through her. She'd insulted the man—to his face.

Simply, there was something about him—this golden lord of

the *ton*—and something in her that wanted to test him and see if there was a chink in his armor.

For that was what she'd detected behind his amiable eyes.

Armor.

One only needed armor if one was guarding something precious or...secret.

What was the Marquess of Ormonde's secret?

Ahead, he cut a quick right onto a quiet side street, and Tessa was left with a decision to make—continue along Piccadilly and on toward home, which was where she'd been heading with her choice batch of tea. Or...

Make a left onto Sackville Street.

Which she shouldn't do.

But a few seconds later, that was exactly where her feet found themselves pointing.

Then she had barely an instant to locate Ormonde before he slipped into a shop. Instinctively, she crossed to the other side of the street to minimize the chance of running into him. He could've been paying a quick visit. After all, she knew nothing about his daily life or the sort of business he conducted in the course of a day.

She knew nothing about *him*.

And yet...here she was, following him.

As she passed the shop from across the street, she cut a glance over and read the discreet sign.

Blanton & Co.

A jewelry shop.

She reached the end of Sackville Street with another decision to make. She should walk on to the next street over and make her way back to Piccadilly. But wouldn't it be much simpler to double back?

And, really, why shouldn't she cross the street to get a better look into the shop? She was a lady, and it was no uncommon occurrence for ladies to peer through windows when pretty baubles were on display. No one would question her presence or her interest.

When she reached the shop, however, the glare from the midday sun made it impossible to see inside. Perhaps a proper lady wouldn't cup her hand onto a windowpane and press the tip of her nose to the glass to peer into a shop—but Tessa was only a lady come-lately.

Her inspection revealed several cases placed about the shop and a single occupant. A woman of middling years...who was observing Tessa with curiosity.

No sign of Ormonde.

Without a staying thought, Tessa reached for the door handle. The door didn't budge, which only made sense. Jewelry stores didn't leave their doors unlocked for all and sundry to stride through and steal their wares.

From the other side of the glass, the proprietress inspected Tessa for thirty additional seconds before she moved. She must've deemed the unusual lady worthy of entry, for she took the key hanging from a long chain around her neck and turned in it in the lock. The bell jingled lightly overhead as Tessa crossed the threshold.

"How may I be of assistance to you, Miss...?" asked the proprietress leadingly.

Tessa opened her mouth to reply with her usual *Miss Siren*.

Except...She was no longer Miss Siren.

She was now Lady Tessa.

Further, she quickly surmised that being Lady Tessa in this fine jewelry shop would get her farther than being a mere *Miss*.

"*Lady* Tessa Calthorp," she said with an abundance of confidence used only by those bent on absolute virtue or absolute vice.

The proprietress's smile broadened, and Tessa could see she'd been wise to wield her title. What use was it, anyway, if not to be applied as a crowbar to prise open all the places one wished to enter?

Come to think of it, a title could be bloody useful.

The key turned in the lock behind Tessa as she gave the shop a quick scan, confirming no sign of the marquess. If he was here, he would be obvious. There was no hiding the Marquess of Ormonde.

The metaphor of the ox in the china shop came to mind.

The proprietress smiled at Tessa. She was waiting.

Right.

Tessa drew herself up to her fullest height, which was several inches taller than the other woman. "I would like to see your, *erm*, jewels."

Jewels?

Was she now the Queen of England?

"And what sort of jewels would suit you, Lady Tessa?" asked the proprietress, moving behind a case with a glass top, waving her hand to indicate a few said jewels.

Would she have to buy some jewels before this was all over? And all because she'd let her curiosity get the better of her and followed a marquess into a jewelry shop?

She supposed it would serve her right.

"Perhaps," began the proprietress, her gaze doing a slow up-and-down appraisal of Tessa's person, "a signet ring?"

Tessa could see why the woman would suggest that piece of jewelry. Not every woman—or, indeed, *lady*—strode about London wearing cravat and waistcoat with her skirts. In fact, she only considered it a shame that she couldn't wear trousers, too, for they called to her innate sense of practicality.

But, alas, trousers would've been a step too far beyond society's narrow view of appropriateness for ladies.

"Oh, yes," she began, only noticing a narrow doorway in the opposite corner of the shop. Perhaps Ormonde had somehow squeezed his broad shoulders through...

The proprietress's eyes lit with delight. "Oh, those are my favorite."

Tessa glanced down and found that her finger was pointing...

Toward a necklace of pink pearls.

The proprietress opened the case and slid the pearls off black velvet, the strand long and sinuous, each perfectly round orb glowing with iridescence. "They're so lovely and feminine, aren't they?" she asked, a dreamy quality had entered the woman's voice.

"*Erm*, yes," said Tessa, unable to pretend much interest—*what had a strand of pearls to do with her, anyway?*—as she leaned back and craned her head around for a glimpse down that corridor. "Do you have another room in your shop?"

The proprietress glanced up, sharply. "Why do you ask?"

Tessa's brow wanted to lift with curiosity. The question had been a simple one—and the expected answer equally simple: *yes* or *no*.

Was the proprietress protecting something...? Or...someone?

Perhaps the man who had slipped into this shop not five minutes ago?

Lord Ormonde.

And Tessa knew: She wasn't leaving this shop until she found him.

"This is quite indelicate of me," she began. "But do you have a ladies' retiring room that I might use?" She gave a dainty, self-effacing laugh that didn't suit her at all. "I'm afraid I find myself in desperate need of a bourdaloue."

The proprietress smiled, sharpness softening. "Of course. I'll show you the way. An afternoon of shopping will do that to a lady."

Not thirty seconds later, Tessa found herself alone in the privy room with not the slightest inclination to relieve herself and feeling three ways a fool. What was she doing here, following the Marquess of Ormonde? How was his business any business of hers?

Then she heard it—a low, muffled sound through the walls.

Voices, low and masculine, engaged in conversation, both muted. One low and agreeable. The shop owner, presumably.

The other deep and commanding...a familiar voice.

Ormonde.

Tessa poked her head into the dim corridor. The proprietress had returned to the front of the shop, which was where Tessa should most definitely go. Instead—and predictably, it must be admitted—her feet pointed in the opposite direction, and she was creeping down the corridor, one slow step at a time, praying she didn't locate a creaky floorboard.

She found the door cracked a sliver wide enough for her to peer inside, her heart racing. Two men, as she'd suspected—the proprietor and Ormonde. Floor-to-ceiling cabinetry on every wall, no chairs. And upon the few open shelves...

Objects.

She blinked and attempted to comprehend what she was seeing in this room with all manner of strangely shaped objects. Some glass, others jeweled...Some bulbous and squat...Others long and slender...

The pull of curiosity drew her closer, her face now firmly pressed against the door, even as strange sensations fluttered through her body.

Those *objects*...They were utterly foreign to her and... evocative.

She squinted. What was that he was holding?

Long...cylindrical...

Phallic.

She knew enough of anatomy to know that much.

Ormonde slipped the object into an interior pocket of his greatcoat.

Whatever it was, it wasn't for public viewing.

His head turned to the side, his profile presented as if his ear had picked up a sound. The breath caught in her lungs. His gaze slid over and met hers through the crack in the door. Eyes locked, her heart became a heavy hammer wreaking havoc through her chest, and his face went dark as thunder.

Right.

Then he was crossing the room, and, at last, Tessa's survival instinct kicked in. She jumped back from the door as if it had caught fire, just as it swung open. Panting, they stared at each other.

"*You?*" he said, utterly bewildered.

Well, he wasn't alone in the emotion.

Survival of this moment pushed to the front of Tessa's mind, leaving her no option but to leg it.

She'd taken two steps when she felt it—a large, masculine palm, planted between her shoulder blades, marching her down the corridor, like a child who had done something shameful.

When they emerged into the sun-bright front of the shop, a feminine voice sounded behind them. "*Lady Tessa?*"

Tessa didn't slow. "If you could please unlock the door," she tossed over her shoulder, "I'll be on my way."

She needed to get out of this shop and away from Ormonde—away from the press of his solid, unyielding palm—*tout suite.*

"Shall I set the pearls aside for you?" asked the proprietress, bemusement clear in her voice. It wouldn't have been every day that a marquess marched a lady out of her shop.

"*Pearls?*" asked Ormonde at the very moment Tessa said, "That won't be necessary."

Her eyes caught his over her shoulder. The look in those sky-hued depths had her feet stuttering over themselves.

Challenge.

This man was the amiable Marquess of Ormonde? A man liked by all, with not a single enemy in the world?

Yet he didn't feel precisely like an enemy…

Nemesis.

That descriptor felt more accurate.

"Let's see these pearls, shall we?"

His hand fell away from her back.

And strangely, she felt the loss.

Unexpected, that.

The proprietress swept into action. "They're absolutely divine, my lord. Just arrived from the South Seas two days ago."

Ormonde directed smiling, summer-blue eyes toward the woman. She didn't stand a chance—no woman did.

"Is that so?" he asked.

The distinct feeling came to Tessa that he was toying with her. "Truly, I must be going," she attempted.

Her protest landed on deaf ears.

Pink pearls slinked through the proprietress's fingers as she held them to the light. "They would be so lovely with Lady Tessa's peachy skin and strawberry-blonde hair."

"Let's see them on her, shall we?"

Now, Tessa *knew* Ormonde was toying with her—positively intent on doing so, in fact.

If he meant it as some sort of punishment, well, he was succeeding.

The proprietress stepped around the case, pearls in hand. As she made to drape the necklace around Tessa's neck, Ormonde reached out to stop her. "Please, allow me."

"Oh," gasped the woman on a giggle as he deftly slipped the pearls from her hands and stepped into her place before Tessa.

Her gaze had no choice but to lift and meet his. Within those clear blue depths, she detected a hot white blaze.

Oh.

He unlatched the amethyst clasp. Then, an end in each hand, he reached around her neck. Goose bumps cascaded up her arms and across her body. Though her lungs had forgotten how to breathe, she knew his scent—*cedarwood*. As if through cotton, she heard the tiny clasp click and lock into place.

Time stayed its inevitable advance into the future and held still—for them.

Which was empirically impossible.

Yet...she was presently experiencing that very impossibility, at this very moment.

It was as if with the click of the clasp he'd cast a spell and bound her to him.

"Methinks," began the proprietress, "the pearls would complement a different sort of dress, perhaps?" The words emerged with hesitant diplomacy.

But they were enough to push Tessa from this strange, neverending moment with the marquess. She cleared her throat. "You mean a long strand of pearls doesn't complement a cravat and waistcoat?"

The proprietress didn't notice the irony in Tessa's tone. "Oh, no," she said with a firm, definite shake of the head. "A silk ballgown, to be sure."

Ormonde didn't release Tessa's gaze. "We'll take them."

Shock strummed a harsh chord through her. "*We* will?"

The blue of his eyes darkened to indigo. "My gift to you."

Tessa opened her mouth, only to snap it shut.

"And the clasp, milord?" asked the proprietress, taking the pearls from Ormonde, who had already removed the necklace and stepped away from Tessa, leaving her standing in the center of the room, stunned. "Shall we switch the amethyst to sapphire to deepen the blue of her eyes?"

He shook his head. "The amethyst will bring out the violet hue, did you notice it?"

The proprietress nodded her approval. "Oh, lovely eyes, Lady Tessa has."

And that was the matter settled without Tessa having been consulted once.

Not five minutes later, she was stepping onto Sackville Street cobbles, a bundle of tea in one hand and a jeweler's box of pearls in the other. She thrust the box forward, toward Ormonde. "I cannot possibly accept such a gift." She hoped her absolute tone would settle it.

He stepped backward and waved the box away. "You *can*."

She exhaled an irritated sigh. "I *cannot*. I don't even know you."

Something unknowable flashed behind his eyes. "Now, you do."

She tried for a different angle. "I don't wear jewels."

"You should."

No other angles available to her, she said, "I shall have my bank deliver a cheque to you."

"It will be returned."

Was anyone else aware of how blasted stubborn this man was?

A hackney coach rolled to a stop a few yards away, depositing a lady and gentleman onto the cobbles. Before Tessa could gather her wits, Ormonde had neatly arranged for the hackney to drive her home.

After she gave the coachman her address, Ormonde very properly handed her up into the carriage. She tried not to think about the hand holding hers—the very hand that had tucked the intriguing glass object into an interior pocket of his greatcoat...the very hand that had pressed into the place between her shoulder blades.

Her gaze narrowed on that hand, and her brow crinkled. The knuckles were bruised, and a few abraded.

Then she was settled inside the coach, the door shut behind her, and rolling down Sackville Street. Unable not to, she glanced out the back window, only to find Ormonde striding in the opposite direction.

She didn't at all like the feeling of disappointment presently swirling through her, as she settled against cracked leather squabs and set her gaze ahead. The marquess had left her holding tea, pearls, and a thought.

In all the kerfuffle about the pearls, she hadn't time to ask him about the private room…and the objects housed within.

And she suspected that was rather his intention—obfuscation and distraction.

What was it she'd seen? What was it the marquess didn't want her to know about him? And why did he sport a different injury every time she saw him?

Until this afternoon, she hadn't wanted to know anything about the Marquess of Ormonde beyond what she already knew.

He was a member of The Archangel—for social rather than gaming reasons, she suspected, for she'd never once seen him partaking in the club's vices.

And he always paid his quarterly dues on time.

Those had been all the facts she'd cared to know about the man.

Now, she wanted to know more.

For, now, there was something she very definitely didn't know.

Something unrevealed in his eyes.

Latent.

That was the word for the Marquess of Ormonde.

Much lay hidden within this golden lord, waiting to be revealed.

Last week, when he'd barged in to The Archangel, demanding better odds, she'd dismissed him as a spoiled aristocrat—one of many she came into contact with on a daily basis.

But she saw now he wasn't a spoiled aristocrat.

Well, doubtless he *was* a spoiled aristocrat, but he wasn't *only* that.

He was something more…*different.*

And he was hiding something.

Against her better judgment, Tessa was intrigued.

CHAPTER FOUR

THREE DAYS LATER

*1*7 Sloane Street

The address Lady Tessa had provided the hackney driver.

The address Julian was presently standing opposite at six in the morning.

From his place propped against a plane tree across the street, he'd watched her enter the townhouse fifteen minutes ago.

He shouldn't be here.

Epsom Downs was where he belonged. It was only a few days until the Derby. The entirety of his thoughts should be concentrated on making merry and ensuring that Filthy Habit was safe and would fulfill his promise and win.

Annoyingly, however, an increasingly sizeable part of his brain wouldn't stop thinking about Lady Tessa Calthorp.

The woman had come as a shock when he'd gone to confront The Archangel's bookmaker. He'd formed a very definite idea of the sort of man he would be dealing with—*older...balding...wire-framed spectacles perched atop his nose...possibly hunched over...*

What he hadn't expected to encounter was an actual siren.

Fire in the belly...You don't seem to have that.

How dismissive she'd been of him—as a horse owner...

As a man.

Even now, those words sparked something elemental to life inside him.

Oh, he felt a fire all right.

To prove the woman wrong.

She thought him a spoiled lord, which, in truth, took him aback.

Everyone immediately liked him.

His lived experience had borne out as much.

Everyone—except Lady Tessa.

You are content not to win.

He would simply have to prove the woman wrong.

Which was why he was here.

Well, if he was being honest with himself, that wasn't the only reason.

Three days ago...

Blanton & Co...

She'd seen him in the jeweler's private room reserved for the select few who knew of its existence.

There was that reason, as well.

She hadn't known what she'd seen. Of course, she hadn't. For all she was a gaming hell owner, Julian sensed Lady Tessa remained an innocent about what went on between men and women behind closed doors.

Someday, however, she wouldn't be quite so innocent, and she would understand what she'd seen and what sort of wares were being purchased by the Marquess of Ormonde.

Yet, strangely, he wasn't embarrassed.

It was a secret between them—a bond, however slight and tenuous.

And he might like sharing a secret bond with Lady Tessa Calthorp.

So, here he was at six in the morning, standing opposite her townhouse when he should be in Epsom.

And why?

To make a wager with her.

Since he was going to prove her wrong, he wanted to make sure she felt it.

Right.

He pushed off the plane tree, dusted off his greatcoat, and crossed the street. Up the short flight of stairs to her doorstep and he was giving the brass knocker on her glossy black front door three solid raps.

He waited.

A small part of him insisted it wasn't too late to leg it down the street. He could easily round the corner before the door opened.

And none would be the wiser.

Except him.

He would know.

The door cracked open a scant sliver, and Julian experienced a wave of relief that he'd left it too late to leg it. A confused silver-blue eye peered out at him, followed by the gathering of a single eyebrow. The door swung wide to reveal Lady Tessa in full.

He'd thought to see her as he always had—waistcoat buttoned, cravat neatly knotted, hair pulled back into a tight chignon. The self-contained Lady Tessa he'd become accustomed to.

But standing before him with a quizzical expression on her face was an altogether different Lady Tessa. Waistcoat and cravat gone...hair looser, possibly in a plait down her back...shirt narrowly parted, revealing a V of ivory skin—skin that suggested curves beneath white muslin...

Her throat cleared, and his gaze startled up. He'd been caught staring, and blast if he didn't experience a sheepish flare of heat.

Of a sudden, the reality of the moment struck him, and he felt his brow crinkle. "It's dangerous for a woman to be opening doors at odd hours. Don't you have a butler?"

An eyebrow winged toward the sky. "Do you intend me harm, Marquess?"

"Of course not."

An unbothered feminine shrug. "There you have it."

"You still haven't answered my question."

She sighed. "The housekeeper and cook will arrive in a few hours for their duties. Mine is a late-rising household, particularly since—"

"*Since?*"

"Since my sisters moved to my brother's mansion in St. James's Square."

By way of explanations, Julian liked this one even less. "You live here—*alone?* Without a man in the house?"

"And yet somehow I manage." No mistaking the sarcasm in her voice.

"Your brother is a duke, Lady Tessa." Julian wasn't leaving this be. He was absolutely in the right. "You need protection."

She stifled a yawn. "Is there a reason you're knocking at my door at dawn and haranguing me about my living arrangements?"

She made no move to invite him in.

He offered her the amiable, lopsided smile that so charmed every lady in the *ton*—and many a gentleman, too. "May I come in?"

She remained uncharmed and unmoving in the center of the doorway. "I was just about to retire to—" She frowned. "You're not leaving until you've stated your business, are you?"

"No."

She released a heavy sigh and stood aside, granting him entry, and shooting the bolt behind him. As she swept around him, her

48

shoulder just brushed his in the narrow receiving hall. As he had in the jeweler's, he caught her scent—*crisp lemon.*

That would be her scent, of course.

He followed her down a dimly lit corridor to the kitchen and noted the tidiness of the house. The furnishings were fine, but without a sign of lace doilies or such fuss. He saw, too, he'd been correct about her hair. It fell in a long, thick red-gold plait down the center of her back, the ends just touching the small of her back. Unbound, they might reach the top of her arse.

A sweet arse, too, he knew without yet knowing.

Yet.

Now there was a presumptuous word.

Yet suggested he would.

He didn't *yet* know—and never would, of course.

He shouldn't be here.

But as they entered a kitchen as neat and tidy as the rest of the house, and she told him to sit anywhere he pleased, he found he couldn't quite make himself leave and, instead, lowered into a straight-backed kitchen chair.

"What sort of tea do you prefer?" she asked, her back to him as she began gathering dishes and various foods.

The question caught Julian on the back foot. "Whatever you have will do."

She stopped and turned. "I presently have eleven varieties of tea in my cupboard. You'll have to be more specific."

"*Erm...*" Flummoxed, he shrugged.

"Black or green?"

He understood she thought she was helping. Except..."There's *green* tea?"

She considered him for a moment. "How about a lovely jasmine?"

Julian nodded. "Sounds...lovely."

He was fairly certain he'd never uttered the word *lovely* in all his life.

The fact was, he'd come here with a plan—and matters were not proceeding according to it.

Instead, he was watching a woman with whom he'd spoken on two occasions prepare him tea. She flitted about the kitchen like an especially industrious bird, setting teacups, plates, and cutlery on the table, cutting four thick slices of spice bread and placing them on a white oval plate. Next came a bowl of lumped sugar and a tiny pot of cream.

And she performed it all automatically as if it were what she naturally did in the course of her day—how she lived her life.

How was *this* Lady Tessa? Was *this* the same woman who ran a gaming hell?

She kept coming at him from different angles, each time revealing an unexpected part of herself. Beneath her forbidding exterior and fiercely intelligent mind lay yet another part of her...a deeper part of her.

A woman not displeased to be serving him a *lovely* tea.

Quick on the heels of that thought came another.

This woman who appeared to be hard as nails...

She was a nurturer.

And Julian couldn't help warming to the idea of being nurtured by her.

Tea prepared and assembled on the table, she lowered into the seat opposite him. Her gaze drifted down his face and rested on his jaw for the flicker of a second. So quickly he might've missed it, except he knew what she was looking for.

The bruise.

She busied herself with pouring the tea and transferring a slice of bread to his plate, but he'd caught the glint of intrigue in her eyes. Though the bruise had disappeared, she was wondering about that bruise—and what it meant about him.

Well, let her wonder.

He rather liked that he held some intrigue for this woman who was becoming more complicated with each time they met.

Usually, the very idea of being known—truly, fully known—had the muscles of his jaw tensing.

This woman with whom he'd shared a single conversation and whatever that was in the jeweler's shop...how easily she peered beyond the façade and saw him.

In fact...

She might see him for who he actually was.

And the conclusion she appeared to have reached was she didn't like him all that much.

Right.

"Would it be presumptuous of me to infer that you have some business to state?" she asked and tore off a corner of spice bread.

"It would be only natural."

She nodded. "As I thought."

Knowledge flickered within her eyes, and a sense of unease rippled through Julian. She wasn't speaking of the Derby or the odds on Filthy Habit. She was speaking of...

"You are, of course, welcome to have them back," she said.

"*Them?*"

"The pearls."

The pearls.

He'd bought this woman pearls.

He'd even placed them around her neck, unable not to.

It had been a curious form of embrace. A feeling of being locked inside a moment...at the mercy of its whim.

At the time, and even now, it felt very much like a moment whose vagaries could lead somewhere unexpected.

"Have you worn them?" he couldn't help asking.

She gave a curt, dismissive shake of the head, pursed her generous lips, and blew a cooling breath across the surface of her tea. A shallow sip later, her eyes closed for a moment's bliss. The woman was serious about her tea.

Julian found himself staring. He cleared his throat. "I don't want the pearls."

Her eyes startled open. "No?"

He cocked his head and waited.

Her gaze turned assessing. "Then what—?" Her mouth snapped shut, and a light blush pinked the roses of her cheeks, as another reason for his unexpected appearance at her door occurred to her. "For my behavior at Blanton and Company, I must apologize."

Julian's lungs refused to draw breath—or release it. Was she actually speaking of what he thought she was speaking of?

"Everyone," she continued, "is entitled to privacy, and for my violation of yours, I offer my sincerest apology."

In all his life, Julian had never met a more direct and honest person than Lady Tessa Calthorp.

Yet, while he doubted not the sincerity of her apology, a flicker of something a mite more complicated remained in her direct, honest eyes. *Curiosity.* She was still wondering about what she'd witnessed.

And though a part of him wanted to confess to her—show her...*demonstrate upon her*—he wouldn't.

"I appreciate your apology," he said and wondered if she detected the telling rasp of desire in his throat. "I'm not here about that, either."

"It's simply that I have a question—"

"It's not up for discussion," he said, firm, even as an unhelpful image flashed across his mind—of the object and the myriad uses it could be put to upon Lady Tessa's body.

"*Oh,*" she said. No mistaking the flicker of disappointment in her eyes—and the curiosity that yet remained.

Oh, Lord.

His mouth gone dry, he took a sip of tea.

She was watching him more closely than a sip of tea strictly warranted. "How do you like it?"

"It's..." In all honesty, he hadn't tasted it.

"It's my own blend."

He took another sip, determined to have something to say about it this time. "It's...delicious."

And it was.

A smile of delight lit across her face, and he realized this was the first genuine smile he'd seen from her. It had a smile of his own wanting to join in.

"It's a simple composition of Chinese oolong and jasmine."

He took three more gulps. "Truly, it's, *erm*, lovely."

There was that word again—*lovely*.

And here was another unexpected moment whose vagaries he wanted to follow.

Soon, however, her smile faded, and she said, "I suppose you'll state your business," and that was the moment gone.

No more beating about the bush..."I'm here about the Derby."

Her brow gathered. "*The Derby?* Why would we discuss—?" Realization dawned across her face. "Is this about the odds on your horse?"

"Yes."

"I did shorten them."

Julian shook his head. "Not enough."

Lady Tessa's teacup suspended in the air, mid-lift to her mouth. Her eyes flashed with irritation. One positive about her directness and honesty was that her emotions weren't difficult to read.

"And here I thought you weren't merely a spoiled lord," she said.

Julian blinked.

She'd done it again.

Insulted him directly to his face.

A chuckle startled out of him.

When one broke the insult down, it contained multitudes. Fundamentally, it acknowledged as established fact that he was a spoiled lord.

Only, she hadn't thought him *merely* one.

Another chuckle rumbled through his chest.

Head canted to the side, bemused expression on her face, she watched him and waited.

Best he stated his business before she turfed him out. "Filthy Habit will win the Derby."

She didn't bat an eyelash. "Doubtful."

At last, they'd arrived at the reason for his visit. He'd almost lost track of it himself. "I'll wager you that he shall."

"Feel free to place your wager at The Archangel."

"This wager is private," he said. "Between us only."

A surprised beat of time ticked past. "Why would I do that?"

"You're part owner of The Archangel, correct?"

"*Co*-owner," she corrected.

"Your brother is known as one of the richest dukes in the *ton*."

"Given the profligate spending habits I observe in The Archangel every night of the week, I imagine he is."

"Your own wealth must be comparable."

She took a sip of tea and remained silent.

"So, what difference would a friendly wager make to you?"

Friendly? Who was he trying to fool?

She considered him over the next decade of seconds. "I can't decide if you're spoiled or simply foolish."

"I've found the two usually go hand in hand, but I'm neither."

Now, it was dry laughter startling from her. "Is that so?"

"It's the principle of the matter."

"*Principle*," she repeated. "You mentioned that word the other night."

"One thousand pounds," he said, lest she doubt his seriousness.

"Pardon?"

"*One thousand pounds*," he repeated.

"A great deal of principle in that amount of blunt." No doubting the shrug in her voice.

"Two thousand."

Her brow lifted, and she shook her head. She might be enjoying denying him—*a merely spoiled lord.*

His back teeth ground together.

"Five thousand."

Even as the figure left his mouth, he began to doubt his sanity.

The surprised lift of her eyebrows indicated she harbored the same doubt.

Five thousand pounds?

He never placed such wagers.

But this was different.

Lady Tessa was different.

And he was different with her.

In this moment, the woman felt like a madness in his blood.

"Ten thousand pounds," fell from his mouth.

Silence so thick one would need an ax to cut it filled the air before a stunned laugh escaped her. "Then why not twenty thousand?" she scoffed.

Indeed, why not?

"It's a wager."

She blinked, and a line of distress formed between her eyebrows. She was a gaming hell owner; she understood what had just happened.

They'd made a wager.

She'd only stated the ridiculous amount to get him to leave off, but he'd accepted and now here they were—bound by a wager.

One she was no doubt rethinking.

"And if—*when*—Filthy Habit wins," he began, quickly binding her to it before she could balk.

She cut across him. "I'm good for the twenty thousand, of course."

He didn't doubt it, but he realized something.

He didn't want her twenty thousand pounds.

He wanted..."One night."

"Pardon?"

"One night," he repeated, hardly able to warrant the words emerging from his mouth.

"*One night?*"

"One night in my bed."

Shock traced through Julian. In fact, he might be even more shocked than Lady Tessa.

He didn't spend the night with women.

Particularly not ladies.

And certainly not sirens.

"You cannot be serious."

"You'll find that I am."

Her eyes narrowed, and five long seconds dragged past before decision appeared within silver-blue depths "You have a wager."

How easily she'd agreed. *Too easily...* "You don't think Filthy Habit will win."

"We shall see, won't we?"

Oh, how he couldn't wait for Filthy Habit to wipe that smug expression off her face.

"You'll be attending Derby Day, of course," he said.

"I believe I shall."

Good.

He would see her proven wrong in real time.

For now, best he leave before she thought better of the entire matter and changed her mind. He came to his feet and offered a slight bow. "Lady Tessa."

He pivoted on his heel and saw himself out.

With a light step, Julian's feet hit Sloane Street cobbles. Filthy Habit would win...

And Julian would have Lady Tessa in his bed.

At once, a sharp dagger of panic sliced through him.

What had he done?

This must've been how Pandora felt in the instant before she opened the box.

And yet, like her, he wasn't able to curb the momentum and stop himself—even as he understood his debauched blood drove it.

For the first time in his life, he wasn't able to curb it.

And it had everything to do with Lady Tessa Calthorp.

CHAPTER FIVE

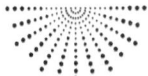

EPSOM DOWNS, THREE DAYS LATER

*T*essa emerged from the King's Head to make her way to Epsom's betting post, the morning yet a soft gray with the final vestiges of night.

The clock hadn't yet struck six, so she should've been one of the rare few prowling about. But this was Derby Day, and Epsom was already abuzz.

Still abuzz, to put it to the nail.

Yesterday, along with about half of London clogging the roads, she'd made the hours-long journey in a cramped coach with two burly men and three ladies who likely wouldn't have been described as *ladies* in the strictest sense—or the loosest, either. Though she could have hired a private carriage, she'd wanted to be in the company of Derby spectators to gain a feel for the mood of the coming day—and to see where their bets were being placed. A horse named Little Wicked had been the overwhelming favorite.

By the time she'd arrived, all she'd hoped for was a restful night's sleep, so her mind would be sharp for Derby Day in all its various insanities.

A hope that, alas, wouldn't come to fruition.

Though she'd arrived late, the carousing had only gotten started. To make matters worse, when she'd passed through the taproom to make her way up the stairs to her room, she'd been recognized by more than a few of The Archangel's patrons. Some had even tried to pull her into their games—and several drunken winky smiles had flown her way, as if to entice her into their beds.

She'd firmly declined all advances. It never did a woman a bit of good to be too polite to a man. A woman's politeness only ever gave a man the wrong idea.

Of course, some men didn't need a woman to be polite to get a wrong idea in their heads.

Ormonde.

He, for example, had gotten exactly the wrong idea—despite her *im*politeness.

Days later, the question kept circling her mind. What in the blazes had happened in her kitchen?

He'd knocked on her door.

She'd invited him in.

He'd sat his imposing self at her kitchen table.

She'd made him tea.

He'd insisted on a wager that his horse would win the Derby.

She'd refused, again and again.

Then...

It all went fuzzy from there.

Tricked.

That was how she felt.

Somehow, she'd been tricked into the wager.

Even so, she could all but start counting her twenty thousand pounds. She felt almost certain of it—*almost.*

Oh, a sticky, little word, that one—*almost.*

Ormonde's horse hadn't lost yet.

And until he did, the chance remained that she would have to spend a night in the marquess's bed.

And yet...had there been a flicker of something in his eyes when they'd shaken on the wager?

Surprise.

Had he surprised himself as much as he'd surprised her?

Or...perhaps the man was a rogue in marquess's clothing.

Late-night, drunken carousing wasn't the only reason for her lack of sleep last night.

Today, she needed Ormonde's blasted horse to lose.

Perhaps she should've slipped a blackleg a few quid to ensure Filthy Habit couldn't run.

Except she couldn't take such action for two very sound, if annoyingly inconvenient, reasons.

First, she couldn't have a horse harmed.

Second, she couldn't win a bet in such a dastardly way.

Neither was in her nature.

She would have to accept the consequences of what she'd set in motion.

And what might those consequences be?

A night with the marquess.

That was known.

But what would occur during such a night?

And why did the very thought send light and variable flutters of sensation racing through her? Flutters that tended to pool in her stomach and...*lower.*

She gave her head a clearing shake and continued her odd journey to the betting post, unable to walk in a straight line for the foxed carousers yet staggering about. She lifted her skirts high enough to step over one passed-out lordling to avoid tripping over him.

Though the night hadn't entirely loosened its grip on the sky, much industry hustled and bustled about in the efficient forms of those who made the day possible—stable lads and grooms rushing to and fro; trainers walking the Thoroughbreds; jockeys discussing race plans with owners.

Tessa tugged her wide-brimmed straw hat low and located a spot twenty or so yards from the betting post, a place where she could observe and avoid the same treatment from others.

Those whose business centered around the betting post were already getting on with the day. The blacklegs setting the touters out to establish up-to-the-minute information on the Thorough-breds. The touters prowling the grounds, sly and quick, picking up every morsel of tattle to report back to the blacklegs, who then lengthened or shortened the odds. And, of course, there was the thickening crowd of bettors, waving their coin about, deter-mined to get the best odds on their favored horse. Though reeking of desperation from the outside, the routine held a fluid order.

All the while, Tessa watched, the only still figure as controlled chaos whirled about her.

It wasn't long, however, before she noticed it—a sensation on the side of her face...The sensation of eyes upon her.

She wasn't the only one doing a bit of watching.

She was being watched.

Unable to ignore the feeling, she canted her head subtly to the side and met the unflinching gaze of a man.

A man she didn't know.

A young man—around her age in his middle twenties, to be fair—his long, rangy form dressed as finely as any gentleman at the Downs for Derby Day.

The word *dashing* might cross the mind of more than one young lady.

Yet he obviously was *not* a gentleman.

The garish gold and blue of his waistcoat...The jaunty angle of his hat...The diamond stud in his left ear...The boldness of his stare, for he didn't flinch or blush or smile when she caught him out.

Instead, he winged his eyebrows at a saucy angle and continued to hold her gaze, bold as brass.

The man's identity struck her with the force of a whirlwind.

Blaze Jagger.

He could be none other.

A young lion—rangy...intense...fearless—that was this man with his intent gaze that could easily bend others to his will.

And when he began walking toward her, Tessa understood she had no choice but to meet him.

More than that, she had no choice but to hold her ground. For if she fled, the chase would be on and that would be her and Gabriel's goose cooked. *No.* She needed to meet Jagger and gain a sense of the man. Only then could she devise a plan for how to deal with him. He wouldn't be easy to best—that truth was plain in the glint of gray eyes fringed by black lashes—but then, neither was she.

A smile formed about his mouth. In the general sense, smiles conveyed joy or delight.

Jagger's didn't.

Feral, that was the word for his smile. The sort of smile a cat gave a mouse as he held the creature trapped beneath his paw—in the moment before his teeth sank into tender flesh.

Tessa could see how such a smile could and would inflict a dual sense of dread and fear in its intended recipient.

Neither struck through her.

To her mind, the man was simply a complex equation that required time, determination, and patience.

Eventually, she would arrive at the solution.

"Imagine this," he said in an accent that spoke of East End origins. "A duke's sister at the Derby Day betting post." His predatory smile didn't slip.

So, this was his first angle of attack. A small skirmish to set her on the back foot and gain a feel for her balance.

"I can't be the first," she said without an ounce of heat. "And I certainly won't be the last."

His smile transformed the slightest increment, shifting from the feral into the assessing. "You're not the usual sort of nob, now are you?"

Another attempt to ruffle her feathers. Blaze Jagger was a man accustomed to getting a reaction from people.

Well, if he wished to get a rise out of *her*, he would have to do better than that.

She shrugged. "I wasn't a nob at all until a few weeks ago."

He gave a broad glance around them. "This your first time at a betting post?"

"Aye." She saw no reason to lie.

"You have a favorite pony?"

An image of Ormonde's Filthy Habit trotted across her mind…*"No,"* she said with more force than necessary.

"Ah, now," he said, the hard glint in his eyes sharpening into a straightedge. "You have to be in the game to win it."

He'd come directly to the point: The Race of the Century…

He wasn't being let in.

Tessa met candor with candor. "The Race of the Century is a single, one-off race. You could leave it be."

"Ah," he tutted with an apologetic shake of the head, "but there you're wrong, pet. If the race was up in Yorkshire, aye, I might concede the post to you. But this is Epsom. It's my home turf, ye ken?"

Tessa suppressed an annoyed sigh. "Aye."

He jutted his chin toward the building beside them. A rather rickety-looking structure, in truth, that proclaimed itself The Royal Reform Club. Tessa could only assume the name ironic. "You a member?" he asked.

Tessa shook her head. "You are?"

He released a bitter snort. "Turns out, if you have enough blunt they'll let you in just about anywhere."

By *they*, he meant the *haut ton*, of course.

That, too, had been her experience with society…

Until she'd been informed she was one of them.

And as much as she tried to resist the fact that it had changed her life, she understood it was irrevocably true.

But that didn't mean she felt like a lady—and it certainly wouldn't do to approach Jagger like she was one, either.

Still, he would have to be dealt with.

That was what the set of his mouth told her.

"Lead the way," she said.

He didn't really want to show her the delights of the Royal Reform Club—not as a gracious host, anyway—but rather wanted to throw his weight around. To have a capital "L" lady in his company only amplified his presence and lent him a bit of panache.

But more than any of that, he wanted to speak with her further.

Which happened to suit her purposes.

Like the rest of Epsom Downs, there wasn't much reforming happening in The Royal Reform Club, with its gaming tables of all varieties strewn about, populated by groupings of lords raucously throwing dice or slamming useless hands of cards onto tables...ladies looking either artfully delighted or artfully bored... more than a few members of the demimonde doing the same. Like Jagger said, anyone with enough blunt to secure admittance to its tawdry, sweat-and-whiskey-soaked environs was welcome.

Though unable to hear a single word spoken over the cacophonous din, Tessa nodded when Jagger tossed a question her way. She immediately regretted her acquiescence when he led her to an especially rowdy Hazard table.

Of course, all Hazard tables were rowdy.

Rowdy was the very nature of the game.

"I don't gamble," she shouted.

"Sure you do," he shouted back, shouldering open a space at the table wide enough for the both of them.

Now that they were closer, he said, "That's what you do every day when you step outside your front door—gamble. It's your choice how you play. Small and safe—or big and bold." He eyed her up and down, not lascivious, but assessing. "And you, Lady Tessa, are not the small and safe sort."

"You do like your word play, don't you?"

Jagger snorted and turned to watch the dice. Somehow, Tessa found a cup of arrack in her hand. She took a testing sip and frowned. Too sweet for her taste. How she longed for a proper cup of tea.

She took in Jagger's profile as he exchanged greetings and light jibes. Most of the men arrayed around the table knew him—lord and codger, alike. Though they stood at a Hazard table, Tessa saw the game Jagger was playing. He was showing her who she was up against.

Except it made no difference to her who came out of their dealings on top. She only wanted him to leave her and, more importantly, her family be.

The time had arrived for them to get to it…"The Race of the Century will have no bearing on your business interests."

Jagger tore his gaze away from the action to cut her a sharp glance. "Do I need to be speaking with the duke?"

"*I'm* the one you deal with." The words emerged hard and implacable, leaving no doubt. "The Race of the Century is for nobs, you know that."

That angle might work.

Jagger shook his head. "If only that were true." He rested his forearms on the table. "All those flyers and booths set up across London selling tickets, they put the lie to what you're telling me."

Tessa didn't like feeling caught out, but she couldn't deny the truth of his words.

"That's not about your sort, now is it?" he pressed. "It's about *my* sort. *My* turf. And you think you can cut me out?"

He had a point. Still…"It's not our intention—"

He cut her off with an impatient wave. "Intentions mean

naught to me. Intentions put into actions have consequences. Some toff said as much."

Tessa felt her brow crease. "Sir Isaac Newton?"

"That's the one."

The crinkle in her brow deepened. "Sir Isaac Newton was talking about apples."

Jagger shrugged. "The sentiment applies here."

Ah..."Every action has an equal and opposite reaction."

"That's the one."

A bad feeling stirred in Tessa's gut.

She saw her mistake. Though she'd known Blaze Jagger to be a dangerous adversary, she'd been underestimating him. He wasn't a feral animal. He was an intelligent man, even if he was a criminal, and a foe different from the one she'd assumed him to be—a more dangerous foe. He was a London ruffian, but not simply a London ruffian.

An important distinction.

Oh, what had Gabriel started?

And what did she have to finish?

For of that she had little doubt: She would have to finish this. Gabriel had become so caught up in the numbers and the business side—not to mention his recent inheritance of a dukedom— he hadn't comprehensively accounted for the human side.

He hadn't comprehensively accounted for Blaze Jagger.

The dice cup found its way into Jagger's hand. When he rolled and didn't throw out on the first toss, Tessa released the breath she'd been unwittingly holding, grateful for breathing room so she could think.

Movement caught the edge of her eye.

It shouldn't have. Dozens of bodies milled about The Royal Reform Club in various states of inebriation, casting greetings this way and that, using any excuse to toast one another and find the bottom of their cups. One more such body shouldn't have made any difference.

Except this body wasn't simply one more body.

Tessa knew it before she discreetly angled her head and caught a glimpse.

Ormonde.

At her side, Jagger became distracted by a small man murmuring in his ear. His tout relating betting post business, no doubt. Then he gave the dice another jaunty toss when the table began hurrying him along.

Leaving Tessa an opportunity—to fully take in the Marquess of Ormonde.

He stood half a head taller than most. More handsome than most, too. But Tessa already knew all that from their interactions.

Interactions?

A rather tame word for what had transpired between them.

And she knew something true about this golden lord whom all the room seemed to admire.

He wasn't simply a golden lord.

Lucifer had been the most beautiful of all God's creations, but beneath the blindingly gorgeous exterior hid a deep well of darkness.

Blindingly.

That was the key. The marquess had learned somewhere along the way how to use his golden exterior to obscure the true him.

And Tessa understood she was the only person in this room who had ever caught a glimpse of the true Marquess of Ormonde —the golden lord who would wager a woman for one night in his bed.

As ever, the thought sent a strange ripple of tension purling up her spine, the fine hairs of her arms and neck lifting, the beat of her heart half a step faster, the need to inhale deeply pulling at her lungs.

No one in this room saw that Ormonde.

As if her thoughts held a gravitational pull, his gaze cut over and met hers. The lopsided smile that lent a boyish air to his Viking features froze in place.

Somehow, after a pair of meetings, they'd become two instruments tuned to one another.

The angle of his gaze shifted an increment, enough for him to register the man at her side.

She couldn't imagine the Marquess of Ormonde knew Blaze Jagger from the next London rough. What he saw was that she was standing at a Hazard table in the company of a man.

That was what the shadow that passed behind his eyes told Tessa.

And the marquess was possibly bothered by the idea.

Tessa felt something being shoved into her hand—a dice cup. She tore her gaze from Ormonde. It was with greater difficulty than made her comfortable, for a stray thought had wandered into her mind...

What would it be like to spend one night in such a man's bed?

She shook the question away and focused on Jagger, who waited with a shadow of amusement in his eyes. "Your toss."

"Truly, I don't—"

"You're at the table." His eyebrows lifted with challenge. "Your toss. I'll stand you."

Jagger placed their bets, and Tessa called out a five as she let the dice fly. The next instant, a cheer flew to the rafters. She'd rolled a seven and hadn't nicked or thrown out. Again, the dice found their way to her cup. She cast again—and *again*.

"The dice agree with you," shouted Jagger over the cheers.

A few tosses later, predictably, the dice turned on her and rolled the main. She passed the cup, her heart a hammer in her chest. She wasn't sure if this high-flying feeling originated from the dice play—which was incredibly invigorating, truth told—or if it originated from the sighting of Ormonde. She couldn't say she liked either possibility.

One—if not both—had to be true.

It was how logic worked.

"An unusual sort of lady, aren't you?" asked Jagger, his head cocked contemplatively.

"I think it's been established that I'm not the usual sort of lady." She spread her hands wide. "I do run a gaming hell."

He swept an up-and-down glance over her. "Is that why you wear that getup?"

Ah. He was attempting to backfoot her, again. *"Getup?"*

"Wearing men's clothing."

Tessa considered the man before her. She didn't owe him the truth—or anything, for that matter, contrary to his belief.

Except...

The truth would be good for him.

"I wear this *getup* because I prefer it. I *like* it. And it's my prerogative to do as I prefer and like."

He snorted and smirked. "Not a different sort of lady, but a different sort of woman, too, eh?"

Tessa had long grown accustomed to men's comfort in throwing such words her way. "I'm a person, Mr. Jagger, who will do as she likes. And here's what you need to know." She leaned forward. "I don't allow anyone to stand between me and how I wish to live my life."

Understanding flickered within Jagger's hazel eyes. She'd informed him that she had lines and, if he chose to cross hers, she would stand her ground.

Amazing how direct a person could be in a roundabout way.

Jagger's tout again flitted to his side and murmured in his ear. Reflexively, Tessa's gaze flicked toward where it had left Ormonde. He was no longer there. However, a wider scan of the increasingly close room found him. That towering height of his certainly helped.

Of course, all one needed to do was locate the biggest crowd. He would be at its center, the other aristocrats mere moths, helpless against his light. With what ease he conversed with those lords and ladies, whose smiles and fans were out in full force, competing for a sliver of his attention. How they threw themselves into his path.

Subtly, his gaze shifted and met Tessa's. Not a flicker of surprise.

He'd known she'd been staring.

This man knew his power over others—and used it.

And she saw something else, too.

He'd moved nearer.

The heavy beat of her heart made itself known and her lungs were suddenly all out of air and a fluttery tension entered her body—a *new* tension. A tension specific to the Marquess of Ormonde.

This man affected her, physically, just by sharing a room with her.

Disconcerting...unsettling...troubling...

And yet more, too. For this tension in her body had an additional cause—*anticipation.*

What would it be like to spend one night in such a man's bed?

For the first time, she allowed herself to wonder if, perhaps, she wanted to find out.

CHAPTER SIX

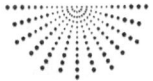

*J*ulian entered the Royal Reform Club and began his usual round of greetings—a task that had begun to feel as dull and ordinary as old shoe leather, as the years went on—expecting to be bored to bits within the half minute.

Then it happened.

His gaze flicked left, and there she was.

Lady Tessa.

And the blood sparked alight in his veins.

His feet took one instinctive step and stopped.

She wasn't alone, for standing beside her at the Hazard table was a man…A man who looked to be a blackleg from the ostentatious style of his clothing and the diamond stud the size of a large pebble in his left ear. Legs liked to flaunt their newfound wealth.

A frown began to form about Julian's mouth before he remembered Lady Tessa ran a gaming hell. She would count such men as associates.

Except she and that man didn't have the look of mere associates. From the defensive, possibly acrimonious way they faced one another—the clench of her hand at her side; the tight pull of his jaw muscles—they weren't making idle conversation about the day's weather or Epsom's turf conditions. They were locked in intense conversation.

Her shoulders lifted and dropped, as if she'd heaved a great breath. Then from below the wide brim of her rather dashing straw hat tied with a blue ribbon, her gaze slid right and found his.

Julian understood he had a choice. He could tip his hat and continue making his way through the club, greeting one and all— or he could pursue the path his feet were already initiating toward her.

It wasn't much of a choice.

Even as he knew he shouldn't.

While it was true he'd struck a private wager with the woman, he didn't have the right to insert himself into her business. But neither could he leave it. If his presentiment was correct and the man beside her was a blackleg, that also meant despite his diamonds and fine clothing—or perhaps because of them—the man was a rogue.

An unexpected feeling reared up inside Julian—*protectiveness*.

Which was wrong, wrong, wrong.

Lady Tessa wasn't his to protect. The sum total of their acquaintance came down to three conversations.

Yet the feeling wouldn't be denied, and with every brief conversation with this or that lord or lady, his feet brought him closer—so close he might've picked up her crisp lemon scent.

He caught the instant she registered his presence. It was there in the way her shoulders squared with tension and how her gaze remained steadfastly fixed before her. When, at last, she realized the very large man at her side wasn't going anywhere and she would have to acknowledge him, her gaze shifted right and met his. Within her eyes blazed a hearty desire that he keep moving.

Too bad.

"Lady Tessa," he said, practiced smile tipping his mouth.

She swallowed, as if her throat had gone suddenly dry. "Lord Ormonde."

The other man lifted his eyebrows. "Lofty as all that, are we?"

The man was, indeed, an East End blackleg. It was there in his accent and the flinty glimmer in his eyes.

"Lord Ormonde," began Lady Tessa, "may I introduce Mr. Jagger to you?"

Jagger snorted. "And such a *proper* introduction, too." He was thoroughly enjoying himself.

Julian gave the man a curt nod and directed his next words to Lady Tessa. "Are you finding the day to your satisfaction?"

Such a question was what one asked in a social setting, but it seemed to stall Lady Tessa. "I, *erm*, yes, it's a satisfactory day as days go."

Jagger let out a loud guffaw. "I always wondered how nobs talked to each other." It was clear he wasn't too impressed. "Proper titillating, it is, right down to the short scrofulous hairs of me nether—"

"That will be enough," said Julian, low and firm.

A smile curled to one side of Jagger's mouth, even as he shut his mouth.

Lady Tessa was observing Julian with a slight cant of the head and a glint in her eyes—*appreciation*.

And the feeling it produced within him told him something about himself.

He liked being the object of this woman's appreciation.

It meant something.

Then she blinked, and the moment broke. "I…," she began, "I have other matters to attend."

Jagger sucked his teeth. "Oh, you go and attend those other matters, *Lady* Tessa. We'll be conversing again."

The words rang more threatening than conversational.

As Julian bent in a shallow bow, Lady Tessa swept around him, leaving him alone with this Jagger character, who appeared to be no piece of good news. Though he lacked Julian's bulk, the man reached the same height.

"You have business with Lady Tessa?"

Even as Julian asked, he understood she wouldn't appreciate him interfering with her affairs. As if he had the right...

As if their wager bound them in some way.

"More like parallel business interests," replied Jagger.

"*Parallel business interests?*" What in the blazes was that supposed to mean?

"Just seeing if they're going to intersect." Jagger smirked. The younger man certainly possessed an abundance of swagger—perhaps more than his years warranted. "It's simple—" Dark eyebrows crinkled. "What's the maths that's all lines and angles?"

"Geometry?"

Jagger snapped his fingers. "That's the one. It's simple geometry."

With that, he pivoted on his heel and strode away, leaving Julian contemplating the space left not by him, but by Lady Tessa.

A jolly "Ormonde!" cut through the din, and Julian suppressed a reflexive flinch. Even as he engaged in greetings on the surface, his thoughts remained latched onto the encounter just finished. What sort of parallel and possibly intersecting business interests did Lady Tessa have with a man like Jagger?

No lawful business interests, that was certain.

A woman who didn't have a man in her house—who, in fact, opened her front door to men she hardly knew, as he'd learned firsthand only a few days ago—had somehow made an enemy of this Jagger ruffian.

It was all Julian could do to keep his feet planted and not hie after her and demand a full accounting—and that she hire a butler who happened to be handy with fists, knives, and firearms.

He pulled his watch from his waistcoat pocket. *Two o'clock.* An hour until the start of the race. He made his way to the stables for one last conversation with his jockey, Smithwick, about the race plan for Filthy Habit before the weigh-in. The Thoroughbred had a tendency to become bored and distracted during a race—a habit known as daisy cutting—and he wanted to make sure Smithwick was clear on the trainer's strategies for eliminating it.

After a quick conversation that did a fair bit to alleviate Julian's concerns, he was exiting the stable when a shock of auburn hair in the last stall caught his eye. He recognized the man—*Liam Cassidy*, an up-and-coming jockey whose sister, Gemma, was the very same woman his best friend, the Duke of Rakesley, had run off with and married only a week ago. News that Julian hadn't enjoyed delivering to the Duchess of Acaster earlier today. Though she and Rake hadn't been officially betrothed, there had been an understanding that Rake would soon propose marriage.

As for Gemma, she'd been one outstanding jockey, riding Hannibal—a horse deemed unrideable by all but her—to victory in the Two Thousand Guineas, the first race of the season.

Her brother was just as good. Cassidy had steady hands—light and sensitive, yet strong—and a loose, but firm demeanor that didn't let one into his thoughts or intentions. Liam Cassidy would be crowned the best jockey of his generation. It wasn't a matter of *if*, but *when*. Within five years, Julian guessed.

Of course, Julian knew he shouldn't be fraternizing with another man's jockey, but he stopped anyway. After all, Cassidy's sister had just married Julian's best friend. He should greet the man.

"Good Sir Longshanks is a fine goer," he called out.

Cassidy glanced up from the magnificent black Thoroughbred whose saddle strap he'd been tightening. Instant recognition glinted in Cassidy's hazel eyes before he straightened and ran a soothing hand along the horse's withers. "Aye."

"Will you be staying with him after today?"

"I committed to him through the Derby," said Cassidy, wary.

"Few jockeys exhibit that sort of loyalty."

An understatement.

Horse racing was like a game of shuffle with jockeys and trainers jumping from one stable to another, depending on whose purse paid more.

"I like to follow through."

"If you're looking for a new opportunity, my stables at Nonsuch Castle would have a place for you."

Cassidy smiled and snorted. "I've been wanting to give Hannibal a ride."

Of course.

The refusal was polite, but firm. After the Derby, Cassidy would switch his allegiance to Rake's stables at Somerton, like a loyal brother should.

Instead of beating about the bush, Julian decided to sweep any awkwardness out of the way. "How does it feel to have a duchess for a sister?"

Cassidy chuckled. "Gemma's been a duchess all our lives, so no great surprise there."

Julian joined in the laugh, even as an unexpected feeling ribboned through him. A pang of loss for his own sister— *Clarissa*. Perhaps he would've joked about her just so.

Something the universe had denied him.

He swallowed back the sudden surge of bitterness.

"Gemma seems like a salt-of-the-earth sort to me."

At least, that had been Julian's impression from the few times he'd met her. An unexpected sort of woman...a woman Rake hadn't seen coming. Of course, that would be the only sort of woman who could bring Rake to his knees and make him defy society to have her.

Rake was braver than Julian. That was the truth of it. Rake had the courage to follow such feelings where they led.

Julian wished his friend well, but what Rake had, he never could.

"Oh, she is," said Cassidy, "but my sister does as she pleases, always has. She'll make a fine duchess."

Julian caught something in Cassidy's voice he hadn't noticed before. He didn't speak like a lad who grew up in stables. His intonation was decidedly schooled. There was something more to Gemma and Liam Cassidy than what showed on the surface. A story Rake would know.

A story that was none of Julian's business.

Right.

Julian inclined his head. "Best of luck with your ride today," he spoke in farewell. "But not too much luck."

Cassidy's laugh echoed down the central aisle after Julian as he exited the stable and was immediately conscripted into the dense and raucous party that was Derby Day. One couldn't fight it. One's only choice was to enter the jubilant flow and give over. He'd once heard the Derby described as all wild hordes and chaos, and he couldn't think of a more fitting description for Epsom Downs on this day—all hedonism and excess.

And though Julian was part of the day, he wasn't truly. He didn't gather with the masses at the betting post or play the odds or enter a rooster into the ever-popular cockfights or play Loo, Brag, Gleek, or Quinze. He didn't drink the plonk or punch thrust into his hands. He was a man who had defined his boundaries and never strayed from those confines.

Except...was that quite true?

Lady Tessa...

The wager.

As a gentleman, he should pray for Filthy Habit to lose the race—and thus lose him this wager. Then he could return to his well-defined life and leave the moment of madness that had him proposing one night in his bed well behind him.

For that was what it had been—*madness*.

Yet he couldn't quite utter that prayer.

He wanted to win.

Perhaps more than he'd ever wanted to win in his life.

The promise of Lady Tessa in his bed for one night did something to his blood—pushed it hot through his veins.

"Ormonde!" came a jolly shout.

Julian looked up to find a group of lords waving him over to their place outside the periphery of the crowd. When he found two footmen shedding their coats, he knew what was afoot.

"Houghton reckons his man Smith can best my Foley," said a young earl.

Julian smiled. Though the horses were the official draw on Derby Day, here was yet another sport popular amongst lords: The pitting of their footmen against one another in a race to see whose was fleetest of foot. The side betting had already commenced as the servants pulled off their boots, shed their cravats, and rolled up their sleeves. Both men were young and lean as whippets. It would be a close contest.

"Since you're not a betting man," began the earl, "would you declare the winner at the finish line?"

Julian smiled and agreed—as everyone had known he would.

In the end, Houghton had been proven right. His man Smith had bested Foley by a clear yard.

Riding a wave of good humor following his footman's win, Houghton called out, "Ormonde, come and watch the race with us in Prinny's stand."

"You have access?" asked Julian. It had been years since King George's voracious appetite for the races had cooled and his famed viewing stand centered inside the racing course had remained empty—after the Escape Affair, specifically.

Decades ago—in the previous century, in fact—when the King had still been the Prince of Wales, he'd become embroiled in a horse racing scandal that yet lived on in infamy. The prince's horse, Escape, started as the heavy favorite in the first day's race at Newmarket—and came in dead last. The next day, the odds on Escape were lengthened to five-to-one, and the horse won easily, even beating two of the horses from the previous day's race.

The scandal lay in the fact that Escape's jockey, Sam Chifney, didn't bet on Escape on the first day, but bet heavily on him on the second day—and walked away with a small fortune.

As did the Prince of Wales.

The Jockey Club banned Chifney from the sport with immediate effect. Meanwhile, all the papers endlessly mocked and lampooned the Prince of Wales. His reputation, such as it was, never quite recovered from his close association with a known cheat—neither did his appetite for horse racing. He did, however, publicly stand by Chifney and even granted him a pension of £200 per year for the remainder of his days—a gesture which likely stemmed more from self-serving impulse to protect his reputation rather than loyalty in his heart.

"Prinny and Papa were old carousing mates when they were young," said Houghton.

Julian usually spent Derby Day in the company of Rake and Artemis, Rake's younger sister. However, since Rake had eloped with his jockey and Artemis had fled to her Yorkshire estate after the loss of her most beloved Thoroughbred, he found himself at loose ends and saying, "Lead the way."

Unlike Newmarket and Doncaster, Epsom Downs didn't yet have a grandstand, so Prinny's stand was the only elevated place from which to view the race, with three sides offering unimpeded views of the horseshoe-shaped course from start to finish. Julian navigated the room in his usual manner, smiling and offering greetings to one and all. Though a few were here for the race itself—and the outcome of bets placed—most came for the socializing and brandishing about of wealth and status.

Still, no one was immune to the vibrancy that enlivened the air and made the blood sparkle through the veins as Thoroughbreds began to assemble at the starting line, jockeys bedecked in an array of colorful silks.

While Julian experienced all those feelings of anticipation, it was another reason, one entirely novel and slightly troubling, that had his blood pumping hot and hard.

Lady Tessa.

This anticipation had to do with possibility.

Given the structure of his life and the same few hundred lords and ladies populated within it, it had been years since he met someone who offered the unknown...Someone who offered possibility beyond what he could predict.

Where was she, anyway?

He stepped to the wide balcony overlooking the starting line. Somewhere, amid the ten-thousand-strong scrum of Derby Day attendees, she was out there—to watch the race...to know her fate.

To find her in that massive horde was another matter. It wasn't only aristocrats who enjoyed the pleasures of Derby Day, but any Londoner who could make their way from Town to Epsom—by carriage, horse cart, foot, or any other conveyance at hand—for the event that was known as the Londoners' Day Out.

He made his way to the middle balcony with its view of the course's turns, including the infamous Tattenham Corner.

No sign of Lady Tessa there, either.

It wasn't until he stepped to the third balcony with its view of the finish line that his eye caught upon a wide-brimmed straw hat with its fluttery blue ribbon, escaped red-gold tendrils waving in the breeze...

Lady Tessa.

He leaned forward, squinting against the sun-bright day. It was definitely her, side pressed against the white railing, conversing in a tight bunch with three ladies. One of the ladies, Julian knew. *Mrs. Fairfax*, a widow and a popular figure in society. He'd never met the other two ladies who were of a height with Lady Tessa, one even sharing the same red-gold hair. They were clearly her two younger sisters. Even from this distance he could see they were beauties—like their sister, as well.

He noticed something more. How Lady Tessa behaved with her sisters—attentive...smiling without tension...protective...

Nurturing.

That word again.

Memory stole in—of how she'd served him tea.

How natural it had been for her.

Beneath her mannish mode of dress and forbidding exterior beat the heart of a woman softer than she wanted the world to know.

And here was another word returning to him—*possibility*.

What possibilities lay within the enigma that was Lady Tessa.

"Your Filthy Habit is looking in fine form, I'll say," came a voice behind Julian.

Julian tore his gaze away from Lady Tessa and pivoted. "Aye, that he is."

Along with the rest of the stand's occupants, he gravitated to the window overlooking the starting line. Jockeys shuffled, shouldered, jostled, and muscled their horses into their preferred starting positions. There were Good Bottom, Squirrel, and Old Bugger. All three fine goers, but all three lacking the nonspecific magic required to win a major race. Filthy Habit possessed that magic, but so too did a few others. Good Sir Longshanks could tear up the turf, and with Liam Cassidy as his jockey, he might do just that. And the Duchess of Acaster's Devil's Spawn held a competitive glint in his eyes that spoke of grit. But it was a filly who possessed the most magic on today's turf.

Little Wicked.

Upon her foaling, she'd been declared the best of her year—finely sculptured head that spoke of her Arabian lineage...long legs...sound hindquarters...silky coat...But beyond those not-so-unique physical characteristics, she held an additional special something—a brightness. Though horses couldn't smile, one would think Little Wicked was ever smiling.

She'd been lost in a card game by that wastrel Lord Clifford to a man named Blake Deverill. Many in society viewed Deverill as a chancer and interloper who was using his newfound wealth to muscle his way into the *ton*—a man who had no business owning a serious racehorse like Little Wicked.

But Julian viewed Deverill differently. He'd made a success of himself through ingenuity and hard work with his steam engine enterprise. How many members of the *ton* had achieved their status in life through their own grit, intelligence, and determination?

Certainly not Julian—or anyone else in this royal, elevated room.

The fact was, though he'd never met the man, Julian felt a respect for Deverill. Upon acquiring Little Wicked, he'd sent for the best trainer in France to take her in hand for the three-year-old racing season, which was the most important season in the career of a Thoroughbred. Deverill had also used a king's ransom to lure away the Duke of Richmond's favorite jockey, which the duke was still grousing about.

But that was horse racing. The rules were few and far between, and even then, good luck to anyone trying to enforce them.

Julian leaned forward and gripped the balcony rail, his gaze locked on the anxious line of horses and riders now ready for the firing of the starting gun.

He should want Little Wicked to win.

As a gentleman.

But as only he knew, his wanting knew no limits.

And *this* wanting—the wanting of Lady Tessa—respected no boundaries.

He wanted to win...

He wanted *her*.

Barring any false starts, he would know in less than three minutes if he was to have her.

Though he couldn't see her from this side of the stand, he

knew she would be watching as intently as he—and for the same reason.

At last, the starter lifted the gun into the air. The crowd fell as silent as ten or so thousand people could. The trigger pulled, and the shot cracked through the air an instant later. Impelled by their jockeys, the horses lurched forward and were off.

Little Wicked jumped to the fastest start, taking the lead by a nose, for Filthy Habit was right there with her. Working him through his paces before the race had taken effect, for the Thoroughbred was more focused than Julian had ever seen him. For all his defense of Filthy Habit, he'd harbored a few doubts. But now as the horse thundered up the slight ascent of Epsom's first furlong, he believed with every cell of his being.

Filthy Habit could win the Derby.

As the horses made the first turn, Julian and everyone else moved left with the action to the next balcony. Several horses, including Squirrel and Old Bugger, got their legs tangled and fell, but Julian's gaze didn't linger there. Rather, it held steady on the leaders—Filthy Habit and Little Wicked. The Derby was now the two-horse race Julian had hoped it would be.

Here, in the middle portion of the racecourse, it was essential to hold the lead position before the sharp, precarious turn of Tattenham Corner, where many a horse fell every year. Filthy Habit and Little Wicked approached the corner, and Julian's heart pounded as hard as their hooves on the turf, their bodies brushing against one another, each angling for the tightest line around the curve. Then they were around without incident, leaving the remainder of the field to their fates.

Now, the race was gaining heat, for the final stretch was downhill, as the jockeys all leaned forward and allowed their mounts to stretch out and have their head. Filthy Habit's turnover picked up, as did his speed. So, too, did Little Wicked's.

As Julian moved to the third balcony overlooking the finish line, his gaze cut away from the action and found Lady Tessa, her gloved hands gripping the white railing, her full lips pressed into a straight, firm line. The elation of the crowd had no effect on her as the horses blazed toward her, the finish line now in their sights. In fact, the nearer the horses sped, the more pinched her expression. The possibility—nay, *probability*—that Filthy Habit was going to win this race and she would be left with a debt to pay was writ plain there.

One night in his bed.

Still, perhaps a sliver of hope remained, for Little Wicked, with her smile and clear joy of racing, wasn't ceding ground. The filly refused to lose.

Filthy Habit would have to win it.

Then he stretched at the right moment at the finish line and did precisely that.

Slaps on the back and cheers of congratulation began pouring Julian's way, but it was fast upon Lady Tessa that his gaze remained.

In a jubilant crowd of thousands, she alone remained the only still figure, staring sightlessly where the horses had crossed the finish. Even from this distance, he could see she'd gone pale as a sheet—a siren's hopes dashed against the rocks.

As he became swept away by the ensuing celebrations—a failed attempt had even been made to lift him into the air—Julian understood he should call off the bet and let Lady Tessa off the hook.

It was what a gentleman would do.

But the blood rushing hot through his veins felt decidedly *un*gentlemanly.

That blood wouldn't hear of it.

To claim his win—to claim his one night—was the worst thing he could do.

And he couldn't not do it.

CHAPTER SEVEN

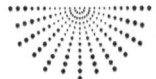

*T*he logic went thusly.

 Filthy Habit had won.

Which meant…

Lord Ormonde had won.

Which could only mean…

Tessa had lost.

Her eyes, stubbornly affixed to the finish line, refused to believe what had so clearly and definitively transpired before them.

Ormonde's Filthy Habit had nosed just ahead of his closest competitor at the crucial moment and won the Derby.

So many around Tessa were ripping loose with wild whoops and roars, jumping up and down, waving jubilant arms in the air. Even Gabriel was hugging—*hugging!*—the Duchess of Acaster, who was the widow of the late Sixth Duke of Acaster and, as such, now a tangential part of their family.

Tessa had only seen her brother hug one person—their mother—and that had been when she was near to drawing her last breath.

And now she'd seen him hug two people.

Right.

The point was that everyone was caught up in the moment.

Everyone—except Tessa.

She'd decided it best to remain very, very still...while her mind spun and raced through the order of events yet again.

Ten seconds ago, Filthy Habit won the Derby.

Which meant...

Ten seconds ago, the Marquess of Ormonde won the Derby.

Which meant...

Tessa had lost the wager.

Which meant...

She would have to pay her debt.

One night in the marquess's bed.

A shiver traced through her, crawling through nerves, pooling in an uneasy pit in her stomach.

How arrogant...how smug...how *sure* she'd been that he would lose.

How...*foolish.*

She had no one to blame but herself.

She'd provoked and goaded Ormonde—*unnecessarily.*

Except...it had felt utterly necessary to provoke and goad him.

A golden marquess needed to be provoked and goaded.

Now she would have to suffer the consequences of her provocation.

Suffer?

Though she had no evidence to support this theory, she harbored the inconvenient doubt that anyone had ever suffered in the Marquess of Ormonde's bed.

Again, the bothersome shiver.

"Tessa!" The exclamation was quickly followed by a bouncy hug from her youngest sister Viveca, pulling her from the prison of her worries. Though seven years younger, Viveca could've been Tessa's twin with her silvery blue eyes and silky red-blonde tendrils that ever wanted to escape and run off with the breeze—hair that Tessa tamed into submission every day with a tight chignon that brooked no arguments...hair that Viveca let do as it willed. Viveca was ever the sister who expressed herself with freedom and not the slightest hint of self-consciousness.

The opposite of their other sister, Saskia, who was stepping back and regarding Tessa with a slight cant to her head and a narrowing of the eyes. "Sister," she said, "is something amiss?"

Saskia—ever observant, ever reasonable, and ever direct with her observations.

Beneath the question, however, lay concern. Through childhood, Tessa had been as a second mother to Saskia and Viveca. Every member played a role in a family, and that was hers. As a result, Saskia and Viveca were attuned to her moods in the way of daughters with their mothers.

"Oh," she began, trying for breezy, "I need to be getting on to the betting post."

Saskia's eyebrows gathered. Viveca's followed. Tessa wasn't known in the family for *breezy*.

Mrs. Fairfax, the widowed cousin of the Duchess of Acaster and the woman who had taken up the cause of introducing Saskia and Viveca into society alongside the duchess, didn't seem to notice the tension vibrating between the sisters as she asked in her perfectly easy way, "Did your horse win, Lady Tessa?"

Such an innocent question.

"*Erm*, yes," said Tessa, before instantly doubling back on herself. "*No.*"

All three heads canted in question.

"It's a matter of some complexity."

"Oh, speaking of horses," said Viveca of a sudden. "Lord..." Her eyes squinted as she searched her mind. "Oh, what was his name?" Viveca never had been exact with names. "Anyway, a lord invited me to stroke his stallion behind the Royal Reform Club after the race. Shall we go?"

An aghast moment passed as Mrs. Fairfax gasped, Saskia snorted, and Tessa blinked.

Stroke his stallion.

Surely such a proposition could have but one meaning.

Tessa met Mrs. Fairfax's luminous brown gaze and found confirmation there.

"I believe," began the other woman in her sensible way, "now that the race is over, we should begin making our way toward our carriage so we can avoid the traffic back to London."

Viveca gave a little frown of disappointment. "I'm certain Lord Whatsit's stallion must be quite glorious."

"Lady Viveca," said Mrs. Fairfax in as stern a tone as Tessa had ever heard from the woman. "Every gentleman on God's dear earth thinks his stallion quite glorious."

Tessa suppressed the snort that desperately wanted release.

"Well, anyway," continued Viveca, "the gentleman himself is somewhat dashing, even if his one front tooth is showing a spot of rot." She shrugged a resigned shoulder. "We all like a little sweet, don't we?"

Oh, how Tessa dearly loved her sister.

But, oh, how her sister needed to be gone from this den of iniquity.

Mrs. Fairfax apparently thought the same, for with clear purpose, she stepped between Saskia and Viveca and neatly threaded her arms through theirs. "Shall we locate my dear friend Mr. Lancaster, then find my cousin and your brother to let them know we're leaving?" They'd taken a few steps when she tossed over her shoulder, "And Lady Tessa, I look forward to you and I furthering our acquaintance in London—*soon*."

Tessa knew a command when she heard one.

Three seconds later, Mrs. Fairfax disappeared into the raucous crowd with her sisters.

Which left Tessa alone with thoughts that circled and spun like a whirlwind...

Filthy Habit had won the Derby.

Ormonde had won the Derby.

Ormonde won their wager.

And she would have to pay.

She couldn't run from it.

Although, as her feet began moving, that felt precisely like what she was attempting as she shouldered and shoved her way through the dense crowd that flowed toward the racecourse like a spring river rushing wild with winter's heady snowmelt. She needed open air where she could draw a proper breath and have a proper think. So, she kept her head down and kept pushing, one determined step at a time, tamping down panic.

Panic would get her nowhere.

At last, she reached the outer edge of the crowd and broke free. Winded and surprisingly sore, she braced her hands on her knees and sucked in a deep breath.

There.

At last, she was able to breathe.

Now, perhaps, she could think and find a way out of this mess she'd waded into with Ormonde.

"Lady Tessa?" came an unfamiliar feminine voice at her back. Tessa braced herself before turning to find a woman she'd never met approaching, a smile on her mouth, but business in her eyes.

Dark of hair, the woman was of middling height and so slight a strong gust of wind could blow her away. But her piercing gray eyes sent a clear message that she was more than the sum of her physical parts. Like a thin blade of steel that gave the appearance of fragility, this woman held substance and the honed ability to cut. Tessa would wager on it.

She nearly groaned.

Nay.

She was never wagering again.

"You *are* Lady Tessa Calthorp, correct?"

"Correct," admitted Tessa, grudgingly. How she longed for the days when she'd merely been Miss Tessa Siren.

"I thought you must be."

"Was it the cravat and waistcoat that twigged you to my identity?"

A corner of the woman's mouth lifted into the semblance of a smile. "Your reputation as a sharp one precedes you."

"And you are?" Tessa was in no mood for games.

"Lady Beatrix St. Vincent," said the other woman.

A beat of silence ticked past as Tessa waited. The lady had three seconds to state her business before she started walking.

"You don't often attend racing meetings, do you?"

Tessa blinked. Unexpected question, that.

"I mean, given your business interests, one would think to see you around the racecourses."

Who was this woman, anyway? "I'm part owner of a gaming hell. I have nothing to do with the races."

"Ah, but your gaming hell is heavily invested in the Race of the Century."

"That's my brother's venture."

Lady Beatrix's head canted, contemplatively, as if she were carefully storing away each and every word issuing from Tessa's mouth for future use. "So, you're not aligned with your brother, the duke? Is there a rift at The Archangel?"

Uncharacteristically, Tessa snapped before she thought. "Of course not."

The other corner of Lady Beatrix's mouth lifted, the smile feline and keen. She wasn't the least affected by Tessa's show of temper.

The time had arrived to end whatever this was transpiring between them.

An interrogation?

Before parting words could pass Tessa's lips, however, Lady

Beatrix held up a finger and said, "The Duke of Rakesley's Hannibal won the Two Thousand Guineas." A second finger joined the first. "And the Duchess of Acaster's filly Light Skirt won the One Thousand." A third finger. "Now, the Marquess of Ormonde's Filthy Habit has taken the Derby. That's three of the five entrants for the Race of the Century secured."

Although Lady Beatrix wasn't telling Tessa anything she didn't already know, the facts spoken aloud had her heart jumping into a sudden gallop and a pit of anxiety opening in her stomach. There was her breath coming shallow and unsteady again.

It wasn't the facts in the plural sense, but rather a single fact.

Ormonde's Filthy Habit had won the Derby.

And she had a debt to pay.

Lady Beatrix's brow gathered with concern. "Lady Tessa, are you feeling all right? You're looking rather peaked, if I may say."

"Oh, well—"

"Here." She threaded an arm through Tessa's. "What you need is a lemon ice."

Not two minutes later, the sweet had been procured from a nearby stand and Lady Beatrix was watching to make sure Tessa ate it. Tessa wasn't sure why, but she felt strangely touched.

"Feeling better?" asked Lady Beatrix, her intelligent eyes missing nothing.

"Much," said Tessa, handing the sweet over. "You can finish it if you like."

As Lady Beatrix took the ice, an abrasive aristocratic voice that sounded sauced to the gills cut through the air, "If it ain't my dear, sweet daughter!"

Now, it was Lady Beatrix gone pale as her eyes squeezed shut. As if in doing so she could will away the man presently barreling toward them, offering the crowd no choice but to give way.

The Marquess of Lydon—a habitué of The Archangel, his

specialty being betting heavily and losing at every game he put his hand to. The man was a wastrel to his dissolute core.

And he was Lady Beatrix's father.

The resemblance was visible in the gray hue of their eyes and their long, straight noses. But there the similarity ended. Where Lydon was ruddy with drink, Lady Beatrix was pale with a smattering of freckles across her nose. Where the father carried a keg of weight around his middle, the daughter was thin and lissome as a stalk of wheat. Where Lydon laughed in forced merriment, Lady Beatrix observed her father in quiet judgment.

She didn't like her father, that was clear.

"Father," she said, her mouth so tight it could hardly emit the word.

A long and boisterous laugh rumbled from Lydon's belly. "I see you're the same as ever."

It wasn't a compliment.

Tessa decided now would be the perfect opportunity to take her leave. She'd taken two steps backward when Lady Beatrix's gaze shifted and pinned her in place. "Father, may I introduce you to Lady Tessa—"

Lydon's jollity fell away like a mask. "I know the chit."

"Lord Lydon," said Tessa in greeting.

"Now what?" he blustered, his ruddy face gone beet red. "You're here haranguing my daughter about a few flimsy pounds of blunt?"

Tessa didn't consider a sum of one thousand to be a few flimsy pounds but considered it best to keep the observation to herself.

"I told you," he continued, "I would settle up on the first of the—"

"Father," exclaimed Lady Beatrix, who had gone almost as red as her father with a blush that surely reached the tips of her toes. "'Twas *I* who introduced myself."

Lydon sniffed and jutted his chin toward Tessa. "You've got to keep your eye on her sort. Those gaming hell folk are money grubbers one and all."

Tessa took no offense. A lord as deeply in debt as the Marquess of Lydon would feel as much.

"*Her sort?*" Lady Beatrix shimmered with distress. "She is the sister of the Duke of Acaster."

Lydon snorted and waved a dismissive hand, shaking his head as he turned on a wobbly heel and shambled into the crowd before disappearing.

Leaving Lady Tessa alone with Lady Beatrix, who looked shamed by the exchange.

Tessa couldn't depart without a mollifying word. "I'll never be a puzzle piece that clicks into place with the *ton*." She added with a shrug, "And that is all right with me."

The last needed to be said, for it was true.

The sharpness reappeared in Lady Beatrix's eyes, signaling a return of her composure. "But, Lady Tessa, that's the beauty of the unique position you occupy in society. You don't have to fit in. You are the rare lady who can be entirely her own woman."

Tessa snorted. "Her own *foolish* woman."

The words had flown from her mouth before she could contain them.

Lady Beatrix's gaze narrowed. "Have you done something foolish, Lady Tessa?"

She would have caught that word—*foolish*.

And, *yes*, she had.

Ormonde.

An answer she would keep to herself.

"You don't strike me as the foolish type."

That got another snort from Tessa. "Apparently, foolishness doesn't have a type."

Lady Beatrix smiled. "May I quote you on that?"

"If you must," said Tessa.

Before she could ask what she'd just agreed to, Lady Beatrix bid her a good day and disappeared into the crowd that had in no way thinned, even now that the race was over.

Tessa hadn't been alone for three seconds when a familiar figure cut across her path.

The Duchess of Acaster.

The woman Gabriel had been hugging minutes ago.

"Your Grace!" she called out on impulse.

The duchess pivoted, turning the blazing glory of her smile onto Tessa. She inhaled a shallow gasp, such was the power of the Duchess of Acaster's renowned beauty, with her thick sable hair and luminous amber eyes and porcelain skin. One couldn't properly brace oneself for its impact.

And Gabriel—a man who wasn't demonstrative with his physical person—had been hugging her.

Right.

As she and the duchess began exchanging the usual greetings, Tessa questioned why she'd sought the duchess's attention.

Except she knew

It was the embrace.

She wanted to understand why her brother had embraced this woman, for he wouldn't embrace just any woman.

Tessa's eye snagged on a figure in the distance—a gentleman half a head taller than everyone else. Had she caught a glimpse of golden hair peeking out from beneath his hat? Or a wide set of shoulders, built for muscling through a Derby Day crowd?

"Did your favorite win?" asked the duchess, cutting into Tessa's thoughts.

She was simply continuing the conversation Tessa had started, but Tessa was feeling suddenly tetchy, her feet itching to move, for that distant figure had been familiar—*too* familiar.

But she must reply, of course. "For me, the horses are incidental. I've never observed Derby Day in person."

"And has the day been to your satisfaction?" The duchess looked as bored as she. Idle conversation was decidedly dull sport.

"Actually, I—" Tessa's gaze caught on the figure, and her mouth snapped shut.

Ormonde.

No longer far away, but in the near distance...and getting nearer, his eyes locked onto...*her.*

He came to a stop before them, and the breath in Tessa's lungs became stuck.

Was he here to gloat? For that was certainly triumph singing in his summer-blue eyes.

Was he...*oh*...was he here to claim his one night?

As the duchess began to make introductions, Tessa interrupted. "The marquess and I are acquainted."

The duchess's eyebrows looked as if they would lift off her forehead as her gaze flicked back and forth between Tessa and Ormonde. She was adding one and one together and clearly arriving at two.

And the subtle smile curved about Ormonde's mouth...

It held more than triumph.

Arrogance.

One would expect as much from a victor.

But his smile held something else, too—something solely for her.

Determination.

If she'd harbored the slender hope that he would forgive her debt without claiming it, like a gentleman should, all such hope was immediately dashed.

Then he bowed, pivoted, and strode away. Was that a swagger she detected in his step?

Who was *this* Marquess of Ormonde?

"You're acquainted with the marquess?"

Tessa realized she was staring at the back of the man.

Or, more accurately, the *backside* of the man.

My, but he was built solid as a marble monument to Adonis.

She tore her gaze away. "He's a member of The Archangel," she said, careful of her words.

Disbelief shone in the duchess's eyes. "So, *that* was about business?"

Dread snaked through Tessa. "*That* was about a debt—a debt that must be paid."

Speaking the words aloud transferred them from the theoretical to the concrete—imbuing them with substance.

This debt...

It existed.

It must be paid.

"Your Grace," came a masculine shout.

A young gentleman with a shock of coppery hair and a too-bright smile was practically tripping over his own feet in his haste to get to the duchess. *The Earl of Wrexford.* Tessa had noted him at The Archangel. Not a spender, this earl. He came for the company of friends rather than the gaming.

Tessa took the opportunity to slip away, unnoticed. She had no intention of being trapped in conversation with an eager young lord who only wanted to bask in the glory of the Duchess of Acaster.

Yet as she moved through the crowd that had finally begun to thin, she realized she was walking in the direction opposite the one the marquess had taken. Instinct urged her to pick up her pace and run.

She stopped.

Run?

When had she ever run?

When had she ever taken the coward's way and patiently waited for the ax poised above her neck to drop?

She couldn't live that way.

She would have this debt settled.

She swiveled and began striding, certainty in every step even as she experienced a wobble in her core.

Ahead, he appeared, engaged in conversation with a small group of gentlemen. Her gaze roved over his back—*again*. Following the width of his broad shoulders and his golden hair between his shoulder blades, confirming he was still as solidly and massively built as he'd been three minutes ago.

Right.

She cleared her throat when she'd drawn near enough and said, "Ormonde," before she lost her nerve.

His name hardly emerged loud enough to be detected above the din of the crowd, but he heard it and glanced over his shoulder. Surprise flicked in his eyes.

"I believe we need to discuss the settlement of a debt, my lord."

The statement emerged clear and direct and without a hint of the wobble quivering through her.

He turned toward the group. "Gentlemen, if you'll excuse me."

Then Tessa was walking—*striding*—in silence by Ormonde's side. They weren't precisely walking as a pair, for her arm wasn't linked through his, but she felt him all the same. A sort of energy that pulsed between them, as he led her through the crowd that didn't make it easy and around the back of a building that appeared to be a stable.

And she was alone with this massive, built man.

She was a tall woman, but her head had to tip back so she could meet his eyes—eyes that gave the impression of openness due to their similarity to a clear blue sky, but which were, in fact, the very opposite.

One couldn't read what lay behind the Marquess of Ormonde's eyes.

She swallowed, her throat gone dry. "About the debt..."

"Yes?" he asked, carefully.

Expectation glinted within those summer-blue eyes.

And she understood what that expectation was.

He expected her to try to beg off.

"Shall we get the debt settlement over with tonight?"

Debt settlement?

She couldn't very well call it what it was.

The one night in your bed.

Though she was being bold and brave, she wasn't that bold and brave.

Debt settlement would have to do.

A subtle smile curved about his mouth. *"Over with?"*

She nodded and tried not to swallow—and failed.

His gaze drifted down and followed the undulation of her throat above her cravat.

Of a sudden, she was too hot.

He leaned forward as if to invade her space, and she offered up a silent prayer of gratitude to her past self who had deemed it practical for her to wear a wide-brimmed hat to the Derby. Even so, she froze, her back pressed against the wall, catching his scent above the horsey smell that permeated the air of Epsom Downs.

He planted his hands to either side of her head and angled his face, the smile on his mouth still there…

Still determined.

Then he shifted and before Tessa understood what he was about, he ducked beneath the wide, distancing brim of her hat and she felt his warm breath on the patch of skin just below her earlobe. Her insides flipped and fluttered before deciding to ignite and now she was thanking the heavens for this wall at her back, for without it she would surely collapse into a molten puddle.

His lips moved against her ear. "Not yet," he muttered.

Then he pulled back, met her gaze one last time, and pushed off the wall.

And he was gone.

Now Tessa knew what a house on fire felt like.

Ablaze.
Entirely engulfed in flame.
Not yet.
If *not yet*, then...
How soon?

CHAPTER EIGHT

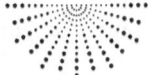

LONDON, A WEEK LATER

*H*e was a heel.

Of that, Julian had little doubt, as he found himself—*again*—on Sloane Street.

He must've covered five miles by now, as he paced up and down its length.

In his defense, he hadn't intended to seek out Lady Tessa at her home. He'd gone to The Archangel first, where he'd been informed by the implacable doorman that this was her night off. A forbidding narrowing of the eyes and the arch of a single eyebrow had accompanied the information.

Which was how Julian ended up on Sloane Street, wearing a rut in the cobblestones.

Steeling his resolve to do the right thing.

To let her off the hook.

To tell her the debt was forgiven…And they could each go their own merry way…And perhaps look back upon the entire misbegotten episode with fondness and a laugh.

That was what he would say, anyway.

And he would say it the way he said everything—with good humor and amiability.

She would believe him.

Even if he didn't.

His entire life was constructed of falsehood. Why should his interactions with Lady Tessa be any different?

Indeed, *why*?

Why did his interactions with her *feel* different?

Feel...*true*?

But what did he know about the truth?

Or how it would feel?

Once he'd had enough of this limbo he'd created for himself, he strode across the street and practically leapt up the five steps to her doorstep. He gave the knocker three firm raps before he could reconsider.

This was the correct course of action.

Of course, it was.

A minute passed, and no answer came, but he could see an orange glow around closed curtains.

She was home and awake.

Unease sheered through him. He clenched a fist and began a genuine harassment of the door. He would give it another minute, then action would be taken. It was a solid enough door, but he didn't like its odds against the heel of his boot.

Of a sudden, the door swung open, and a thoroughly piqued Lady Tessa stood in the center of the doorway, her cheeks flushed, a question in her eyes. Like the first time he'd knocked on her door, she wasn't wearing cravat or waistcoat, but a man's shirt tucked into her skirts, her thick red-gold hair in a loose plait.

She was dressed like a woman not expecting company.

Annoyance flared through Julian. "Do you open your door to every man who bangs upon it?"

"Just you, it seems," she said, dry.

Julian was in no mood to be chastened. "Did you not hire a butler?"

She exhaled a long-suffering sigh. "Seems to have slipped my mind."

Blasted frustrating woman.

"If you could please state your business?" The instant the question was out of her mouth, her brow crinkled and a blush stained her cheeks. "Are you here about—"

"*Debt settlement*, yes," he said, suddenly as uncomfortable as she.

As that had been her term for it, she would immediately take his meaning.

Wordlessly, she stood aside and allowed him entry.

It was the aroma filling the air that assailed him first. If Heaven descended to Earth, this would be how it smelled. "What is that scent?" he was unable not to ask.

Her head canted. "What is the first note that comes to mind?"

"*Note?*"

"Scent."

"Jasmine?"

She nodded, slowly, weighing his answer. "Of course." Her head canted. "And the second?"

Julian considered for a moment. "Smoky...*rice?*"

That answer didn't make a great deal of sense to Julian, but it got an approving smile from Lady Tessa. "*Exactly.*" She led him into the drawing room. "You'll have to excuse the mess. I wasn't expecting visitors."

Here, Julian located the source of the heavenly aroma. Except..."What am I looking at?"

Populated atop two large rectangular tables were individual piles of what appeared to be leaves and dried flowers and...were those citrus rinds?

"Since my sisters moved into Gabriel's mansion, I've started an endeavor I've been itching to try."

She spoke the words as if the goal of the endeavor were obvious to the casual observer.

"Are you in training to become an apothecary?" It was his best guess and not a bad one, given the evidence before him.

A smile hovered within her silver-blue eyes. "Tea."

"*Tea?*"

"Well, the blending of it."

"Ah," he said, remembering she'd mentioned as much the morning she'd made him tea.

"I have a fondness for tea," she said with her customary unapologetic directness. "So many flavors can be blended into it, not to mention the number of varieties of tea itself to be had."

"I'm more of a coffee man myself."

She scrunched her nose. "Coffee is a bit heavy on the palate for my tastes."

"Ah."

She indicated he take a seat on an ancient settee whose damask had been worn to fraying threads from decades, perhaps centuries, of use. She perched on the chair opposite. Before him sat a woman who wouldn't have noticed the state of her furniture, save that it was clean, tidy, and functional. How many sisters of dukes thought thusly?

One, as far as Julian knew.

"The smoked-rice scent you caught in the air?"

His brow wanted to gather at the seeming non sequitur. "Yes?"

"It's a rare green tea that comes from China. *Sencha.*"

"I suppose you buy that at Twinings?"

She laughed. "Oh, heavens no. I have a source who deals with a Dutch trader who procures it directly from a merchant in China. I can only get it once a year."

Before Julian sat a woman who would, literally, go to the ends of the earth for tea.

A useful thing to know about a person.

"Tea is my one indulgence."

"Just the one?" he asked. "You're a lady now; you're entitled to all the indulgences the world has on offer."

Fervor and passion shone in her eyes, and a feeling stirred within Julian—a feeling at odds with what he'd come here to say.

A feeling that held a demand.

Rather than forgive the debt, he should claim his right to payment.

He should claim his right to *her* for one night.

His *right*?

This was the year 1822, not 822.

He had no *right* to her.

But that knowledge didn't prevent parts of him from wishing it were so.

The spark of humor faded from her eyes. Perhaps she'd caught a glimmer of medieval stirrings in his.

She was waiting for him to state his business.

He cleared his throat.

"Someday," he began, "perhaps we might look back on this whole episode with a laugh."

Her brow lifted. *"This whole episode?"*

He'd begun in the wrong place. "After we've each gone our merry way."

"Our merry way," she repeated. Her eyes narrowed upon him. "Have you recently suffered a cosh to the head?"

He snorted. "Not that I'm aware of. But then, I might not remember, mightn't I?"

A little humor never went amiss—except the theory would explain a great deal about his recent, *erm*, wagers.

She watched him for ten held-breath seconds before shifting forward. She'd made up her mind about something. "Let's speak openly, shall we?"

"I believe that would be to both our benefits."

She nodded, her steady eyes trained on him. "Have you come to collect your one night?"

How was that for directness?

"I've come here to—"

Forgive the debt would've been his next words—if the deafening crash of shattering glass hadn't filled the room the next instant.

A large rock whizzed past Lady Tessa's head, missing it by a few inches, and landed at Julian's feet. Instinctively, he lurched forward and reached out to grab the nape of her neck and duck her head down. If the assailant yet lurked, he wouldn't have an easy target.

"Stay here," he shouted, as glass clattered to floorboards.

"But I—"

"*Stay.*"

Her jaw clamped shut; mutiny shone in her eyes.

On a low crouch, he rushed toward the smashed front window that overlooked Sloane Street and peered around the curtain now swinging with the night breeze, ready to give chase at the least sign of the assailant. As he could have predicted, they'd legged it.

"They'll be long gone, won't they?" came Lady Tessa's contralto voice just beyond his shoulder.

Annoyed, Julian half turned. "I thought I told you to—"

"*Stay?*" She shook her head. "You need to know two things about me, Lord Ormonde."

Julian felt the reflexive flinch—*Ormonde*—and saw her take note. Interest sparked in her eyes, but she continued her scold, "I am not a dog who can be commanded, and I make my own decisions about my person."

"Do you know who did this?"

"I have a decent idea."

A few beats of silence ticked by as he waited and she continued to say nothing. "Would you deign to enlighten me?"

"Oh, it's surely Blaze Jagger. Well, not him directly. He would've had one of his toadies throw the rock. But it was done at his behest, definitely."

She spoke as if she were reciting the shopping list, completely without emotion or concern. If she was rattled or shaken, she was doing a bang-up impersonation of someone who wasn't. While he understood and respected her desire for autonomous personhood, now wasn't the time for urbane, rational discussion.

Now was the time for action.

"Well, then I suggest you gather what you'll need for the night," he said, meeting the coolness of her voice note for note. "You're coming with me."

Instinct had a quick refusal poised on her lips. Except Lady Tessa wasn't a person guided by instinct, but rather by good sense. She considered herself a rational and pragmatic woman, and as such, she couldn't quite utter the *no* that so wanted airing.

She pivoted on her heel, tossing over her shoulder before she exited the room, "Meet me at the front door in two minutes."

The thrill of triumph that shot through Julian was completely inappropriate given the circumstances of her acquiescence, but he'd won an exchange with Lady Tessa and he would take his victories where they came.

The reason that had brought him to her door—*the wager*—was no longer the important thing.

Keeping Lady Tessa safe was.

* * *

THE MARQUESS HADN'T BROUGHT her to his primary London address, Tessa understood that much.

That address would've been located in either St. James's or Grosvenor or Berkeley Squares.

Instead, she was crossing the threshold of an unassuming townhouse on Little Thomas Street in Cheapside.

As she followed Ormonde into the drawing room just off the small entry hall, it struck her this townhouse held all the comforts of a home with its low fire burning in the hearth.

Discreet servants accustomed to their master coming and going at whim kept this house.

He crossed the room and lowered himself onto a burgundy velvet settee, resting an ankle on a thigh and stretching his arms along the back of the sofa. Gone was the amiable golden lord of the *ton* and in his place was a man in control, serious and confident.

And attractive.

Oh, he was always attractive, but this attractiveness extended beyond handsomeness.

This was the sort of attractiveness that sent a quiver tracing up a woman's thighs.

Better she remained standing, rather than take the chair opposite him.

"So," he began, the first word he'd uttered in her direction since they'd vacated Sloane Street. "I take it you and Jagger aren't friendly business associates."

She stepped to the back of the armchair and rested her forearms. "I'd never met the man until Derby Day."

"Right."

He was waiting for her to continue.

"It's this Race of the Century business." She didn't owe Ormonde an accounting of her affairs, yet she continued, "Gabriel and the Duke of Richmond are cutting the blacklegs out of the race day betting post."

"That'll be hundreds of thousands of pounds."

"It will."

"Why not let Jagger have a piece of the pie?"

Tessa understood why this golden lord would wonder as much, but he knew nothing of how the London underworld was ordered. "Whether I agree or not, Gabriel drew the line. Jagger knows the rules."

"Which are?"

"If we make that concession, then Jagger will demand another and another until we're thoroughly and inextricably in his pocket. Next thing, we'll be doing his bidding."

Ormonde's brow gathered. If his expression wasn't quite thunderous, then thunderous adjacent. "You're going to fight him."

"*Fight* is a strong word." She gave a shrug. "A fight wouldn't benefit anyone. I don't want to fight Blaze Jagger. I want to solve him."

Ormonde cocked his head. "In case you hadn't noticed, Jagger's a flesh-and-blood man, not a mathematical equation."

Tessa tried not to let her annoyance show. But really, this lord had been—*correctly...irritatingly*—taking her measure.

"I know precisely what he is, Lord Ormonde," she said. "He's angry, ambitious, ruthless, calculating, and capable."

"All qualities which make him a dangerous adversary."

She couldn't disagree. But this marquess needed to understand something vital—something she was under no obligation to tell him, even as the words were flowing from her mouth... "He's the sort of person Gabriel and I could have easily become."

Ormonde's brow gathered with curiosity. "Pardon?"

She would have to explain. "Surely, the *ton's* gossip mill has provided you an outline of our family's history."

Ormonde's gaze remained fixed on her. "A grandfather who cut and ran from his family. A great uncle who died without legitimate issue."

She nodded. "When I was nine years old, our parents died within six months of each other."

"Blast."

"Then Gabriel was given a scholarship to attend Eton College."

Tessa caught the instant the import of that statement sank into Ormonde's mind. "Leaving you and your sisters to fend for yourselves in London."

"Gabriel didn't desert us." That needed to be understood. "Him being educated at Eton was our family's best hope."

"Hope doesn't put food on the table."

"I worked odd jobs and kept us going."

His ankle unhooked from his thigh, and he shoved forward with sudden distress. "What about living quarters?" he asked. "Did you have a roof over your heads?"

She nodded. "After Mama and Papa died, we invented an uncle who never happened to be home when the rent was collected. It was how we were able to keep our small flat of rooms in the early days." She gave a dry laugh. "Of course, the irony isn't lost on us that we did, indeed, have a long-lost uncle. Anyway," she continued, "I dressed in Gabriel's old clothes and did any odd job that came my way to keep us out of the work-house. Chimney sweep…assisting washerwomen…helping mend clothes for resale at pawnbrokers…Some days, I begged. Others, I wasn't above picking a random pocket or two. Whatever was available, and where I could bring my sisters. Nothing that held us together was out of bounds, then or now, if it comes to it. Then Gabriel made a discovery. The lordlings at Eton were willing to pay him for doing their schoolwork."

"Enterprising."

"It might not seem all that impressive to you, my lord, but our luck changed that day." She felt strangely prickly and defensive. "We did everything it took to keep our family together and our sisters safe."

"*You* are impressive, Lady Tessa."

The praise crept through Tessa, warming places inside her long gone cold. She tried to shake off the feeling and continued, "My point in telling you is Jagger's is the life we could've led if our lives hadn't zigged when it could've zagged. Fate is that simple. A different turn here or there can set the course of a life in a whole new direction."

Enigmatic emotion passed behind Ormonde's eyes. Something in her words had affected him. Silence woven through with complex feelings and memories expanded into the air between them.

She'd said too much—revealed too much of her past...of herself. *Exposed*, that was her in this moment.

Right.

"I must send a note to my family," she said, brisk efficiency in her voice. "They tend to arrive unannounced on my doorstep. I can't be missing and put them through that worry."

After Filthy Habit had won the Derby and Ormonde their wager, she'd informed Gabriel of the possibility that she might take an impromptu holiday. He hadn't asked too many questions —save one.

With someone?

She'd snapped a dismissive retort worthy of an older sister to a younger brother and that had been the end of it.

Except that hadn't been the end of it.

Here, she stood in a townhouse owned by the Marquess of Ormonde, poised at the beginning.

Of...*something*.

Exactly *what* yet eluded her.

A few beats of time ticked past before he unfolded his long body and stood. "Of course. Follow me."

Alone in an upstairs bedroom, Tessa dashed off a quick note to Saskia and Viveca and handed it off to the housekeeper who appeared to have materialized from thin air. Ormonde must've sent her.

Only then did she properly take in her surroundings.

The room was surprisingly opulent, all done in gold accents and deep mahogany wood and silken purples that bordered on black.

This was the bedroom of a marquess.

In Cheapside.

A bureau on the opposite side of the room caught her eye.

Curiosity had her closing the distance and considering the solid structure—the top half with two closed doors and the bottom half with three large drawers. Her palm smoothed across the fine surface of inlaid woods worked in an intricate floral motif.

Temptation beckoned...How easily she could slide a drawer open...Ormonde would never know.

She shouldn't.

But what rose above that rather weak objection was possibility—the possibility that within this bureau lay something personal to the Marquess of Ormonde.

Something that would help explain him.

For here was what now gnawed at her about the golden lord —the longer they were acquainted, the less she felt she knew him.

Unbidden, memory flashed.

Of him in the back room of Blanton & Co....

Of the long, jade-green cylindrical object he'd slipped into his pocket.

Was that object in one of these drawers?

Determined fingers hooked a brass pull...

"You might rethink doing that," came a low rumble behind her.

A startled, guilty Tessa swung around. Though Ormonde stood on the other side of the room, his voice vibrated through her as if he'd uttered the words in her ear.

"Why?" she asked, more defiant than she had a right to be.

Of course, he was under no obligation to answer.

"You won't be able to unsee what's in there."

A light scoff escaped her. "Are you in possession of stolen treasure, perchance?"

His scoff answered hers. "Hardly."

Tessa's desire to open the drawer transformed into unrequited physical need. Heart racing, her palms experienced a light slick of perspiration as she pulled and it glided open on silent waxed runners.

Anticipation pulsing through her, it took a full three seconds for her eyes to register what they were beholding. Her brow gathered, and she blinked. *"Feathers?"*

Across the black velvet drawer lining lay every sort of feather —striped pheasant, fluffy quail, dazzling peacock, extravagant ostrich...

"Disappointed?" No mistaking the indulgent smile in the question.

And she understood.

She *was* disappointed.

And that reaction told her something.

Not about him—but about herself.

"Were you expecting to find something else?"

They both knew what *something else* he was referring to—the object he'd slipped into his pocket at Blanton & Co.

He was toying with her.

Of course she'd been expecting *that* something else.

Nay, not simply expecting.

Wanting.

She faced him, and in doing so, faced her wanting. "Since you came to my house about *debt settlement* tonight," she began. "Is this to be our one night?"

CHAPTER NINE

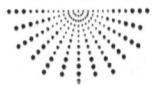

*J*ulian ignored the fact that they were in a bedroom and pulled from a deep well of integrity and, somehow, made himself speak the truth…"No."

Lady Tessa opened her mouth and closed it, incredulous. She opened it again. *"No?* What was all that talk about looking back and laughing about it?"

"Tonight was—*is*—about forgiving your debt."

"Forgiving it?"

She lifted an ostrich feather from the drawer and gave its length a contemplative stroke. He nodded, his mouth gone too dry for speech.

Silver-blue eyes narrowed. "You came to beg off?"

The woman seemed…annoyed.

With him.

"Have I done something wrong?"

Her hand stopped, mid-stroke. "But what if I…" She swallowed. She seemed to be screwing up the nerve to say something.

"If you…?"

He very much wanted her to complete that sentence.

He might want it with every fiber of his being.

Her tongue swiped across her full bottom lip, and all Julian wanted was to replace it with his. "What if I want the night promised me?"

Had she truly spoken the words every fiber of his being wanted?

He didn't trust himself to answer.

"What if...," rasped across her throat. "What if I *demand* you give me my one night?"

Julian's brow gathered. Wasn't it to have been *his* one night?

Yet she was speaking as if it were *hers*.

And he was denying her.

Lady Tessa had lost the bet—but one wouldn't know it.

A powerful surge of desire pulsed to life inside him...arrowed into deep, interior places he kept hidden away, safe from feeling.

"Is this where you meet your mistress?" she asked.

Oh, the questions she kept asking.

He wasn't sure he would survive them.

"Aye."

"I want you to treat me how you treat her...*here*...*tonight*."

She couldn't be more clear.

Except she hadn't the faintest idea what she was demanding.

"You don't."

"Do you think me a woman who doesn't know her own mind?"

Julian should turn on his heel and exit this room...this town-house...and Lady Tessa's life. For if he stayed, he would say, "*Undress.*"

He did—so, he did.

She inhaled a sharp, little gasp of shock. *Good.* Perhaps she would flee.

Her head canted, eyes gone bright with curiosity and suspicion. "Do you think to scare me off?"

She was standing her ground, which left Julian with but one

way to proceed—to stand his. "Don't you wish to receive the same treatment as my mistress?"

The air went electric. He detected her pulse throbbing hard against her throat.

It was the truth—and it was a dare.

Until now, she hadn't known this side of him existed.

There was yet so much she didn't know. So much he could teach her. Still, it was only gentlemanly to offer her one last chance.

"Or…"

"*Or?*" The question emerged more than a mite breathless.

He indicated the door. "Or you can leave."

Her gaze searched his. "This is how you treat your mistresses?"

"Yes." She needed to understand this truth.

"Have any ever left?"

"No."

"You're quite sure of yourself, aren't you?"

"In this way, yes."

"And what way is that?"

"My ability to bring you pleasure unlike any you've ever experienced."

Through her breathlessness lifted a mildly skeptical eyebrow. "With *feathers?*"

"If you like. It's but one method."

"You have *methods?*"

A smile pulled at one corner of his mouth. "Yes."

A confounded laugh escaped her.

Julian crossed his arms over his chest and waited—and watched. He could be a very patient man.

His words—and their effect on her imagination—were having the most interesting influence on Lady Tessa. As she contemplated the ostrich feather held in her hands, a light blush crept up her throat, pinking her cheeks and the tips of her ears. Indecision shimmered about her, but something else, too.

Curiosity.

For all her knowledge of the workings of the world, this woman was an innocent.

An innocent who no longer wished to remain so.

She wanted knowledge—and she wanted him to be her teacher.

A want he was powerless against.

She returned the feather to its place in the velvet-lined drawer and lifted her gaze to meet his, decision in her over-bright silver-blue eyes.

What was her decision?

To leave?

Or...

To undress?

Unhurriedly, she reached up and nimble fingers slipped the single button of her cloak from its loop. The garment fell to the Aubusson carpet.

Anticipation coiled within Julian, muscles tensed, his cock gone half full.

She reached for the band of her skirt, flicked another few buttons, and it was joining the cloak on the floor. Her shirt fell to the middle of her thighs, just above the plain wool stockings gartered above her knees.

Before him stood the sister of a duke—and the most interesting woman he'd ever met. If he hadn't suspected it before, her clothing told him so now. No silk or lace or frills for this lady, but sensible wool.

"Perhaps my boots should go next?" she asked.

"As you like," he somehow spoke through the desire clogging his throat.

She reached down and made quick work of the laces of her practical black boots, before kicking them off.

This woman knew nothing about the art of seduction and it was...charming. So utterly without calculation. He couldn't help wondering if he'd ever encountered this in his dealings with the opposite sex. After all, though he didn't consort with any doxy on a street corner, he did associate with women with whom there would be no entanglements—women from the demimonde... women who benefitted from seducing him with everything in their arsenal.

All this woman wanted from him was the pleasure promised —*one night*.

Her garters and wool stockings quickly followed. When she tossed them aside, they didn't flutter to the floor like their silk counterparts, but landed with a light thud.

Now, it was her clad in naught but a linen shirt and whatever garments that lay beneath. She pulled the shirt over her head, then was standing in nothing but chemise and stays. She didn't attempt to cover herself with her hands. She wasn't a woman to get in the way of her own interests.

Julian's mouth went dry. He might have gotten carried away. Lady Tessa was the sort of woman who had demands—and would see them satisfied. Yes, he could make her scream with pleasure, but that was as far as he could take her.

For he sensed the physical would only be the beginning for this woman.

She would crave and demand *more*—and what this woman wanted, she took.

Even went to the ends of the earth for it.

But he was getting ahead of himself, wasn't he?

What he had now was one night.

He should've been prepared for this—he'd seen a woman's body clad in all varieties of ways—yet he wasn't.

This was *Lady Tessa's* scantily clad body.

Her mode of dress had accomplished its mission to obfuscate

what lay beneath, for her masculine clothes had hidden a secret—and he was the only man in London who knew it.

Lady Tessa possessed the body of a goddess—all lush valleys and peaks and rounded curves, rosy nipples pushed up by the stays and straining against the gossamer muslin of chemise.

She reached for the laces of the stays, which were at the front between her breasts—practical and independent to the last, this woman—and her gaze met his. Within, he didn't detect the uncertainty of a virgin, but decision and daring and excitement.

The pleasure unlike she'd ever experienced—the pleasure promised—she wanted it.

She tugged the laces, and the garment fell loose and joined her other clothes on the floor. Beneath the chemise, curves abounded from her heavy breasts to the indent of her waist, the flare of her hips, the shadowed mound of her sex. She took the hem of the chemise, lifted it over her head, and flung it away.

His cock was no longer at half-mast.

There was no halfway with this woman.

"Now what?" she asked.

Within her eyes shone a dare.

It was his turn—to deliver the pleasure promised.

He pushed off the wall he'd been propped against and crossed the room. He took the ostrich feather from the drawer and stepped forward. Not so close that he touched her, but near enough that he could angle his head and whisper in her ear, "Now you find out what *this* is for."

His lips so close to the cup of her ear…he nearly pressed his mouth to it. But he resisted, knowing that if he started kissing her, he wouldn't be able to stop.

So, he pulled away, but not before inhaling and catching her subtle scent of citrus, jasmine, and Chinese tea. He wondered if her scent changed daily with her teas.

What would tomorrow's be?

Of course, he wouldn't know.

For them, there was no tomorrow.

He reached for a few more feathers before tugging open another drawer.

"Is that...?" she began, hesitant.

He glanced over his shoulder and met curiosity in her eyes. "Yes?"

"Is that where you keep the object that I saw you slip into your pocket at Blanton and Company?"

A smile tugged at his mouth. It couldn't help itself. So, she had been thinking—and wondering—about what she'd seen. "No."

"Will you use it tonight?"

"No."

Was that a flash of disappointment in her eyes?

"You aren't ready for that," he added.

Yet.

He'd almost said *yet*—and he shouldn't.

Yet implied a next time.

And there wouldn't be a next time.

Instead, he pulled a long black silk scarf from the drawer and held it up. "Do you trust me?"

"Should I?"

"Yes."

A heavy beat of the heart later, she nodded her consent.

He closed the distance between them, her head tipped back, gaze holding his, until he reached up and covered her eyes, tying the scarf snugly at the back of her head.

Here was Lady Tessa, so vulnerable...so trusting.

A Lady Tessa only he knew.

Nothing that transpired between them tonight would betray her vulnerability and trust.

Her breath came in jagged catches as he stepped behind her. His fingers longed to touch her, to know the feel of her skin. Instead, he took the ostrich feather and brushed it up her spine. A breathless laugh escaped her as it lightly trailed down. Just as the feather reached the top of her bottom, her back gave a little arch, and she exhaled a shivery sigh.

"The denial of one sense," he said, "only heightens others—like sensation."

He ran the feather lower, over the lush curve of her bottom, down the back of a long leg...up the inside of calf...thigh... leisurely, allowing sensation and anticipation to build with each inch higher, stopping just shy of her sex. He heard her breath catch in her lungs, as she waited.

He moved around to the front of her. A light blush tinted her skin, rosy nipples puckered—a body aching to be touched...by him. The feather traced along her arms, across her delicate clavicle, between her breasts, around her nipples, down her belly, pulling a giggle here, a gasp there, then lower...a light tease at the mound of her sex.

Her sex...

Beneath red-gold curls, her sex would be swollen and wet... begging for a touch firmer than the caress of a feather.

A feather could only take one so far.

"Ormonde," she said, the name a plea.

He froze. *"Julian,"* he growled. "You must call me Julian."

"Julian," she repeated, reaching up and removing the blindfold. Impatient lust shone in her eyes, flared pupils having pushed blue irises into thin silvery rings. "Julian, I need—" She gave him a quick up-and-down and frowned. "Aren't you going to—"

"Undress?"

She nodded.

He shook his head.

Pleasure...denial.

He gave pleasure; he denied himself.

Those were the rules of this game.

But Lady Tessa was asking for more—as he'd thought she would.

She reached out and removed the feather from his hand,

letting it flutter to the floor. Then she stepped so close her puckered nipples nearly pressed into his waistcoat. Her head tipped back, and she held his gaze. Alongside lust shone defiance.

Before him stood a woman utterly unafraid to be herself. A trait incredibly attractive—a trait that shook him to his core.

"Julian," she said.

A feeling, trembly and new, lit through him. His name on her tongue, spoken in her low, contralto voice…It set a fluttery feeling awing inside him.

"The feathers are nice, but…"

"*But?*"

"I want *your* touch on me."

She took his hand and pressed it to the indent of her waist, moved it across her ribs to her stomach. This feel of her beneath his hand—soft and hot and vibrant—wasn't how this was supposed to go.

Of course, he touched women. He brought them pleasure with capable fingers. But this…the feel of her…This brought *him* pleasure.

This wasn't denial but the opposite.

Indulgence.

The control that defined his life and his very personhood was slipping…

She guided his hand to her *mons pubis.* "I need your touch *here*," she said…*begged.*

She was so wet and slick and hot. He should pull away.

But he couldn't.

He held the fruit of temptation in his hand, and he couldn't not graze a thumb along that sweet, swollen slit. Her eyes drifted shut and a groan poured from parted lips. He stroked her again, and she reached up and hooked her hands onto the back of his neck, her body gone molten against him, mindless fingers weaving through his hair. His thumb went firmer, applying more pressure, and she gasped against his neck, then moaned, her breath warm against his skin. He pressed his other hand to the small of her back, to steady her, as driven by instinct and need, she stretched up his clothed body, mindless with abandon.

"This way," he uttered.

Without releasing her, he stepped them to the bed and sat on its edge, pulling her to a straddle atop him. Her face above his, a daring smile tipped about her mouth, curiosity in her eyes. She hadn't the faintest idea what was about to happen next—or the exquisite pleasure he was about to deliver to her.

Again, his thumb slid along her slit and grazed the sensitive nub at the top. "*Oh*," she cried, lifting onto her knees as she strained to offer him more access.

She needed more, and he knew what to give her.

Her knees to either side his thighs, he pressed into her with his forefinger—slowly...deliberately. Her breath caught in her throat as she took him in. "Oh, that feels so...*good*."

Guided by instinct, she pressed down onto him as his thumb continued stroking her nub, and she began to ride him, her head tossed back, her breath hard and sharp. One hand caught around his neck, the other trailed down, between their bodies—hers naked...his clothed—and grazed trembly fingers across his stone-hard length through the superfine of trousers that only just contained him.

How his body urged him to surrender...To allow her to unbutton the falls and free his cock. She was in position above him. All it would take was a single, swift stroke and he would be inside her.

Surrender, came the siren's call.

With a strength of will he hadn't been sure he possessed, he covered her hand with his and removed it from him.

Questioning eyes met his. "Aren't you going to...Aren't *we* going to...?"

"*We* aren't," the statement gravel in his throat. When her mouth opened to protest, he continued, "But *you* are."

He set his near-overwhelming desire aside and focused on hers, one hand steady on her back and the other simultaneously stroking and penetrating her as he established a rhythm—the one that would bring her to climax. A nipple brushed against his lips, and he flicked his tongue to taste its sweetness, sucking it into his mouth. A ragged cry poured from her. He wasn't sure he'd ever experienced a sight as erotic as a naked Lady Tessa straddling him and riding his fingers and being pleasured by him.

Her breath caught and held, and she went into herself like a spring coiled and waiting for the touch that would bring release. "Not long now, my sweet," he muttered. "Just…give…over…"

Another slick graze of his thumb across her nub…another intentional press of his finger inside her…another suckle on her sweet breasts…and she came undone on a cry, her quim pulsing against his hand as he stroked her to satiety, her breath hard against his neck.

His was coming just as hard, his cock demanding he give her what she'd begged for.

It almost had him convinced when she, at last, pulled back enough to meet his eyes. "Julian," was all she said. All she could say, he suspected.

"I did promise to bring you pleasure unlike any you've ever known," he said, the words a raw scrape across his throat.

A light sigh blew between parted lips. "I'd say you delivered."

Even as gratification arrowed through Julian, so did another feeling—*unease.*

He'd adhered to all his rules. He'd remained clothed…no kissing…He'd kept his cock well away from her.

And yet…

This *after* felt different—like he'd given her more than pleasure.

This felt like they'd shared an intimacy.

Too soon, she pushed off him and reached for her chemise.

Alarm sounded through him once he understood what she was doing. "Why are you dressing?"

"Because I'm leaving."

"You've only been here an hour. You're going nowhere."

Mutiny glittered in her eyes. He shouldn't have said that last bit.

"You're in danger," he added as a reminder.

She shook her head. "The stone through my front window was a warning. I'm in no danger."

Julian tested the logic in his mind, and annoyingly, it held.

"I need to send for a glazier to replace the glass," she said, ever pragmatic. "And I need to contact Jagger."

Now, *that* logic didn't hold. He couldn't have heard her correctly. "You're going to *contact* Blaze Jagger?"

She nodded, definite. "To arrange a meeting. It's obvious our last one wasn't to his satisfaction."

"That would be one way of putting it."

She fastened her stays, and Julian attempted not to leer at the pushed-up roses of her nipples.

It was a poor attempt.

"Perhaps what he needs is a nudge to zig instead of zag."

"Do you care to elucidate?"

"It's simple." She gave a one-shouldered shrug, as if it truly were. "I'm going to treat him to tea."

Julian understood nothing he could say would sway the stubborn woman, so he settled back onto his elbows and watched her clothe that lush, glorious body of hers.

A shame, that.

Once fully dressed, she turned and faced him. An uncharacteristic hesitancy shimmered about her, and Julian braced himself for the words perched on the tip of her tongue.

"Was this our one night?"

He knew what he should say—*yes.*

He sat forward and, carefully, asked a question. "Do you want it to have been?"

After a moment's hesitation, she crossed the few feet separating them, placed a hand on his shoulder, and angled her mouth so it met his ear, sending a warm shiver through him. "Not yet," she whispered.

Then she pulled back enough to meet his eyes, so he could see the intention within hers, and pivoted, swiftly exiting the room, her sure footsteps fading down the staircase. A few seconds later, he heard the front door bolt slide as she slipped from the townhouse.

But not from his life.

Not yet.

If her answer had been *yes*, that would've been the end.

But she'd given a very different answer.

An answer that lit parts of him into life that hadn't felt alive... *ever*.

Parts he'd supposed himself lacking.

Parts, it seemed, only Lady Tessa had the power to awaken.

And he understood something: It wouldn't be enough for her —*he* wouldn't be enough for her.

For within her *not yet*, he detected a beginning—and a demand.

That next time he give her more.

That he give her everything.

For she was the sort who would give all—and she would expect as much from him.

Even as it alarmed him to the interior cells of his being, it fired an unexpected thrill through him.

He stood at the precipice, a rolling boulder to his back, which left him with two options.

Stand his ground and be smashed to bits.

Or fling himself, powerless, into the unknown.

CHAPTER TEN

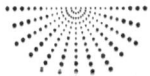

THREE DAYS LATER

oot tapping with impatience, Tessa stood outside Garraway's Coffee House and cast her gaze up and down Exchange Alley. Through the hustle and bustle of every sort of honest working man London had on offer—from ship chandlers to purveyors of navigation instruments to goldsmiths hailing from Lombardy to fashionable physicians who reserved special seats in the coffee room where they consulted with patients—Jagger with his loose, rangy stride and flash clothing would stand out.

She was early.

She gave her pocket watch another glance. Actually, she was on time. But when it came to a negotiation, on time was early. That was certainly the view Gabriel took.

Strategically, she should've been late. But she wasn't one for those sorts of power struggles. A direct approach was ever her way.

Finished standing on a street corner like a doxy, she switched course and stepped inside the coffee house. At least, if Jagger didn't show himself, she would have a proper cup of tea for her efforts. She garnered many second looks as she made her way through the crowded room. Coffee houses were generally considered the domain of men, but one of the benefits of her unique mode of dress was that it promptly communicated that she was no usual sort of woman and would be treated on the terms she dictated.

Upon finding a relatively quiet table in the corner, she sat with her back to the wall and placed an order for tea for two, half an eye fixed on the front door. It had taken two days of back-and-forth messages between her and Jagger before the day, time, and place could be agreed upon.

That he wanted to meet here was an indicator of his ambitions. Garraway's was no low coffee house, but a place where up-and-comers rubbed shoulders with those secure and settled in their business dealings. Jagger had chosen this location to be seen —and possibly to be seen with a lady...the sister of a duke, no less.

With so many angles to the coming conversation to consider, Tessa absolutely should concentrate on them and the man she was about to meet.

But it was a different man who kept stealing into her thoughts.

The Marquess of Ormonde...

Julian.

Three nights ago, he'd set her body ablaze—and the flame yet licked hot within her.

Don't you wish to receive the same treatment as my mistresses?

That was how he treated his mistresses?

To deliver pleasure to them so exquisite their bodies still burned with it three days later?

These last few days, it was as if she'd stepped through a curtain and entered a new world. As if there had been an entire spectrum of color that she'd been blind to—and now the blindfold had fallen away.

Fitting metaphor, that.

Yet she experienced a strange hollowness at its core.

As if one could achieve supreme pleasure and satiety—but not satisfaction.

And therein lay the paradox.

In Julian's giving, there had been a withholding.

Without speaking the words, he'd defined the limits of whatever it was that existed between them.

It wasn't simply that they hadn't coupled—though she'd never done so, *oh*, how her body had begged for it.

They hadn't kissed.

And for some reason, that felt more like a deliberate withholding.

By its very nature, coupling could never be chaste—but a kiss could. A kiss could be many things—a hello...a goodbye...an expression of affection...an outlet for lust.

In the withholding of his kiss, he was withholding something deeper.

He was withholding intimacy.

It seemed the longer she knew him, the less she knew him.

Who was this Marquess of Ormonde?

Julian.

He preferred to be Julian.

A familiar rangy figure entered Garraway's. *Blaze Jagger.* As he'd been on Derby Day, he was dressed in tailored superfine and a flamboyant silk waistcoat—today's a startling orange and teal. As he strode through the coffee shop and threw greetings around, the diamond in his ear throwing sparkling light, Tessa saw with her own eyes how Jagger was rising in the world. Garraway's wasn't an East End coffee shop, full to the brim with characters. These patrons knew Jagger as a man on the rise—a man who likely held no few of their debts.

Hazy recognition struck through her. Something familiar hung about him—something she hadn't noticed before. She couldn't quite lay a finger on it, though. She hadn't taken note of the opaque gray hue of his eyes and long, straight nose on their first meeting beyond the fact that they combined to make him a dangerously handsome man, especially with the long dark lashes that fringed those gray eyes.

Now, they felt distinctive and called to memory just out of reach.

He didn't acknowledge Tessa until he'd pulled a chair to her side of the table, so they sat side by side, facing the room. "You're not the only one who needs to keep an eye out," he said in greeting.

For her welcome, Tessa reached for the teapot and poured. She inhaled the dark brew before taking a sip. *Bitter...nutty...bracing.* Here was a tea that would batten down the hatches and see one striding into a productive day. She took another sip. She needed some bracing, if she was going to deal effectively with the man seated beside her.

Jagger directed an exaggerated lift of the eyebrow toward her. "Up to your standard, *milady?*"

"A bracing brew," she replied, equitably. She wasn't one to be baited, and he would soon know it.

He emitted a hearty guffaw. "You've certainly picked up the knack of playing lady."

She met his boldness and asked, "How's that?"

"*Bracing*, not *strong*." He shrugged. "Not saying what's really on your mind."

"Diplomacy done right is its own form of truth."

Jagger nodded. "I'll buy that for a bob. A truth can be got from different angles, is that it?"

Though he lacked formal education, Jagger was sharp and bright—like the edge of a knife glinting in the sun.

He took a sip of tea and winced before signaling to a serving girl. "Bring me a coffee, pet." He turned to Tessa. "Never did get the knack of tea. Now," he continued, "tell me another truth, *Lady* Tessa."

No mistaking his mocking sneer.

"How about this truth," she began. "You cannot go around having stones thrown through my windows."

He sucked his teeth. "Had to get your attention, didn't I?"

"There are other ways."

He daintily picked up his teacup between forefinger and thumb, pinky out. "Should I have invited you for tea?"

Again, Tessa wouldn't rise to his little provocation. "What do you want?"

"You know what I want."

"Gabriel and I aren't cutting you into the Race of the Century." Even as the words emerged from her mouth, frustration at her brother flared within her. It wasn't like him not to think through potential consequences. In addition to his intelligence and brilliance with numbers, that sense of forethought was a reason for his success. But here, he'd undeniably created a mess.

Jagger shrugged. "Well, then I'd say you have a Blaze Jagger problem."

"You're referring to yourself in the third person now?"

A smile accustomed to charming every soul within a three-block radius tipped at the corner of his mouth. "When it suits." His gray eyes went serious. "The thing is I took note when your little gaming hell opened a few years back. But The Archangel services nobs, so…" Another mild shrug of the shoulder. "Bankrupt 'em all, as far as I care."

Tessa settled back into her chair, waiting for him to continue.

"But the horses," he tsked. "That's another matter. The horses are my game, ye ken?"

"You're not the only blackleg in town." It had to be said. "None of your kind are being cut into the Race of the Century."

"I may not be the only leg in town, but I am a man of the people."

"How's that?" Tessa scoffed. Jagger's capacity for self-importance had tipped into delusion, and it was beginning to irk. "By taking their money?"

She didn't harbor any illusions about the business she and Gabriel conducted in The Archangel, but Jagger's logic defied belief.

The glint in his eyes turned to steel, and he sat forward. "By giving them opportunity. By giving them hope."

"Through horse betting?" Tessa snorted. "The Archangel might take money from the rich, but *you* are taking it from anyone with a penny in their pocket."

His head cocked. "You think if I stop laying and taking odds, gambling on the ponies will cease and we'll suddenly be the virtuous nation we pretend to be?"

Tessa felt her eyebrows lift. "Of course not."

Eyes burning with barely contained fervor, Jagger planted his forefinger square into the table, which gave a little wobble at the force. "Here's what everyone in this room knows about Blaze Jagger, except you. *I...pay...out.*" He enunciated the last three words with slow emphasis.

"Isn't that what you're supposed to do?"

"If I get it wrong or a horse comes up lame, when the time comes to pay, I don't leg it. I pay out, ye ken?" He settled back in his chair and straightened his cravat. "I'm here to stay, Lady Tessa." His arm swung in a wide arc, indicating all the coffeehouse. "That's what they know, and what *you* need to know."

"I understand you have a reputation to—"

His scoff cut across her. "From what I understand *Lady* Tessa, you didn't come up too far from me."

"Likely not," she acknowledged.

"What does compromise cost you in that world? Can you cast your mind that far back?"

She could. "Everything."

"Look around and, tell me, what do you see?"

"Men drinking coffee and conducting business." She didn't need to look.

"Self-made men. No lords here, Lady Tessa. No dukes holding court or flexing their muscle. What these men are today, they created themselves."

Tessa understood what he was getting at. "You're no different."

"And let me tell you something about a self-made man." Jagger's gray eyes blazed with intensity. "Once he's scratched and clawed out a place for himself, he will fight heaven and hell itself to hold onto his patch."

Tessa had hoped to help this self-made man to zig instead of zag, but she had to consider the possibility she'd been viewing the matter from the wrong angle—that her logic was flawed. Still, she'd try one last salvo..."I've been hiding your behavior from my brother, but I shall have to tell him if you force my hand."

The fight in Jagger's eyes stood firm, undiminished.

"You want a war." The words were out of her mouth before she could consider their wisdom.

A smile tipped about his mouth. "*You* want the war. Some are born into their place in the world. Others have to scratch and claw to create theirs, ye ken?"

The threat of this conversation spiraling entirely out of her control had Tessa digging a few coins out of her reticule and plonking them onto the table. She shot to her feet and met Jagger's eye. "No more rocks through windows?"

He heaved a dramatically resigned sigh. "No more rocks through windows. You have my word."

The promise sounded more like a thinly veiled threat.

Frustration seared through Tessa as she hopscotched her way out of the crowded coffeehouse. There would be no more rocks through windows—but their dealings with one another weren't finished.

That was what lay between the lines of Blaze Jagger's promise.

Tessa didn't stop until she reached the post office on Lombard Street, where she waved down a passing hackney cab. "Twinings on Strand, if you will."

The coachman nodded, and Tessa heaved herself inside. Irritatingly, Jagger required much additional thought. He'd given her more information about himself, and she needed space in which to let it stew and brew. So, she would procure a recently arrived Imperial tea from Twinings and consider the matter more closely while she toyed with a few tea blends. She had a few lovely sprigs of dried lavender with the potential to pair nicely.

She'd just paid the coachman and was turning toward the shop with its distinctive white doorway when a trio of ladies just up the block caught her eye. A second glance revealed the trio to be Saskia, Viveca, and Mrs. Fairfax.

Deciding the tea could wait, Tessa waved to catch their attention and called out as she closed the short distance between them. "And what task are you engaged in this afternoon?"

"Oh, we're here to peruse the titles of Dougherty's," said Viveca with a quick hug for Tessa.

At Tessa's blank look, Saskia provided, "It's a new circulating library."

Mrs. Fairfax offered her ever-serene smile. "And you, Lady Tessa? What errands are you about this afternoon?"

In accordance with her vow to keep her dealings with Blaze Jagger separate from her family, Tessa said, "Twinings has a new tea variety in."

"Tessa is positively mad about tea," chimed Viveca as she pushed the library's front door open.

The interior of Dougherty's was as Tessa expected—all brown woods...the only sounds the murmuration of low, masculine voices and shifting of bottoms in plush leather armchairs...the mild, earthy scent of books...*male.* This circulating library—as were most of their kind—was the domain of men.

Her mind was already calculating how best to gain her sisters admittance—no few off-put scowls had already been directed toward Saskia and Viveca—when Mrs. Fairfax made her elegant way toward the gentleman at the front desk, a charming smile curved about her plump bow mouth. "Mr. Dougherty," she began, "how *are* you?"

A sudden blush stained the man's cheeks above his beard as he fumbled to a stand in the presence of a lady. "Mrs. Fairfax, how, *erm*, delightful to see you."

This man who had been chief scowler amongst the gentlemen as Saskia and Viveca had blithely sailed past his desk was reduced to a lad just out of leading strings—such was the charm of Mrs. Fairfax's smile.

"How long has it been?" she continued.

"Your come-out, I believe," he got out in a fluster.

He didn't seem able to believe that a lady like Mrs. Fairfax would remember a gentleman like him. Tessa suspected every man Mrs. Fairfax encountered felt thusly.

Mrs. Fairfax signaled to Tessa to draw closer. "Are you acquainted with Lady Tessa Calthorp?" Before Mr. Dougherty could answer, Mrs. Fairfax continued, "She is, of course, the sister of the Duke of Acaster, as are the Ladies Saskia and Viveca." She pointed toward Saskia and Viveca, who had separated, each pursuing their own literary interests. "Would it be a terrible inconvenience to indulge them with a bit of time in your vaunted establishment? I would consider it a great favor to me."

"Oh, well, *erm*, yes, yes, of course," the man stammered, eager to please Mrs. Fairfax in anything she liked.

The luminosity within her amber eyes increased tenfold. "You have my sincerest gratitude, Mr. Dougherty."

The man looked as if he were having trouble drawing breath as Mrs. Fairfax threaded her arm through Tessa's and led them into the next room.

Once they were out of earshot of the dazzled Mr. Dougherty,

Tessa said, "You can get a man to do anything you like, can't you?" She couldn't help but admire the ability.

Mrs. Fairfax shrugged an unbothered shoulder. "It isn't difficult."

At Tessa's side was a different sort of woman—one who was a force, but a quiet one. She suspected she could learn a few things from this woman. "Mrs. Fairfax—"

"You must call me Eloise."

"*Eloise*," said Tessa. "I must offer my gratitude for taking Saskia and Viveca in hand."

Eloise smiled up at Tessa. "My cousin asked for my help, and I can't deny Celia anything."

Tessa doubted this not one bit. On Derby Day, she'd seen firsthand the high regard and affection Eloise and the Duchess of Acaster held for one another.

Now, as they ambled idly from room to room, startling gentlemen from their reading and greeting said gentlemen in turn, Tessa saw why Eloise was the perfect woman to guide Saskia and Viveca through society. She was well liked and respected, and she knew everyone—*everyone*.

And everyone, of course, would've included a certain marquess who hadn't strayed too far from the top of Tessa's mind these last three days.

Which was how Tessa found herself asking, "Would you happen to be acquainted with the Marquess of Ormonde?"

Eloise shot Tessa a quick, assessing glance. "*Ormonde?*"

Tessa immediately regretted the question. Still, she nodded.

"He's an amiable man," said Eloise, carefully. "According to everyone, the most amiable man in the *ton* with his general good nature and, well, undeniable handsomeness."

In the statement, Tessa detected an unasked question. *And why do you ask?*

Tessa searched her mind for any innocent reason she could be inquiring about the Marquess of Ormonde. "His horse won the Derby, and now he's a contender for the Race of the Century."

The glimmer in Eloise's eye remained unconvinced. "What do you wish to know about the marquess?"

Though Tessa was accustomed to being the most direct woman in any room she entered, she saw that she'd met her match in Eloise Fairfax. Fortunately, she knew how best to counter directness.

With directness.

"Everything," she said.

"Well," began Eloise, "his mother hasn't been seen in London as long as anyone can remember. Decades, I believe. Her absence may have to do with his sister."

"His sister?"

Julian had a sister?

"A tragedy," said Eloise. "A wasting disease took her as a child."

"Were they close?"

"By all accounts."

An ache expanded inside Tessa.

"And the father..." Eloise heaved a sigh. "He spent the next two decades drinking himself into oblivion. A thoroughly dissolute and debauched man."

Dread crawled through Tessa. For Julian to be a marquess, that meant his father must've been..."How did the marquess die?"

"I don't know many details," said Eloise. "But rumor has it that he died in shabby circumstances—and the whispers have that it was done by his own hand."

"*Oh*," Tessa exhaled, both shocked and...*not*.

She'd come to understand that behind Julian's amiable façade lay a dark complexity. But this...

It was surely too much for one man to bear—*alone*.

A stormy Viveca marched into the room, a frown turning down the corners of her typically smiling mouth. Saskia entered through a different door, the same storm cloud on her face.

Rather than lugging stacks of books, their arms remained empty. "We can go now," said Saskia, her voice flat.

"Indeed," added Viveca.

Tessa was certain of an entire silent conversation happening between her sisters—and was equally certain that she would hear all about it the instant they set foot outside Dougherty's front door.

"Well," exclaimed Viveca.

"Indeed," said Saskia.

Eloise darted an amused glance toward Tessa before saying, "*Indeed?*"

"Perhaps a bit more information for the uninformed?" prompted Tessa.

Saskia stared at her as if she'd asked the most dunderheaded question imaginable. "Well, this circulating library is like all circulating libraries, isn't it?"

"Meaning?" Tessa tried not to smile.

"They have treatises on politics and natural philosophy aplenty," said Viveca.

"And every book written on the subject of agriculture," chimed Saskia.

"So?" asked Tessa. "Isn't a comprehensive circulating library what you like?"

Saskia and Viveca continued to glare at her as if she were London's dullest dolt.

Finally, Viveca relented. "It's the principle, Tessa."

"What principle is that?"

"Just as there are all sorts of people," said Saskia, "there are all sorts of books for them."

"And all sorts of people," continued Viveca, "should have access to all sorts of books."

Tessa felt her brow gather. What were her sisters on about?

"And by *people*," said Saskia, "we mean *women*."

"And by *books*," said Viveca, "we mean *novels*."

"And plays," added Saskia.

Viveca nodded.

Something was most definitely brewing between her sisters, Tessa decided. But before she could pursue the thought, a thoroughly charmed Eloise said, "Speaking of plays, I'm escorting your sisters to the theater tonight, Lady Tessa. You must join us."

"Oh, I..." Tessa let her voice trail off, hoping this would be enough to communicate polite refusal.

However, she met no such acceptance in the three sets of eyes watching her.

"I'll be expected at The Archangel." The excuse offered a stronger argument than vague demurral.

Saskia, Viveca, and Eloise appeared wholly unmoved.

It was simply that *theater*, as Eloise would know it, was a society event. It would mean mingling with nobs, which Tessa didn't do. She separated nobs from their blunt—an important distinction.

"All sorts will be there," said Eloise. "Lords and ladies...dukes and duchesses...I even know of a marquess who keeps a box beside my dear friend Mr. Lancaster's."

A marquess...

Tessa knew exactly which marquess.

Ormonde...Julian.

A new angle was needed for her argument. "But I don't—"

"Have anything suitable to wear?" asked Saskia, correctly anticipating her.

Viveca picked up the thread. "I have about thirty new gowns. I'll have one—or five—sent over to Sloane Street." When Tessa opened her mouth to protest, Viveca added, "You and I are the same size, sister."

Eloise's hands clapped together with delight. "That's all settled now. We'll be arriving at Haymarket Theater at eight o'clock."

Tessa's mouth had no choice but to snap shut. She knew when she'd been outmaneuvered.

Eloise escorted Saskia and Viveca to her waiting carriage and turned. "Can we drop you somewhere?"

"I have, *erm*, an errand to run." Even as Tessa spoke the excuse, her mind remained stubbornly blank of just what the errand had been.

Too late, it came to her. "*Tea*," she spoke to the carriage's departing wheels.

Somehow, she was going to the theater tonight.

Dressed in a silk gown.

And she would be seated beside the Marquess of Ormonde's box—which didn't necessarily mean he would be there. It might remain empty or be lent to friends.

She had no reason to believe he would be there.

Yet a feeling had her heart pumping harder, making itself felt as it moved the blood through her veins.

Anticipation—a feeling she was becoming entirely too well acquainted with since she'd met the Marquess of Ormonde.

A man she now called Julian.

CHAPTER ELEVEN

HAYMARKET THEATER, EVENING

*J*ulian approached the newly remodeled stone portico of Haymarket Theater with its impressive Grecian-style entablature and pediment supported by six towering Corinthian columns, and checked his pocket watch again.

Half-past eight.

The night's entertainment started at seven, which meant he was late. That wasn't a crime at the theater, of course, as patrons came and went at will over the course of an evening. And, really, he hadn't even planned on attending tonight's performance.

Then the first note had arrived at his door at four o'clock this afternoon. A request. Would he mind very much having company in his reserved box at the Haymarket Theater this evening? Julian had dashed off a quick reply in the vein of the more, the merrier and forgot about it—until the second request arrived.

Then the third…and the fourth…and the fifth.

By the time a footman had presented him with the eighth note, his curiosity was fully up.

Why was a bevy of lords flocking to the Haymarket Theater

tonight and requesting the use of his box when he knew more than a few of them had boxes of their own?

As he hadn't anything else on tonight—well, nothing that couldn't be endured another night—here he was, unable to resist finding out.

Of the five doors facing him, he entered the one farthest to the left, bypassing the opulently lit, mirrored vestibule, and made for the private staircase that led directly to second- and third-level boxes. He pulled back the curtain to his box and found the space filled to overflowing with lords, most standing, as there were only four seats for eight...*nine* gentlemen. Heads turned, and greetings were freely given. Julian gave the stage a quick glance and thought the play might be *Romeo and Juliet*, if he had his Shakespeare correct, eliciting a curious furrow of his brow. That particular play wasn't one gentlemen gravitated toward, in the general sense.

Except the gentlemen weren't watching the play, which was below and to their left. Instead, gazes—some direct, others furtive—were pointed in the opposite direction, to the right. Julian followed, and the beat of his heart gave a wobbly stutter-step in his chest.

A lady...light red-gold tendrils falling in artful waves down the elegant column of her neck...

Tessa.

The woman he hadn't been able to exorcise from his mind since she'd uttered those parting words.

Not yet.

Words both tease and promise.

After three days, however, perhaps more tease than promise, as he'd heard naught from her.

And here she was in the theater box beside his.

Her head angled just enough to present her profile limned in the soft light of the stage.

Julian's eyebrows dug into his forehead.

The lady was Tessa—and she wasn't. Rather, a discomfiting close approximation.

Observations about this Tessa followed in quick pursuit. She was a very animated Tessa and open—and younger, too. Not that Tessa was old—far from it, as she couldn't have more than five and twenty years on her—but this young lady was possessed of an altogether different demeanor from the Tessa he was coming to know.

Then his gaze shifted to the young lady's conversational partner, another young lady of similar looks, and he remembered. The sisters he'd encountered only in passing at the Derby. Now, Julian understood the requests for the use of his private box. Word that the younger sisters of the Duke of Acaster would be attending the Haymarket Theater tonight in Mr. Michael Lancaster's private box must've spread like wildfire through the clubs today.

Next, he found Mrs. Eloise Fairfax speaking behind her hand to Lancaster, a barrister who had made quite the name for himself in Lincoln's Inn and who many in society suspected of harboring political ambitions. Courting one of the *ton's* most popular ladies and taking her to wife would be a beneficial step in that direction.

The instant before his gaze shifted yet another increment, tension filled Julian. His body knew who he would find to Mrs. Fairfax's right before his mind could register her.

Tessa.

Seeing her in a society setting illustrated how unique a woman she was, as she'd dressed ever as she always did—a man's white linen shirt, lavender watered silk waistcoat, and pristine snow-white cravat. A feeling strummed through him...a feeling of protectiveness. He wouldn't stand for a mocking or cross word about her preference for this mode of dress. Like everything with Tessa, she would have her well-thought-out reasons.

Her head turned a fraction, and she went still, as if she were in deep concentration. Her gaze shifted, and silver-blue eyes met his. Time slipped out of its forward march and stilled.

It wasn't so much what he did see in her eyes that froze him in place—but rather what he didn't.

Surprise.

She'd known Mr. Lancaster's box was beside the Marquess of Ormonde's.

And while she'd had no way of knowing for certain he would attend the theater tonight, she'd known the possibility existed.

And here he was—possibility come to life.

"Ormonde," came a voice behind him.

A black shard of ice sluiced through Julian, even as he turned with a warm smile on his mouth. A young lord stood at his side, blushing furiously, uncertainty shining in his eyes. Julian wracked his mind for the man's name…"Wrexford," he spoke in amiable greeting.

The earl cleared his throat, as if unable to believe he had the full attention of the Marquess of Ormonde. Julian was accustomed to his effect, truth told. "Do you know if the duchess will be attending tonight?"

"The duchess?" Unexpected, that question. "Which one?"

Wrexford's splotchy, radish-red blush crawled to the tips of his ears. "Acaster."

Julian had only met the duchess on a handful of occasions, which made him by no means the woman's keeper. "Why would she be here?"

Wrexford licked his lips and plowed on. *"Those"*—he gave an unsubtle jut of the chin—"are the new duke's sisters."

"Right." Julian was experiencing difficulty summoning the energy to give a toss about this conversation.

"And *that*"—another unsubtle jut of the chin—"is the duchess's favorite cousin."

Julian nodded—he'd known as much about Mrs. Fairfax—but now, and more importantly, he understood the point of this conversation. Wrexford was harboring a tendre for the Duchess of Acaster.

Julian almost felt badly for the man. It wasn't her elevated status as the widow of a duke that made the match unlikely. The duchess was one of the most beautiful ladies in society, and Wrexford...well, the affable earl hadn't much to recommend him beyond his average looks, average intelligence, and future title of marquess.

Beyond the box, the theater's lights brightened, signaling the end of the act. Now permitted to speak freely, the young lords populating Julian's box vied for the attention of the Ladies Saskia and Viveca, who didn't appear to notice all the hubbub they were causing as they bent their heads close together, intent on their own conversation.

As for Tessa...

Aside from that one locking of the eyes, she was keeping her gaze steadfastly away from him, though she must've felt the heat of his boring into her.

"Lord Ormonde," came a soft feminine voice.

Julian turned to find Mrs. Fairfax's luminous brown eyes staring up at him, serene smile in place. He gave a slight bow. "Mrs. Fairfax."

"Are you enjoying the play?"

Julian didn't know Mrs. Fairfax beyond passing acquaintance, so he couldn't be sure if that was a knowing twinkle in her eyes.

If it was...what precisely did she know about him?

"It's..." He searched his mind for something to say about the play. "It's most well executed."

A safe enough statement that shouldn't land him in any difficulties.

"Are you acquainted with Mr. Lancaster?" she asked.

The barrister gave Julian a nod by way of greeting, his shrewd gaze assessing before shifting its angle and softening upon Mrs. Fairfax. The man was openly besotted.

"And perhaps you met the Ladies Saskia and Viveca at the Derby?" she continued.

The strained smiles the ladies directed at Julian denoted clear annoyance at having their conversation interrupted. He saw the family resemblance extended beyond looks and into personality.

"Are you enjoying the play?" he asked, as was polite and expected, when all he wanted was to shift the entirety of his attention onto their sister, who continued her assiduous avoidance of his gaze.

It was the blonder of the two younger sisters who answered. Lady Saskia, he believed. "In all honesty, we are not enjoying the play."

That startled a laugh from him. "Oh? And why is that?"

A look passed between the sisters before the younger said, "The play has been Bowdlerized."

Julian felt his brow gather, even as he snuck a glance toward Tessa, who appeared in no way confused by her sister's words. "*Bowdlerized?*" he asked.

"There are these siblings," began Lady Saskia.

"Thomas and Harriet Bowdler," provided Lady Viveca.

"And they claim to love the works of Shakespeare," continued Lady Saskia.

"But...," said Lady Viveca, ominous.

"*But?*" asked Julian, feeling it his duty to ask.

"But they decided Shakespeare's *indelicacy of expression*—"

"Their words," Lady Viveca cut across her sister.

"—needed softening," continued Lady Saskia. "So, they created *The Family Shakespeare.*"

"Ah," said Julian. He'd heard of it, but had paid little mind, in truth.

"They've removed all the *offensive* and *indelicate* parts of the Bard's work, while keeping the plots intact."

"Surely, you'll have noticed all exclamations of *God!* and *Jesu!* were replaced with *Heavens!*"

"*Erm...*" Julian hadn't, but he was more than willing to take their word for it, for the ladies' eyes glowed with the light of young crusaders, and he'd long deemed it the wise course to let such women have their way.

And these two crusaders weren't finished.

"Just now on the stage," said Lady Viveca, outrage in every syllable, "Mercutio was to have said, *the bawdy hand of the dial is now upon the prick of noon,* but instead said—"

"*The hand of the dial is now upon the point of noon,*" finished Lady Saskia.

Julian didn't see the change made all that much difference, but knew enough to keep his mouth shut.

"Well, we can't have any talk of pricks," scoffed Lady Viveca. "Even though half the population has one!"

A few stunned beats of silence followed.

Julian cleared his throat and said, "Right."

More fraught silence, then it was Mrs. Fairfax to the conversational rescue with her easy smile. "And Lord Ormonde, I believe you're already acquainted with Lady Tessa?" She asked the question as if the round of introductions had proceeded uninterrupted by talk of pricks.

And Julian was grateful—*truly*—for it navigated the conversation away from talk of pricks and lent him the excuse he needed to direct his full, undivided attention where it wanted to be.

He bowed. "Lady Tessa."

CHAPTER TWELVE

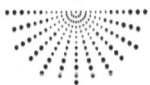

To her everlasting shame and annoyance, Tessa blushed. The slow crawl of heat through her body had begun the instant Julian had walked into his theater box and hadn't stopped since, even as she gave the appearance of ignoring his presence.

As if that were a possibility.

And now, here she was, exchanging greetings with the marquess, her cheeks hot and eartips flaming for all and sundry to witness, from the legion of suitors vying for the attention of Saskia and Viveca to the quietly observant eyes of Eloise to...

Julian.

He would've noticed.

"Lord Ormonde," she said, as was proper.

The flash of a wince crossed his features—a reflex. *Julian.* He'd demanded she call him Julian, and this was why—he harbored a deep loathing of being called by his title. A title, she'd learned only today, he'd inherited from a father who had dissolved into licentiousness and taken his own life.

She nearly corrected herself and said *Julian.*

In the nick of time, she stopped.

In the eyes of everyone around them, they'd only just met. They were nothing to one another.

She couldn't call him Julian.

However, she was saved from further having to call him anything at all when the theater lights dimmed and the audience muted their conversations.

Tessa affixed her unseeing gaze onto the stage and, from the corner of her eye, watched Julian settle into a chair.

Relief couldn't quite come. This was simply a brief respite. For inevitably the play would end, and she would be exactly where they'd left off—expected to behave civilly with a man with whom she'd behaved most *uncivilly*.

And wanted to again.

Not yet.

She could've claimed that night as their one night.

But she hadn't.

Not yet.

Foolishly…recklessly…she'd spoken those words to him.

Because she wanted another night.

Of their own accord, her eyes stole toward him and followed a broad shoulder down his arm to the hands resting on his thighs.

She'd straddled those thighs.

And those long, masculine fingers…

They'd been inside her.

Those long, masculine fingers had pleasured her so that even three days later, she was still a bundle of ache and need.

Uncivil.

Oh, she was hot—*too hot*—and of a sudden, the dark theater felt small—*too small*.

Instinct drove her to her feet and muttering hasty excuses to Eloise and fleeing from the box, out of the dark and into the infinitely reflected light of the mirrored vestibule, its chandeliers and sconces throwing luminosity, giving the appearance of openness. The pressure around her ribs released, and at last, she could draw breath again.

Blessedly alone, she stepped to one of the many mirrors and pressed cooling fingers to her flushed cheeks. A hunted quality still flickered in her eyes. What had she been thinking by coming here tonight? What had she expected?

Her gaze drifted downward in the mirror. At least, she'd done one thing in the interest of self-preservation.

She'd worn her usual attire.

As promised, Viveca had sent five silk gowns for her to choose from. In the privacy of her bedroom, she'd even slipped one on—an iridescent dove gray that pulled silvery violet from her eyes. She'd stared into the mirror and hardly knew herself.

Who was this woman with the creamy shoulders and bosom that threatened to spill over the delicate bodice that hardly seemed up to the task of containing her?

Though she didn't think this of other women who dressed thusly, she felt too exposed.

So, in the end, she'd opted for her usual attire. A youth spent building a life from scratch had taught her a female was safer the less she revealed of herself. She and her sisters had escaped having been treated violently by a man, but she didn't fool herself that fact was anything but a combination of strategy and luck.

Not, of course, that she would have to fear being treated criminally at the theater, but she wasn't ready to wear such a dress.

Perhaps for Saskia and Viveca's upcoming debut ball— *perhaps.*

Then her gaze had drifted over the dressing table—toward what lay nestled within the box atop its surface.

The pearls.

She hadn't worn those tonight, either.

Movement appeared behind her. Before her gaze shifted, she knew—*Julian.*

Their eyes locked in the mirror. He'd come for her, that was what the resolution in his eyes told her. Without a word, he drew near enough to slip an arm through hers. She drew a quick breath and caught his scent—*cedarwood.*

He tended to fill every sense when he was near.

They began walking through the vestibule, as if he played the gallant escort. If any society eyes happened on them, they might form a curious thought. *Was that Lady Tessa Calthorp walking arm in arm with the Marquess of Ormonde?*

But likely not.

They wouldn't suspect their golden lord, the Marquess of Ormonde, of hidden motives. Just look at the amiability of his smile and the open blue sky of his eyes. Surely nothing ulterior could hide behind them.

"Perhaps we should converse?" she asked.

"If you like."

He sounded like a man determined—but not one determined to talk.

Too bad.

"Will you be attending the come-out ball my brother is throwing for Saskia and Viveca?" She couldn't resist a snort. "And me, apparently." The very idea hadn't ceased being ridiculous in her eyes.

"Of course," was all he had to say on the matter.

"Do you not take pleasure from small talk?"

He flashed her a glance that once would've been unclear to her. But that was three days ago, and this was tonight—and tonight, she recognized the heat within, and it sent a responding flame of desire licking straight through her. "Lady Tessa," he said, "you know very well what brings me pleasure."

Rather than shock, it was a question that hit her...Was he trying to throw her off balance?

Well, that was a game for two...

"Do I?" she asked. "I seem to remember being denied the opportunity to gain such knowledge about you."

*Three nights ago...*It was here between them, the clench and release of his jaw said.

She decided to switch tack and not pursue the matter—for now. He would've gotten the message. She wasn't a woman easily rattled. "Perhaps you would like to know how my meeting with Blaze Jagger went?"

"I don't want to talk about Blaze Jagger," he said, definite. "I'll have him under control soon enough."

An alarm bell sounded through Tessa. "Blaze Jagger is none of your concern."

Julian snorted.

Pique flared inside her. "I am serious. He's not your problem to solve. He's mine."

"And you think a conversation over tea will solve him?"

Outrage provided Tessa a needed emotional outlet. "How do you know about my tea with Jagger?"

Had he been following her?

Cool eyes met hers. "You said that was your plan, and you're the sort of woman who follows through with her intentions."

That settled Tessa—a bit.

She hadn't at all liked the idea of being followed.

He led them down a short corridor, testing the first door handle they reached. Next thing, Tessa was being pulled into a room.

"If this isn't about Jagger, then what is—"

"*Tessa.*"

Her mouth went dry. In the gray dark of the tiny room, the only source of illumination was the rectangle of light framing the door, so she couldn't see his shadowed face.

But she didn't need to.

It was her name gone to a velvet rasp in his throat.

She knew that rasp.

A slow, sinuous shiver twisted through her, and she realized his arm was still twined through hers. With his other hand, he reached up, calloused fingertips brushing across her cheek. It was all she could do not to sway into his touch like a cat.

Because she must, she fought the feeling and spoke the first tangible thought that crossed her mind. "Is this about the pearl necklace? All you had to do was ask if you wanted it returned."

"It wasn't about the necklace three nights ago, and it isn't about the necklace tonight. *This* is about *you*."

"*Me?*"

When she made to continue the question, he pressed a silencing finger to her mouth.

"You'll see."

The promise embedded within that gravelly rumble was all it took to set her irretrievably ablaze.

He angled forward and pressed his mouth to the sensitive skin of her neck. A melting occurred within her, and she tipped her head to offer him more access…

And she swayed.

There was no help for it. The need to touch him—to feel his muscled body beneath her hands—drove her, as she pressed trembly palms to his chest and began to trail lower, reveling in the feel of him. She reached the waistband of his trousers—and lower her fingers explored…to the thick length of his manhood.

Oh, how she wanted to see it…touch it…*feel* it.

Of a sudden, his hand clamped around hers, stilling its progress. Her gaze flew up, and he shook his head. Then his hands were around her waist and he was lifting her. The next instant, her bottom was perched atop a table she hadn't even known was behind her.

Still, the wanting remained. "Julian, I want to feel you."

Paltry words for what that wanting was coming to mean for her.

"Tessa," he said, low and rumbly and she knew that whatever he next asked of her, she would agree to. "May I taste you?"

The question had another question forming on her lips, but since it was Julian asking, she said, "Yes."

He shifted forward, pushing her skirts up, over her knees, and parted her thighs with slow intention. Anticipation skittered through her as he stepped into that V, her sex throbbing with utter ache. But he didn't press against her...*into* her, as she so desperately needed. Instead, he fell to his knees, and she understood his meaning.

May I taste you?

It was the warm release of his breath that met the wet slick of her quim first. She gasped, and he chuckled. Then all thought was chased from her mind by the slow, deliberate swipe of his tongue. Lightning licked through her—one hand clutched the edge of the table and the other reached for his hair—the pleasure of his tongue upon her tipping the balance of her world topsy-turvy.

Nothing in her life had prepared her for *this*—a man between her legs, pleasuring her with his tongue...effecting a magic upon her that surely originated beyond the heavy bounds of earth. This was air and light and ether. Only *this* mattered—where he touched her...his tongue flicking, stroking, pulling moans from her so his hand reached up and covered her mouth, which only intensified the forbidden pleasure, rendering it a slight transgression.

Her hips rolled back, her legs widened, as this pleasure overtook her. Then, of a sudden, it was upon her—*release*—and she was crying out into his palm as she broke against his tongue, climax fluttering through her, sending her spiraling into some sort of oblivion.

But only a moment's worth—oblivion was short-lived for the earthbound being.

Eyes yet closed, she felt him move between her legs and rise to a stand before pulling her skirts over her knees.

Her eyes were left with no choice but to open. She longed to reach out and confirm the reality of his shadowed presence before her. Instead, she said, "I could do the same for you."

It was what she wanted—to take his manhood in hand and feel him in her mouth. "*I* want to taste *you*."

"That won't be necessary." The words emerged tight, curt. Gone was the velvet rumble.

"*Necessary?* Don't you want—?"

"*Want you?*" The question was a hard scrape across his throat.

Tessa nodded, though she didn't think he could see the movement.

"I've had you," he said, flat. He'd regained command of himself.

"Is that what you tell yourself?"

The air pulled taut with the answer he refused to speak. He'd been seen—and he didn't like it.

"We shouldn't be observed exiting together," he said, at last. "I'll go first."

"Oh, we're not going anywhere just yet. Not until…"

She hopped off the table and closed the handful of inches between them. Before he could intuit her intention, she hooked her hand around his neck and wove her fingers through his hair, lifting onto the tips of her toes…pulling his head down…

And pressed her mouth to his.

For an instant, his lips remained an unyielding line beneath hers, and she thought he might push her away. Then a growl sounded at the back of his throat, and he grabbed hold of her and really, truly, thoroughly kissed her, the full length of his body against her…the full length of his manhood, too—hard and thick and long.

Oh, how she wanted it inside her.

This man had delivered pleasure upon pleasure, but she wanted *more*.

And as she poured all of herself into this kiss, it felt like *more*

—even more fulfilling than everything else they'd done and had been done to her.

For this kiss was mutual—a sharing...an equalizing of power and control.

Then, as suddenly as the kiss had begun, he shook his head and tore away. A cry of protest flew from her as he pivoted and exited the room without another word.

Tessa's mind spun circles as her feet remained rooted in place.

Through the whirl emerged a thought...The two selves of the Marquess of Ormonde...

The marquess the world knew—and the Julian only she'd been allowed to glimpse.

He wore the mien of a man people were disposed to like. A quality he used to his advantage—to hide his other self.

The self who winced at the sound of his title...The self who wouldn't allow her to see him...or touch him...The self who hid in plain sight.

And here was the part she couldn't solve without more information—*why?* Why did he hide himself away? It wasn't as if he were a monster. Yet...

He might think himself so.

Strange, that.

He was like a mathematical equation that lacked all the necessary numbers to solve.

And he was more than that.

He was a human being...a man. One whose denial of self had grown a taproot so deep and strong it might never be dislodged.

She could send him twenty thousand pounds and walk away. If she were going to, this would be the time.

But she wouldn't.

She understood that about herself.

When had she ever turned away from a complex equation in need of solving?

So, she retraced her steps to Mr. Lancaster's box and bore the heat of Eloise's inquiring stare on the side of her face without meeting it. Quickly, she ascertained that Julian hadn't returned to his box. The action of a scared man.

Good.

She wasn't entirely sure why she felt that way, but she did.

As one, Saskia and Viveca turned. "We can go."

"Before the end of the play?" whispered a puzzled Eloise.

"We've seen enough," said Saskia.

"It tries one's soul to sit and watch a masterpiece be butchered," said Viveca.

The most unforgivable crime in the eyes of her sisters.

Eloise hadn't yet experienced the petulant side of Saskia and Viveca that they'd mostly left behind with childhood—that trying moments could still conjure. So, Tessa extended their thank yous and goodbyes to Eloise and Mr. Lancaster and bid a relieved farewell to Haymarket Theater.

Not yet.

Those were the two words—and single concept—whirling around her brain throughout the ride home.

They were more than a promise.

They were a bond.

Her one night with Julian was still outstanding.

And she would have it.

As a gentleman, he was honor-bound to give it to her.

From this—or her—he couldn't run.

CHAPTER THIRTEEN

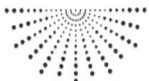

ST. JAMES'S SQUARE, TWO WEEKS LATER

*J*ulian had no business at the Duke of Acaster's ball.

That, he understood with crisp clarity.

But he hadn't been able to stay away.

He understood that, too, as he moved through Acaster's mansion, the building filled to the rafters with lords and ladies, conversation and music, and free-flowing laughter—an atmosphere glittering with bright effervescence.

For weeks, the *ton* had been panting with anticipation of this ball—and to be the recipients of the new duke's hospitality. To the disappointment of some, to be sure, a better ball couldn't be asked for. But for the many, the duke had passed the test with flying colors. After tonight, not a single doubt would linger that he was one of them. The title of duke had been only the first step. His bottomless wealth and willingness to spend it on frivolity for all was the finish line.

Julian took a left down a corridor that would lead to the card room, given that only gentlemen were taking this turn. The other direction surely led to the ballroom, where he would be immediately conscripted into dancing, and he wasn't ready for that.

A stray thought wandered into his mind.

Was Tessa out there now...*dancing*?

She might've been an unconventional lady, but she was the sister of a duke *and* a beauty *and* intelligent. Surely, a few gentlemen in the *ton* valued such qualities in a woman.

Further, she would have a dowry. But then, she would have her own money, wouldn't she? She was half owner of a popular, high-stakes gaming hell. If her brother was rich as Croesus, it only followed she was, too.

Yes, Julian would wager his finest filly that many a gentleman in attendance would be willing to overlook Tessa's idiosyncrasies to get his hands on her blunt.

The very thought had his stomach turning as he entered the mostly male domain of the card room, the last refuge of many a gentleman.

Quickly, however, he found he couldn't escape Tessa that easily. All the talk was of the Calthorp sisters.

"They're a serious lot aren't they?" said one lordling, struggling with the idea.

"As serious as ladies can be, I suppose," cut in another lordling.

That got a round of laughter. Julian saw the humor not at all. Clearly, none of these gentlemen had ever conversed with the ladies in question.

"That Lady Viveca is a sweet bit of fluff."

Julian only just didn't snort. *Fluff...Lady Viveca?* This gentleman had obviously never discussed *The Family Shakespeare* with the sweet bit of fluff that was Lady Viveca—or he would understand that kitten had razor-sharp claws.

Society was in no way ready for the sisters Calthorp.

Again, the feeling thrummed through him. He shouldn't be here. The impulse to come had been a bad idea—a weakness.

However, as he turned to leave, an amused voice rang out, "And the odds on the other sister? Lady Tessa?"

The question stopped Julian dead in his tracks.

Or, rather, the one word—*odds*.

With an efficiency borne of practice, he schooled his face into amiability and asked, "What's this about odds?"

No gentleman would question an inquiry related to sport and betting.

"Haven't you seen the book at White's today?" asked the amused voice.

"The odds on the Calthorp sisters being married by year's end," chimed another.

"Of course, Lady Viveca will be snapped up by some lucky chancer right quick," said one lord with a morose twist of the mouth.

"And Lady Saskia, too," spoke another, albeit with a smidge less certainty.

"That chancer might be a hair less lucky."

Another round of laughter.

"Her dowry will be enough to warm one in the night."

"But Lady Tessa..." A doubtful shake of the head was enough to complete the gentleman's sentence.

"She's an altogether different proposition."

"Fifty to one?"

"Odds that fair?" came a snark.

"A thousand to one."

"Have you seen the mode of dress she parades around in?"

"The cravat and waistcoat, you mean?"

"Unnatural."

Another word that bristled across the fine hairs of Julian's neck—*unnatural*. When gentlemen started pronouncing a woman *unnatural*, it usually didn't bode well for the woman in question.

Defensiveness surged through him. Tessa was her own woman—the sort who didn't give two tosses about the opinions of society. Her journey through life had fashioned her thus—and he wouldn't change that about her, as blasted frustrating as the woman could be.

"But have you seen her *tonight*?" asked a young viscount with a knowing waggle of his eyebrows.

Other knowing eyebrows joined in waggling chorus. Julian's smile slid to the floor. "What do you mean?"

"You haven't seen her, then?"

"I've only just arrived."

"One could be tempted into thinking her a diamond of the first water."

"We're speaking of Lady Tessa Calthorp, correct?" Julian clarified.

Of course, he knew that truth for himself—*intimately*—but he'd thought himself the only one to know it. When had society begun thinking of her so?

Those knowing waggles of male eyebrows...*Have you seen her tonight?*

What was he missing?

Only one way to find out.

He pivoted on his heel and strode from the card room, purpose in every step, his driving thought that he find Tessa. She'd become the subject of gossip, and he would know why—and protect her, if necessary.

"Ormonde!"

Julian tensed at the sound of his title and as quickly released it when he found Lord Wrexford barreling toward him.

"She's here," the excitable earl exclaimed.

Julian's brow gathered. "*She?*"

"The duchess."

Oh, this again.

The Duchess of Acaster.

"Should I ask her to waltz?"

Julian didn't hesitate. "Yes." The duchess would reject Wrexford outright and put the man out of his misery. It was the kinder course.

Impatience itched at Julian as he scanned the ballroom.

Still, no Tessa.

A footman bearing a silver tray topped with bubbling coupes of champagne appeared. Out of habit, Julian lifted a glass and held it without taking a drink. Wrexford downed half the contents of his in a single gulp. The boisterous belch that followed held not a hint of abashment. "For courage."

Julian snorted.

A familiar figure moved into view—*Tessa.*

His hearing became muffled, as if he'd entered a very long tunnel and she was the light at the end.

It was only when he began to follow the elegant curve of her neck that the obvious struck him...

Tessa wasn't wearing her usual uniform of cravat and waist-coat, but rather a silk evening gown of pale lilac, its cap sleeves of the same sheer ivory fabric as the fichu at her décolletage. A modest dress in the eyes of society, but one that suited Tessa, who wasn't given to displays of her person.

Her person?

Was that how he was describing the body he'd seen... touched...and *pleasured?*

Then he noticed it—the strand of lustrous pink pearls, flowing across her collarbone and down the front of her bodice.

The pearl necklace he'd bought her.

His mouth went dry. Pearls were known for their iridescent beauty. But they had other uses, too. Uses he wanted nothing more in this moment than to demonstrate—*thoroughly*—upon her person.

Without thinking, he took a step in her direction, shoving his champagne coupe into Wrexford's empty hand.

"Ah, yes," said the earl. "More courage."

The words fell on deaf ears.

Tessa's gaze shifted and found Julian's—as if she'd long since spotted him and had been monitoring his movements.

Of course, she would. Nothing got by Tessa.

By the time he reached her, the string quartet struck up a waltz. He lifted her hand, twined his fingers through hers, and pulled her into his arms and the stream of the dance.

He hadn't asked for permission.

Her eyes told him he didn't need to.

* * *

TESSA HADN'T BEEN sure Julian would come tonight.

Though she'd known he was invited.

A discreet scan of the guest list yesterday had confirmed as much.

But the night had proceeded along like clockwork with Gabriel introducing himself to society as the new Duke of Acaster and his sisters in their come-out. The congratulations had poured in and the dancing commenced—and there had been no sign of the Marquess of Ormonde.

His absence had produced an ache of yearning inside Tessa unlike anything she'd ever experienced—or could have predicted.

What havoc the man had wrought within her—body and mind.

She'd been keeping half an eye out for him wherever she went. The Archangel...on the street...even in her house, as she kept an ear out for his knock. Then tonight, she'd, at last, spotted him—the dashing Marquess of Ormonde in his evening blacks.

To her, *Julian*.

When he'd started walking toward her, with that glint in his eyes, she knew they wouldn't be able not to touch one another. That momentum flowed in an inevitable direction.

They would touch.

Fortunately, this was a ball and dancing was a useful excuse— touch sanctioned by society.

The sure grasp of his fingers wrapped around hers...the firm hold of the hand upon her ribs...as they entered the silken *one-*

two-three of the waltz. Her body responded to being held in his strong arms in the only way it knew how—to surrender. They danced as if they were the only two people who mattered in the world.

It was a problem.

But not, surprisingly, one which Tessa felt inclined to solve.

Which was a problem in itself.

They'd done a circuit of the dancing floor before he spoke. "You're wearing—"

Her snort cut across him, and curiosity flicked in his eyes. She experienced mild relief in the reaction—in the distance it provided. "A proper ballgown?" she finished for him.

A quizzical cant to his head, he said, "The pearls."

Degree by degree, Tessa grew hot. She shouldn't have worn the pearls.

But she had.

Because the possibility had existed that Julian would be here, and she hadn't been able to leave them in their velvet box.

It didn't follow logic, but that was the fact of the matter.

She liked the feel of them against her skin—something of *him* against her skin.

The fact was she might be a little obsessed with the marquess.

Which had been her way for her entire life. When something intrigued her, she gave her whole being over to it until she solved it.

And the man holding her in his arms intrigued her.

It was because of what he appeared to be—and how he wasn't that man.

It was what he did to her body.

It was what she wanted him to do again.

So, she'd worn the pearls.

She'd wanted him to notice—and see his reaction when he did.

She wanted to produce reactions in him—*seismic* reactions.

Reactions that quaked him to his core.

They took another swirling turn about the dancing floor before he said, "They've put marriage odds on you, you know." She just caught the tentative note in his voice.

"They'll put odds on any tired, old nag, won't they?" she asked lightly. "As part owner of a gaming hell, I should know."

His brow lifted in undisguised skepticism. "*Tired, old nag?*"

"Yes, well, figure of speech."

"Surely, you don't think of yourself that way."

"As a matter of fact, I don't." She gave a self-effacing laugh that emerged more giggle than intended. "I think entirely too highly of myself and my abilities to harbor such a reductive idea of femininity."

Julian snorted, skeptical clouds somewhat receded.

"Still," she continued, "as far as the action those gentlemen will see out of me, I may as well be a tired, old nag."

That funny look entered Julian's eyes again.

"Tessa, if you were a horse, you would be a Thoroughbred."

Another giggle wanted to bubble up, but she didn't allow it its head.

It was the look in his eyes that stopped her.

The very earnestness within.

He'd just paid her a very high compliment, and she couldn't toss it aside with a laugh, like some bit of rubbish.

And this compliment…She could see it wasn't easily spoken, and a thought struck her an instant later—one that seemed impossible.

Through caught breath, she asked, "You're not accustomed to courting ladies, are you?"

He hesitated only a moment. "I *don't* court ladies."

Tessa felt her brow gather, meeting his in seriousness. Words, by their very nature, were an ephemeral bit of nothing that, once released, floated out to join all the infinite others in the ether.

But these words, spoken by this man, held a weight—a weight solidly yoked about his shoulders.

These words...

They emerged with a rote finality that held the ring of closely held truth.

These words...

They were a burden.

"But...*why?*"

Julian tensed his jaw and directed his gaze over her shoulder and led her through the steps of the dance for the next thirty seconds.

Confusion tumbled through Tessa. She was close to something, but she wasn't sure what.

And when she was close to a truth, she knew of but one way to proceed—forward. She'd never been one to let confusion stand.

"*You* are the Marquess of Ormonde," she said.

He flinched.

She was getting closer...

"Why wouldn't *you* court ladies? Surely, they must compete for your attention." She made a point of glancing around the crowded dancing floor. "I can count five unmarried ladies staring at you from behind their fans."

"It's not your concern," he said through clenched teeth. "Leave it."

Oh, but Tessa couldn't..."*I*," she said, "am a lady."

Impenetrable emotion flashed behind his eyes, but nothing more passed between his lips. Somehow, that simple truth—*I am a lady*—was a provocative statement.

Which only notched up her curiosity another degree.

"So, to be clear," she pressed, recklessness running zigzags through her. "Whatever it is you and I have been doing is *not* courting."

That got his attention.

Behind narrowed eyes usually so clear and blue marched a jumble of emotions that would take Tessa a decade of years to untangle. But it all added to one certainty: His mask of amiability and good nature hid a man tortured down to the bones of his very existence.

She still wasn't sure what the mark had been, but she'd hit it dead center.

Instinctively, her hand tightened around his and she stepped so close not even a whisper of air came between them, so close her mouth could've touched his neck, and said, "Julian…"

That instant, the violins struck the final flourish of the waltz. Before Tessa could gather what he was about, he broke free of her grasp, took a step back, and bowed, his face implacable granite. Then he pivoted on his heel and left her standing alone in the center of the dancing floor, her mouth agape with unconcealed shock.

What in the blazes had just happened?

Her feet wanted to chase after him—even started to—but a voice at her back stopped her. "Sister."

CHAPTER FOURTEEN

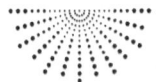

*T*essa released a frustrated sigh and glanced over her shoulder.

There, not five feet away, stood Gabriel, head canted as he regarded her with an inquisitive glimmer in his eyes.

To follow her instinct and chase after Julian would only spark inquisitiveness into a full-on inquisition.

Which wouldn't do.

"How are you finding your newfound position as the most popular duke in the *ton*, brother?" she asked. That should set him back on his heels a bit and dampen any embers of curiosity that might be tempted into conflagration.

He snorted, as she'd known he would. "Expensive."

A responding snort sounded from her. They ran one of the most exclusive gaming hells in London together; they understood precisely how expensive it was to entertain these people.

Without stating their intention, they moved to a quiet stretch of unoccupied wall and stole a few moments to assess the room and its general mood and any needs that might be arising—as they did every night at The Archangel. It was second nature. The *ton*, as they'd learned over the years, needed a watchful eye kept on it.

On the dancing floor, Viveca swept past in the arms of her partner, followed five seconds later by Saskia. Tessa knew without having to glance at her brother that his eyes followed, too.

"But anything for them," she said.

"Anything," he agreed.

It had been sixteen years since their parents perished within six months of one another—and sixteen years since Tessa and Gabriel had stepped into their roles of *de facto* parents at the ages of nine and eight, respectively. Somehow, through sheer grit, determination, fear, and audacity, they'd kept the family intact. Life in London held sharp, jagged edges at every turn and one slip was all it took to sever the tie that bound a family and send them sprawling in every direction. Even at the age of nine, Tessa had known that much.

So, they'd done anything to provide a roof over their heads and scraps of food for their table. It was a role neither she nor Gabriel had ever resented. Life had been too busy for such pettiness and instinct too strong. *Anything* for each other became the mantra that drove them forward. It was simply what one did for those one loved.

Anything.

Unbidden, Julian stole into the thought and she wondered if he'd ever had anyone feel thusly about him. Had anyone ever been willing to do *anything* for him?

From what she knew of his past, she suspected an answer she wouldn't much like.

And yet...He held himself away from any such relationship.

I don't court ladies.

What drove his desire to be utterly alone?

To be...*lonely*?

For that had become clear to her.

Julian was lonely.

By his choice.

Why?

"You, *erm*," began Gabriel. He looked suddenly out of his depth as he cast about for a way to finish the sentence he'd begun.

"What about me?" she asked. Sisters could demand such answers from brothers.

"You look...," he began again.

She supposed an additional word—a verb, no less—was progress. "I look...?"

"You look...lovely."

A sudden flare of heat blossomed through Tessa, and she knew high spots of color stained her cheekbones. "*Erm,*" she began. "Thank you," she finished with an uncomfortable clearing of her throat.

It was the dress, she understood. Feminine and silky, it pointed out features of her body that her customary mode of dress hid. Take her skin, for example. Before tonight, no one in this room had known that she had a small pink mole on the underside of her upper arm, just above the reach of silk gloves.

Another flare of heat pulsed through her.

Well, one other person had known.

Julian.

He'd even dusted it with a feather before pressing his mouth to it.

The heat pooled deeper, low in her body, within that place she'd become all too familiar with since Julian had charged into her life and rendered it insatiable.

Unable not to, her gaze flicked across the room, her heart in her throat, though she knew she wouldn't find him.

"I saw you dancing," said Gabriel.

"Oh?" She tried for breezy—and failed.

"I didn't know you could dance."

"I couldn't until a few days ago." When Gabriel waited for more information, she continued, "I dropped by St. James's Square during Saskia and Viveca's dancing lesson one afternoon."

"Ah."

"And Mrs. Fairfax insisted I take part."

"She's a difficult person to refuse."

"Indeed." Difficult was an understatement. Impossible, more accurately fit. Tessa lifted resigned hands. "And that's how I know the waltz."

Gabriel's gaze landed on the side of her face. He had more to say, and he wanted to gauge her reaction when he spoke his next words. "With the Marquess of Ormonde."

"He asked," she said on a shrug.

Actually, he hadn't.

But Gabriel didn't need to know that.

"The two of you looked as if you'd, *erm...*"

And here was her ever cool, ever composed brother stumbling over his words again.

That could be no good thing.

Gabriel was as clear-minded a person as one was ever likely to meet.

Gabriel didn't stumble over his words.

Tessa kept her gaze trained directly before her, as if riveted by the twirling pairs of couples gliding past.

"Well," Gabriel continued, as if seeing no way forward but through, "it looked as if you'd waltzed before."

Oh, the snort that wanted release.

It looked as if you'd waltzed before.

That was certainly one way of putting it.

If Gabriel only knew.

Which he wouldn't.

Not ever.

She turned to tell her brother to mind his own affairs, but the scold went stodgy in her mouth. Gabriel was no longer looking at her, but at the dancing floor, his eyebrows digging deep trenches into his forehead.

An alarm bell clanged through Tessa. "Is it Saskia?"

She wouldn't put it past that sister to call a lordling a nodcock for his vacuous stupidity in the middle of the dancing floor and incite a minor scandal.

When Gabriel didn't answer, she asked more urgently, "Is it Viveca?"

She wouldn't put it past their other sister to do the same, except that vacuous lordling likely wouldn't know it until he was lying in bed later.

And here she'd thought Saskia and Viveca's introduction into society was an unmitigated success. In fact, she expected dozens of invitations to society gatherings to flood into the St. James's mansion by dawn, with a few proposals of marriage thrown in, too.

No. That didn't explain the scowl on Gabriel's face.

She followed the direction of his thunderous gaze, and now it was her brow furrowing. Her brother was tracking a single couple around the dancing floor.

That young whelp, the Earl of Wrexford, and...the Duchess of Acaster.

"A surprising couple, to say the least," she said, delicately testing the temperature of the water.

"It's simply a dance, Tessa."

The words and their tone were dismissive, caustic even, but the glare in Gabriel's eyes revealed they were a lie. Her brother was feeling anything but dismissive of Wrexford and the duchess as a couple.

"Someone should tell Wrexford as much," said Tessa, unable to resist poking her brother.

Gabriel's jaw clenched. Recent experience had taught Tessa that only a woman could provoke such a reaction in a man.

And she had her answer without even having asked a question.

The Duchess of Acaster was that woman for Gabriel.

Interesting.

Of a sudden, Wrexford pulled the duchess to a stop in the center of the dancing floor and fell to one knee. Foreboding traced through Tessa. Beside her, Gabriel went still—too still. She wouldn't have been at all surprised to learn he'd forgotten how to breathe.

"I cannot live another day without you," Wrexford all but shouted to the rafters as if he were both proposing marriage and performing on a Drury Lane stage. "Will you...Will you consent to be my bride?"

A shocked breath of a laugh escaped Tessa. Gabriel, however, reacted not at all, his eyes trained on the duchess. He was clearly willing an answer from her.

Tessa's sense of foreboding went from a trace to a solid object. She suspected the answer her brother willed from the duchess, but she wasn't sure that was the answer the duchess would give.

"Yes," said the duchess, ghostly pale, the answer emerging breathy and unaccompanied by a smile. To Tessa's eye, the woman looked as if she'd just signed her own death warrant.

A strangled sound emerged from Gabriel's throat.

That a goddess like the Duchess of Acaster would join her life to a man like Wrexford—not that he was a bad man—defied belief. But then, he was an earl and a future marquess and exceedingly wealthy, and she was a beauty and penniless from what Tessa had pieced together and in possession of a brain in that beautiful head of hers.

Tessa supposed the logic of her acceptance only followed.

Except to Gabriel, it seemed, as a battalion of emotions marched behind his eyes. He appeared to be having trouble working out the solution that was all too clear to Tessa.

"Gabriel," she said, laying a hand on his arm, "are you all right?"

He pivoted and blinked, as if surprised to find her standing there. He nodded slowly, as if a solution to an equation of his own was only now arriving to him. "It will be," he said, still nodding. "It will be," he repeated, each word composed of a more solid substance than the last.

And with that, he shook off her hand and crossed the room, doggedly skirting the crowd that was pressing toward the center of the room to congratulate the *ton*'s newest and most improbable affianced couple. Then he passed through the open French doors leading onto the terrace and vanished from sight, leaving Tessa on her own and no small amount bewildered.

What in the blazes was *that* all about?

Actually, she suspected the answer to the *what*, but the answers to the *when* and *how* were as elusive as her brother.

Blasted frustrating man.

Like all men, it would seem.

And speaking of men who frustrated...

For the thousandth time tonight, she scanned the ballroom, on the lookout for the broadest pair of shoulders.

Still, Julian wasn't here.

Annoyance sparked through her.

She had unfinished business with that blasted frustrating man.

Unerringly, her feet pointed in the direction of the card room. That was, of course, where he would be—tucked away in his safe, all-male domain.

She snorted.

Well, tonight, it wasn't safe from this female.

If he thought he could simply leg it and be rid of her and her inconvenient questions, he hadn't learned a single thing about her.

At the threshold to the card room, she paused and took in the scene. Five tables arranged with different games at play, those gentlemen not engaged in play standing about and socializing. Her eye glided past the scene she beheld every night at The Archangel and found her quarry exactly where she'd expected—shoulder propped against a wall, arms crossed over his chest, idly conversing and watching.

It struck Tessa there was a reason she'd found him so easily, for this was how she usually found him at The Archangel—watching...set apart.

A hot blush threatened to stain her cheeks as another scenario presented itself in her mind where he liked to set himself apart...and watch.

As quick as she could question it, she intuited all the *whys*.

Why he watched...Why he set himself apart...Why he ran...

For safety.

Within those actions he sought shelter.

His gaze lifted, and the storm within his eyes, directed squarely at her, betrayed his studied indolence.

But what she didn't see within those summer-blue depths was surprise.

He'd known she would follow.

The realization set a warm frisson pulsing through her.

He did know her, after all.

And she liked it.

She wanted to be known by him.

And, perhaps, from somewhere within his solitary shelter, he wanted to be known by her.

Except he didn't know how to let himself.

Right.

Without another staying thought, she strode through the room and collected more than a few lifted eyebrows along the way. Most of these gentlemen knew her as the dragon of The Archangel, anyway. Why not burnish her reputation a bit?

As for Julian, he watched her approach with subtle wariness.

Good.

A woman on a mission, she shouldered her way through the gentlemen gathered round and planted herself squarely before the Marquess of Ormonde, golden lord of the *ton*. Eyebrows would have to be scraped off the ceiling come morning.

Whirring chatter and low whistles sawed through the air—*a woman...in the card room!*

Julian, alone, remained utterly composed.

And it was his unrelenting composure that gave him away.

CHAPTER FIFTEEN

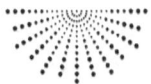

*J*ulian wasn't sure which he found most attractive about Tessa.

Her fearlessness…

Her arrogance…

Her utter indifference to the opinion of the many…

Her attractive qualities competed for best as she stood planted before him. Her eyes shone bright, her cheeks flushed, her rather bounteous bosom heaving and making a minor spectacle of itself for all the gathered to see and, frankly, admire.

Here was a woman who didn't give a toss about these gentlemen clamoring around, waggling their eyebrows and pulling comic faces like schoolboys. The look in her steady eyes said they could stuff their nonsense straight up their collective bum.

It should have annoyed him. After all, there were rules, and the rules stated that ladies keep away from the card room. Of course, some ladies insisted on being exceptions to that rule. Widows…married ladies…All ladies of a certain character—untamable in the eyes of society.

Tessa was neither married nor a widow, but she might well be untamable.

And it was that last quality that he found most attractive.

That made him want to claim her.

That made him want to leg it to the Thames and jump into the river and let it wash away the wild impulses the woman inspired within him.

"May I be of assistance to you, Lady Tessa?" he asked, smiling amiably and playing the marquess the gentlemen in this room expected.

She didn't waver. "You and I have a debt to settle, my lord."

She wasn't in for a penny.

She was in for a pound.

His body registered the double entendre before his mind caught up to it, but that split of a second was all his cock needed to fill to half-staff.

His smile broadened, even as his eyes narrowed. "The debt has been forgiven." The words emerged more tightly than he would've liked, and she would've detected as much.

The gossipy buzz of the room quieted to a low murmur, curious ears attuned to the entertainment being provided by the Marquess of Ormonde and Lady Tessa Calthorp, and all Julian could think was he'd brought this upon himself.

He'd underestimated Tessa.

Of course, she would follow him into the card room and create a scene.

Her gaze steady and cool, she gave a slow shake of the head. "The possibility of debt forgiveness wasn't laid out in the original terms."

She wasn't letting him off the hook.

His amiability didn't slip a hair. "Consider it a gift, then."

He was all magnanimous marquess. How could she possibly refuse in the face of such lordly generosity?

Yet he knew without a doubt, she would.

And that certainty sent such a hard throb of anticipation spiking through him, he nearly lost his breath.

"Perhaps," she said, "this discussion would be better settled in private."

A few beats of stunned silence loped past before a voice three sheets to the wind rang out, "Oh, it's off to the naughty chair with you, Ormonde!" And the room broke free of its tension and into riots of relieved laughter, guffaws, and whistles.

However, Julian and Tessa remained unmoved, their eyes only breaking contact when she pivoted and began striding away, the gentlemen happily clearing a path for this woman on a mission, if only to be rid of her. Julian was to follow, of course, and he caught several rueful, sympathetic shakes of the head and jocular pats on the back as he did so, a man nobly walking the plank so many men in this room had trodden before him.

He'd thought she would lead him into the ballroom, perhaps to a quiet alcove. But, no, she led him straight through that happy chaos without a single backward glance.

She knew he followed.

Across an empty foyer, they strode. It would have been a private enough location for a discussion regarding the settlement of a gambling debt.

But still they walked on.

Down an even quieter corridor, the roar of the ballroom and the buoyant strains of music fast fading, they continued, ignoring the paired off couples stealing a private moment for themselves. Julian only caught them from the corner of his eye, having no inclination toward gossip, his attention solely for the woman leading the way.

Up a set of stairs, she ascended, her hips a subtle sway, the moonlight streaming through the skylight above setting the silk of her gown alight in shimmery lilac ripples.

Here, there was no one else.

Only them.

She hesitated at a door at the far end of another corridor, grabbed the handle, and pushed it open. Beyond the doorway, Julian's eyes were magnetically drawn to a single piece of furniture—*the bed*.

She'd led him to a bedroom for the settlement of their wager.

A slick of sweat pinpricked his palms.

Lady Tessa was playing dirty.

"Won't someone be needing this room tonight?" he asked. It was worth a try, anyway.

"As it happens, this bedroom is mine."

He felt his brow knit. "Have you given up your Knightsbridge townhouse?"

Disappointment pinged through him. He rather liked her independent streak and didn't want to see her give it up.

Also, it had to be admitted, he rather liked that he could happen down Sloane Street and knock on her door at any time and she would likely let him in.

That wasn't a possibility at the ducal mansion.

Rules would apply here.

She shook her head. "This room has been designated mine if I ever choose to use it."

Ridiculous relief struck through him. "Ah."

"I'd never thought to have a use for it," she continued, propping a shoulder against a bedpost, "But tonight…"

She allowed the sentence to finish itself in the quiet air between them.

Tonight… There was a use for it.

Right.

"Tonight, you and I aren't leaving this room until we've settled our wager." A beat. "To my satisfaction."

A supremely wrong impulse had a supremely wrong question leaving his mouth…"Have I ever left you unsatisfied?"

Her head canted, and her eyes narrowed. "That's a very interesting question with a very complex answer."

Blast.

This conversation was careening toward the edge of a cliff. He didn't want this woman's complex answers.

Or he wanted them too much.

Either way, simplicity was his only hope. "The twenty thousand pounds is yours."

"But *I* lost the wager."

"I'll have it delivered to your townhouse by noon tomorrow."

"Let me see if I have this straight." Her head canted quizzically. "You would rather pay me twenty thousand pounds than bed me?"

Most men would pay this woman twenty thousand pounds *to* bed her.

But he couldn't tell her that.

It was a wrong thought on many levels.

She wasn't finished. "Should I be insulted?"

The metallic tang of danger scented the air.

The truth was he would give up everything to bed her—titles...lands...wealth...his fleetest yearling...*everything.*

Except that isn't quite true, is it? asked a small voice.

What he understood her to be asking for, he couldn't give.

And it wasn't a matter of choice.

"Why don't you court ladies?" she asked. The brightness of her eyes told him she sensed the danger, too—and insisted on striding into the thick of it.

"I don't see any logic in it."

"Why is that?"

"Because I would only be leading them on." He considered leaving it at that. He didn't owe her more. Yet..."I don't intend to marry."

Tessa's brow crinkled. "You don't intend to marry?"

He shook his head.

"But you're one of the most eligible lords in society."

He spread his hands wide, a man helpless to the facts. "Even so."

She pushed off the bedpost in a burst of unconcealed irritation. Lady Tessa wasn't accustomed to being thwarted, and she liked it not one bit.

She began pacing about a bit, deep in thought, and Julian used the opportunity to settle into a chair and observe this utterly unladylike woman, with the elegance of her movement and her long stride and indifference to how she appeared. Yet, still, she was all woman—her curves undisguised by shimmering silk, hair tumbling about her shoulders, golden tips spiraling into curls. This woman hadn't the faintest idea how feminine she was.

How exquisite.

At last, she stopped and planted herself in the center of the room, facing him. Her eyes said she'd arrived at a conclusion. Tension grabbed Julian's breath and refused to release it.

"No," she said.

"*No?*"

She shook her head. "That won't do."

A second later, a laugh of disbelief burst from him. The audacity of this woman.

"You'll have to do better." Not the scantest hint of a smile played about her mouth. The woman was dead serious.

And Julian understood.

He would have to give her a truth. Not all of it, but a morsel— and hope it would be enough to satisfy her.

"My past," he said.

"We all have a past," she retorted.

It was then that he saw it.

Within her eyes shone knowledge.

"You know of my past."

It wasn't a question, but a confirmation.

Her head canted. "Not yours so much, but some of your family's."

Such gossip would be easily come by, as the broad strokes of the tragic House of Ormonde would be known to all.

"There isn't one without the other," he said.

Another truth.

She nodded, and he saw not only understanding but something more—*connection*. The feeling vibrated through him to the marrow of his bones—connection to this woman. He'd felt it from their very first conversation, and it shook and rattled him, even as it made it impossible to stay away from her.

"That is true." She believed those words, for this woman didn't speak words she doubted.

He felt understood.

Dangerous...It was dangerous to feel this way—to let such feeling sink below the surface and warm him. He might want more of that warmth...

Then what?

"Still," she continued, "you haven't answered my question. Why don't you court ladies?"

"You'll just have to settle for the answer I've given."

Mutiny shone in her eyes. She wasn't about to settle.

And Julian saw he had no choice...

But to seduce her.

Distraction had succeeded before.

Why not again?

He pushed to his feet. The shift of her body wouldn't have been noticeable if he hadn't been watching her so closely. She'd tensed. It was subtle, but there in the set of her shoulders.

He detected something more, too, within the flare of her pupils—*desire*.

"What are you doing?" she demanded.

"Don't you know by now?"

He took another step closer.

She tried for indignation. "You would rather seduce me than answer my questions?"

He snorted, and a smile curled one side of his mouth.

She tried for outrage. "You simply can't seduce your way out of this."

The thing about her indignation and outrage was it rang hollow. Not even she believed a word of it.

Desire for what he offered was too strong a pull.

"Can't I?"

So close he could pick up her scent of crisp lemon, he reached out and cupped the nape of her neck, the fine hair silky against his calloused palm, before angling his head so his mouth met the sensitive skin of her neck. A breathless sigh escaped her parted lips, whispering her responding desire into his ear. His other hand found the indent of her waist, wrapping around to the small of her back, a simple contraction of muscle bringing her body, all lush curves, into his. The feel of her against him—all feminine woman.

The tetchy sense of danger fell away in the inevitability of this seduction. *This*—Tessa in his arms...being seduced by him—he understood. This sparking of desire into a full-on conflagration of lust...of pleasuring her...of making her cry out in climax. In the seduction of Tessa lay control and safety.

This was what he knew—and what she wanted.

He removed one silk glove, then the other, stealing a kiss on the pink mole on the underside of her arm. Next, his fingers were unbuttoning her dress. It fell to the floor in a silken *shush*, leaving her clad in chemise, stays, stockings, and pearls—all delectable woman.

He cupped heavy breasts and sucked nipples through gossamer muslin chemise. A tremble of desire rippled through her. Without breaking contact, he eased her backward until they reached the bed, with a single intention—to pleasure this woman to within an inch of her life.

Then he felt them—her hands—no longer wound tight around his neck, drawing the soft length of her body against the rigid line of his. Instead, her hands had gone slack—and had begun moving, her fingernails a light scrape along his neck, sending goose bumps cascading down his arms, desire a hot streak straight to his cock.

Her fingers reached his cravat and curled around the knot. Reactively, his hand flew up and covered hers.

Him undressing wasn't part of his seduction plan.

Her gaze lifted. Not a hint of surprise shone in those silver-blue depths.

What he saw was defiance.

This woman—for reasons unfathomable to him—was determined to push his every boundary tonight.

Why?

Why couldn't she leave matters be?

Why couldn't the pleasure he would deliver to her body be enough for her?

"I want to see you," she said. "All of you."

She was speaking of his body, yes, but also of what lay deeper —*his soul.*

Of the two, the body was simpler.

So, he released his grip and let her fingers unknot his cravat. Less than thirty seconds later, white silk was fluttering to the floor and his shirt had fallen open in a V, revealing the light dusting of golden hair across his chest. She didn't hesitate, but pushed the evening coat off his shoulders, nimble fingers moving to the buttons of his waistcoat. Then the garment was off his body and joining the growing heap on the floor. When this woman set a goal, she reached it.

Her gaze drifted down and landed on his feet, where they remained for a full five seconds. "I don't see any help for it."

"Help for what?"

"You'll have to sit."

"*Sit?*"

"It's the only way to get your boots off."

Before he could offer resistance to her plan, she had them pivoting around and was pushing him onto the bed. A laugh escaped him. He couldn't help himself.

Not one to dawdle once a decision was made, she reached down and grabbed a boot.

"You must understand the removal of my boots is quite unnecessary." It had to be said.

"Oh, it's quite necessary." She planted herself and pulled with all her might.

*This woman...*There wasn't another like her. What other woman dressed in chemise, stays, stockings, and pearls would insist on pulling off a pair of men's boots. This was the work of a burly valet.

At last, the boot came loose, the release sending her stumbling backward. Without missing a beat, she let the boot thud to the floor as she lifted his other foot.

This woman wouldn't let a pair of boots defeat her.

With a bit more finesse, she had the second boot off in half the time, with half the effort. The woman was a fast learner, which came as no surprise, of course.

She went still and let her gaze rake over him as he remained propped on his elbows...Her eyes skimmed up his thighs...the demanding bulge straining against his trousers, lingering there long enough that a blush crept up her throat...and up further, over his chest to meet his gaze. He was the object of her desire— and he found he rather liked that.

A new truth sank in.

He was no longer in control of this seduction.

CHAPTER SIXTEEN

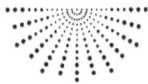

essa placed her hands on his thighs, parting them and stepping between, and Julian realized a truth vital to this moment.

He didn't need to be in control.

She reached down to grab his shirt, giving it a few tugs until it pulled free of his waistband. Then it was up over his head and tossed away.

"Oh, my," she said at the sight of him. "How many muscles does one man need?"

A wave of gratification washed through him.

A shallow line formed between her eyebrows. "What is…" Light fingertips trailed across his shoulders to a point just below his clavicle. "Is that a bruise?"

"It's nothing."

"It very much looks like something." Her fingers trailed across him to another spot, lower. "And is this bruise nothing?"

"I spar."

"As in boxing?"

"Aye."

She leaned forward and pressed her mouth to the bruise

beneath her fingertips, her lips so soft and generous against him, touching and warming his skin…touching and warming a place deeper.

She found another bruise, then another, exploring his body with her mouth and hands.

All he wanted was to reach out and touch her.

But he couldn't.

If he surrendered to that urge, then he would surrender to another, then another, and down that path lay destruction—he felt the certainty in every cell of his body.

Already, he'd let it go too far.

She kissed a bruise just below his bottom rib and hesitated. She'd reached the final and lowest bruise.

His cock throbbed.

Light fingertips brushed along his waistband, and her gaze lifted and met his across his reclined body.

"I want to taste you."

His cock *begged*.

Too far.

Here she was, again, pushing him too far—determined to do so.

"You shouldn't."

No. He should've spoken a flat, final *no*.

But the simple fact was he couldn't make himself.

"Don't deny yourself the pleasure you so freely give," she said. "Not tonight."

Not tonight.

As if tonight were different from any other night.

And yet…

Perhaps it could be.

What was one night in a lifetime of thousands, anyway?

"Don't deny me the pleasure of pleasuring you."

And he knew it wasn't in him to deny this woman anything.

A dangerous woman, indeed.

Though it was the worst thing he could do, he nodded.

She settled back a few inches and considered what lay before her—the buttoned falls of his trousers and what throbbed beneath...the thickened length barely contained by black superfine.

Trembly fingers grazed across him, and he sucked in a sharp breath. He could spend here.

His eyes drifted shut. He couldn't watch her as if she were a vassal in worship to his cock and not spend.

But as her nimble fingers worked the buttons of his trousers, he wasn't sure it was better to have his eyes closed. For now, all he could do was *feel* and anticipate, which only heightened the lust coursing through his blood, fizzing it into bright effervescence.

He knew the instant the final button was freed and the falls tucked back. He felt a whisper of cooling air across his length—and her gasp that held the trace of a giggle.

Gratifying, that gasp and giggle, and he squeezed his eyes tighter.

Then he felt them—feathery fingertips brushing across him. A groan escaped his parted lips. So much contained within that vocal release—pleasure...a sweet sort of pain...impatience...want...*need*...

The need for *more*.

Driven by instinct, he reached out and covered her hand with his. Unsteady fingers became firmer, tightening around him.

Or was that tremble coming from him?

Impossible to tell, for what he was experiencing with her and she with him and they together was a oneness.

His tremble or her tremble...it mattered not.

For tonight.

Together, they stroked up, then down, his length, and another ragged moan poured from his throat as she found a rhythm. He released her hand, his tutelage no longer needed.

Then he felt it—a soft, slick glide all the way up his length.

He shouldn't open his eyes—truly, he shouldn't—but how could he not when her tongue was teasing and flicking and stroking his length.

His gaze slitted open, and he watched her taste him, even as her hand used the slickness to move up and down. Her eyes lifted and met his across his reclined body, her black pupils pushing irises into thin blue rings, as she wrapped her mouth around the crown of his cock.

It was the most erotic sight of his life.

He was in trouble.

This magnificent, logical, fearless woman, who was clear about what she wanted out of life, wanted him.

He'd never encountered a greater aphrodisiac.

She shifted backward, and her mouth slid off him. A groan of protest escaped him. Silver-blue eyes fast on his, she languidly fingered the strand of pearls, caught the amethyst clasp and flicked it open.

Intention and mischief sparking about her, the pearls swung from her forefinger. "You like playthings, don't you?"

He gave an unhurried nod. No use denying it.

"What if we used these for..." Her gaze moved between his cock and the pearls.

"*For?*" He hardly knew his own voice, so rumbly and ragged it had gone.

A secret smile curled about her mouth. "You'll see."

She slid the pearls across her lips, wetting them with her tongue, and all Julian could do was watch, transfixed, as she took the strand and grazed them across him and began wrapping them around his rigid length, layer upon stacked layer. She interlaced her fingers and closed around him and began rolling the slick stack of pearls up and down.

Yet another groan scraped across his throat. "That feels so... *good.*"

He'd used pearls on a woman's body—had, in fact, fantasized about using these very pearls on *this* woman's body—but never on his. The absolute pleasure of slick, rolling pressure as she moved them up and down, her mouth taking in his crown as she did so.

A notion—one he'd been avoiding—came to him.

He'd met his match in Lady Tessa.

A distinct and known feeling began to build inside him—the build toward release—and he felt himself resist the momentum.

He should allow it to happen. Then he would return pleasure for pleasure, and they would both end the night satisfied.

Except he wouldn't be satisfied. He understood as much on a fundamental level.

For tonight...he wanted...craved...*ached* for an outcome he'd long denied himself.

For tonight, all he wanted was the relief of surrender.

He reached out and covered her fingers with his, staying her hand before it was too late.

Before his mind got in the way of capitulation.

Her gaze lifted and met his, his cock still in her mouth.

Heaven help him.

With care, he pushed himself to a sitting position and slid from between her swollen lips. She unwound the pearls from around him, dropping them onto the coverlet, and stood. Her hands found his shoulders, and she leaned forward, her gaze steady on his. "I need *you* inside me."

She wasn't one for equivocation, this woman.

Even as he questioned his sanity, he grabbed her waist and pulled her against him, so her breasts pressed into his chest. She lifted onto her toes and swung one knee, then the other, to either side of his thighs, so she straddled him, her quim a hairsbreadth above his length, her mouth nearly touching his, her shallow breath a whisper across his lips.

Then her mouth lowered onto his in a slow, languorous kiss

that said they had all the time in the world, even as urgency pressed in at the edges.

He'd kissed her once and had known it to be a mistake—and even now he wasn't sure he'd been wrong. It was simply that her lips were too soft and too sweet and too irresistible. Now, as then, he wanted to tumble headlong into her kiss and never break surface again.

A note of fear shimmered through him, for within a kiss lay intimacy beyond pleasure.

Pleasure could be a cold object.

But not a kiss.

There was no place to hide within a kiss.

On an impatient moan, she shifted closer, pressing her slick cunny against his rigid length and ground up and down him. They wouldn't have all night, but a mere few seconds, if she kept that up.

Right.

His hands tightened around her waist as he half stood and swiveled them around in a swift, efficient motion that had their places on the bed reversed—it was now her lying on the coverlet and him hovering above her. Her long legs crooked at the knees before reaching out and wrapping around his hips, squeezing him closer, demanding his surrender.

"Please, Julian," she said. "Give me this one night."

This woman didn't beg easily.

And it wasn't in Julian to refuse her.

One forearm propped to the side of her head, with his other hand he reached between them and positioned himself at the entrance to her sex, so wet and swollen and ready...

With slow deliberation, he pushed inside, the feel of her hot and tight...so deliciously tight...

He stopped.

Blast.

"You're a virgin." He'd forgotten the possibility.

Her eyes told him he wasn't telling her anything she didn't already know.

Right.

"I want this," she said, her voice a raw, fervent scrape across her throat. "I want *you*."

I want you.

She wanted the pleasure his body could bring to hers.

That was what she wanted.

She didn't actually want him.

And he told himself this not because he wanted to hear it.

But because he *needed* to hear it.

On a single, swift stroke, he thrust into her sweet, slick cunny, and she pinched her eyes shut for a quick instant.

He shouldn't be doing this.

She was a lady.

She was a virgin.

He was in no way, shape, or form worthy of her.

And here he was, surrendering to the weakness he'd known was lying in wait inside him.

Waiting for the right woman to test and expose it.

Waiting for Tessa.

And now they were joined, his head bent, mouth pressed against her neck, her breath quick and shallow in his ear, and there was no retreating.

Slowly, he began to move inside her, trying for tenderness, but a hard cock was a blunt instrument of force and ache and demand, no subtlety to it, and she was responding, her hips finding a rhythm with his, as they moved together with the unified goal of delivering and extracting pleasure from one another's bodies.

He wouldn't last long.

It had been how many years since he'd experienced a woman's body in this way? Six...? Seven years?

But this wasn't any woman's body.

This was Tessa beneath him, demanding everything he had.

The movement of her hips became focused and intentioned. Though it had been years since he'd bedded a woman in this way, he knew what she was reaching for. He kept his rhythm slow and shallow, even as she clawed at his back for more.

"Tessa," he spoke into her ear. "Be patient, my—"

He flinched, the next word sticking in his throat.

Love.

He'd almost called her *my love.*

And he couldn't help wondering.

If he'd said it, would he have meant it?

Another thought for another moment.

"Oh, Julian," she cried, straining against him, her head arched back in frustration and pleasure and incompletion.

Still, he penetrated her steadily, letting her meet her need on his body.

Then the breath caught in her throat, and she went still in the specific way just before climax. He gripped her hips, unwilling to let her lose this. He moved in and out, dragging cries from her, his control slipping from his grasp. He was only a man, and she was a woman bent on pulling him over the edge with her.

Then she broke, her cunny pulsing its release around him, a ragged cry tearing from her throat and toward the ceiling. And that was all it took for his own release to nip at him and demand its due.

Never had surrender felt so sweet and so...*right.*

It was only when he began to spend that reality crashed onto him, and he pulled from her and spilled the rest of his seed onto the rumpled coverlet.

Blast.

Then it was one reality after another collapsed onto him as he stilled and the final reality of what he'd done seeped in.

He'd made love to Tessa.

He'd spilled his seed inside her.

Neither was supposed to happen.

In fact, he'd carefully fashioned a life where none of this would happen.

Then Tessa had come along.

And nothing had been the same since.

With the clearest eyes he'd had since their first conversation, he saw the inevitability of this outcome.

They'd been careening toward this all these weeks.

It had never been about a wager.

He'd been deluding himself.

It had been about his desire to have her.

He felt her steady gaze on the side of his face. "Julian?"

He couldn't look at her.

Not if he wasn't going to take her in his arms.

Not if he was to leave.

Without a backward glance, he shoved off the bed and grabbed his shirt, donning it in a few efficient movements. His other clothes quickly followed, and he was striding across the room. His hand closed around the door handle, and he heard at his back, firm, "Julian."

He hesitated.

If she called him back to her bed, he wasn't sure he could resist.

"Our wager is settled," she said.

Disappointment sheered through him.

He'd wanted her to call him back to her bed.

He'd wanted to be weak.

Then he was through the door, the catch clicking behind him.

They were free of each other.

He was free.

Then why didn't he feel free?

Why did he feel utterly, irrevocably, irretrievably bound?

* * *

FOR THE NEXT THREE MINUTES…OR three hours—it didn't much matter—Tessa lay in bed, alone, eyes fixed on the ceiling, silken strains of violin seeping through the walls.

She'd let him go.

She'd set him free.

Except he didn't walk like a free man.

He walked like a man with the weight of the world yoked to his shoulders.

And she didn't understand why.

He had it all—wealth, looks, the rare gift of having people genuinely like him, fast racehorses…All the trappings a marquess could ask for to navigate the world as he liked.

Didn't the Marquess of Ormonde possess all the necessary ingredients to combine into a fulfilled man?

Yet he wasn't.

He was alone…*lonely.*

By his own choice.

Something was broken within Julian.

And though Tessa longed to know what, she accepted she might never know, for nothing bound them now.

An ache pulsed through her and settled in the center of her chest.

Yet…

Did *nothing* truly bind them?

The ache in the center of her chest seemed to suggest otherwise.

CHAPTER SEVENTEEN

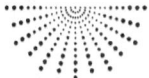

THREE WEEKS LATER, SLOANE STREET

*T*essa took a step back, pencil poised above her journal, and contemplated the table centered in the middle of the drawing room.

Well, she wasn't contemplating the table so much—it was of sturdy, reliable oak—but rather the three mounds of tea blends, composed of black tea, bergamot, and vanilla, piled upon its surface. Bergamot was a typical enough infusion with black tea, but the addition of vanilla added a special something. Except she hadn't quite gotten the mixture correct. The vanilla was overwhelming the other flavors, giving the tea a distinct shortbread-biscuit aroma.

Lately, she preferred the green teas, but they were too delicate to stand their ground against bold infusions like bergamot and vanilla.

As she recorded her observations as related to the scent notes —taste testing would come later—she couldn't help thinking that if she'd been a man, she might've attended Cambridge and made a chemist. Well, there was no changing that and, anyway, the house smelled a treat.

Pounds and pounds of tea, however, was the result of such a hobby.

She hadn't the faintest idea what to do with it all from a practical standpoint. Perhaps she would introduce tea time at The Archangel. She could just envision it: Peers of the realm at Hazard tables, teacups preciously held between thumbs and forefingers, pinkies out, while the other hand threw the dice.

A laugh bubbled up. She reckoned strong spirits were more conducive to the ambience of a gaming hell environ than tea. Unless...

The Archangel could have lady's hour.

Another chuckle followed, bounced off the four walls of the drawing room and faded away, leaving behind a silence that was somehow more silent than the silence had been ten seconds ago.

The house was so very quiet. Saskia and Viveca had been gone for weeks now—it was nothing new—but how she missed the general vibrancy of them. Missed the sound of Viveca humming as she cleaned her teeth...Missed Saskia's disapproving sighs over something she'd read—the Greeks could have terribly antiquated notions about the female sex...Even missed the muted crackle of pages turning, for one or the other sister ever had her nose buried in a book.

Or, perhaps, she was feeling this way because Gabriel had done something she couldn't have predicted in an eternity of years. He'd up and married the Duchess of Acaster—on her wedding day to another man, no less—and made her *his* Duchess of Acaster. While Tessa couldn't have predicted that turn of events, she couldn't say it surprised her. She couldn't think of a single instance in their entire lives that Gabriel wanted something and didn't attain it. And from the way she'd caught her brother looking at the duchess at the ball, he'd wanted her— *badly*.

Tessa liked the duchess. The woman had backbone and intelligence to go with her legendary beauty. Gabriel had married his match. And Tessa wished them well, she did...

But the townhouse felt lonelier since they married.

Which made no logical sense, for nothing had materially changed. She'd been living alone for weeks.

And yet, at some point she couldn't pinpoint, *alone* had turned into *lonely*.

Except...was that true?

If she cast her mind back—which she'd been avoiding for weeks—didn't the tip of the arrow hit the bullseye on a single night?

Right.

She tucked the pencil into the binding of the journal and snapped it shut. It was late enough now that perhaps she could grab a few blessed hours of sleep and freedom from that thought. She stepped to the front door and checked the deadbolt, then tested the lock on the front window overlooking Sloane Street. The heat had been sweltering today, so the housekeeper had thrown open the windows and the back door to tempt a cooling breeze to blow through the house—and with it a healthy dose of Thames summertime stench.

She was stepping away from the secured window when a figure caught her eye just before it disappeared around a corner onto Exeter Street. *Male...tall and broad-shouldered...*

Ridiculous flight of fantasy.

Every tall and broad-shouldered man couldn't be Julian.

And, really, matters between them had become exceedingly clear in these last three weeks of complete silence.

The terms of the wager had been met.

They were finished.

They were free of each other.

As she made her way up the stairs to her bedroom, she shooed the thought away and began removing her clothing. She opened a drawer to grab a night chemise, and her hand passed over the stack of folded white linen squares—her menses cloths. Her mind performed a quick calculation. She was overdue by a week. Or was it two?

No matter.

Though a rarity, this wasn't the first time her menses hadn't arrived on time.

Night chemise in hand, she shut both drawer and thought away.

After she'd slipped into the chemise, she stepped to the window overlooking the garden shared by all the neighboring townhouses. A little cooling night air would be just the thing.

A light *tap-tap-tap* hit her ear. A second later, she registered it was coming from the front door. An image filled her mind—a tall, broad-shouldered figure disappearing around a corner...

Julian.

Her heart fluttered into a cascade of light *pitter-patters*. That man and his penchant for "happening" past her townhouse at any odd hour of day or night.

Yet her feet were already on the move as she grabbed a dressing gown and all but flew down the stairs. She would let him in, but that didn't mean she would make it easy for him. The man had some explaining to do.

She slid the deadbolt and swung the door wide, a ready scold on her lips.

The scold and every other part of her froze, as it took a moment for her mind to understand the sight before her. Two men, burly and florid-faced, one smiling, one frowning, both cracking their knuckles.

"You aren't Julian," she said, nonplussed.

Later, she would think about what a stupid use of her lungs those words had been.

She should've screamed.

The frowny one switched the knuckle cracking to his other hand, and Tessa had the sense that he was a man accustomed to letting his knuckles do the talking for him. The smiley one said, "Naw, where we come from, we don't get names like *Julian*."

A shift occurred in the air, like a tiny spark of lightning, and Tessa understood that was the end of the greetings. The frowny one took a step forward, and she whirled around and bolted for the drawing room. While she didn't live her life in fear of happenings such as home invasions, she had formed a plan, and she enacted it now as she ran straight for the fireplace and grabbed the iron poker. She swung around, brandishing it before her.

That got the men's attention as their pursuit came to a screeching halt, hands extended, wariness in their eyes as they each took a different side of the room, cutting off her access to an exit and began calmly closing in on her. They were disturbingly well practiced at this. "Now, now, Lady Tessa, let's have none of that."

Lady Tessa?

"How do you know my name?" she shouted. A wobble had entered her voice, one composed of fear, frustration, and anger. And she knew…"Blaze Jagger sent you."

Again, she swung the poker as a warning to keep away.

"Ye'll be wantin' to put that down, milady," said the smiley one.

"I think I won't be wanting that at all," she said, swinging the poker again to prove her point.

Except this time, the frowny one caught the poker in his over-sized, meaty paw. Tessa planted her feet and pulled with all her might. The ensuing back-and-forth game of tug was quickly over, however, when he gave a mighty pull and she lurched forward and came entirely unbalanced, knocking into the table holding her tea blends, sending leaves, twigs, and petals flying every-where. Her assailant roared a mighty sneeze, relinquishing his grip on the poker for the split of a second, but long enough for Tessa to seize the moment and scramble away.

But she wasn't quick enough. The smiley one—she'd forgotten about him for that hopeful split of a second—grabbed her arm from behind and twisted it painfully up her back as he clamped his other hand over her mouth. Tessa caught the stench of beer-and-onion breath just before he said, "Jagger said ye might be a handful."

Tessa attempted to wriggle out of his grasp, but he only twisted her arm higher up her back, eliciting a sharp cry of pain. She went still and attempted to recover her breath and *think*. Surely, there was some way out of this mess...

Though she didn't make it easy, between them, the two men were able to tie her arms behind her back and a gag around her mouth. She gave the frowny one a hard stomp on the foot for good measure. On a low growl, he gave another crack of the knuckles, but before he could fulfill the evil intent in his eyes, the smiley one cut across him, "Ye go find the cellar and open the door."

Frowny grunted, clearly annoyed that he wasn't about to teach Tessa a lesson about stomping on feet that didn't belong to her, but he nodded and set about his orders.

Smiley turned toward Tessa. "Now, ye'll want to stop with that foot stompin' nonsense and keep quiet and no harm will come to ye."

She snorted, her only viable mode of communication that made it clear what she thought of his assurances.

Smiley shook his head, bemused. "A right handful," he said. "Now, Jagger wants ye to think about how ye've arrived at these circumstances and how ye can avoid them in the future, ye ken?"

Tessa gave another snort. Smiley began talking again, but a flash of movement beyond his right shoulder caught her attention. A figure had stepped into the doorway between the drawing room and the foyer and filled it. *Tall...broad-shouldered...*

Tessa blinked.

Julian.

"What in the blazes is happening here?" came his furious roar.

* * *

TEN MINUTES EARLIER

It was only after Julian determined he was in danger of wearing a path into the cobblestones of Sloane Street that he summoned a fading remnant of willpower.

He wouldn't pace up the street—*yet again*.

And he certainly wouldn't knock on Tessa's door.

He wouldn't.

Instead, he would round the corner onto Exeter Street and get himself home and on with the day ahead.

A day that filled his gut with dread, even as he knew it to be a necessary day—and if he avoided meeting it head on, the dread would only amplify into self-loathing. He'd tried it one year. Avoidance only made the feeling worse.

Reflexively, his hands tightened, and he remembered the sheaf of papers. His feet came to a sudden stop. Thankfully, it was five in the morning, so no one collided into his back.

These papers...

They contained vital information regarding Blaze Jagger. Tessa needed to see them. The Bow Street Runner had earned his fee, having done a thorough job of his investigation into the East End blackguard. Once Tessa read through these papers, she would know who and what she was dealing with.

He pivoted and began retracing his steps.

This wasn't about *that* night—or any particular need to see her.

After all, their wager was settled. They owed one another not one thing.

Except...couldn't he have sent a footman to deliver the documents, accompanied by a concise, explanatory note, without him having to see her at all?

It could've all been so neat and tidy.

Neat and tidy.

He snorted. His and Tessa's dealings had taken many forms, but *neat and tidy* wasn't one of them.

Even now, after twenty-one days, two hours and twelve or so minutes, all he had to do was shut his eyes for the sliver of a second and an image came to him—Tessa propped against the headboard, coverlet gathered just below her chin, red-gold hair love-tousled all about her shoulders, silently watching him dress with wary eyes. The image possessed a clarity as if it were imprinted on the back of his eyelids.

And there she waited for him every night when he could no longer hold his eyes open...waiting to haunt his dreams.

She was patient in that regard.

Nay, he wasn't beating a path to her doorstep for that reason. Simply, he needed to place this information directly into her hands and impress upon her the importance that she not set it aside and ignore it. She'd been underestimating Blaze Jagger, and Julian was here to see that wrong righted.

Determination impelling every step, he found himself again on Sloane Street, a plan of action forming in his mind. He would knock on her door. And when she answered, and after he'd— *again*—scolded her for not employing a manservant for that task, he would keep the conversation focused on the Blaze Jagger findings. He would impress onto her the importance of the Bow Street Runner's information. He would wave away her inevitable annoyance that he'd had the rogue investigated.

He wouldn't enter the townhouse.

He wouldn't bring up the fact that for the last three weeks she'd occupied nine of ten of his waking thoughts.

He would leave.

Neat and tidy.

He couldn't stay, anyway, he reminded himself. He'd instructed the head groom to have a coach-and-four readied by eight o'clock for the day's journey to Suffolk.

Today was Clarissa's birthday—and Clarissa didn't spend her birthday alone.

Familiar darkness pressed in at the edges of his mind.

He gave himself a mental shake. He couldn't go down that road now.

Later.

There were two days in the year that inevitably drove him to drink—and this was the second of them.

Oblivion was necessary.

But first, *Tessa.*

A small voice suggested he could've left this errand until tomorrow, upon his return to London.

Another voice suggested the two might even be linked. Perhaps he was here...pacing Tessa's street...*today*...because all that held the encroaching darkness at bay was the idea of seeing her.

Another thought that needed shaking away.

He'd made it halfway across the street when he noticed it— the front door at Number 17 open a crack.

Tessa's townhouse.

That door hadn't been ajar ten minutes ago.

He would have noticed.

His feet kicked into a near run, taking the short flight of steps in two long strides. When he reached the front door, he stopped himself from shouting through the crack, a feeling of portent crawling up his spine stopping the words in his throat. He pressed his palm against

solid oak and offered a prayer of gratitude for silent hinges.

The low mutter of voices drifted on the air. On feet as quiet as he could make them, he followed the sound across the small receiving room, then toward the drawing room.

At the open doorway, he came to a sudden stop at the sight before him, his brow furrowed, the breath arrested in his chest.

Tessa...huddled on the floor, her knees pulled into her chest, her hands tied behind her back, gag in her mouth...A great lump of a man, squatting before her, speaking in a low, menacing voice...

Her gaze lifted and met Julian's over the lump's shoulder.

Red blazed across his eyes, and he was shouting, "What in the blazes is happening here?"

He didn't wait for an answer as three great strides carried him across the room. Pure instinct had him grabbing the man by the scruff of his coat with one hand and with the other delivering a great walloping blow to the center of the man's face. Blood sprayed in the wake of his fist. There was no doubt in Julian's mind he'd just broken the man's nose—which was only the first bone he intended to break.

A screeching howl sounded from the ruffian, "Hey, what'd'ya do that for?" The man staggered on his feet and attempted to gather his bearings, even as blood dripped down both his first and second chins. It was clear he understood this game as he held up his fists and attempted a punch that was half-hearted, at best.

Julian followed his first blow with a left hook that hit its mark on the man's ear. Then it was a jab to the gut that had the man doubled over and gasping for air. Though he'd never expected to use his boxing skills outside the ring, a feeling of blood-thirst roared through Julian. He felt as if he'd been preparing for this moment all along.

To protect Tessa.

He grabbed the front of the man's coat and pulled him straight enough to receive another blow. This one had the man collapsing into a heap on the floor. It would be a while before he was of use to anyone.

Julian stepped over him and squatted before Tessa, first pulling the gag from her mouth. "Is all right with you?"

It might not be.

The possibility stirred places inside him he hadn't known he possessed.

Places that needed Tessa to be all right.

She nodded. "Julian, you should know—"

He reached around her, working at the rope binding her hands. "*Shh, shh*, sweet, it can wait."

"No, it can't," she said in an urgent whisper. "Julian, there's another—"

Her eyes went wide, and in the instant before he was coshed over the head, Julian understood there was a second assailant he hadn't accounted for.

The last thing he heard before he fell into unconsciousness was Tessa's cry. "*Julian!*"

CHAPTER EIGHTEEN

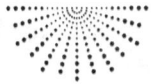

*T*essa squirmed left, then right, testing her wrists against tight hemp rope.

To no avail.

By her calculation, Smiley and Frowny had left five minutes ago, which made it imperative that she free herself and see to Julian, who still hadn't regained consciousness.

It had taken Smiley and Frowny a full ten minutes to drag Julian down here to the cellar, and in case they'd thought to do him more violence, she'd informed them that this great barge of man—their words—was, in fact, the Marquess of Ormonde.

That had snapped them to attention. "Jagger didn't say naught about a lord," said Frowny.

Smiley directed an obsequious smile toward Tessa. The man was rattled. "Now, when this fellow wakes up, ye tell him there was no harm intended to ye or him. A small fright was all that were meant."

"Then ye had to pick up a poker," groused Frowny.

Smiley nodded. "Aye."

Tessa snorted with no small amount of disbelief. "Are you saying *I* am at fault?"

Smiley nodded, pensively, as if he'd given this question a great deal of consideration. "Lots of folks would see it that way, aye."

"*You*," said Tessa, "invaded *my* house."

"And ye couldn't leave it be." This, from Frowny.

Tessa attempted to follow the logic…"So, to your mind, we're even?"

Smiley tested his nose. He'd stuffed a handkerchief up each nostril to stop the most profuse of the bleeding. Now, it was the occasional trickle. "Not quite."

Tessa sighed. "When are you going to untie me?"

Smiley was already halfway up the narrow staircase leading to the ground floor. "Yer servants will be here soon enough," he tossed over his shoulder.

And that was Smiley and Frowny gone.

Which left Tessa alone with Julian, who had emitted the odd groan but hadn't come to full wakefulness.

She tamped down the fear that wanted its head. Fear would do neither of them any good and only cloud her mind. She needed to *think*.

A few hours yet remained until the housekeeper and cook arrived. Since Tessa didn't have enough duties to keep a full staff occupied, especially with Saskia and Viveca gone, they only came for a few hours a day to see the house cleaned and the kitchen provisioned. She didn't entertain, and there was only one of her. The logic only followed.

Of course, servants in the house would've been useful in the present circumstances. A few hours was too long to wait. Julian might need assistance, but she couldn't tell right now as they were propped against a crate, their backs to one another.

"Julian," she said, testing.

That got a groan.

It was better than nothing, but not enough to assuage the fear increasing with every beat of her heart.

She shimmied her bottom until she'd positioned herself at the corner of the crate, where she began moving the rope up and down. A few seconds later, she realized it would take hours, perhaps years, for blunt wood to rub through thick rope. Julian might not have that sort of time.

Testing fingers fumbled around the crate, picking up a few splinters for her trouble. She wasn't sure what she was looking for...

Until she found it.

The head of a nail that hadn't been fully knocked in. Though it was sharp enough to scratch through skin—that would need to be tended later—it wouldn't be enough to cut through rope.

Think.

And she had it.

She lifted her arms enough to snag the knot of rope on that sharp bit of metal and caught her first bit of luck. She didn't need to cut through the rope if she could simply unknot it.

She went to work—scooching, shimmying up and down, side to side...working up a great big sweat.

"Tessa?"

She stopped, panting from her exertions. "Julian?" she asked, never so relieved to hear her name in all her life. "Are you all right?"

"Someone's taken a hammer to my head," rumbled low from his chest. "And my hands and feet are bound."

"You were struck on the head by my fireplace poker."

"That would explain it," he said. A hesitation. "Where are we?"

"In my cellar."

"Why?"

"Apparently, I needed time to think."

"Jagger."

"Aye."

"He's gotten out of control."

Tessa grunted in agreement and kept working at the knot. It seemed to have loosened an increment...

"Have you considered involving the law?"

Tessa stopped. "It wouldn't do."

"Why?" No mistaking the wariness in the question.

"East End rules." Of course, a marquess would know nothing about those. "The law doesn't get involved. We sort it between ourselves."

"And that's working for you?"

Tessa snorted and continued tugging at the nail, praying she didn't actually pry it loose.

"You're going to have to take him seriously."

"Aye." She'd already decided that much. It was only a matter of time before Jagger got the bright idea to go after Saskia and Viveca.

And that could not be allowed.

"What are you doing back there, anyway?" Julian tossed over his shoulder.

"Trying to work the knot loose," she said, really digging in. "I think I'm...almost...*there.*" Of a sudden, the knot came loose, and Tessa was able to shake free of the rope. "Got it!" she exclaimed with no small amount of triumph.

"Good lass."

After clenching and unclenching her hands to get the blood flowing again, she bent forward to untie the rope binding her feet. Then she was in a crouch and scrambling around to Julian's side of the crate. She grabbed his face between her hands and stared deep into his eyes.

"What are you about?" he asked, cautiously, as if he were wondering if she, too, had been coshed on the head.

"When I was a child," she said, searching his eyes, "a neighboring man was knocked silly by a falling piece of limestone on Fleet Street. The construction had been new and shoddy. He said it was nothing, but one of his pupils was dilated to the size of a penny and the other tiny as the head of a pin. He laid his head on his pillow that night and never woke up."

"And my pupils?"

"They look like they should," she said, relief soaring through her.

"Tessa," said Julian, holding her gaze steady. "I'm all right."

Her throat went suddenly tight. She could only nod, even as she realized her hands were shaking. He would feel that.

Then she caught it—the scent of him. *Sweat...the tang of blood from Smiley's bleeding nose...cedarwood...him.*

She still had his face clutched between her hands, and she couldn't seem to let go.

And all the while his gaze remained steady on her...*steadied* her. His gaze the only thing keeping stark fear on a leash.

"I was so scared," she whispered around a suppressed sob.

"It's understandable," said Julian. "There were two of them."

She shook her head, adamant. "I...I wasn't scared of them." He needed to understand this. "I was scared *for you.*" She swallowed the bile that had suddenly risen in her throat. "I thought you might not wake up."

His eyes searched hers. "Tessa, I'm awake. I'm all right."

She inhaled a trembling breath and felt the press of tears behind her eyes.

"Now," he said, "if you would untie my hands..."

"Oh, yes, yes, of course," she said, sparking into action, relieved to have something practical to do.

She shifted around to his back, her fingers setting to work. The rope was loose in ten quick seconds, and while Julian shrugged his shoulders and shook his hands to encourage feeling back into them, Tessa moved to his feet. It wasn't until the rope went slack that she felt it—Julian's gaze upon her.

Somehow, she said, "You're free."

A beat of time crept past before he said, "Am I?"

Time...space...the elements of the physical world slowed and fell away. Her lungs forgot how to breathe, and her heart forgot how to beat. He shifted forward and reached out, his hand finding hers, fingers tangling together. A strong hand...a sure hand...a capable hand...The sort of hand that held a woman steady in place and didn't let her fall, even if she stumbled on occasion.

A woman would never want to be free of such a hand.

Then he tugged, and that movement, so small as to be almost insignificant, was enough to flip time over and send it speeding through the air around them. It was a release of fear...a surrender to the moment...*Unexpected...fierce...demanding...*A release into each other borne of the primal. She was on top of him, straddling him, her dressing robe falling off her shoulders, and taking his face in her hands and pressing her mouth to his, pouring all of herself into this kiss, even as he grabbed and pushed her chemise over her hips. And still she held and kissed him, his fingers unbuttoning the falls of his trousers, the cloth shoved aside, leaving his hard velvet length exposed, sliding along her slit.

Desperation.

There was no other word for it as Tessa lifted several inches, reached down, and wrapped her fingers around him, positioning him at the entrance of her sex. "Oh," she breathed into his ear, "how I need you inside me."

An addict speaking words of madness to her craving.

She lowered onto him, inch by inch, stretching around his thick length, taking him deliciously inside. A long animal groan slid from her throat. His hands held her hips all the while, forcing her to take him slowly, not give in to the mindless ache and impatience clawing at her. She was a woman unleashed.

She hardly knew herself.

Except she did.

"Easy, darling," he spoke into her mouth.

"I don't think I can, Julian," she said in a rushed whisper. "You're all I want, and I'm greedy."

She'd been doing all sorts of things these last three weeks—spending her evenings at The Archangel...making tea blends—

but *this...oh...this* was what she'd been wanting to do—*again*—every second of every day. Join with this man...feel him inside her...know for certain that what she'd felt the first time had been *real*.

It was.

Further, it was as good as she remembered.

Nay.

It was, somehow, better.

This instinctive, primal drive toward one another was *real*...and *right*...and *inevitable*. Even as she was having him, she couldn't get enough of him.

She didn't pretend to understand these forces, but she understood *this...here...now*...Her, atop him...penetrated by him...holding onto him as if he were the only safe harbor in the world. Perhaps he was...

Even as her mind wanted to insert logic into this act, as she did with all other areas of her life, she might have to accept that logic held no sway in the air that existed between two lovers. This wasn't a place for reason...It was where one surrendered to feeling. Logic would only push away this desperate intimacy...of his kiss...of the feeling of him inside her...

They were alive, so very alive...

And this act was a celebration of that fact like none other.

They were fated for this.

She'd never believed in fate—until this moment.

Tension began coiling inside her, and her body took over and she rode him along the razor-fine edge between pleasure and pain. His mouth on her neck...trailing to her decolletage...giving a nipple a long, languorous stroke with his tongue...Pleasure streaked through her. He did it again, and she grabbed his hair and held tight as he continued to pleasure her nipples. Then, without warning, the coiling tension burst free, and she was crying out and pulsing her climax around him, and the next instant, he was shouting his release into her clavicle, his breath a warm rush across her skin, and they were tumbling over that edge together—only one another to cling onto as the void claimed them as a single entity.

Such was the power of this act—this union.

An act of the body...an act of the soul...an act which transcended both.

An act which contained a mystery that ever held a bit of itself out of reach.

But, oh, now Tessa saw. How one would ever seek understanding—its path pleasure, but its destination...what?

A celebration of being alive...

Connection...

Completion.

As she descended into her body, leaving such lofty thoughts in the ether where they could wait, she shifted an increment back and met Julian's summer-blue gaze, already upon her. The look within held both satiety and challenge.

"You're coming with me."

She wasn't sure what she'd expected his first words to be, but it hadn't been those. "Am I?"

"Aye."

"Is this to be my second kidnapping of the day?"

His jaw clenched and released. "Not a bit humorous."

"And where, pray tell, are you taking me?"

"To my family seat in Suffolk—Nonsuch Castle."

A laugh of disbelief escaped her. "You're absconding with me to your castle?"

"If you choose to see it that way."

He was utterly serious, and for reasons she couldn't quite articulate, she didn't feel like arguing about it. In fact, she rather thought she'd like to see Julian's castle—to see him in his native element.

"May I change clothes first?" she asked. "And I need to send word to the servants not to come today."

A *no* looked poised on the tip of his tongue, but he glanced down at her scantily clad form and said, "Ten minutes. The ruffians might come back." Clearly, she looked as ravished as she felt.

She nodded and, reluctantly, unwound her arms from around his neck, and slid off him. A pang of loss winged through her. The opaque emotion that passed behind his eyes said he might have felt it, too. Then she pushed to a stand, her legs just able to support her, and he shifted his attention to the falls of his trousers and the sliver of a moment was gone.

Right.

And now she was off to his castle—but not for the reason he supposed.

She didn't fear for the safety of her person from the likes of Blaze Jagger, the invasion of her home notwithstanding.

But here was an opportunity to know Julian better, and she'd never been one to shy away from opportunity when it presented itself.

Before she returned to London, she would understand the vital piece of the equation of this man that she'd been missing.

The piece that would solve him—and perhaps make him whole.

CHAPTER NINETEEN

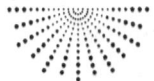

NONSUCH CASTLE, SUFFOLK, AFTERNOON

A chorus of *shouldn't-have-done*s whirled through Julian's mind.

He shouldn't have brought Tessa with him to Suffolk.

He should have deposited her at her brother's St. James's Square mansion—the man was a duke, after all, and could command an army if he chose.

But he hadn't been able to make himself do it.

He'd needed to have her with him—to see she was safe with his own eyes.

So, he'd brought her here, and after introducing her to Mrs. Morningstar, Nonsuch's capable housekeeper, he'd taken himself off to the study, grabbed a decanter of whiskey, and made his way to the family plot.

Almost too many *shouldn't-have-done*s in that last sentence to enumerate.

Of course, all those *shouldn't-have-done*s paled when compared to the whopping *shouldn't-have-done* running riot and wreaking havoc through his mind.

He'd tupped her.

Again.

Hadn't been able not to.

And, still, he wanted to do it again...and again...and again... Wanted to spend the rest of his days tupping Tessa...*properly*.

Better not to focus on the *shouldn't-have-done*s.

Presently, he was stretched on his back on a gently sloping hillside beneath a sprawling, five-hundred-year-old oak tree. Sun-dappled light filtered through breeze-fluttered leaves and soaked into his outstretched body.

This was the single thing in his wasted life that Father had done right—Clarissa's gravesite, placed on this hillside, over-looking the estate's stables and Thoroughbred training track... giving her *this*, her favorite view for eternity.

Julian propped himself onto an elbow and took a swig of whiskey, the decanter now half empty.

A *shouldn't-have-done*, of course, but he'd found no better way to slog through this day than to seek and find blackout oblivion and wake the next day feeling like utter shite, of course, but having the previous day done and behind him.

Until the Earth circled the sun three hundred and sixty-four more times and he did it all over again.

He'd made his peace with the inevitability.

Unlike Father.

Julian took another swig. The thing was he couldn't actually stand the taste of whiskey. But the only other method for blackout oblivion that he knew of was opium, and *that* was a step too far. Unlike whiskey, he suspected he would like it too much. A risk he couldn't take.

So, whiskey.

Clarissa would have been thirty-three years old today. She would've been a wife...a mother...likely the owner of a horse racing stable and Julian's fiercest competitor on the track.

Or perhaps, she would have been none of those things.

Perhaps she would've gone her own way.

Perhaps she would've led a surprising life.

As long as it would've been a happy life, it wouldn't have mattered to Julian. The point was she would've been *here*, sitting beside him, instead of lying beneath a headstone. Perhaps at this very moment offering running commentary about various horses as the jockeys took them through their paces. Over the years, that was the hardest fact for him to reconcile—Clarissa's life, unlived.

He turned his head and caught sight of a figure at the bottom of the hill, hand held to her forehead as her gaze cast about the grounds. Recognition had him rising to a fully seated position.

Tessa.

She was looking for something or…someone.

Him.

He waited, tension twisting through his gut, and saw the instant her gaze lit upon him. She stilled for half a beat of time before she began marching up the hill, determination in each stride. Of course, she wouldn't take the hill any other way.

Quite a woman was Lady Tessa Calthorp, former Siren.

He snorted and propped onto both elbows as he took in her approach. The whiskey should've provided a barrier, a remove, from which he could watch her and maintain a distance. But whiskey had no dulling effects when it came to Tessa. It wasn't how matters worked with her. When she entered his orbit, it was he who circled around her. Her pull was that strong.

She looked her usual self in many ways, with her usual attire, her hair pulled back into a prim knot. Except the wind caught at it and tempted it free, wispy tendrils burnished gold in the sunshine, her eyes bright and silver as the puffs of cloud above, her full mouth soft and tempting as ever.

A pulse of desire thrummed through him. *Complicated*, this desire. Physical, yes. Overwhelmingly so, at times. But more than physical. A feeling inside him, like a yawning black chasm that wanted to take all her sunshine and light and swallow it whole—wouldn't be satisfied until it did…until he had it for himself…

No *former* about it—the woman was a siren through and

through, tempting him toward the rocks...toward his destruction.

When she was halfway up the hill, she called out, "There you are."

"Here I am."

An only slightly civil response. But he wasn't yet sure how he felt about her joining him here. Even the servants knew to keep respectfully clear of him on this day.

She didn't stop until she'd come within ten feet of him, a little winded, hands planted on her waist. One half siren—the other half harridan.

He didn't mind.

In fact, he rather liked it. That she could look the way she did —diamond of the first water, if anyone peered closely enough... and he had—and be the way she was...It was a rare thing in a woman.

Her gaze raked over his supine form, missing nothing as it hesitated on the decanter of whiskey, but didn't rest until it fell upon the headstone to his right.

"Clarissa," he said.

"Your sister," she said, soft, all harridan vanished.

"She would've liked you."

He hadn't the faintest idea why he'd said it, except he thought it would be true.

Tessa lowered herself to the grass and settled a few feet away. Far enough that she wasn't within easy reaching distance, but close enough that he could feel her presence...the restless vibrancy that ever radiated from her, so bright were the cells that constituted her being.

"It's lovely here," she said, taking in the view below of Nonsuch's Thoroughbreds going through their paces on the practice course. "They're so strong and fast...so beautiful with their shiny coats and the muscles working beneath." Her voice held a note of self-consciousness. "I didn't grow up around horses or *this*." The sweep of her arm indicated *this* was all Nonsuch—grand English country estate.

"As a child," he said, picking up the thread, "I was a scrawny little lad."

This got a lift of her eyebrows. "Oh? I would've assumed you a boy who was always large for his age."

"Nay, I didn't grow until I was eighteen. Then it was six inches that year and another three at nineteen."

"That must've come as a welcome surprise."

She didn't know what he was on about, so she was humoring him.

"*Scrawny*," he repeated, "and scared of everything. Clarissa hadn't a fearful bone in her body. And horses? She loved them. Amongst my earliest memories are her riding her pony and me watching, her little shadow."

"How much older was she?"

"Three years," he said. "I didn't like horses. They were too big. Made me feel too small."

"How did that change?"

"One day, Clarissa led me to her pony and just had me look into his eyes. Wouldn't let me stop for ten straight minutes. *Stop whining and tell me what you see there*, she commanded. *Does he want to harm you?* I shook my head, hoping for reprieve. Then she had me run my palm along his nose. The pony's eyes went soft, and he swayed forward, into my hand, and I experienced this sensation in the center of my chest, like my heart was trying to lift free of my body. *Now you won't ever be afraid again.* Her words." Julian shook his head. "If only it were that simple."

"You were still afraid of horses?"

A bitter laugh escaped him. "Oh, no, that fear was cured." His smile fell. "But there's so much more out there, you know?"

He caught Tessa's silvery gaze and saw she might—and, further, he hoped it so.

* * *

So much more out there...

To fear.

Julian left it unsaid, but Tessa heard it anyway.

They hadn't experienced similar upbringings, not by a mile, but they'd had upbringings fraught with the sort of dangers and uncertainties that caused the ground to wobble beneath their feet.

Which, of course, didn't at all square with the golden lord she'd thought him when they'd first met, but it did with the man sitting beside her now. This golden lord knew of pain and struggle. Not in the ways she knew, but in ways she sensed were somehow worse.

His gaze skimmed across the racing course below. She intuited he couldn't be looking into her eyes when he continued. "Clarissa began getting tired. Where her skin had always been sun-kissed from so much time spent outdoors, it became pale and wan. In the course of a few months, she was a shadow of the lively girl she'd been all her life." Before Tessa could ask, he said, "A disease of the blood according to the doctors." He shrugged, a gesture helpless to the past. "A trip to the coast was prescribed. When that didn't do any good, Father took her to a spa village in Switzerland. No joy there, either. She just kept growing more and more frail." He lifted empty hands. "Then, one morning, she didn't wake up."

The words, full of grief and helplessness to the cruel whims of the universe, held a note of surprise, as if all these years later, he still couldn't quite believe them.

"And you were a devastated boy, alone in the world."

He swallowed. "No one was more grief-stricken than Father. Clarissa had been his favorite. I never held that against him. She'd been my favorite person in the world, too."

"I'm sorry."

The words felt so paltry Tessa felt almost embarrassed to speak them. They were what one said in the face of utter devastation. Yet they were necessary for their very simplicity. What else sufficed when an entire universe had been blown to bits?

"Father responded by diving straight into the sea of iniquity and never resurfaced, the meaning to his life obliterated." No masking the pain that yet remained. "Nonsuch has long stood as one of the preeminent racing stables in England. Father almost ran it into the ground by making one bad bet after another. It was as if he wanted to set it, everything, and everyone ablaze and wreak utter devastation. I took control before it could entirely implode."

That he remained in possession of one of the finest racing stables in England spoke of his grit, determination, and talent. Qualities he didn't wear on his sleeve as the golden lord of the *ton*, but were there, nonetheless.

"And your mother?" It only struck Tessa now that he hadn't yet mentioned her.

Julian gave a dry snort. "Mother did come for the funeral, I'll give her that."

Tessa's eyebrows burrowed into her forehead. "*Came for the funeral?*"

"Oh, yes, Mother and Father had an arrangement. Their marriage had been decided at birth, but Mother didn't like the man her family determined she would marry. The only way she would agree to marry the Marquess of Ormonde, whose debaucheries were breathlessly reported all the way up in Edinburgh, was that once she delivered his heir, she could return to Scotland and set up her own household."

Tessa nearly gasped. "What woman would do such a thing?"

"All parties involved must've thought exactly that, for they agreed. After all, what mother would leave her newborn babe behind, especially when she had a three-year-old daughter, as well?" He was unable to contain a bitter snort. "Mine, it turned out."

This time, Tessa did gasp, her gaze flying to meet his, but all he gave her was his profile. "*No.* She left you when you were a babe?"

Though she'd been young when her mother had died, Tessa remembered her—her scent...the feel of her affection. Julian had been denied that, and she experienced an ache for him.

"Without a backward glance," he said. "The aristocracy plays their games by rules they make up as they go along."

Tessa felt no surprise at that last part. Long nights at The Archangel had taught her as much.

"Can't say I blame her," continued Julian, resignation to the past clear in every syllable. "You've yet to meet a wastrel aristocrat as debauched as my father. Born that way, so why wouldn't his heir be the same? She didn't stay to find out."

"No one is born debauched," said Tessa. "*You* aren't debauched."

"No?" He took a long swig of whiskey, his face etched in defiance.

A warning, that swig of whiskey. He wanted her to understand who she was dealing with.

And she did.

But she wasn't at all sure they were seeing the same man. He'd been left to raise himself, without the guidance only a parent could offer. And even so, he'd become a man who was resilient and kind, capable and possessed of grit.

Yet he didn't acknowledge those qualities in himself.

A question came to her, one she very much wanted to ask— whose answer she sensed lay beneath the way Julian managed his life and saw himself when he looked in the mirror.

He cut her a glance, his expression telling her he was waiting for her to ask it.

"Your father," she began, "he..."

Oh, how to ask such a question?

Julian knew how to answer it, though. "Took his own life."

He spoke the words—*flat...distant*—as if he'd long locked any feeling related to it in a deep, inaccessible corner of his mind.

The statement settled into the air for a few beats of time before she asked, "When?"

"Three years ago." He blew a harsh breath. "On the anniversary of Clarissa's death."

Tessa's hand flew to her mouth. Julian cut her a hard glance. "He'd been working up the courage to pull the trigger on that death for twenty years." The facts emerged in no particular order and without emotion. "A single gunshot to the head. In a cheap East End bedsit. A small blessing, that."

"How do you mean?" None of Julian's life sounded like a blessing. Tessa didn't believe in family curses, but the history of the House of Ormonde might tempt the possibility.

"So he would be found by strangers."

Tessa glanced at the all-but-forgotten decanter in Julian's hand. No one would blame him for downing a bottle of whiskey every day.

But he didn't.

And that said something about him. Life had made him strong, yet he didn't seem to know it.

"We have bad blood in this family, in case you hadn't figured that out yet."

"*Bad blood?*"

"The sort that dies with me."

Tessa's stomach fell to her feet. "How do you mean?" Before he could answer, she said, "Is that why you don't court ladies?"

He didn't need to nod. The flex of his jaw was answer enough.

"Is that why you don't..." Oh, she couldn't make herself finish that question. "Why you pleasure women in ways other than..." Another sentence she couldn't finish.

He cut her a penetrating glance. "I won't father children."

"But…" Oh, she had no right to say this, but it was occurring to her that this impressive man was harboring some beliefs that needed to be challenged. "Isn't that your one job as a marquess? To marry and breed?"

He shrugged his indifference. "They can give the marquessate to someone else for all I care."

She wasn't letting him off the hook that easily. This man definitely needed challenging. "Did Clarissa have bad blood?"

"Of course not."

"But she had the same blood flowing through her veins as you. The logic only follows…"

How she hoped he would follow it.

"She was the white sheep of the family," he said, as if he'd given it some thought. "Every family has one exception, even bad families."

Oh, he was clinging onto this belief with both hands. Well, he wasn't the only one who could latch onto a notion and not let go. This man needed a good shaking up.

And she was the woman to give it to him.

"Would Clarissa have liked *that*?" She pointed at the decanter of whiskey lolling loosely in his hand.

"She hadn't yet developed a taste for drink," he said, dry. "She was ten years old when she died."

He was deliberately misconstruing her question…which only meant she'd hit close to the mark. Time to move even closer… "Would she have liked you feeling pity for yourself?"

His head whipped around, his summer-blue eyes sparking heat. "I don't pity myself."

"Don't you?" Tessa wasn't about to let up. "What is that whiskey all about?"

"It's about getting through the day."

"You mean, it's about *avoiding* the day."

He flinched.

Now, she had the bit firmly between her teeth. "I see it every night at The Archangel. Lords using every vice at their disposal to avoid the reality of their lives. How is *that*"—her finger turned accusing—"any different?"

He ran a hand through his hair and exhaled a frustrated breath.

He didn't have a ready answer.

But Tessa did.

"Has it ever occurred to you to do something different with this day?"

Defensiveness shimmered off him. "I won't have Clarissa spending it alone."

"But is *this* what she would want? You wallowing in drink and grief? You could give her the birthday *she* would want. You're *here*, Julian. You're alive."

He went utterly still, a riot of conflicting emotions passing behind his eyes, as he turned her words over in his mind and tested them for truth.

She could say more, Tessa understood that. But the fact was Julian had a right to his feelings—and how he got through this day was his business.

It was no worse than what others did.

How utterly alone he was in the world, forced to navigate his life alone, without the care and love of family—family that Tessa took for granted every day of her life. How he was able to get out of bed and put one foot in front of the other, day after day, she wasn't sure. He might appear weak in this moment, but he was the strongest man she knew.

And this wasn't the moment to say any of that to him.

She pushed off the ground and stood. While she dusted off her skirts, he settled onto one elbow, his long body half twisted at the torso, and silently watched, contemplative. She met his eye, all brisk efficiency. "Mrs. Morningstar sent me out here to inform you that the evening meal will be served at seven of the clock—*sharpish*, she instructed me to say."

The suggestion of a smile hovered at the corner of his mouth. Already, the world felt brighter. "I make it a point to always do as Mrs. Morningstar instructs."

"And she said to remind you there will be guests."

He gave a slow nod, as if he'd forgotten, but now remembered. "Rake."

"*Rake?*"

"The Duke of Rakesley. He's my oldest friend, and his Somerton estate shares a border with Nonsuch." He hesitated before adding, "He always takes the evening meal with me on Clarissa's birthday."

An unexpected feeling of relief strummed through Tessa. Relief that Julian had someone in the world who cared about him —who saw him through this day.

Relief that Julian understood that, to at least one person in the world, he mattered.

Not just one suggested a small voice.

And Tessa didn't try to deny it.

Julian mattered.

To her.

"Then," she said, "I'll see you at supper."

His head canted subtly, his gaze inscrutable and searching. "You don't have to join us. If you prefer to take your meal in your room, that is."

"Is this your way of gently telling me not to join the meal?"

An unspoken *yes* echoed in the air between them.

"After your ordeal with those ruffians, I thought you—"

"It was your ordeal, too," she cut across him. "I wouldn't miss this evening meal for the world."

And it was true.

She wanted to meet this Duke of Rakesley...*Rake*. This man who cared about Julian.

The expression on Julian's face shifted into one more serious and intent. "Speaking of the ordeal," he said. "We need to discuss Jagger. I hired a Bow Street Runner, and—"

"You had him investigated?"

"Aye."

Irritation prickled through her and found its way into her voice. "You had no right. It's none of your concern."

"Tessa," he said, low and intense, "it concerns *you*. It's my concern."

She swallowed against the sudden lump in her throat.

"There's information you need," he continued. "That's why I came to your townhouse this morning."

This morning? It felt like a lifetime ago. Nonsuch Castle seemed to exist in a realm so very far away from London and all its concerns.

"It can wait."

With that, she swiveled, her skirts swishing about her ankles and made her way down the hill, her long legs wanting to gain momentum with every step. Out here in the Suffolk countryside, the blood ran lighter in her veins. This air...She was a London girl, born and bred...through and through...but this Suffolk air, diffuse with golden sun, that star's warmth soaking through cloth and skin and into every fine cell of her being, it could almost convince her of exotic possibility...That she could be another sort of woman...The sort of woman whose feet picked up that momentum and kicked into a gallop to match the Thorough- breds in the distance. If she could get her feet moving fast enough, perhaps they could race faster than her mind.

But she tamped down the feeling as best she could.

Julian's eyes were following her all the way.

They were also why the blood fizzed in her veins and untamed thoughts whirled through her mind.

Julian.

With everything that had happened to him in his life, his brain had somewhere made a faulty connection. It was like when one arrived at the wrong answer at the end of a long algebraic equation. One had to retrace each and every step to find the error. For the solution was there, in the open, waiting to be fixed.

Yes, a flaw existed in Julian's thinking.

All one had to do was trace back and nick the error that had led him to the wrong conclusion about himself.

And she was the woman to do it.

CHAPTER TWENTY

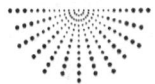

*J*ulian was late for his own supper party.

He finished buttoning the falls of his trousers on that sour thought.

How had it come to this? How was he hosting a supper party on *this* of all nights, anyway?

Tonight was a night when he got sauced to the gills and sought blackout oblivion. He'd been doing it for years. Rake would come by—later and with no expectation of a formal meal —and see him through to the morning with a second or third decanter of whiskey.

And that was this day done.

Would she have liked you feeling pity for yourself?

The memory of those words pulled a flinch, even as a defensive note still echoed through him. What did Tessa know of it, anyway? She knew loss, yes, but not like his.

Yet, another feeling had been expanding through him since their conversation…

You could give her the birthday she *wants.*

That…the very idea of it…sparked a feeling inside him…A *good* feeling, which was an emotion he'd never associated with this day. It had always been a day of grief—of getting through. But...

What if it could be something else?

What if Clarissa's birthday could be a day of *joy*?

Of...*celebration*?

His mind couldn't comprehend all that would mean or entail —it needed time to brew—but the idea had him between its teeth and would be working on him for a while, for it had conjured another feeling—one fragile and easily scared away...

Hope.

He reached for his cravat, and the back of his hand brushed the whiskey decanter. It remained at the halfway mark—exactly where it had been during his conversation with Tessa. He hadn't taken another sip since, and felt himself to be sober, mostly.

And shockingly uninterested in taking another gulp.

Once he'd finished dressing, he grabbed the decanter and left the dressing room to join his guests. He'd lost all use for the whiskey clutched in his hand but didn't want to return to his bedroom to find it there later.

A mixture of voices met his ear in the corridor outside the drawing room. Rake...his new bride Gemma...and Tessa. His next heartbeat delivered a wave of relief and that new, fragile feeling, too—*hope*.

All eyes shifted toward him the instant he entered the room. Tessa assessing...Gemma smiling...Rake wary. His friend's gaze immediately fell and landed on the decanter. Rake expected him to be completely foxed.

Julian strode to the whiskey cart and nonchalantly deposited the decanter before saying with his best charming smile, "I hope I haven't kept you waiting too long."

Rake and Tessa held similar quizzical cants to their heads, but Gemma returned his smile. "Not at all," she said pleasantly.

From Rake and Tessa's twin expressions, they remained unconvinced. They hadn't expected him like *this*—sober.

WAGER WITH A SIREN

Or mostly so.

"Now." He crossed the room and extended a hand toward Rake. "I believe congratulations are in order on your marriage."

Rake stood, and they gave each other manly claps on the back. As Julian kissed Gemma's hand, he said, "I wish you every happiness and all the luck in the world"—a jut of the chin toward Rake —"with *that* one."

Rake snorted. The wariness hadn't entirely receded from his eyes, but it was fading fast. He still didn't know what to make of *this* Julian on *this* day.

That made two of them.

This was unknown territory for him. His steps held a slight ambivalence as he ventured forth, but he was finding he didn't mind it.

"It'll be Gemma keeping me on my toes," said Rake. "I can assure you."

Julian rather suspected it would—and that Rake wouldn't have it any other way.

"We were just discussing The Archangel," said Gemma. "I was about to ask Lady Tessa which game was her favorite."

Rake caught Julian's gaze with an easily interpretable question in his eye. *What in the blazes is Lady Tessa Calthorp doing at Nonsuch?*

Yes, well, one would have that question.

And Rake would have to settle for not getting the answer.

"That's easy," said Tessa. "Hazard."

"Like a toss of the dice, do you?" asked Rake.

Julian heard the protective note in his friend's voice. One who preferred Hazard was a certain type of person, to put it delicately. The type of person Rake had no use for.

"And why is that, Lady Tessa?" asked Gemma, instinctively smoothing over her husband's rough edge. Julian saw how they fit together as a couple.

"Hazard earns The Archangel the most blunt on any given

night," answered Tessa, a slight sneering curl to her mouth. "Naturally, it's my favorite."

As a delighted laugh escaped Gemma, Julian watched Tessa rise in Rake's estimation by several degrees.

"Shall we dine?" asked Julian.

Thankfully, when they walked into the cavernous dining room, every surface polished to a high shine reflecting the light of four fully lit crystal chandeliers, Julian saw the capable Mrs. Morningstar had instructed the table be set all to one end. Otherwise, as the table seated thirty, they would be shouting the evening's conversation from one end to the other. As master of the house, he was seated at the head. Mrs. Morningstar must've decided Tessa was the guest of honor, for she was seated to his right. And since they were newlyweds, Mrs. Morningstar had seated Rake and Gemma side by side, to his left.

Rake held up a glass of water and opened the conversation. "To your win at the Derby."

Julian nodded and drank. "Filthy Habit is a right goer, and Smithwick gave him a good ride." He settled back in his chair as a footman set a bowl of soup before him. He met Gemma's gaze. "Your brother is an impressive jockey himself."

A competitive glint sparked within her eye. "He'll be riding Hannibal in the Race of the Century."

Rake snorted. "That's the small talk all finished."

But Gemma wasn't. "Don't want you getting a hope in your heart about poaching him, is all."

"Wouldn't dream of it," said Julian, a smile curling about his mouth.

Gemma snorted. She didn't believe him, and why should she? Horse racing wasn't for the timid of spirit. Bold moves characterized the sport as much off the turf, as on.

"Speaking of the Race of the Century," said Rake, nonchalant, as if he weren't bursting to speak on the subject. "The field is nearly all set. Just leaves the St. Leger to be run, and that'll be that."

"Bruising race, the St. Leger," said Gemma.

"Any race in Yorkshire would be," said Julian. "Men from the north have a reputation to uphold."

A snort from Rake.

From the corner of his eye, Julian stole a glance at Tessa. She appeared content to observe the conversation, rather than engage with it. Still, there were moments when he could feel the heat of her gaze on the side of his face.

"And how is Artemis faring in the north?" asked Julian, testing the ground.

The fact was Rake was one of his oldest friends, but so, too, was his younger sister. And last time Julian had seen Artemis, she'd been in a bad way.

"She has the horse sanctuary now," said Rake, tightly.

"Oh, it's not limited to horses, mind you," said Gemma. "The locals have learned they can leave any animal, and Artemis will take them in."

She didn't speak with a scold, but rather with a great deal of respect. Julian remembered that about Gemma. She had a special bond with animals. When Hannibal wouldn't let anyone on his back, she'd been the one who had found a way.

Still, he sensed something unspoken about Artemis. "I figured she would have a horse in the running for the St. Leger, seeing as how the racecourse is only a stone's throw from Endcliffe Grange."

Rake and Gemma shot each other a look. A look confident it knew precisely what was in the other's mind. A look only an in-love couple could exchange.

A look that unleashed an arrow of envy straight through Julian.

Again, he felt the heat of Tessa's gaze. Except this time when he turned, she didn't avoid him. She'd seen that look, too, and known it for what it was. That was what her eyes were telling him.

And it struck him full in the chest with no small amount of irony. That look…

He and Tessa were sharing it now.

* * *

"Artemis has vowed not to race again," came the Duke of Rakesley's unhappy voice.

Somehow, Tessa made herself tear her gaze away from Julian and rejoin the surface conversation that had nothing to do with the deeper conversation that was occurring between them with their eyes.

"Dido left her in a bad way," said the duchess.

Tessa cleared her throat of any telling rasp and asked, "Dido?"

"Dido was Artemis's prized Thoroughbred," supplied Julian. "A real goer."

"I wasn't about to admit it at the time," said Rakesley, "but I expected Dido to take the Triple Crown this season."

There were solemn nods all around.

"But…" Rakesley sighed, helpless to the immutable facts of the past.

"Her first race was the Two Thousand Guineas," said Julian. "She was leading the entire race."

"I'm not sure she even broke a sweat," Rakesley cut in.

"I didn't have a hope of catching her," said the duchess.

"Then in the last furlong, she fell."

"*Fell?*"

"And didn't get up again."

"It was her heart." The devastation of that day was writ plain upon the duchess's face all these months later. "It gave out."

"An occurrence not as rare as one would like," said Rakesley.

"Most of the time, heart defects are detected before race day, and those horses can be put to other uses. But..."

"But sometimes, the problem outs on race day," said Julian.

Silence descended as servants set the table with the fish course. Tessa knew little about the world of horse racing, but she could see the genuine pain and respect these three had for the animals. She'd only seen the sport from the tawdry moneygrubbing angle, never from this side.

A sparkle entered the duchess's eye. "But there is a horse up in Yorkshire."

Julian's head whipped around. "What horse?"

Tessa couldn't completely suppress the smile that wanted out. Oh, horse folk...

"You know the stories," said Rakesley, dismissive. "Everyone's always banging on about lost Arabians and Thoroughbreds up in the wilds of Yorkshire."

The duchess shook her head and finished chewing her bite of food. "I've seen the horse. His name is Radish."

Julian's eyebrows shot together. "*Radish?* Who names their Thoroughbred *Radish?*"

The duchess held up her finger while she finished another bite of fish. She knew this answer, too. "Sir Abstrupus Bottomley, that's who."

"Should I know him?"

Rakesley shook his head. "Eccentric old neighbor. Nothing Artemis can't handle."

"Is this Sir Abstrupus racing Radish?"

"That's the question of the day," said the duchess. "Not if Artemis has a say."

Rakesley met Tessa's inquisitive gaze. "My sister has the will of a Roman legion once she digs her heels in for a fight." He smiled. "I'm happy to see it. For a while there, I was worried."

The duchess reached out and squeezed her husband's hand.

Tessa glanced over to see that Julian noticed the small act of intimacy, too.

"Little Wicked is a fast little filly and likes the longer courses," said Julian. "She might take the St. Leger if Deverill chooses to race her there."

"Which he will," said the duchess, sounding none too pleased. She turned toward Tessa. "According to *some*"—she shot her husband a playful glance—"Deverill doesn't have any business owning a Thoroughbred, because he doesn't know horses."

"All true," said Rakesley.

"Further, he doesn't exercise proper judgment about when to race her."

"He races her on back-to-back days," said Rakesley. "No judgment whatsoever."

"In Deverill's defense," said Julian, "the filly has the energy of ten horses. She seems to love it out there. With its few extra furlongs, the St. Leger will be her sort of race."

Rakesley shrugged. "I'll give you that Doncaster is a broad, galloping course, like Newmarket, but there are the Yorkshire weather conditions to consider, too. Half the years, it's the mudders who take the St. Leger."

"If Little Wicked takes the St. Leger, that'll be just four horses in the Race of the Century."

Everyone appeared to have the same thought at once. A one in four chance of winning, instead of one in five—shortened odds.

"Of course," said Julian, "you're aware Lady Tessa's brother, the Duke of Acaster, is an investor in the Race of the Century with the Duke of Richmond."

Tessa couldn't say she liked the experience of the room's attention shifting in her direction. "We've met your brother, actually," said the duchess.

Tessa felt her brow lift. "Oh?"

"Oh, yes, at the Great Yarmouth racecourse several weeks

back," she continued. "He was with his, *erm...*" The rest of the sentence seemed to get tangled in her mouth.

"Future duchess," provided Rakesley, with so faint a whiff of irony that it almost might not have been there.

But Tessa caught it.

Lover.

Gabriel and Celia would've been lovers then—everyone in this room knew it.

Tessa wasn't one to avoid a subject when it needed going at directly. "I think we can all agree my brother and his *future duchess* had a short and unconventional courtship."

Tessa wasn't apologizing for Gabriel's *unconventional* courtship and marriage to Celia. There was nothing to apologize for. Gabriel and Celia were blissfully happy and well suited.

The duchess turned a mischievous smile onto her husband. "Rake and I are certainly no strangers to a short and unconventional courtship, are we, dearest?" she asked, all innocence. "I was your jockey, after all."

Tessa was no prude and certainly no snob, but if the duchess had been looking to shock, she'd achieved her goal. A laugh, irreverent for the elevated company at the table, bubbled up and she was just able to swallow it back. However, the next instant, it spilled over. Then the duchess joined her, and it didn't feel so wrong anymore. And even less wrong when the duke joined in. Then Julian was smiling and a laugh, deep and genuine, rumbled from his chest.

And it struck Tessa for all they'd shared, they'd never shared this—slightly inappropriate laughter that was utterly and completely lost to joy. The magic and intimacy of such laughter felt wonderful as it soaked into her.

It felt *right.*

On the wave of collective laughter, Julian stood and lifted his glass of water. The smile on his face...It was one she'd never seen from him. It wasn't the golden-lord-of-the-*ton* smile. It was free and from within.

This smile wasn't *for* anyone else.

It simply *was*.

"On Clarissa's eighth birthday," he began, laughter still in his voice, "Father woke her up at dawn and led her straight out to the stables. She was wearing her nightgown, but Mrs. Morningstar insisted she pull on her boots." He chuckled wryly. "Of course, I wasn't too far behind, Clarissa's little shadow that I was. Anyway, when we got to the stable yard, there was a groom holding the reins of a chestnut pony. Clarissa's scream of delight must've echoed all the way up to Shetland as she flew across the cobbles and introduced herself to the pony and immediately named him King Arthur—the Knights of the Round Table being our particular favorite nighttime stories. Then she mounted King Arthur and refused to get down for the entire day."

Rakesley smiled. "I remember your father escorting them into the house to take her birthday meal."

A shocked laugh escaped the duchess. "A horse at the dining table?"

Julian's smile increased with the memory. "Oh, yes. Father got a grand old laugh from it. He even handfed birthday cake to King Arthur."

"What happened to King Arthur after...," began Tessa, the rest of the question dying a quick death in her mouth. What was she thinking by asking such a question?

"Father couldn't bear the sight of him," said Julian, his voice taking on the familiar flat quality that struck a warning signal through Tessa. "So, he gave King Arthur to a local family." One could hear that second loss in his voice all these years later. "But," he continued, "he was a sweet, little pony, and I'm certain he brought immeasurable delight to the family who took him in."

A sudden onslaught of tears filled Tessa's eyes. "A legacy of Clarissa that lived on."

Julian nodded. "Indeed." His smile turned wistful. "If it weren't for the portrait of her, I'm not sure I'd remember her face. But I remember her smile and her laugh. She liked to laugh. So, I propose on this day of her birth that we celebrate Clarissa, rather than mourn her." His gaze slid toward Tessa. "The mourning has gone on too long." He lifted his glass. "To Clarissa."

"Hear, hear," said Rakesley.

The duchess swiped a tear away. "To Clarissa."

Tessa joined the toast, impressed by Julian. Just as he had all his life, he was doing his best—and his best tonight was profound.

He was attempting to break free of the shackles that had been binding him all these years. In truth, she didn't know if he could fully. His family and all their tragedies were no small thing of the past. They shadowed him every moment of every day. But perhaps he was willing to try a different way of navigating them.

And that meant something.

It wasn't long after the toast that Rakesley and the duchess spoke their farewells. The duke met Tessa's gaze for a full five meaningful seconds, his message clear—he was leaving Julian in her hands. She gave a discreet nod, and within a minute, it was only her and Julian and they were walking side by side without touching, through the castle until they reached her bedroom door.

"Do you need someone to stay with you tonight?" she asked.

He shook his head. "I don't think so."

Disappointment sheered through her. She'd thought he would've escorted her to, well, *his* bedroom.

Her body wasn't taking the disappointment lightly.

She could see he was deep in his mind. Tonight had represented a complete revolution in his thinking. He needed time to allow it to steep and soak in.

She nodded her acceptance of this and shut the bedroom door

behind her. But she'd barely undressed and slipped into bed before she was tossing about, unable to sleep.

It was Julian.

She needed to see him—see he was all right with her own eyes. She could sleep in a chair in the corner. She didn't need to share his bed.

She needed him to know he had a friend.

In his bedroom, she found him in bed, flat on his back, hands behind his head, chest bare, coverlet at his waist, staring at the ceiling.

He turned and met her gaze in the moonlight. "Come here."

She slipped into his bed, and he reached out and took her in his arms.

The kiss was slow and thorough, the sort of kiss that reached deep and could steal one's soul, if one wasn't careful. And the thing was—Tessa didn't feel like being careful.

In truth, pure intentions hadn't been her sole motivation for coming to his room—and here was the truth out. She needed his large, masculine hands on her...his mouth on hers...

"Oh, Tessa," he spoke against her lips, "my body is a temple of ache for you."

She moved so her body pressed against the length of his. How she loved the feel of his rough, calloused hands moving on her skin. The fact was she'd become addicted to this man.

She didn't only want to solve him.

She wanted him.

Though she'd become obsessed with many a mathematical equation brought home from Eton and Cambridge, she'd never once wanted to tup one.

Julian had introduced her to the novel idea that before the needs of the mind came the needs of the body.

On a pained moan, he broke away, panting. "I know how to do this—pleasure you."

A smile tipped about her mouth. "Indeed, you do, my lord."

He didn't return her smile. "But I don't know how *not* to do this."

His eyes searched hers, hoping to find understanding.

And she did.

How easily they could fall into established pattern and make love.

But, tonight, Julian was striving for a new pattern.

What was happening within him—and between them—was delicate and required careful handling.

New...fragile...uncertain...

"I don't know how to do *this*."

Be with another person, he didn't have to say the words.

They both heard them.

She delivered one final kiss to his lips before slipping from the bed. She hesitated. He was so beautiful in the moonlight. "This Monday night," she began. "I'll be at Vauxhall Gardens with my sisters."

"Would you like me to be there?"

"Yes."

"Then I shall be."

As she made her way to her own bed, a feeling, bright and ephemeral, glittered through her.

Hope.

The words she and Julian had spoken—even the ones left unspoken—felt like a beginning.

As it had so many times this last week, her hand brushed across her stomach. Still, her menses hadn't come.

Another beginning—perhaps.

The thought she'd kept tucked in the back of her mind remained there—for now left uncertain.

But that possibility was, in truth, a welcome one to her.

And for the beautiful man she'd left lying in the moonlight, it wasn't.

Right.

CHAPTER TWENTY-ONE

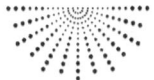

LONDON, MONDAY

*J*ulian wrapped a layer of linen around his knuckles, tugged it taut, then added another layer. There was nothing new to wrapping his hands before his Monday bout of sparring with Brewster.

But the feeling that had been expanding in his body these last two days...

That *was*.

He felt different in ways that were difficult to quantify or even name.

A feeling of...lightness.

A lightness of body.

A lightness of spirit.

A fanciful notion, to be sure, but the only way he could think to characterize it was that before yesterday morning he'd been a gray man. Naught more than a shadow stalking his own life as he went through the motions of it.

Then yesterday, he'd awakened feeling...*lighter*. As if the cells composing the air were brighter, and when they filled his lungs, he went buoyant from the effect. Where he'd been gray in the days and years preceding this one, he now felt as if the sun had risen after a decade-long night and filled his world with warm, golden light.

Of course, it could've been as simple as he'd awakened sober and refreshed after Clarissa's birthday for the first time in years.

But that wasn't it.

Tessa.

She'd commandeered a coach-and-four yesterday and left Nonsuch Castle with the arrival of dawn. He could've hardly stopped her, short of kidnapping, and she'd already experienced enough of that for a lifetime. So, he'd told the footman, who had drawn the short straw to inform the master of the lady's intention, to let her proceed.

Of course, that hadn't been his first instinct.

His instinct demanded he keep her close—within sight at all times, preferably.

But instinct could be wrong.

What he needed ran deeper than reactive instinct.

What he needed was solitude. Only then could he begin to understand the novel feeling unfolding within him. This feeling that wobbled on unsteady feet as it tried to find its footing to take the first step blind into unknown territory, the fledgling idea of lightness filtering through him.

Until two days ago, he'd thought—*known*—the only contribution his past had to offer his present and future was grief—the sort that caught body, soul, and spirit in its black unyielding grip and never relinquished its hold. Grief that turned one into a gray man—a shadow of oneself.

And even now, in this nascent state of lightness, he understood grief would always walk beside him. But what if...

What if grief's only form didn't have to be soul-destroying sorrow?

What if one could flip that coin and find on the other side...*joy.*

The feeling that had compelled him to celebrate Clarissa at

her birthday supper hadn't subsided. If anything, it had found purchase in his mind and taken root. He hadn't been honoring his sister all these years by holding onto her death so tightly. Rather, the time had arrived to take joy from her life.

And it had been Tessa who had made him see it.

She may have left him to think on his own, but she'd made it clear that he wasn't alone.

If he chose not to be.

He would see her tonight at Vauxhall Gardens—at her invitation.

That mattered.

But first, he had some business to deal with.

Blaze Jagger.

Julian had sent a note first thing this morning requesting— less request than summons, in truth—his presence at Brewster's Boxing Salon at three o'clock. His fists clenched and released several times to test that the linen wraps would hold for sparring and made his way into the ring where Brewster waited. He'd hoped to get a sparring session in before Jagger arrived. Perhaps then he would have purged all his aggression and wouldn't act upon the need to pummel the rogue to a pulp, like his hands were itching to do.

No physical harm had come to Tessa. Further, Julian didn't believe true harm was intended. But those facts didn't make him feel any less murderous toward Jagger. Tessa's home had been invaded under Jagger's orders to scare her into submission of his wishes.

No one treated Tessa thusly.

Not while Julian still drew breath.

Jagger could refuse the summons, of course.

But he wouldn't.

An invitation from a marquess wouldn't arrive on his doorstep every day, and a ruthless and ambitious young man wouldn't be able to refuse—especially given his complicated parentage.

Jagger would want to hear what Julian had to say.

As he entered the ring, Julian gave Brewster a nod of greeting and went light on his feet. As the sparring commenced in its customary routine, he experienced the same invigorating lift as usual, but today something more, too. Today, as he dealt and received blows, it didn't feel like a purging or a punishment or like he was numbing himself.

Today, he wasn't making his body pay for the blood running through his veins.

Today, he was having fun.

In some way, this was a celebration—a celebration of being alive.

They'd been at it for half an hour when a figure appeared in the open doorway. *Tall and rangy.* Though the man was standing in shadow, Julian knew him.

Blaze Jagger.

He stepped into the light, and the diamond in his left ear winked its brilliance.

Cocksure.

Sudden fury flared through Julian. He wanted nothing more in this moment than to wipe that arrogant smile off Jagger's mouth. His fingers coiled into tight fists with anticipation of that very act.

"Do you box?" asked Julian in greeting.

Jagger shrugged off his greatcoat. "Been known to go a few rounds."

He began unknotting his cravat, before working the buttons of his waistcoat. Then he was tugging his shirt from the waistband of his trousers and pulling it over his head.

Julian took in his opponent. Rangy, yes. A man who appeared composed entirely of sinewy muscle. But it wasn't the fact of his muscle or the potential long reach of lanky arms that would make him a tough opponent.

It was the glint in his eyes.

Jagger liked a fight.

Brewster handed him a length of linen. "There'll be no bare knuckles in the sparring ring."

Jagger flashed Julian a quick grin even as he accepted the wrap.

He shouldn't have invited Jagger into the ring. It was simply the thinnest of excuses to pummel the cocksure smugness off Jagger's face.

This wouldn't be a mannered bout of sparring.

It would be a fight.

Jagger entered the ring and began moving like a man in his element—a man comfortable throwing punches and receiving them. That was the give and take of boxing. One had to be willing to sink into its rhythms and take some blows in order to be able to mete them out. A minor sacrifice of the body for the victory at the end.

Or, at least, that was what one went into the ring thinking. One had to—or one should stay clear of it.

Confidence in one's abilities was one half; respect for one's opponent the other half. Lack of respect was the same as under-estimating, and underestimation of one's opponent led to defeat nine times out of ten. Julian wouldn't be underestimating Blaze Jagger. He was young, bold, and fearless.

It was Jagger who landed the first punch. A quick feint to the left before landing a swift left-handed jab to Julian's jaw. Julian ducked, and the follow-up right hook missed. A southpaw. A good thing to know about one's opponent.

Jagger was light and fast on his feet and understood that to be his advantage against a larger opponent. His strategy would be to run circles around Julian and wear him out. He thought he had Julian all figured out. His smile said as much.

While Julian was a big man, it was a wrong assumption to think him slow. It was that young man's arrogance in him. Along with his fists, Julian could use that against him.

Within ten seconds, Julian devised a strategy and began implementing it. He would never land a solid punch on the quicker man in open space. He had to, first, corral Jagger against the ropes. As he went to work on the younger man's torso, he landed a few solid hooks to Jagger's face, while he was at it.

That got Jagger's attention, and he pushed away from the ropes. A killer left hook landed solid on Julian's jaw. That would leave a bruise. Still, Julian kept to his strategy and managed to maneuver Jagger into a corner. This time, he began working him over in earnest, emotion taking over, as a torrent of anger surged through his fists for all Jagger had put Tessa through.

He'd pulled back for another blow when an unyielding hand closed around his elbow and held, preventing him from delivering his next blow.

"That'll be enough for today," came Brewster's voice behind him.

The red haze that had fallen over Julian's eyes began to fade. Jagger was watching him cautiously as he accepted a towel from Brewster and began dabbing at his bloodied mouth. He'd be lucky not to need a suture from a barber in his bottom lip.

"You'll want a cut of meat for that," said Julian, swiping the sweat from his brow.

Of course, violence was never the answer to one's problems, but in all honesty, it felt cleansing to have had it out with Jagger in the ring. Now, perhaps, they could say what needed to be said in a productive manner.

The cocksure glint had already returned to Jagger's eyes. "You've got a right proper lead hook on you. You could go a few rounds with Jackson himself, if being a marquess stops paying your bills."

The arrogance was still there, but a new measure of respect

shone in Jagger's eyes, too. Julian snorted. "Afraid I don't have a choice in that matter."

"Oh, I'd say you have more choice than you give yourself credit for," mused Jagger. "Imagine the headlines." Jagger splayed his arms wide. "Gentleman Jackson takes on the Mad Marquess of Mayfair. You could fill the whole of Hyde Park with spectators."

Julian snorted again. "With you running the odds, of course."

Jagger gave a one-shouldered shrug. "Naturally."

While the two men dressed, Julian kept half an eye on the younger man. He was an unexpected sort of person. He'd noted it at the Derby and saw it now, too. Uneducated and brash, but fiercely intelligent, too. He took in every detail of a situation or conversation and stored it up for future use. But skating alongside those qualities was a ruthlessness and raw ambition that bred overconfidence. Therein could lay his downfall, if he wasn't careful.

None of which was Julian's concern beyond how it affected Tessa.

Julian had a quick word with Brewster about giving him and Jagger fifteen minutes of privacy. When Brewster left, Julian leaned against a ring post and crossed his arms over his chest. He got directly to it. "You've made your point, now leave it and walk away."

Jagger shifted on his feet. He knew what and who Julian spoke of—*Lady Tessa Calthorp*—and he wasn't yet convinced about his best interests in this situation.

Julian would convince him.

"No more nonsense will be tolerated," he said. "Or the consequences won't be to your liking."

Jagger snorted, indicating a foolhardy lack of concern. "What? A high and mighty peer of the realm coming after an East End nothing-worth like me?" That got a chuckle. "I fight dirty, and you have too much at stake, what with your marquessly reputation and all."

And here it was—exactly what Julian had suspected.

Jagger was underestimating him.

He felt the menacing smile stretch his mouth. Jagger blinked, a flash of uncertainty flicking behind his eyes.

"Ah, that's where you've taken a wrong turn, Jagger. I don't care about society or you. I only care about Lady Tessa Calthorp," he said, low, the threat in his voice clear. "You see, I've lost much in life, and I won't tolerate any more losses. I'll burn London to the ground, and you with it, without batting an eyelash, if it will keep her safe. Now, do you truly think I won't meet you blow for dirty blow?"

All traces of arrogance fell away from Jagger as he took Julian's measure.

"I'll tell you only once more," said Julian. "Walk away."

As Jagger weighed the gains and losses of such an action, Julian decided to help the man with his choice. "I've recently happened across some interesting lines of information about you."

That got a lift of Jagger's brow. *"Happened across?* Or you had me investigated?"

Julian shrugged. It was the wrong question. They both knew the answer. "In addition to your odds laying and making for the Ring, it's become known in certain circles that you've been buying debt all over Town."

Jagger spread his hands wide. "It's what chaps like me do. Buy the debt of nobs. A diversity of interests for the rogue on the rise, if you will."

Julian nodded. "I can see the logic," he said. "Except here's where it doesn't follow. It's the debt of one nob, isn't it?" He let a beat of time slip past. "The nob who happens to be your father."

Jagger's gray eyes went flat with repressed emotion.

"The Marquess of Lydon," continued Julian. "He's a known

wastrel, to be sure. In fact, I doubt he has a ha'penny to his coffers. Dead broke, it's said. Vice and debauchery aren't cheap when one puts one's head down and goes at it with single-minded purpose the way he has over the last few decades. I believe he's down to the entailed properties of the marquessate."

"There's a townhouse in Mayfair."

"But not for long, am I correct?"

Jagger sniffed and kept his mouth closed.

"One might not think much of it except for this other snippet of information I happened across," said Julian. "Your mother was quite a beauty. It was known far and wide. And her father was the proprietor of a tavern in Wapping. Now, when I put my mind to it, I can see how it happened. The Marquess of Lydon was out making merry with one and all when he happened into your grandfather's tavern. At some point, he must have noticed the proprietor's fair daughter—and decided he would have her. And we have the proof he did, because, well, there's you."

The clench of Jagger's jaw said he didn't like this story, but he could hardly deny it.

"But Lydon being Lydon, he was soon on his merry way, and your mother—"

"That'll be enough," said Jagger. "We won't be discussing my ma."

"You're trying to ruin him."

"That man was ruined long before I walked God's dear earth."

Likely true, except…"You have a sister. Aren't you concerned what will happen to her when you call in Lydon's debt?"

Jagger gave a bitter snort. "She'll just marry a nob, and that's her life all sorted."

Julian had his doubts. Lady Beatrix St. Vincent was a different sort of lady, one for whom life wouldn't proceed as straight as line. Now that he was looking, Julian could see similarities between the two siblings. A glint of gray eye that suggested they didn't play by rules that weren't of their own devising.

Jagger sucked his teeth. "Speaking of fathers who happen to be wasters."

Julian braced himself.

"Yours used to tear the East End right up," continued Jagger. "At least, your old marquess had the good grace to shed his mortal coil."

A shocked laugh escaped Julian. "That's one way of putting it."

Of course, Jagger would know about the late Marquess of Ormonde. He'd only been dead for three years, and his legacy of vice and debauchery would long live on.

"You're not much like him, you know," said Jagger.

Julian went still. "Oh?"

"Yeah, you look like him and all, but in here—" Jagger knocked his fist against his chest. "No resemblance."

"You knew him?"

"Aye, I may be five and twenty, but I've been on the rise these last ten years." He nodded contemplatively. "Yeah, your pa wore his sadness like a cloak. Like you, I'd say. That's where you're like for like."

Like for like.

The words struck Julian at a wrong, sideways angle.

He'd spent all these years trying to be the opposite of his father, and yet, he couldn't deny Jagger's observation. Just as his father had, he'd let grief turn to sorrow and destruction of the self.

It was a difficult reality to swallow.

Jagger pushed off the post and grabbed his greatcoat, making ready to leave. "Fathers," he said, shaking his head.

"Yeah," was all Julian had in him to return on the subject.

"Dance a number on your head, they do." The words floated lightly on the air, but the serious look in Jagger's eyes held them to the ground. "You can be better than him."

With that, Jagger pivoted on his heel and strode across the

room. Before he passed through the open doorway, Julian called out, "And I would say the same to you."

A scoff floated over Jagger's back. "I already am."

Then he was gone.

And Julian was alone with his thoughts for company.

You can be better than him.

Those had been Jagger's words, but they could've as easily been those of someone else—*Tessa.*

She thought him worthy of those words.

And it struck Julian for the first time in his life—perhaps he could be.

Perhaps...he was.

For all her sharp edges, Tessa believed in the good in others— believed it of him.

And if a woman like Lady Tessa Calthorp could believe it of him...

It felt like too fragile and too bright an idea to behold directly.

But, perhaps, left alone within all those *perhaps*es, it could find purchase.

CHAPTER TWENTY-TWO

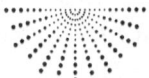

VAUXHALL GARDENS, NIGHT

"*W*ell, it certainly appears wet."

"You do have a way with words, Lady Saskia," said Eloise after a tick of discreet silence.

"All matters of perceived wetness aside," said Viveca. "It's quite the mechanical marvel, isn't it?"

Tessa stood back, along with Saskia, Viveca, Eloise, and Mr. Lancaster, and properly *ooo*-ed and *aah*-ed over the artificial landscape that was The Cascade, along with a few hundred other spectators.

The grand Monday-night concert at Vauxhall Gardens built to this moment when, at ten o'clock, the bell rang to announce the end of the first act. The audience then assembled behind the stage and waited for the curtain to lift. When it did, gasps and claps of delight sounded all around as the scene of a bridge, miller's house, watermill, and waterfall appeared before them. Clever lighting and the sound of roaring water gave the effect of a natural scene. It was, in fact, entirely artificial down to the actors playing soldiers crossing the bridge.

But it was the cascade itself that was the wonder as it gave the appearance of an actual waterfall by fluttery tin sheets attached to moving belts, turned by a team of men hidden behind the manufactured ruin.

Though Tessa thought she wouldn't be much impressed, she found she was—even through the light and variable feeling that kept tossing about her stomach and sent her gaze skittering over the crowd, unable to keep still for five seconds strung together.

The reason wasn't difficult to discern.

She'd invited Julian to join their party tonight.

And he hadn't yet arrived.

Further, the possibility existed he might not altogether.

I don't know how to do this.

He might've decided he didn't want to learn.

He might've run.

She'd understood she would have to give him the space to decide, which was one of the reasons she'd left Nonsuch Castle at dawn yesterday.

The other reason was that she'd needed to return to Sloane Street before the servants arrived to find the drawing room in shambles. Further, Tessa wouldn't have put it past Saskia and Viveca to pop their heads in for a little impromptu visit.

The drawing room was as she'd left it—chair on its side… table pushed at a wrong angle to the settee…tea and papers haphazardly scattered about the floor…fireplace poker lying at an odd and ominous angle before the hearth. She hadn't thought much of the papers until she began gathering them up and an image of Julian charging into the room flashed across her mind. He'd been holding papers—*these* papers.

A quick scan of a few pages revealed their importance. This was the report on Blaze Jagger. She perched on the edge of a chair and took it all in.

The bastard son of the Marquess of Lydon.

Well, that would stand out.

Further, along with his murky business dealings with the Ring and various other ventures, Jagger was buying Lydon's debt all over London. Somehow, Tessa didn't think this an act of familial charity stemming from the goodness in his heart.

No.

Jagger had a purpose.

She would have to wade deeper into the weeds.

A gasp, followed by a giggle, sounded at her side, shaking her from her thoughts. "There's the Duke of Wellington," whispered Viveca.

Tessa followed her sister's gaze and found the duke, his tall, arrogant bearing and hawkish profile impossible to mistake. He wasn't a man to be ignored in a crowd.

"It truly is too bad we missed the unveiling of the Achilles statue at Hyde Park Corner a few weeks ago," said Saskia. "We absolutely must view it before they put a fig leaf over his nethers."

Tessa's eyebrows shot toward the stars above. "*A fig leaf over his nethers?* Have I missed something?"

Saskia and Viveca exchanged a wry, long-suffering look. "*Have you missed something?*"

To Tessa's annoyance, her sisters giggled.

"What is it?" she asked. While she usually didn't attend to the whims that gave her sisters the giggles, tonight, for a reason that yet eluded her, she felt the strange, hysterical urge to giggle, too. She could feel the ready smile already tipping about her mouth.

"So," began Saskia, "a gaggle of ladies put their heads together and decided the Duke of Wellington must have a statue to commemorate his heroism in defeating that troglodyte Napoleon."

"I contributed fifty pounds," cut in Eloise.

"The esteemed sculptor Mr. Westmacott was commissioned," continued Viveca. "Whereupon he melted down thirty-three tons of captured French cannons and created an eighteen-foot-high Roman colossus for view in Hyde Park."

"The form is Roman in inspiration, yes," said Eloise. "But the head is based on none other than Wellington himself. No one could mistake his distinctive profile."

Tessa almost didn't want to ask…"And where does the fig leaf come in?"

Mischief glittered in Saskia's eyes. "Well, you know how we mentioned the Roman inspiration?"

Tessa's hand flew to her mouth. "*No.*"

As one, her sisters nodded. "Oh, yes," said Viveca.

There was that giggle just peeking around the words.

"London's first nude statue," confirmed Saskia.

"One lady suffered a fit of the vapors and fainted on the spot at the unveiling," added Eloise. "I was there."

Saskia snorted. "So, a fig leaf has been commissioned to protect the virtue of England's ladies."

"It won't have to be all that big," said Eloise, matter-of-fact.

A loaded beat of silence ticked past, and Tessa thought she might be able to contain the laugh that wanted release. Then Saskia and Viveca exchanged a look, and next Saskia met Tessa's gaze and Viveca's found Eloise's, then Eloise's eyes cut left and caught Tessa's, and they all burst into a fit of the giggles.

Oh, what a relief to release her nerves into buoyant night air.

She should giggle more often.

A few moments later, she was still giggling when she realized she was giggling alone. In fact, the others had ceased giggling altogether and were watching her. Eloise wore a mildly curious expression on her face, while Saskia and Viveca were observing her with twin cants of the head and narrowed eyes. Only Mr. Lancaster didn't notice as he moved closer to The Cascade to discern its inner workings.

The thing was Tessa didn't giggle—*ever.*

But tonight, she'd gone absolutely giddy with nerves and excitability.

"Sister," said Saskia, the note in her voice both quelling and maternal. "You're different these days."

"Am I?" Tessa swiped tears from her eyes with the back of her hand.

Viveca nodded with certainty. "Oh, yes."

"You've smiled more tonight than in the last decade of years put together," added Saskia.

"I've never seen so much of your teeth," observed Viveca. "They're quite lovely, but alas I think you might have a spot on a back right molar. It could be food, but shall I check just in case?"

"*Erm*, no," said Tessa.

Only seconds ago, she thought she might be carried away on a river of giggles, but now she felt sobered, even as jangly, excitable nerves continued to skitter through her veins.

"Shall we adjourn to our supper box?" asked Eloise, her arm twined through Mr. Lancaster's, their feet already moving.

Tessa noticed the curtain had closed over The Cascade and the crowd was dispersing to return to their boxes for the second half of the night's entertainments.

Eloise reached out with her other arm and slipped it through Tessa's, Saskia and Viveca leading the way. "Will anyone else be joining our party tonight?" she asked.

Tessa didn't like the discerning glint in Eloise's eye.

"I know for certain Gabriel and Celia won't be here," Saskia tossed over her shoulder.

"They much prefer one another's company to anyone else's," said Viveca. "I don't think they left their bedroom today."

A smile twitched about Eloise's mouth. "Allowances must be made for the newly wed."

Though Eloise wasn't looking directly at Tessa, she couldn't help feeling very much observed by the other woman, as if her question had been intended solely for Tessa. She was waiting for Tessa to answer—and there was but one answer that would suffice.

"Well, I…" Tessa didn't feel like giggling anymore. "I might've mentioned it to, *erm*, Lord Ormonde."

The hope that those words wouldn't garner much notice was completely dashed when three sets of eyes landed on her. Mr. Lancaster even leaned forward to spare her a glance.

"The *Marquess* of Ormonde?" asked Saskia, the question a demand for a load more information than Tessa had yet provided.

"The very same," said Tessa.

"Sister," said Viveca, "what have you been playing at?"

It was clear she spoke for all.

Tessa opened her mouth to reply when a figure ahead caught her notice, his arms crossed over his chest, shoulder propped against a wall of their supper box. An easy smile curled his mouth, his eyes open as a summer-blue sky as he laughed at a story being related by one of the three young bucks gathered around him.

Tessa's heart decided to beat mayhem in her chest.

Julian...here.

His gaze shifted and unerringly found Tessa's. His smile remained, but it took on a deeper quality. Within his summer-blue eyes shone pleasure—pleasure at the very sight of her.

A feeling blossomed within Tessa. It was almost drunken, this feeling fast and hot as a lightning strike, making her breathless. And though she felt keenly observed by her sisters and Eloise, all care for others' observations fell away.

It only mattered that she was centered within Julian's gaze.

Mr. Lancaster led the way with greetings, filling his role as host of this supper box. "Ormonde," he said, taking Julian's hand in a manly shake.

"Lancaster," returned Julian, even as he nodded in dismissal of his companions, who offered parting greetings to Saskia and Viveca before disappearing into the jolly night.

"Lord Ormonde," said Eloise, falling into her role as hostess with practiced ease. "I'm sure you'll remember the Ladies Saskia and Viveca?"

Saskia and Viveca offered shallow curtsies of greeting and pretty light blushes on their cheeks. It was the rare woman who would be immune to the golden handsomeness of the Marquess of Ormonde.

And Tessa was no rarer than any other woman in that regard.

"And I believe you and Lady Tessa are already acquainted, as well," continued Eloise, the disingenuous glint in her eye suspect. "Didn't I see the two of you dancing at Acaster's ball?"

A smile twitched about Julian's mouth as he bowed toward Tessa. "One wouldn't soon forget the occasion of holding Lady Tessa Calthorp in one's arms."

Tessa didn't have to look at her sisters to see their brows lifting to the heavens—or in a mirror to see the high spots of crimson staining her cheeks.

She'd been in his arms in more ways than simply on a dancing floor—and the implication running just below his words said as much.

She might never draw breath again.

* * *

JULIAN WAS DOING the one thing he'd vowed never to do in his life.

He was courting a lady.

It was undeniable fact.

Tessa's gaze drifted down his jaw, and her smile fell. "Have you been boxing?"

"Aye," he said on a light note. "Just a bit of sparring."

Her silver-blue eyes lifted and searched his before she reached out and touched light fingertips to the bruise shading his jaw. If he'd been dark of hair, he might've gotten away with it.

Only a lady one was courting would touch the bruise purpling one's jaw in full public view—far less set tongues wagging on a daily basis.

The possibility existed it might feel good—both her touch and this courtship.

Like two things at once—both wrong and right.

The one feeling old and worn-in, a feeling he'd been carrying with him for years.

The other feeling new and attractive, a feeling that conflicted with everything he'd built his life around—a feeling that had him unsteady on his feet.

He didn't know how to court a lady, but even he knew he and Tessa had gone about it all backwards.

Well, tonight could be, perhaps, a step forward.

"I hope you didn't come hungry," said Mrs. Fairfax. "We'd hardly entered our box for the first act when the servers began arriving with all manner of meats. There was even a lobster. Perhaps we can order another round of meats for you?"

Julian's mouth curved into his best soothing-the-hostess smile, and he glanced at the table set with all manner of libations from tea to coffee to Vauxhall's famous arrack. "A cup of coffee will suit me perfectly."

He'd just settled into conversation with Lancaster about a piece of recent legislation he'd been involved in seeing passed through both Lords and Commons when he felt *it* on the side of his face—a stare. He turned to find not one, but two intense pairs of eyes fixed decidedly upon him. He immediately intuited his boyish smile wouldn't be up to the task of withstanding the scrutiny of the Ladies Saskia and Viveca Calthorp. Into dangerous waters he would have to wade…"Are you finding the evening to your satisfaction, my ladies?"

The flat, unsmiling lines of their mouths told him they wouldn't be following his lead into impersonal pleasantries.

"What do you do, Lord Ormonde?" asked Lady Saskia.

His smile didn't falter. "*Do?*"

It was what any aristocrat would ask—and it was worth a try, anyway.

"When you're not busy marquessing," said Lady Viveca. "Or boxing."

Ah. They understood what he was about—courting their sister. And they would have him prove himself worthy of the privilege. "I run a horse racing stable in Suffolk, which commands much of my attention."

The Ladies Saskia and Viveca had been mostly brought up under the care of Tessa. And what they were doing now—feeling him out to the point of interrogation—was informing him that river flowed both directions.

Tessa was under her sisters' care, too.

In that vein, Lady Saskia asked, "In horse racing for the high-stakes gambling, are you?"

Julian felt his brow lift. "I don't gamble."

"Which would make you a rarity in that world."

"A unicorn, if you will." Though no less serious than Lady Saskia, Lady Viveca had a readier sense of whimsy.

A laugh burst from Julian, and he rubbed his forehead. "When do you think my horn will grow in?"

That got an appreciative smile from Lady Viveca, and even a twitch of the lips from Lady Saskia.

The lights of the stage began to dim. "Oh, the play is about the start," said Lady Viveca with a clap.

"I wonder if it will be performed as the Greeks performed it," said Lady Saskia, her gaze sweeping across the as-yet empty stage for a clue.

From her place on the other side of Mrs. Fairfax, Tessa leaned forward. She must've recognized a note in her sister's voice, for her eyes narrowed. "And how was that?" she asked, low and firm, her voice leaving no room for anything but the truth.

Lady Saskia exhaled a long-suffering sigh. "You know what *Lysistrata* is about, don't you, Tessa?" She sounded almost disappointed in her sister.

"A battle or some such?" asked Mrs. Fairfax. "A favorite subject of the Greeks, if memory serves."

Lady Saskia nodded, consideringly. "At the start of the play, a war is being waged, yes, but that's happening off the stage. What's happening on the stage is a different sort of battle—between men and women."

"I'm not sure about the sound of that," said Mrs. Fairfax.

Tessa held her peace and waited. She knew more was coming.

"So," continued Lady Viveca, "the women are sick to death of the men constantly waging war, so they band together and refuse to perform their wifely duties."

"Like...," said Mrs. Fairfax. "Pouring tea for their husbands?"

Lady Saskia didn't hesitate. "Duties of the *conjugal* variety."

Stunned silence filled the air. "That's the play we're here to see?" asked Mrs. Fairfax, the question holding a slightly out-of-breath quality.

"Oh, yes," said Lady Viveca, breezy as the summer night air.

"And what was that bit about how the Greeks used to perform the play?" Tessa's gaze remained fixed on Lady Saskia. She hadn't lost hold of the main thread.

Lady Saskia held Tessa's eye. "The actors playing the men would affix giant, red..."

Julian heard each word as if from the end of a very long tunnel—as if he stood too far away and therefore powerless to stop their inevitability.

"...leather..."

Lancaster, too, seemed to have caught hold of what the next word would be for he moved forward as if to stop it—but its momentum was too strong.

"...phalluses..."

Mrs. Fairfax's hand flew to her mouth. Tessa kept her gaze steadily affixed to her sisters.

"...to the front of their costumes—"

"And prance around the stage like that during the performance," finished Lady Viveca. "Isn't it delightful?"

"That's certainly one word for it, but not the one I would use," said Lancaster, dry, but not particularly shocked. He would've been spending enough time around the Calthorp sisters to expect as much by now.

Mrs. Fairfax, however, was having difficulty recovering her usual sangfroid. "And you think the play might be performed thusly tonight?"

Lady Saskia gave the question a few seconds of consideration. "In nineteenth-century England? Likely not."

"Society isn't nearly as bawdy as it was a thousand years ago," chimed Lady Viveca. "Or even a few hundred, come to think of it. Have you seen King Henry the Eighth's armor? That codpiece is one for the ages."

Mrs. Fairfax blinked and turned to Tessa. "Perhaps this play isn't the proper setting for your sisters to be seen—"

Lady Saskia held up a hand and stopped the words in Mrs. Fairfax's mouth. "We stay until the end."

Mrs. Fairfax exhaled a delicate, long-suffering sigh and let the matter be. Tessa flashed Julian an amused glance.

Just as it had occurred to him at supper at Nonsuch, the thought again struck him.

They no longer much needed words to speak.

A thought that should've sent him running.

"Besides," said Lady Viveca, "even if they did parade around the stage clad in fully erect red leather—"

"*Viveca*," said Tessa in a quelling tone that brooked no arguments.

"Well, even so," continued Lady Viveca, "it would be historically accurate, which is only a version of the truth and how can the truth ever be bad?"

It was clear from the crinkle of her brow that Tessa harbored deep doubts regarding the soundness of her sister's argument, but she hadn't time to voice it before the stage lights dimmed, then brightened the next second, signaling the impending start of the play.

Julian took a seat in the last row of the box. Ladies Saskia and Viveca sat at the front, eager as puppies for the play to start. They took their theater seriously, those two. Lancaster and Mrs. Fairfax settled into the middle row. One couldn't miss their utter ease with one another, both in their relaxed physicality and the private glances.

A spark of longing lit through Julian—soul-deep longing. He craved what they had—with Tessa.

And he could see it within reach, except...

What he wanted and what he should have were two separate entities.

And he hadn't yet worked out how the two could coexist within him.

While propriety might've dictated that Tessa sit beside her sisters or Mrs. Fairfax, she instead settled into the chair beside Julian's. The players began filling the stage and speaking their lines and he registered none of it, the entirety of his attention instead trained on the woman to his right. Something about the darkness made her feel more present beside him, though they weren't touching.

A truth, one he never could've known until this very moment, dawned on him.

Courtship was a torturous process.

Intentionally so.

Which, of course, was its value to society.

To drive would-be lovers so wild for one another that they had to marry.

He felt it—a light brush across his knuckles. So slight he could've taken it for a whisper of night air. Except he wouldn't have felt that through his kidskin gloves.

This brush was composed of more solid substance.

Tessa.

His hand responded without a staying thought, turning to catch elegant, feminine fingers in his.

His gaze shifted to find a little smile perched upon Tessa's mouth. She leaned over as if to conspire with him. "It seems we won't be treated to the Greek rendition of *Lysistrata* tonight, after all." The note of disappointment in her voice was unmistakable.

Only then did Julian see the players were, indeed, modestly clad in clothing more fit for English rather than Greek climes—and not a red leather phallus in sight.

All the while, her hand remained in his, perfectly fitted.

It held a weight more substantial than the sum of skin and bone.

Her fingers slid from his, but before he could voice a protest, they began tugging the tips of his gloves, efficiently sliding the glove off his hand and tucking it beneath her skirts. Then she held her hand out, flat, fingers splayed. He realized she was waiting for him to return the favor.

A few seconds later, her hand was bare against his, skin against skin, warm and humid. It could be an innocent touch—it *was* an innocent touch—but with Tessa, it was more, too, for nothing with her was ever so simple as one thing.

Both impulse and intention had him pulling her hand and lifting a quieting finger to his mouth. "Come with me."

CHAPTER TWENTY-THREE

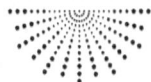

*J*ulian guided Tessa out of the supper box on silent feet, and they slipped into the night, his hand fast around hers. Muted steps crunched on Vauxhall's winding gravel paths, each more dimly lit than the last the farther they moved from the stage and orchestra, lilting drifts of music following in their wake.

While the impulse was simply explained—it was a fine night, and the dark walks lent the desirous couple a bit of privacy to... *court*—the intention was more complex.

He wanted to have her to himself—*simple.*

But to what end?

Complex.

To keep holding her hand?

Certainly.

To talk?

Possibly.

They should talk.

They had much to discuss.

But the feel of her hand in his only made his arms want more —to feel her within their embrace.

They rounded a bend on the darkest path, and he pulled her into an indent in the shrubbery that could serve as a makeshift alcove in a pinch, one that would protect them from view. Her head tipped back to meet his gaze. Though they'd come as far from the entertainments as the perimeter of the garden allowed, the music wafted around them, imbuing the air with the feeling that it was only they two in the wide world.

He lifted her hand to his mouth, pressing his lips to her knuckles. An innocent kiss—*simple*—but made more complex when he turned it over and pressed his mouth to her warm palm. A fire lit within her eyes as he followed inclination to the delicate skin of her inner wrist, her pulse beating a skipping rhythm beneath.

No more exposed skin available due to her blue wool spencer —hardy wool...for a night at Vauxhall Gardens where the ladies wore gossamer silk to impress...The woman was practical to the marrow of her bones—he lifted his mouth and shifted forward, the one hand refusing to relinquish hers, while the other found the small of her back, bringing her body against his. He angled his head so their mouths were only inches apart, so close her breath skittered across his lips.

And he kissed her.

It felt novel and wondrous, this kiss witnessed by only the moon and stars glittering in the inky sky above.

Yes, they'd kissed before.

But this time was different.

It was the first time he'd initiated a kiss.

And it felt like another wobbly step forward.

Intimate, this kiss.

It wasn't only its physicality—her lush body pressed against him, her curves molding themselves to his hard length, curves that all but begged to fill his hands, to offer pleasure and be pleasured in turn...his cock, hard and full, painfully straining against his trousers, demanding he hike up her skirts and bury himself deep inside her.

Oh, those physical demands were nothing new, though no less precious to him.

Yet this kiss tapped into a different side of him, too.

But his wasn't the only hand on the move. Hers caressed his bruised jaw, before trailing down his neck and chest, giving the solid muscle of his chest beneath a testing squeeze. She liked his heft. Then she was pushing his overcoat back from his waist, his cock straining with anticipation as to where her hand would next venture.

A curious, little sound erupted from her throat, and she went still. She pulled away enough to break the kiss, and now it was a sound erupting from his throat, one that resembled nothing so much as a dissatisfied grumble.

"What is it?" he asked, the question gruffer than intended.

She glanced down, and he saw that she still clutched his coat. Even before she reached into the pocket, he knew what her hand would emerge holding.

Blast.

Tonight, he'd worn the same overcoat he'd been wearing at Blanton & Co on the day she'd followed him.

And that day's purchase had lain forgotten in the pocket all these weeks.

The jade phallus.

He watched her slide it from his pocket and go stone still. Eyes wide with recognition flew up to meet his. *"This..."*

He remained silent, even as his every muscle tensed. She would have questions, and he would answer every one of them. For he understood why he'd allowed her to remove the phallus from his pocket.

He wanted to be known by this woman—*fully.*

And this jade phallus was part of that composition within him.

"*This...*" She held it up, its seven-inch length glowing a mellow otherworldly green. "This is the item I saw you purchase at Blanton and Company."

He nodded.

Improbably, she brought the phallus closer to her face and gave it a thorough inspection from varying angles. A host of sensations beset Julian—*bewilderment...amusement...lust*—but mostly a jittery assortment of nerves that might have him crawling out of his skin.

"It's rather long," she said, at last, having arrived at a few observations. "And thick and, *erm*, hard." Her gaze lifted to meet his. "But, perhaps, not quite as long and thick and hard as *you*."

Oh, lord.

He would combust.

There would be nothing left of him but a spent pile of ash.

"And you use this..." She hesitated. "On women?"

Of course, Tessa would ask.

"I've never used that one on a woman." And he didn't hesitate. "There has been no other woman since you, Tessa."

And there will be no other woman if there is an after-you, he didn't say.

He didn't know how to speak such words.

Skittish thoughts flashed behind her eyes, but alongside them slid others he recognized—*desire...curiosity.*

"Would you like a demonstration of its capabilities?"

* * *

A BLAZING ripple of lust shuddered through Tessa.

Her mouth gone suddenly dry, all she could do was nod.

A wicked glint flickered in Julian's eyes. But that wasn't what had her thighs squeezing together with utter ache and need.

It was the dark intention within.

Here was a man about to take control of her body.

He eased the jade phallus from her hand. "Let's put that aside for the moment." It disappeared into a pocket.

"But I thought—"

The slow shake of his head, and the knowing smile curling his lips had the rest of her words fading in her mouth.

"You have permission not to think, Tessa," he said, both the words and the way he spoke them, *oh*, so seductive. "All that is required of you is that you feel."

Again, his mouth claimed hers, firm and demanding, his tongue skating across her bottom lip before sliding suggestively into her mouth, tangling with hers, all her senses filled with this man—his cedarwood scent...the ragged in and out of his breath...the taste of coffee on his tongue...the feel of his hard, demanding length against her.

She wasn't the sort of woman who went through life being a vessel for a man's needs. She was a woman with drive and agency —a woman who took control of the path she followed.

But here she was, nothing more than an empty vessel, desperately aching to be filled by him.

To cede all control of self.

Large, masculine hands took hold of her skirts, hiking them over knees, up thighs, exposing them to the night air.

A hoyden...a wanton...That was her in this moment.

Instinctively, she lifted a long leg and wrapped it around his waist, drawing him nearer.

She felt his smile against her mouth. "Now," he muttered, "let's get you ready."

Anticipation shimmered through her as rough, calloused fingers trailed across the sensitive skin of her inner thigh, grazed over the slick slit of her sex, lighting fire through her. A quick inhalation suspended in her lungs as his fingertips grazed across her sex. It felt so...*good*. Her back arched, and her legs trembled as she pushed forward and opened herself more fully, greedy for the pressure of his touch.

Then a long finger slipped inside her and a long moan poured from parted lips. Oh, this need...It would consume her. His finger slid, deeper with each stroke, playing her body like a well-tuned instrument. "You're so wet and ready," he muttered, and somehow, improbably, the anticipation within her spiked to a higher level.

He took the jade phallus from his pocket. "It's going to feel cool. But you might like that."

Inch by inch, jade entered her, so smooth and slick—an altogether different sensation from him.

His eyes remained concentrated upon her face as he pushed the phallus deeper inside her, watching her as he carefully controlled the movement, which was different from how he moved when he was inside her. Here, this way, he was in total command of her pleasure. The phallus pushed to the end of her, and she closed her eyes, imagining his hand squeezed around the base, thrusting the jade deep and her desire spiked higher, and a familiar feeling began picking up momentum inside her. "Oh," she exhaled. "*Oh.*"

He increased the rhythm, moving the phallus in smaller increments, but faster. It was hitting a specific place inside her—one created for pleasure.

Then the build became suddenly and impossibly too much and impending climax beckoned and teased, her cries lifting to the heavens, he moved the jade relentlessly, her arms tight around his neck, clinging on for dear life as the hand pressed at the small of her back tightened, holding her steady as release burst through her and dissolved into starry glitter almost as quickly. His head bent, and he caught her mouth with his in a slow, languorous kiss as he slid the phallus from her.

Then he eased back, and her lashes lifted. She met his gaze so steady and knowing upon her. "That was..." Oh, there weren't words to describe what *that was*. "And you're so..." However, there was a word for him. "*Skilled.*"

How the smile perched upon his lips—a smile that acknowledged precisely how *skilled* he was—made her want to kiss him again.

Until this very moment she hadn't the faintest idea how attractive a man's arrogance could be.

A shiver traced across her skin, tightened her nipples. She lifted onto the tips of her toes with one foot, and dug her other heel into the indent of his taut buttock, and did exactly as she pleased and pressed her mouth to his.

Oh, how she loved his kiss—its surrender to intimacy.

One of her hands unhooked from around his neck and trailed down his torso, reveling in the solid, bulked muscle of his chest and stomach. He could've done the nation a service and posed as the model for Hyde Park's Achilles statue himself.

Lower, her hand explored until it reached his shaft, her fingers gone trembly with the desire to wrap around him.

"I want you inside me."

How attractive was the smile curled about his mouth, the serious intent within his eyes. "Haven't you received enough pleasure for one night?"

She gave her head a slow shake. *"That"*—there was no mistaking the meaning of *that*—"is no substitute for *you*."

On a low growl, his hand slid to her bottom and pulled her against his length, unyielding beneath the thin superfine that barely contained him, he angled his head, and his mouth met her neck, as if he'd only needed her permission to devour her.

Her swift fingers worked the falls of his trousers. After the havoc and pleasure he'd just wrought upon her body, how could she want more?

You have permission not to think, Tessa.

The falls released, and his cock fell forward, a turgid, heavy weight in her hand. She couldn't resist wrapping her fingers around that hard length she so badly needed to have inside her.

"Julian," fell from her lips and into his ear, a breathless whisper devoid of sound. *"Please."*

His fingers replaced hers around his shaft, guiding it to her sex, her arms tight around his neck as he slightly bent his legs, a better angle for when he, at last, pushed inside her on a sure, slick stroke. The breath caught in her lungs, her heart in her throat. He lifted his mouth from her neck and caught her gaze, refusing to release it as he began moving in and out of her.

Oh, that length of jade had been capable of delivering great pleasure—there was no doubting its effect on her body—but *this*...this was the genuine thing.

So *hot...visceral...urgent...real.*

This mingling of sweat and breath and tangling of tongues and limbs and intentions held an immediacy that nothing else in life came close to achieving.

This was intimacy.

Their bodies found a rhythm, sinking into it, and as frenzied as it was, their urges were in sync.

As if she had a choice to think her way out of this.

As if she would want to.

Him in her arms...him inside her...

Feel.

To feel...*him*...was all she ever wanted.

Another feeling that he'd made so familiar to her began to pool and coil within her. "Oh, Julian," she gasped, her leg wrapping tighter around his waist, imploring...*more.*

"Tessa, wrap your other leg around me."

His feet planted wide, both hands clamped tightly around her bottom, he began driving into her with focused intention. Her mouth found his neck, so her cries of pleasure would be muffled and not carry on the night air.

Her quim, at last, could take no more and, for the second time tonight, broke in release, pulsing around him, and this time a cry did break free as lightning bolted through her veins and tingled through nerve endings to the farthest reaches of fingers and toes, at once utterly alive and deliciously enervated.

His mouth found hers again as he continued his relentless drive inside her, his climax following hers, her mouth closing on his and muffling his shout of release.

Slowly, his hips stilled, their chests heaving, the sharp in and out their only movement.

"That was…"

She couldn't seem to finish a descriptive sentence tonight.

"Aye, it was," he rumbled into her neck, punctuating his agreement with a kiss.

His head lifted, and their eyes met. Neither seemed able to look away, each understanding that when they did, reality would begin to assert itself.

But…

What if this could be reality?

Not illicit trysts in Vauxhall Gardens, as such.

Though she wasn't in the least opposed to it.

But…

This.

Them…together.

She unwound one leg from around his waist, then the other. Her feet on firm earth, her dress fell into place down her legs. He buttoned the falls of his trousers.

And that was them—respectable again.

It was only when he didn't immediately run that she realized she'd half expected him to.

Instead, he stood before her wearing a bemused smile.

When he'd said he didn't know how to do this, he hadn't been lying.

He didn't.

But neither did she.

And the fact that he remained, opened the possibility that, perhaps, they could learn together.

But even as the comforting thought drifted through her mind, it cut across her at the wrong angle.

What came next for them wasn't that straightforward.

"We have a matter of some importance to discuss," she somehow forced herself to say.

Uncertainty flickered within his eyes. "Oh?"

"I might have some news." Only by sheer dint of will did she not touch her stomach.

His gaze narrowed. "Is this about Jagger?" Before she could reply, he continued, "Jagger can wait."

"I'm not sure he can, but that wasn't—"

He twined his fingers through hers, their solid strength pushing all matters of *some importance* from her mind.

All matters lost the urgency of importance when he was touching her.

So, she didn't tell him what she knew with near certainty.

That she was with child—*his* child.

It was a fact that could wait one more night, for it was going nowhere. If she told him now, it might be too much, too soon. What they'd done, after what he'd confessed to her—he didn't court ladies…he abstained from intimate relations…

The fact that he was doing both, with her, meant something important.

But it was new and fragile.

So new and fragile it could collapse beneath the weight of what she had to tell him.

So, it would keep for one more night, but it wasn't something that could wait forever.

Soon, there wouldn't be a choice.

Soon, there would be a child.

A child she knew to the core of her being that she wanted very much.

A child whose blood she knew to be pure as the driven snow.

But Julian…He'd harbored the idea for so long that his blood was intrinsically bad, it felt elemental to him—like a foundational part of his being.

But it wasn't.

He hadn't been born with bad blood.

Life had taught him to believe that—and he'd taken the lesson to heart.

The problem was he couldn't see that his belief was fundamentally flawed. It happened with mathematical equations—and it happened in life.

But a seedling of hope had sprouted that this belief could be changing within him.

And if it did, with a little more time, there could be hope for them.

CHAPTER TWENTY-FOUR

NEXT EVENING

*J*ulian entered the fashionable Mayfair residence of Mrs. Eloise Fairfax and felt the immediate urge to lie through his teeth and politely inform the manservant he'd gotten the wrong address, pivot on his heel, and exit before anyone noticed his presence.

One glance into the drawing room circulating with a handful of guests comprised of family and close friends of Mr. Lancaster and Mrs. Fairfax communicated a single fact—he'd dived into the sort of perilous waters that were placid on the surface but roiling with dangerous currents unseen until it was too late.

Which left him with but one option.

Carefully swim parallel to the shore and remove himself from the rip current.

He was on the verge of coaxing his hat back from the manservant who was regarding him with a mostly impassive face when two happenings occurred simultaneously: His gaze landed on the one figure he sought—an elegant Tessa at her ease while conversing with Mr. Lancaster—and a delighted feminine voice rang out, "How lovely of you to join our little soirée, Lord Ormonde."

He understood as his hostess closed the distance between them with a warm smile on her face that there was no turning his back on Mrs. Eloise Fairfax—or this evening.

Its inexorable pull had the feel of Fate about it—a feeling that fizzed through one's veins, sparking nerve endings alight as it effervesced through.

Even as he returned his hostess's greeting with a smile of his own—the charming one that got him into everyone's good graces whether they liked it or not—Tessa's gaze shifted and met his. A hint of amusement glimmered therein, as if she'd correctly intuited his thoughts.

By now, Mrs. Fairfax had expertly twined her arm through his—as if she were all too well versed in wrangling nervous bachelors—and led him into her stylish drawing room that was all pleasing hues of coral, amber, and walnut, a natural combination of the masculine and feminine mixed with a light scent of honeysuckle that invited one to feel at home.

Of course, Mrs. Fairfax's home would make one feel thusly. It was simply an extension of the woman herself.

"I believe you're acquainted with my cousin, the Duchess of Acaster?"

Julian supposed it would've been too much to hope she would lead him directly to Tessa.

The duchess standing before him was precisely what he'd meant by perilous waters. The last time he'd conversed with the Duchess of Acaster, it had been to inform her that Rake had eloped with Gemma. But the duchess and Mrs. Fairfax were close as sisters. Of course, she would be included in any intimate supper parties. When he'd received the invitation this morning, he'd been too blinded by the possibility of being in the same room with Tessa to consider the other potential guests.

His general amiability slipped not a notch as he offered a polite bow to the duchess. "Your Grace."

"Considering the informality of the party," she said, a joyful lift to her voice, "I believe you can call me Celia for tonight."

When she'd been the Sixth Duchess of Acaster, Julian had always viewed her as aloof—cold, even. A calculating sort of woman who, in all honesty, possessed the necessary ingredients to make a perfect wife for Rake.

But, as it turned out, that hadn't been the case at all.

In fact, now that she was the Seventh Duchess of Acaster, he suspected her to be a much different woman from the one he'd assumed her to be.

He gave another bow. "Celia."

Immediately, he was flummoxed as to what his next words should be to this woman. Across the room, Tessa was now deeply engaged in conversation with both Lancaster and Mrs. Fairfax.

Actually, come to think of it, he did know what he should say to the duchess. "Perhaps I owe you an apology."

Her brow lifted with surprise. "For?"

"For, *erm*, Rake."

It only took half a beat of time for her mouth to curl into a smile that reached her eyes. "There is certainly no need for that. Rakesley did me a most kind service by begging off our potential engagement."

Julian wasn't sure Rake had been motivated by kindness—in fact, he knew his friend very definitely hadn't been—but he was content to let that observation pass unspoken.

"If Rakesley hadn't," continued Celia, "I would have missed out on..." Her hot gaze cut across the room and landed on her husband, Gabriel Calthorp, Seventh Duke of Acaster, a man several years younger than her. A man with whom she was clearly besotted. *"Him."*

Acaster met his wife's gaze, and Julian had to glance away. It was the only gentlemanly course when witness to such naked intimacy between a man and a woman.

Of course, given a moment's freedom, Julian's eyes wandered

the room and found the only person they wanted to behold. Now, Tessa was engaged in conversation with Mrs. Fairfax and Lady Viveca.

The hairs on the back of his neck prickled to a stand, and when he turned, he found that Acaster's gaze had shifted and the duke was now silently watching him...

Silently watching him watch his sister.

Right.

Acaster was an intelligent man. A fact well-known in society. Further, he was a man who hadn't made up his mind about Julian in relation to his sister.

Fair play.

A throat pointedly cleared behind Julian.

He turned, and there stood Lady Saskia, patiently regarding him as if she'd been doing so for some time. "Lady Saskia," he said with a shallow bow. "Are you finding the evening to your satisfaction?"

Her head canted subtly to the side. Julian tried not to brace himself—tried to tell himself this was merely an evening of socializing, not a running of the gauntlet. But the suspicion had begun to form that this evening was most definitely the latter in the guise of the former.

"I have a question for you," said Lady Saskia in the firm, factual tone she employed to great effect.

"Yes?" he asked, slowly.

"Are you here to court my sister?"

Julian's mouth began to open before he immediately clamped it shut. These Calthorp sisters...Nothing could prepare one for them.

Before an answer could occur to him, a feminine voice piped up, "Oh, no, Saskia, Lord Ormonde wouldn't be courting me. We've hardly strung together five sentences of conversation between us." To his left, the wide, disingenuous eyes of Lady Viveca stared up at him. "Isn't that correct?"

Lady Saskia to the right and Lady Viveca to the left, he felt like an animal stalked in the wild, neatly caught. Such happenings occurred on the wide savannahs of Africa.

Lady Viveca's head canted to the exact angle of her sister's. "Unless..." She tapped a considering finger to her mouth.

"*Unless?*" asked Julian, dread creeping through him.

"Unless, of course, you're here to court Saskia?"

"I can assure you that is not—"

"*Or,*" interrupted Lady Saskia, her eyes gone bright with sudden realization.

In the twin feline glints of the sisters' eyes, he couldn't see how they differed much from their African big cat counterparts, as they teased and toyed with rather expert finesse.

"*Or,*" said Lady Viveca, as if completing her sister's thought, "you're here for..."

As one, the sisters' gazes shifted and moved across the drawing room before landing squarely on Tessa, who was now engaged in conversation with Celia.

A hot flush burned through Julian, and the Ladies Saskia and Viveca exchanged a quick, secret smile.

Their work here was done.

"Everyone," came Mrs. Fairfax's voice from the far end of the room, "I've been informed supper is ready."

Julian was the last guest to cross the foyer into the dining room where Mrs. Fairfax was ushering everyone toward their assigned places. "Oh, no, Celia," she was saying to her cousin with a laugh, "I cannot have you and Gabriel sitting beside or even across from each other, or we'll have no conversation from the two of you for the rest of the evening."

So, it was that Julian found himself seated between Celia to his left and Lady Saskia to his right, Acaster directly across, Lady Viveca diagonal right, and Tessa diagonal left. As hosts, Lancaster and Mrs. Fairfax took their seats at opposite ends of the table.

Like the drawing room, the dining room conveyed utter

elegance with its half-lit crystal chandelier sending golden light across the gleaming mahogany table, imbuing every surface it touched with a warm glow.

"You might be wondering why we invited you here on such short notice," said Lancaster, speaking to the room at large, but his eyes fixed on Mrs. Fairfax.

The air sparkled with anticipation. An announcement was about to be made, and everyone could guess its content.

"We couldn't wait a single day to share the news," said Mrs. Fairfax, her eyes radiant with both joy and a rush of unshed tears.

"I've asked Eloise to be my wife," said Lancaster in his rich barrister's voice, "and she's done me the great honor of saying *yes*."

At Julian's side, Celia gasped and took her cousin's hand. "I'm so happy for you, my dear."

Through the round of cheers and hearty congratulations around the table—Julian's included—he caught Tessa's gaze. For an instant, happiness of the purest variety shone out at him. Then she blinked, and an emotion that he couldn't interpret complicated it.

Mrs. Fairfax whispered something in her direction and Tessa responded, and the moment was gone.

Champagne and supper were served, and the conversation centered around the happy couple's plans for the future. As course after course passed by, Julian had to reconcile himself with the scantest flickers of Tessa's attention.

It was sometime during the fourth course that Mrs. Fairfax said, "And who at this table shall be next to marry?"

Mid-chew on a bite of roast lamb, every muscle in Julian's body locked into place. Only by reaching deep into his well of self-control did he not attempt to catch Tessa's eye.

That would be a bad idea…A *very* bad idea for a multitude of reasons—some crystal clear in his mind and others hazy and indistinct and the sort he preferred to leave be for the moment.

"Lady Saskia? Lady Viveca?" continued Mrs. Farifax. "Any fine prospects amid the mountain of flowers and invitations that arrive daily at your doorstep?"

The sisters exchanged a look of mutual understanding, and pure reflex had Julian bracing himself yet again. The Ladies Saskia and Viveca were on the precipice of saying something the room hadn't yet prepared itself for.

He knew, from recent experience.

"We've been thinking for a while," began Lady Saskia.

"And dreaming," added Lady Viveca.

Now, it wasn't only Julian holding his breath, but the entire room.

"That we would like to open a circulating library."

As the statement settled into the air, the collective breath released. As potential scenarios went, this wasn't a bad one at all. Julian's money would've been on big game hunting in Africa.

"And we'll serve your tea blends, Tessa," said Lady Viveca. Another exchange of glances between the sisters. "There's more, too."

Of course.

"We've been inspired by Vauxhall Gardens, as a matter of fact," said Lady Saskia.

"You wish to put on musical entertainments in your circulating library?" Acaster's mouth twitched with humor. "Perhaps do them one better and show *Lysistrata* in the tradition of the Ancient Greeks?"

Julian snorted.

Lady Saskia's eyes rolled toward the ceiling. *Brothers*, that roll of the eyes said. "In the way Vauxhall offers patronage to musicians and artists, we shall champion writers selected by us."

Acaster nodded, not quite approving, but assessing. He was known as a man who would have to evaluate a business plan before he gave it his full approval.

"Then we shall publish and offer their works for circulation and purchase." Lady Viveca's eyes shone bright with fervor.

"Exclusively, at first." Lady Saskia's fervency matched her sister's. "To build anticipation."

"Then, after the shops and other libraries come begging, we will offer our publications to them for distribution."

"Ambitious," said Acaster, approval in every syllable.

Mrs. Fairfax clasped her hands together. "How delightful!"

"What sorts of publications?" asked Tessa. Like Acaster, she was taking her sisters seriously.

Again, it occurred to Julian what a unique sort of person Tessa was. To the world at large, she presented as a sharp, hard woman with her slightly mannish manner of dress and keen intelligence that wasn't afraid of appearing unfeminine—a forbidding exterior that put people off the true scent of her.

For at her core, this woman was a nurturer.

Inside the circle of her care was a special place to be.

That the outside world couldn't see her for who she truly was due to their prejudices—and it was their loss.

"Oh, we will offer the usual sorts, of course," said Lady Saskia.

"Periodicals and philosophical treatises and such," said Lady Viveca.

Skepticism yet hung about Tessa. "But those publications won't build excitement of the sort you speak of."

Twin secret smiles curled about the mouths of the Ladies Saskia and Viveca. They possessed the furtive air of conspirators who had been found out. "*Novels*," they said in unison.

"What sort of novels?" asked Acaster. He'd picked up the scent alongside Tessa. They knew their sisters.

Another exchange of glances—of secrets about to be revealed. Again, they spoke in unison. "*Romances.*"

While that settled into the air, Julian's gaze slid toward Tessa, who was wholly concentrated on her sisters, her mind at work.

A mulish set to her jaw, Lady Saskia continued, "Jane Austen and Walter Scott have proven two things. Novel writing is a respectable art, and there is a public appetite for it. King George, when he was still the Prince Regent, even left Miss Austen with no choice but to dedicate her novel *Emma* to him."

"But what we're actually after satisfying is the appetite of the *female* public for books," said Lady Viveca. "Women comprise half the world's occupants, yet any art created for us is deemed second-rate and therefore inferior."

"Viveca and I have decided that we can have a hand in changing that opinion."

"You will need investors, of course," said Acaster.

"Of course," said Lady Viveca, her gaze steely and unflinching.

The sisters had come into this conversation prepared for Acaster and Tessa.

Julian took in Tessa, as her mind worked through all the angles of her sisters' budding enterprise. They were placing their hopes and dreams into her hands—and better hands Julian couldn't think of.

Those hopes and dreams were safe with Tessa.

A thought struck him from an unexpected angle.

What a wonderful mother Tessa would make someday.

Reflexively, he tamped the idea down. It was too complex a thought. And yet...

It lit a warming ember in a dark, cold corner of his soul.

A place of possibility he'd thought wasn't for him.

CHAPTER TWENTY-FIVE

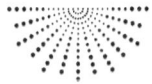

*T*essa swallowed back a surge of pride.

This was what she and Gabriel had been working toward all these years—first in scraping by with nothing but their own wits, then by using their wits to fleece the rich.

This... So Saskia and Viveca would have the opportunity to choose their path in life—to have the confidence and financial backing to pursue their interests and talents.

The same knowledge and pride shone in Gabriel's eyes when they flashed to meet hers, which were stinging with unshed tears.

"We do, however...," began Saskia.

"Have one teensy request to make of you, sister," finished Viveca.

Tessa found two pairs of inquisitive blue eyes trained on her. "Yes?" she asked, wary.

She knew that look—her sisters wanted something.

And if their past track record predicted future, they would have it.

"The Sloane Street townhouse...," began Viveca.

"We would like it for our use," finished Saskia.

"*Please*," added Viveca with her sweetest smile, the one that never failed to melt Tessa into a puddle.

The next instant, Tessa's brow was crinkling as the import of their teensy request sank in. "You're asking me to leave my home?"

Her sisters didn't lack for audacity.

"Yes," said Saskia.

"We've talked it over, and," said Viveca, "Sloane Street is an ideal location for our library with its proximity to Hyde Park."

"And where would I go?" asked Tessa, aghast. Her sisters were seriously making plans to turf her out of her townhouse.

Saskia gave an indifferent shrug. "Gabriel's mansion?"

"St. James's Square is quite the fashionable address," said Viveca, as if she were an estate agent.

Tessa cut a glance over to find Gabriel and Celia making hot newlywed eyes at one another. "*No.*"

She couldn't live in the same house with those two, even if it was a mansion possessed of separate wings. Gabriel and Celia were occupying their own private planet for two.

There was no room for her there.

"Oh, I know." Viveca snapped her fingers. "You can take that giant pile of gold you must have from The Archangel and purchase a fashionable townhouse in Mayfair."

"I don't care about fashionable townhouses in Mayfair," Tessa retorted in a tone that held a whiff of fractious toddler.

But her protest was weak, and she saw it was no use. She'd lost before this conversation even began. The knowing smirks presently being exchanged between her sisters only confirmed it.

She reckoned she would be turfed out before the month's end.

She met Julian's gaze. He'd been watching with a smile in his summer-blue eyes.

He reckoned it, too.

The meal progressed through the courses, and the conversation returned to Eloise and Mr. Lancaster's future nuptials. Tessa was delighted for Eloise, a woman she now considered a friend. Eloise and Lancaster possessed that rare mix of ease and tension that boded well for a couple.

Ease and tension...

Just last night, she'd experienced the same with Julian.

A glimpse of what could be...*perhaps.*

Supper concluded, the party adjourned to the conservatory that opened onto the back garden. The men and women didn't separate so the men could smoke cigars and have manly conversation without offending delicate, feminine ears. Tessa gravitated toward Julian in an ambling arc so as not to draw attention to her intention, while Mr. Lancaster led the conversation further into the business details of the circulating library. He knew a solicitor who was the best at setting up such ventures.

When she'd, at last, found a straight line to Julian, a throat cleared behind her. She turned to find Gabriel regarding her with an expectant look on his face. "Yes?" she asked, letting her irritation come through.

He lifted an unfazed eyebrow. "Why don't you join me on the terrace? I believe you and I could do with a chat."

Tessa inhaled an annoyed sigh and followed her brother outside. It wasn't a clear night, but then night skies in London rarely were. They turned their backs to the party and gazed out in parallel across the dark garden. This little chat could begin at one of a thousand different points, so she waited.

"Blaze Jagger," said Gabriel.

Tessa almost sagged with relief. She'd thought her brother had surely picked up on the tension that vibrated between her and Julian. She'd thought it a nearly tangible thing.

"He's making a great deal of noise in our circles."

"Aye," she said. "I've been learning more than I ever wanted to know about Blaze Jagger."

"Such as?"

"He's the bastard of a marquess."

Gabriel nodded. "Lydon."

Tessa's head whipped around. "You knew?"

Gabriel shrugged. "I had him investigated."

A snort borne of frustration at all the men in her life sounded from Tessa. "He's buying up Lydon's debt all over Town."

"Aye."

"Julian says he won't be a problem anymore."

With lifted brow, Gabriel turned and fully faced her. "*Julian?*"

Tessa didn't flinch. Instead, she stared her brother down. "That's his given name."

Gabriel might be married and a duke, but she was still the older sister. She wouldn't be teased by her little brother.

Neither would she be distracted from the topic at hand.

"Jagger's a lone wolf," she said.

"Apt description."

"And how does one stop a lone wolf?"

"We can't exactly shoot him. There are morals and laws and such."

"Bring him into the fold."

Suspicion flickered within Gabriel's eyes. "And how do you propose to do that?"

"I'm knocking around a few ideas."

"Don't act on any of them without speaking to me first."

Tessa gave a noncommittal shrug that she knew would fiddle on Gabriel's last nerve. "You're selling me your share in The Archangel, remember? Just an old married man settling your markers and getting out of the game, right?"

"Tessa—"

Now, a change of subject suited her. "Do you have an opinion on Ormonde?"

Though his given name had been entered into the conversational canon, she couldn't bring herself to speak it. To say it aloud —here and now...to Gabriel—would be akin to speaking an intimacy aloud.

"Have you had him investigated, too?"

Gabriel didn't smile at her attempt at levity. Instead, his head canted in that particular way he had when considering a matter of importance. "Should I?"

All pretense of levity between them fell away.

"No."

In quiet assessment of one another, they stood immobile. The casual observer could take them for adversaries in this moment.

It was Gabriel who relented first. "Ormonde was several years ahead of me at Eton. A lad who was and is well liked by all. He doesn't get himself into gambling debt that I know of."

"He doesn't."

"His father, however, was a legend in that department," continued Gabriel. "And what do *you* know of Ormonde?"

"A bit."

"More than a bit, perhaps," he said, testing.

"More than a bit," she confirmed.

"You'll want to be careful, sister."

"I'm not asking for permission or advice." The words didn't precisely snap, but they did hold an edge.

"And I can't give you either," said Gabriel, evenly. "But you must've gleaned something of his family by now."

"I have."

"A past like that leaves a mark on a person. It can define his entire existence. Examples of that sort shamble and gamble their way through The Archangel every night."

"That's not Julian." Tessa didn't like the defensive tone of her voice—but there was no help for it.

Gabriel let a calming expanse of silence tick past before he spoke again. "Such pasts can get in a man's blood."

Tessa scoffed. "I don't believe any of that blood nonsense."

Gabriel didn't shift position. "But, Tessa, he might."

The breath caught sharp in her lungs. The truth could have that effect on a person.

"All he's been taught and all he knows is that love brings pain."

Tessa shook her head. "That's the past. It doesn't have to be the future. Isn't that what you and I believe, Gabriel? Aren't the lives we fashioned for ourselves and our sisters examples of that?" She didn't know if she was pushing against Gabriel or against immutable laws of the universe, but she must. It was important that Gabriel—*anyone*—share this belief with her.

"Aye, they are," he said, as if he were soothing a feral cat.

"He's a good man, Gabriel. He's worth the effort."

"But does he know that?"

And there was her fear voiced aloud.

"Ah," came a feminine voice at their backs, "I'd wondered where you'd wandered off to."

Tessa turned to find Celia crossing the terrace and understood in an instant that Gabriel was already forgetting what they'd been discussing, his eyes only for his wife. When she drew near enough, Gabriel reached out and took Celia by the waist, pulling her into a loose embrace at his side that spoke of ease and familiarity.

A pang of envy arrowed through Tessa.

She wanted that with every cell of her being.

With Julian.

Celia held a hand to her forehead in a gesture that looked a mite too practiced. "My love, I find that my head has a little ache tonight."

"Shall we go home and cure it?"

Tessa was no squeamish miss, but she almost groaned. To hear Gabriel speak thusly, and with such hot fervency...well, she couldn't unhear it.

"Aye," said Celia, her fingers curling around his cravat.

Tessa cleared her throat to remind them of her presence. The looks they shot her held not the faintest hint of abashment.

Gabriel pushed away from the low terrace wall, one arm still around Celia's waist. "Sister," he said by way of farewell.

"Let's have tea soon," Celia tossed over her shoulder.

And that was Tessa left alone with her thoughts.

Her feet moved across terrace stones, down the short staircase, and onto the springy, close-cropped turf of the back garden, still summer night air holding a pleasing nip of cool.

The conversation with Gabriel pulled at her mind, refusing to let it settle. He'd only spoken her own anxieties regarding Julian aloud. As it did several times a day now, her hand moved across her lower stomach in a caress that was filled with no small amount of awe. At this very moment, a child lay curled inside her —a child, she found, she wanted very much.

But Julian...

As if her mind had the power to conjure him, he appeared on the terrace above, limned in light from the house at his back. When he'd walked into the drawing room earlier, the breath had caught in her chest. It was the sight of this too-handsome man dressed in evening blacks—but it was more, too.

It was the immediate possessive thought that he was *her* too-handsome man dressed in evening blacks.

Hers.

Until tonight, she'd never known herself to harbor a possessive bone in her body.

But she did.

When it came to him.

She stepped into the center of the lawn, where he would see her even in the dim light. He descended the stairs, and without a word, took her hand and led her beneath the canopy of an apple tree in summer bloom. Here, no one would be able to catch a casual glimpse of them from the house.

Here, it was only them.

Calloused fingers grazed across her jaw and cupped the nape of her neck, bringing her mouth to his. The kiss immediately took on a bright sense of urgency, for it came to her in a crushing instant—this kiss might need to last her a lifetime.

Her senses began to take in everything as if it were the last time—his cedarwood scent…the tensile strength of his arms…the hard length of his body against her, essential and demanding, leading her down a path she so badly wanted to follow.

She was tempted.

Oh, so tempted to give in to desire and put off the inevitable for yet one more night. After all, he'd come so far in these last weeks.

But was the distance reached enough to bridge all the damage done over the years?

Had he come far enough?

Her control and this opportunity were slipping, and the answer could no longer wait—to wait would only complicate matters…more than they already were.

It was when her back was against the tree and he was hiking up her skirts and her leg was instinctively wrapping around his waist that his mouth came away from hers, sliding to the sensitive skin below her ear. "Tessa," he murmured, "you're all I can think about. The way I feel about you…I think it must be more than lust."

The breath caught in her lungs.

They were adults.

They both knew what *more than lust* meant.

And she knew what she must do.

She must stop him before he spoke it aloud.

"Julian…"

"Yes?" The velvety gravel of his voice nearly undid all her intention.

She inhaled and tried again. *"Julian."* His name emerged firmer this time.

He pulled back a few inches and met her eye. He'd caught that firm note.

"We must talk."

"Must we?" the question a low, seductive rumble.

She swallowed, intention wavering, and nodded.

He took a step backward, and his body came away from hers. She suddenly felt too light without the grounding presence of him against her and remained slumped against the tree until her feet steadied beneath her. One side of his face was illuminated by remnants of light from the house, the other side cast in darkness —all of him inscrutable as he waited for her to explain.

"There is something I must tell you, and…and…" Oh, this was difficult…"And I think the only way to say it is simply to say it."

The air between them understood her words would change everything.

He waited, unmoving.

"I am with child."

And there it was—the change in the air as it moved around her words and attempted to understand and incorporate them into reality…A new reality that neither of them was prepared for.

One that offered no return to the life that came before.

There was only *after*.

He'd gone still. Like hers, his lungs would've forgotten how to function. The instant she wished she could read his features for his reaction, she experienced a weak relief she couldn't.

"You're certain?"

She supposed the question logical. Still, she couldn't help wishing he'd reacted some other way. That against everything she'd come to know and understand about this man, she'd thought—*hoped*—perhaps, he would.

"I am," she managed.

Time both stretched and compressed as he took in those words. "How long have you known?" he asked, his voice devoid of emotion.

"I've suspected for a week or so."

He turned that over in his mind. "Since before Clarissa's birthday?"

"Around then, yes."

A laugh carried on the night air, dry and humorless. "So, that's what all this has been about."

The words struck her at an odd angle. "What *all this?*"

"Making me fall in love with you."

And here it was…

Love, spoken aloud.

Like the child nestled within her, she'd been carrying that feeling inside her these last few weeks, too.

Love for this damaged man.

Love that she'd known couldn't go anywhere.

And, yet, she'd hoped.

A hope that faded with every beat of her heart.

"You've fallen in love with me?" she asked.

Either Julian didn't hear or didn't want to hear, for he pressed on. "That day at Nonsuch…the night at Vauxhall Gardens…They were all *what?* To secure a father for your child?"

Tessa's brow furrowed. "*You* are the father of my child."

Julian snorted. "You know what I'm speaking of."

"I can't say that I do," she said, wary.

"I would've thought better of you than a marriage trap."

Utter disbelief pulsed through Tessa, and her feet firmed beneath her. "*Trap?* You should listen to yourself, Julian. Yes, you are trapped. But not by me. You're trapped in your own mind, and no one can free you from that snare but yourself."

In the dissipating light, she saw his jaw clench and release.

"It's not of particular importance to me that you and I marry," she said with as much patience as she could muster. "Let's refresh your memory with a few facts about me." She held up a finger. "I'm a woman of independent means." A second finger joined the first. "And I'm very much accustomed to making my own way in the world. You have a choice, Julian. I'm not taking that away from you, but I thought you should know."

"*Thought I should know?*" he scoffed. "Don't you care if the child is a bastard?"

"There are ways to avoid such a fate for a child. Do *you* care?" This point needed to be pressed. Julian needed to hear it with his heart—not his fear. "You can allow yourself to feel."

"You know nothing of it."

"I know fear when I see it. Deep inside, you're still that scrawny lad full of fear, aren't you? Afraid that if you ever allowed yourself to feel, it would consume you whole."

He remained silent.

"Isn't fear preventing you from doing what you know deep down you have to do?"

"What is that?"

"Leave those wrong beliefs behind." A thought occurred to her. "Or..."

"*Or?*"

"Or are all those wrong beliefs and fears a comfort for you?"

"Leave it, Tessa," he warned. "I'm not one of your equations to be solved."

But she wasn't finished—far from it..."Your wrong thinking makes you safe. You never have to step beyond your fear and into the unknown. Your past causes you great pain, but that's known pain and safer than taking a risk on an uncharted future."

Before her, he stood, taking her words in, translating them through the damage the past had wrought in his mind.

And she was powerless to do a thing about it.

She could only speak the truth.

It was up to him to test its veracity for himself.

How she wanted to reach out and place her hand on him, bridge this distance between them.

But she couldn't.

She understood that.

There were two sides to every river and each side must do its equal work to support that bridge.

How very alone he appeared on his side.

"I know you're accustomed to being in the right, Tessa, but in this case you haven't the faintest idea what you're talking about."

"Enlighten me."

"When my father put a bullet in his brain, do you know what I felt?"

The bluntness of the words caused Tessa to flinch. She shook her head and braced herself.

"*Relief*," he said, his voice weary as if unloading a burden too long held. "Relief down to my bones. I could've melted to the floor with it."

"It would only be natural considering—"

He held up a hand and stayed the words in her mouth. "Don't try to rationalize or justify it."

Tessa clamped her mouth shut.

"What sort of son feels that way, Tessa?" He didn't wait for her answer. "The wrong sort. But it taught me something about myself. I shouldn't be husband to any woman or father to any child, for all this time I've known what no one else has—that sort of defect is passed from father to son. It runs in the blood."

The words settled into the air, heavy and implacable, yet Tessa had more to say…"We are what we make of ourselves, Julian. The products of day upon day of living—some good, others bad. The blood flowing in our veins has nothing to do with who we are. Life is a tougher challenge than that. Life demands that we make something of ourselves—and there we find our freedom. We are *free* to make of ourselves who we are. Only you can set yourself free from who your father was and all his influences. Only you can fashion yourself into the man you are meant to be, Julian."

He blinked, incredulous. "With everything I've just told you, do you truly believe me to be a worthy father for this child?"

Tessa understood the sudden rush of emotion elicited by his question would find its way to her voice, but there was no help for it. "No, I can see you wouldn't be," she said, the awful certainty sinking in with each beat of her fractured heart. "But not for the reason you think." She swallowed. "My child—*our* child—won't go through life bearing the burden of believing he or she carries a stain on their soul. My child will have no father, rather than that sort of father."

With that, she moved past him.

Though each step expanded the crack in her heart, she went on.

I'm not one of your equations to be solved.

She'd thought she could fix Julian, like she'd always fixed everything.

But she'd been wrong.

It was up to Julian to fix himself—or not.

Of all the truths revealed tonight that was the deepest one.

So, she had no choice but to leave him alone with his past and his own truth.

Which left her alone.

Except...she wasn't alone.

Her hand settled on her stomach, even as the tears broke free and streamed down her cheeks. She had a companion and a responsibility as she stepped forward into the future, though it felt as if her heart fully broke in two as a determination solidified within her.

Julian would no longer be involved in her life in any shape or form.

So, though the future that lay ahead was uncertain, she carried that single certainty with her into it.

Though she wanted the man she was leaving behind with every ounce of her being...

She must let him go.

CHAPTER TWENTY-SIX

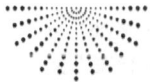

A FORTNIGHT LATER

*J*ulian's day started with solid intention.

The first in a string of ten that had.

It was a Monday, and that helped.

All he had to do was follow the usual Monday momentum from home to Tattersall's to White's to Brewster's Boxing Salon to the Cheapside townhouse.

The last stop wouldn't be the same considering he'd called off the arrangement with his mistress. He hadn't seen her in weeks— since the night he'd met Tessa, actually. So, he'd sent her a note, putting an official end to their dealings. The one hundred pounds that had accompanied the missive would've softened the financial blow.

Anyway, he'd lost the appetite for a mistress.

Really, his appetite had narrowed its craving to a single woman—no other would do.

He supposed he could go to the townhouse and catch up on his reading.

First, in accordance with the established Monday flow, it was Tattersall's.

A disaster from the start.

He hadn't bothered to research a single horse, leaving him unprepared to enter the bidding—which left him standing around, unoccupied and available for conversation with any and every young buck, old lech, and in-between waster who shambled his way.

After all, who didn't enjoy the company of the Marquess of Ormonde?

Except today something was...*off*.

He wasn't sure if it was that his smile didn't reach all the way to his eyes or that his responses tended toward a grunt or a generalized air of malcontent, but conversations were dying away as quickly as begun, those young bucks, old leches, and in-between wasters fading into the crowd and scratching their heads over this sudden and inexplicable change in the Marquess of Ormonde.

Without joy, Julian had taken himself off to his next stop—*White's.*

So it was, equally without joy, at White's he'd remained long past the midday repast and deep into the afternoon hours as they made their turn toward evening, well past his appointment at Brewster's and whatever reading he'd thought to accomplish in the Cheapside townhouse, holding an as-yet untasted tumbler of whiskey in his hand and a thought in his mind.

Nothing in his life was clicking into place.

Not since Tessa.

The life he'd led before her introduction into it no longer shrugged onto his shoulders like a well-worn, familiar coat.

It refused to fit.

Simply, she'd rendered his old life useless to him.

He considered the whiskey in his hand. He wouldn't be the first to quell an unsettled mind with spirits.

Still, he couldn't make himself bring the tumbler to his mouth.

Not yet, anyway.

So, he sat in this worn-in leather armchair and waited for the need to seek sweet, blessed relief to overwhelm him.

Word must've reached White's that Ormonde had taken to a foul and morose state of mind, for beyond the servers seeing to any needs or whims that struck his fancy, he hadn't been approached by a single, solitary lord.

No one knew what to do with an openly morose Marquess of Ormonde.

Himself included.

How long could one realistically contemplate the hue and viscosity of whiskey swirling inside a crystal tumbler, anyway?

Tessa was with child.

That was the long of it.

And the short of it.

And the everything in between.

Since she'd revealed the fact, he hadn't experienced a moment's peace. The reasons were myriad, but the main one—the one haunting his every moment, waking and sleeping—was that she'd absolved him of responsibility.

He snorted, no humor in it. She'd more than *absolved* him of responsibility. She'd determined—*resolved*—he would have none.

The fact kept battering him without cease.

My child will have no father, rather than that sort of father.

It was the last four words that wouldn't let up.

That sort of father...

Him.

He'd made a child with Tessa—and he would have no part of his or her life.

Inconceivable.

Yet...hadn't she been in the right?

His firmly held belief had long been that it would be wrong to sire a child, yet...this child would be with Tessa. How could a child with her be wrong?

That was the question that rattled long-held, firm beliefs apart.

Still, more plagued his mind—his reaction…his words…

I would've thought better of you than a marriage trap.

Even as they'd flown from his mouth, he'd known them to be altogether false. They bore no resemblance to what he truly thought in his mind—or felt in his heart. Pure reflex, borne of fear.

You're still that scrawny lad full of fear, aren't you?

She'd been right about that, too.

"Ah, Ormonde," came a jolly voice.

The Earl of Wrexford lowered himself into the chair opposite, the smile on his face as ever affable and pleasant. If there was a man in England who wouldn't notice the forbidding aura radiating from another man, it would be him. In the face of such persistent affability, Julian had no choice but to pull together the semblance of a smile and offer it in response. "Wrexford."

When a few ticks of time beat by and it became apparent that Julian would say no more, Wrexford forged straight in. "Word has it you recently attended a night's entertainment at Vauxhall Gardens in the company of some rather delightful ladies."

"Oh?"

Julian's memory of that night contained delight aplenty—painfully so—but nothing Wrexford would know anything about.

Wrexford uncrossed and recrossed his legs the other direction, looking as if he wouldn't mind loosening his cravat, too. "The company of the Calthorp sisters, that is."

Julian reacted before he could think, shoving forward in his chair, palms planted on the low table separating them. "If you think Lady Tessa would ever consider you—"

Wrexford's brow crinkled with confusion and horror, and Julian understood two things at once: He'd got it wrong—and he'd been on the verge of making a fool of himself.

Neither of which was an unusual experience of late.

"*Lady Tessa?*" asked Wrexford, flummoxed.

Julian settled back into plush leather. "She is one of the sisters."

"True," said Wrexford, as if the fact had only now occurred to him. "But perhaps she's a little too..." A suitable adjective to describe Lady Tessa eluded him.

"Complex for your tastes?" provided Julian.

Wrexford's face brightened. "Precisely," he said, clouds dispelled. "Besides, I'm not sure how anyone would go about courting her."

"The usual way?" Julian's sense of umbrage was utterly unreasonable—and he cared not.

"Well, yes, I suppose so," laughed Wrexford. "But it might be difficult since she's moving."

"Ah," said Julian. "I knew of the possibility."

It sounded like the Ladies Saskia and Viveca had gotten their way and would have Sloane Street for their circulating library, after all—as if there had been any doubt.

"I suppose the sister of a duke should have a fashionable Mayfair address, anyway."

The edge of bitterness wouldn't keep out of Julian's voice. He'd rather liked the less fashionable Sloane Street address— fewer prying eyes. Now, that lost time had the faraway feel of a dream that grew fainter with every passing moment.

He considered the whiskey in his hand. What was keeping him from it, anyway? The reasons became less clear the farther from the dream he traveled.

"*Mayfair?*" asked Wrexford. The man must've spent three of every four minutes in a state of confoundment.

"Not Mayfair?" asked Julian, understanding he'd forfeited any right to know Tessa's whereabouts. "St. James's Square?"

Surprising, that. He wouldn't have thought Tessa willing to share a roof with her brother and his duchess. They were so newly wed as to be tolerable only in small doses—especially first thing in the morning across a breakfast table, for example.

Wrexford snorted. "Try the Continent."

Julian snapped to. *"The Continent?"*

"Rumor has it that now she's a lady, she has a great yearning to do the Grand Tour." Wrexford shrugged, helpless to confounding facts. "I suppose dressing like a lord has given her some lordly ideas." His brow creased with sudden distress. "Do you suppose the Ladies Saskia and Viveca harbor such notions?"

Julian didn't hesitate. "Yes." But he didn't want to talk about the Ladies Saskia and Viveca. "Where did you come by this rumor?"

Some sources of tattle were more reliable than others.

"Oh, the news has been bandied about every drawing room in London these last few days. Surprised you haven't heard."

Julian understood.

This was about the child—*their* child.

There are ways to avoid such a fate for a child.

Tessa's child wouldn't be a bastard.

She had a plan.

Julian felt like he'd been punched in the gut.

This wasn't right.

Tessa had accepted the reality of the situation and was pursuing a solution.

And what was he doing?

Wallowing.

Wallowing in the past…Wallowing in regret.

This was worse than *not right*.

This was wrong.

He'd been wrong.

And it came to him in a flash.

Relief wouldn't be found at the bottom of this whiskey tumbler. His father's life and death had taught him that much.

Whiskey was a cheap escape.

Life is a tougher challenge than that. Life demands that we make something of ourselves.

He set the whiskey down.

If he drank, there would be no turning back for him.

At last, it sank into him what Tessa had seen all along.

He was nothing like his father.

He never had been.

He never would be.

The relief he sought wouldn't be found in escape—not when Tessa was offering him her hand.

No one can free you from that snare but yourself.

Yes, his father's blood flowed through his veins, but that fact didn't condemn his soul—or his child's.

Set yourself free, Julian.

The time had arrived to seize life...To seize the life Clarissa had been denied...To seize the life his father had been too much of a coward to face.

He was alive.

And now he must live.

Before it was too late to have the only life that would make living worthwhile.

A life with Tessa...

If she would have him.

CHAPTER TWENTY-SEVEN

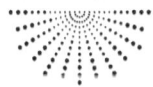

*T*essa kept her step light and her eye sharp about her.

It had been years since she'd ventured into Whitechapel environs—environs that took instant stock of interlopers and disposed of them quickly and quietly.

The address she sought still lay a few winding turnings of pocked cobbles ahead.

Blaze Jagger would be at this address—or, at least, that was what the Bow Street Runner had reported. Since Gabriel and Julian had seen fit to have Jagger investigated, why not her, too?

But it hadn't been his past or his business interests she'd sought information about. This report had been in regard to his private time. *Was he married?...Did he have siblings?...What was his favorite meal?...How did he spend time not engaged in business or slumber?*

The answers were: *No...Just the one half sibling from the correct side of the blanket—Lady Beatrix St. Vincent...Eel pie...*It was the answer to the final question that yielded a fact so unexpected and interesting that she'd had to see it with her own eyes.

Hence her now striding down a dark Whitechapel alleyway trying to keep her wits about her and her throat intact. The coming conversation with Jagger was a vital step toward being able to leave England.

She rounded a bend and slowed her pace. The address she sought would've passed unremarked but for the crowd of women and children gathered before it. A woman with a low-slung bosom and a forbidding scowl on her face was shouting, "Now, no need for all that, Nan. Have ye ever walked away with an empty basket?"

This was the place.

The interesting bit of information she'd received about Blaze Jagger was this: He funded the distribution of food and provisions one day a week to women and children in dire straits.

Half of Tessa hadn't believed it, but here was the proof before her eyes.

Steeled with purpose, she elbowed and shouldered her way to the front of the crowd, using her height and determination to her advantage. She reached the matron, who was quite emphatically not looking her way. Tessa waited...and waited. She cleared her throat...and cleared it again. "I need to speak to Jagger," she called out.

That got the cut of a suspicious eye. "Wants ain't needs."

Tessa wasn't sure what that meant or how it applied to her circumstances, but it meant something to the woman who stood between her and Jagger. She went for a different angle. "Tell him Tessa Calthorp needs to see him about some business."

She'd left off the *lady* part of her name, but the other woman heard it, anyway, as she cast a slow appraisal over Tessa's person, taking in the fineness of her garb and the high gleam of her boots. Tessa didn't shrink. Her adversary would understand this lady wasn't ceding an inch of ground until she'd had her say with Jagger.

At last, the woman snorted and disappeared inside the building, eliciting frustrated groans from the crowd. Tessa sensed her popularity diminishing by the second. To her relief, a different woman appeared at the door holding a basket full of vegetables—potatoes, carrots, leeks, turnips, parsnips, and such—and another woman crowded at her side with a basket of meats that ranged from pork joint to whole chickens.

The first matron appeared, catching Tessa's eye and giving a curt nod that spoke of both annoyance and resignation. She'd wanted to send Tessa packing.

When she disappeared into the dim recesses of the building, Tessa took it as her cue to follow, brushing past the women handing out provisions and stepping directly into a long, narrow corridor. Muted voices drifted from the other end, growing in volume as they approached a square room, its walls lined floor to ceiling with baskets and boxes containing all manner of foods. From the few snippets Tessa had caught, Jagger was listening to an accounting of inventory.

It was only after the conversation concluded that Jagger turned to Tessa. "So, you've discovered my dirty secret, have you?" The roguish grin that accompanied the words didn't make it to his eyes.

Any sense of pique Jagger might harbor made no difference to Tessa. "You and I need to talk."

"Before you're off to the Continent?"

Of course, Jagger would've heard.

"Aye," she said. "In private."

He lifted an ironic eyebrow before leading her into an adjoining room, this one smaller and appearing to serve a variety of functions—walls of shelving that indicated storeroom; cot in the corner indicating sometime sleeping quarters; rectangular table indicating impromptu office. The door clicked shut behind him, and he propped a shoulder against the doorjamb, crossing his arms over his chest.

Tessa cocked a hip onto the edge of the table. Before she spoke, she took one last measure of Jagger. It wasn't too late to change her mind.

SOFIE DARLING

Actually, it was.

She was to be a mother. The trajectory of her life was irrevocably altered.

"I've given the problem of you some thought."

A shocked laugh escaped Jagger. *"The problem of me?"*

Tessa didn't crack a smile. She was here on serious, life-altering business—and he would soon know it.

"Really, the solution to the problem of you has been before my eyes the entire time."

Any lingering amusement turned quizzical. "There's a solution to me?"

Tessa nodded, quite certain. "I finally arrived at what it is you truly want."

"And what is that?" he asked with the condescending air of a man humoring a woman.

"Legitimacy."

His condescension fell away in an instant, and his jaw tensed. Tessa had hit the mark dead center.

He gave a shrug that would suggest indifference to the casual observer—but Tessa wasn't observing him casually. "So," he said, "you know about my interesting parentage."

"Aye," she said. "But that's not the legitimacy you want—at least, I don't think it is—and it's certainly not the sort of legitimacy I can offer you."

His brow lifted. "You're here to offer me legitimacy?"

"I am."

"I'll humor you." *But not for long*, his eyes said. "What sort of legitimacy is that?"

"I'm here to sell you a share of The Archangel."

The air went dense, the sudden tension a near solid object. Emotion flickered behind Jagger's eyes, and she knew it for what it was—*hunger*. She was speaking to the deepest desire hidden within the darkest corner of Blaze Jagger's heart. The desire he kept concealed even from himself, but which drove and fired his relentless ambition every waking hour. To make a place for himself in the world—and for that place to be deemed worthy of respect.

The London streets were a tough life for a lone wolf.

His eyes narrowed with suspicion. "What's your angle?"

She'd expected the question. "No angle."

"You think because I give food to the poor, that makes me a worthy man?"

Tessa shook her head, firm. "I spent enough of my youth in the rookeries. I know better."

His air of suspicion abated not a whit. "What is this, then?"

Time to get to business. "You're buying Lydon's debt all over Town, and you need to stop."

"Now that you're a nob, you're protecting your own?" he asked in false affront.

"You need to stop for yourself."

Jagger snorted, but the hunger hadn't faded from his eyes.

"You have a sister," continued Tessa.

"She doesn't have the faintest idea of my existence." No mistaking the bitterness in his voice.

"But you know of hers. If you call Lydon's debt, you will destroy her, too."

Jagger's jaw clenched and released. "She's a *lady*. She'll be all right."

Tessa wasn't so certain. After their conversation at the Derby, she'd been left with the sense that something in Lady Beatrix St. Vincent's life wasn't quite right...

But she wasn't here to sort the family problems of others. Her own were enough to keep her fully occupied presently. "So, do you want it?"

"You're offering to sell me a share of The Archangel," said Jagger, slowly, as if needing to hear the words aloud again to confirm their authenticity.

"Aye."

"What about your dear brother?" he asked, following the logic. "I would be in business with a duke?"

Tessa shook her head. She already had this part sorted. "A portion of his share is being sold to Mr. Dupratt, floor manager of The Archangel, and Monsieur Ricard, our doorman."

"Is that the brick wall of a Frenchman?"

"The very one."

Jagger snorted. "You think he'll be enough to keep me in line?"

"Perhaps."

He gave that moment's consideration. "What would my share be?"

"Dupratt and Ricard will each have a ten percent share. Gabriel and I will each retain five percent."

"Which leaves me with seventy percent." Jagger cocked his head speculatively. "I thought you were getting out."

"This *is* us getting out," she said on a wry laugh.

"So, you won't let me have the whole lot, eh?"

"You will want us somewhat in." She'd thought this through, thoroughly.

"And why is that, milady?"

Tessa noticed Jagger enjoyed putting on a thick East End accent when it suited him, to see if he could catch her on the back foot.

"Your own good sense." She held his gaze steadily. "Dupratt and Ricard know the patrons and the business of a gaming hell that caters to the highest tier of society. They will ensure continuity. You will need them. As for Gabriel and me…" She lifted her hands, helpless to the ways of the world. "You'll have the title of the Duke of Acaster at your back."

Jagger went stone still, his mind turning each and every one of Tessa's points over. His mouth gave a bitter twist. "I'll always be the dirt under their feet, though, won't I?"

"It's your choice."

"*Choice?*" he scoffed. "You think the life I've led has been by *choice*? It's been survival from the moment I squalled my first breath. But then, what would you know of that, *my lady*?"

"A bit," Oh, where to start..."The death of my parents six months apart when I was nine years old. Then it was scratching and clawing for years to keep out of the workhouse and pick-pocket gangs and hold my family together. You're not the first or the last person who has gotten through days and years just surviving." Her hands were clutching the edge of the table. Finger by finger, she released them. "Of course, the *ton*—the lords and gentlemen The Archangel caters to—they know nothing of that. Success scraped up from the dirt doesn't make you noble in their eyes. Only blood can make you noble, and you came by yours on the wrong side of the blanket."

She didn't believe in mincing words when they were the truth.

Jagger gave a dry snort. "And yours was come by on the correct side."

"Through some improbable twist of fate, yes," she acknowledged.

"And this choice you speak of?" he asked, returning to the main conversational thread.

"It's not complicated." Tessa spread empty hands wide before her. "You can prove them right—or you can prove them wrong."

Jagger sucked his teeth in dismissal. "You said it yourself. I don't have the right sort of blood."

Ah. This very intelligent man who never missed an angle was missing this one. "But isn't all this in the eye of the beholder? You can prove them right or wrong in *your* eyes, Blaze." It was the first time she'd called him by his given name, and it felt right for this conversation. "When you look in the mirror, who is the man you see? A man who is the dirt beneath their feet? Or a man who is worthy?"

Though she was speaking these words to Blaze Jagger, there

was another man to whom she could be speaking with very few alterations.

She couldn't think about that man right now.

His head canted subtly. "And you think I could be a worthy man?"

She held his gaze without wavering. "I do." She went on. "You're intelligent and capable, Blaze. You're a man who sees what he wants out of life and goes after it. Gabriel and I are much the same as you."

He considered those words for a solid minute, and Tessa waited. Then he pushed off the doorjamb and closed the distance between them, his hand extended. She was meant to shake it— and that handshake would be the true point of no returning. Life as she knew it—the life she'd built brick by carefully placed brick —would irrevocably alter. In an instant, that life would be the past.

But wasn't it already? Wasn't the child curled in her belly proof of that?

This child was her future—and she would have it no other way.

Her hand met Jagger's halfway, and they shook on the deal.

"I'll be keeping Lydon's debt," he stated.

She'd expected as much. "But hold it just for now. It only makes good business sense."

"Ah," he said on a nod that took Tessa's meaning. "If I call the debt and bankrupt one of their own, I'll be branded a villain by the very nobs I'm fleecing at The Archangel."

"The club would fail within a year."

"I'd only be cutting off my nose to shame my face."

"And that's not a face you'd be keen to have staring you down in the mirror every day." Tessa pushed off the table. "My solicitors will have the contract delivered to you by evening."

As she exited the room, Jagger's voice sounded at her back. "Why me?"

Her step didn't falter as she said over her shoulder, "Everyone deserves the chance to fulfill their potential."

Easily, she retraced her steps out of the building, sparing a nod for the matron guarding the door. Her feet hit cobblestones that had grown slick from the light mist that had enshrouded the city while she'd been dealing with Jagger.

Now the final item was ticked off her list. Nothing was stopping her from leaving England and proceeding with her plan.

And no one stopping her, either.

The unresolved knot she'd carried with her this last fortnight tightened in her chest. But she'd learned how to walk on with it by putting one foot in front of the other. She'd point herself in the trajectory of her altered life and follow its logic to inevitable destinations. The first had been arrived at easily.

Simply, being a gaming hell owner and a mother weren't compatible roles for her, a hurdle easily surmounted by the deal just struck with Blaze Jagger.

Next for her and her child was a destination quite literal—the Continent. There, she would remain for the duration of her confinement and a few years beyond. A fictional husband of convenience would be invented and almost as quickly killed off by a swift-moving fever, leaving her a widow and, most importantly, her child legitimate.

The plan was decently sound, as long as she stayed away from English society abroad. Further, it was a plan that allowed her to proceed with her life.

Even if it did nothing to soothe the riot of emotions that yet scrambled through her. *Hurt...anger...frustration...ache...*And that other—*annoying*—emotion that yet—*improbably*—remained.

Love.

She now understood why love was so precious. To experience, then lose it, was no small thing. Love was nothing to bandy about. One must gift it with great care.

But how did one go about being careful with love? Didn't its arrow take a trajectory of its own deciding?

It seemed to Tessa the two participants had little choice in the matter.

Except…

There was a choice.

To accept love—or turn away from it.

Julian had made his choice.

And now she was making hers.

CHAPTER TWENTY-EIGHT

NEXT DAY

*T*essa stepped foot inside the Sloane Street townhouse and knew she wasn't alone.

And she should have been.

The house had been empty of servants these last three days.

Blaze Jagger, her mind provided the next instant.

No. They had an understanding and had shaken on it. Jagger wasn't the most upstanding citizen, but he had a code.

Her ear picked up a muted *clank* from the back of the house—a kitchen sound.

She left the door unbolted behind her in case she needed a hasty exit and made her step light as a cat's. Instead of making directly down the corridor, she took a quick detour into the drawing room. Beside the fireplace, she found it—the iron poker.

No one was taking it from her this time.

Slow and quiet, poker held high, she made her way down the corridor, kitchen sounds becoming more distinct with every inch forward. The low roar of water coming to the boil...the glassy *clink* of teacup against saucer...It sounded very much like...

Someone was preparing tea.

Which begged the question...

Who would break into her house to make tea?

She stopped shy of the doorway, tightened her grip around solid iron, stilled her breath, and ducked her head into the room. Her eye instantly lit upon an imposing male form incongruent with a small kitchen, his back to her, facing the stove but also well away from it, as if trying to figure out what to do with a pot of boiling water. Her heart performed a neat little trick and flipped over in her chest, and she lowered the poker.

Julian.

The immediate emotion was joy unlike any she'd ever experienced, so bright and so buoyant within her chest that she might float away with it. But the emotion that followed quick on its heels was much more complex—an emotion that held her feet firmly to the ground. Her brow crinkled into a deep furrow, and a notion slammed into her.

She was furious with this man.

In fact, like that pot of water on the stove, she was boiling with it.

She gave her throat a light clearing, so as not to startle him. No scaldings would happen on her watch.

He tossed an unconcerned glance over his shoulder before half turning, rueful smile curving his mouth, tempting the anger within her to cool. "I seem to have reached an impasse," he said, apologetic.

She'd been determined not to speak, but she found herself saying, "A kettle would've made it easier." She'd never been able to resist imparting a bit of instruction.

He nodded. "Ah."

The man had obviously never made tea. But then, he was a marquess, why should he have?

"You'll want to slide the pot off the heat."

He did as instructed, and Tessa tried not to let the well-worn rhythm of teamaking soothe her. She didn't want to feel at ease with this man.

She was too angry with him.

"I brought tea," he said.

It would've been a superfluous statement, except he jutted a stubbled chin that hadn't seen the sharp side of a razor in days toward the kitchen table. Arrayed on its surface were all manner of meats, cheeses, breads, pasties, and mysterious other foods wrapped in linen.

"I wasn't sure what you would have the appetite for, what with your, *erm*, condition," he said, stumbling inelegantly over the words.

"My *condition*?" she asked, knowing full well his meaning.

"I've heard women get cravings for this or that." He looked as if he might begin perspiring. "I wanted to be prepared."

She might've found his thoughtfulness sweet—if she hadn't a rather large bone to pick with this man.

Even so, an annoying part of her still might.

Her eye caught on a tin—*tea*. She was moving before she could catch herself, her curiosity too strong to resist. "Is the tea black or green?"

"It's from Japan, if that helps."

She cut him a surprised glance. "*Japan?*" Goods from Japan were incredibly difficult to procure as the Japanese only traded with the Dutch and Chinese.

"Through a merchant in Limehouse."

That got a lift of Tessa's eyebrows. The truly excellent rare teas could be found in Limehouse, if one knew the right people. She reached for the tin. "It'll be green, then," she said, taking refuge in facts rather than the emotion this—*sweet...thoughtful*—gesture sparked inside her. "The water needs to cool for four or five minutes before you pour. The leaves will be too delicate to stand up to water just off the boil."

She prised the lid off the tin. It was the aroma that hit her first —fresh and grassy, like the scent lifting off a spring garden on a dewy June morning. Her eyes drifted shut with pleasure, then opened. Contained within the tin weren't leaves, like she'd expected, but a green powder that held an otherworldly glow.

Julian saw the question in her eyes and answered. "Matcha tea."

"I've heard of it from various traders, but I've never been able to buy it." She hesitated. "You can't have known this tea existed."

A smile at once wry and boyish curved his mouth, lit within his summer-blue eyes. An ache twisted through her gut. "I didn't."

"Then how did you know to track it down?"

"I simply asked for the rarest tea in the world." A dry laugh sounded through his nose. "The answer was more complicated." Another laugh. "I thought I would need to hire a Bow Street Runner. But I managed, in the end."

And Tessa saw the tea for what it was.

A gift—and an apology.

She wasn't ready for the apology yet, but she very much wanted to taste this tea.

"I'm not sure how to prepare matcha," she said, contemplatively. "My finest strainer, I think."

Julian stepped back and ceded the space to her, as she assembled the tea-making essentials. She felt him standing awkwardly behind her. The mistress of this kitchen hadn't asked him to take a seat—and she wasn't about to.

Not yet.

Not until she was good and ready.

She spooned a few dollops of matcha into the strainer and reached for a large ladle before pouring sufficiently cooled water over the powder.

"The merchant said it only needs a minute to steep," Julian provided.

The minute dragged by in silence, each second keenly felt. But years of running a gaming hell and existing just on the correct side of the law—and a few times on the other side of it—had taught Tessa many important lessons.

One of them was the usefulness of silence—to gather one's thoughts...to draw them out like a poultice on a wound...to sweat out one's adversary.

All three, if managed correctly.

Even a gift of the rarest tea in the world wasn't enough to solve the issues that lay between them. If they were to stand a chance, it was what lay *within* them that would have to be drawn out.

But first, perhaps, best to begin with the obvious.

She removed the strainer from the teapot and set it aside. At last, she turned and indicated Julian take a seat at the table. She poured for both of them before sitting in the chair opposite, facing him.

Now, for the obvious question..."I take it you'll tell me why you've broken into my home?"

* * *

To TELL *you I love you and can't go on existing another day without you.*

Julian couldn't very well say that.

Tessa would toss him out on his ear—and rightly so. He didn't have the right to speak such words to her.

Not yet, anyway.

Instead, he settled for, "To bring you sustenance."

Her eyebrows lifted. "In the form of the rarest tea to be found in London?"

"Aye."

"That's...extravagant."

Julian held her eye. "Not when it comes to you."

Her gaze slid away and took in the feast spread across the table. She wasn't ready to hear those words.

He tore off a hunk of bread and paired it with a slice of

cheese. He hadn't been sure which foods to bring, so he'd asked Cook to pack a little of everything in the kitchen.

A little of everything in a marquess's kitchen—even one who lived alone and didn't entertain—was considerable.

He cleared his throat. "An interesting rumor about you is spreading through London."

"Oh?" she asked around a bite of mutton and potato pie.

"That you're leaving for the Continent."

Somehow, he'd been able to speak the words that had been clogging his throat for twenty-four straight hours.

She swallowed. "Italy."

Like that, rumor turned to fact, and the dread churning his gut turned into a solid object.

Of course, he'd known it for the truth the instant he'd entered the townhouse today. Though Tessa hadn't been home, it had felt empty of her in a greater way—as if cleared of her essence.

"Not keen to see summer end, I suppose," he said, lightly, to fill the unbearable silence that had drawn out.

A complex mixture of emotions passed behind her eyes. "All seasons come to an end."

Julian's stomach twisted like a towel wrung dry.

Pleasure...joy... That was all he wanted to bring this woman. And he'd seen as much shining in her eyes when she'd opened the tin of matcha tea. But what shone out at him now was the very opposite. *Wariness...pain...hurt.*

And now she was speaking of seasons coming to an end—*their* season coming to an end.

He must make it right.

Two simple words were the correct starting place..."I'm sorry."

Of a sudden, her chair scraped across pine floorboards, and she was shooting to her feet, anger blazing within her eyes, illuminating them with a white-hot flame.

Anger she had every right to.

With determined efficiency, she gathered dirty dishes and brought them to the sink where she began rinsing. Julian supposed it was no accident she chose a task that kept her back to him.

He settled into his chair and watched her in silence. She looked very much like herself. The signs of pregnancy weren't showing yet. He thought of the months to come, of the changes they would bring to her, and he wanted to be there for every single one of them.

At last, the clattering at the sink fell silent, not a dish left to be done. Yet she continued standing with her back to him.

"Tessa," he said, her name a soft susseration on quiet air.

Turmoil radiated from the too-still lines of her body.

"Tessa," he repeated.

Her head canted to the side, presenting him with her profile.

"Let me have my say," he said. "Then I'll leave if you like."

A moment's hesitation, then…"You can talk while I pack."

Swiftly, without a backwards glance, she was out of the kitchen and halfway down the corridor before Julian pushed to his feet. Up the stairs she went, him careful not to follow too closely at her heels or stare too openly at the sway of hips beneath skirts.

It was only when they were standing in the room that it occurred to them both at once that she'd led him to her bedroom.

"Well," she said.

And hiding just behind the word Julian detected bemusement and, perhaps, the hint of a smile.

How he wanted to close the distance between them and kiss that slightly kicked-up corner of her mouth.

Wanted it with every cell of his being.

So, he propped a shoulder against a bedpost and said, "I've been a fool."

Those were the words he should've led with earlier.

The blaze of anger in her eyes cooled a few degrees. "Fear can do that to a person." Still, a guarded quality hung about her.

"*Fear*," he said. "I'd lived with it for so long, it felt like a natural part of me. It would've gone on that way for the rest of my life, if not for one fated occurrence."

A slow moment beat past until her curiosity drew her into asking, "Which was?"

"I met you."

Silence fraught with the words spoken and the ones yet unspoken stretched the air thin and tight.

"I wanted you, Tessa. The wager wasn't more than that—a chance to have you. I had to have you." He swallowed. "Which made you all my fears come to life."

The hard edge in her eyes softened. "I hadn't realized I was such a gorgon."

The hope held tight in his chest peeled back a layer—but it hadn't yet received permission to fully expand. He needed to keep talking…"I loved you—I *love* you. But the old fear…" He gave his head a shake. "It didn't know what to do with love."

Her eyes shone with empathy, as she said, "All it knew to do was turn it into pain." She took an unconscious step forward. "A reflex protective of the self, because there is no safety in love."

She was now close enough that he could reach out and touch her if he chose.

He kept his hands at his sides.

Not yet.

"But, Tessa, you showed me another side of love—its true side."

The hope he felt now shone in her silver-blue eyes. "Oh?"

"Love is not only how one feels about another person. It's as much what one feels about oneself."

She reached out, bridging the distance between them, and took his hand. "I do love you, Julian."

He swallowed against the sudden lump of joy in his throat.

"But," she continued, "love might not be enough for us."

Of a sudden, he couldn't breathe. The very real possibility existed that he might lose her. He searched his mind for the right words before he realized they wouldn't be found there.

The right words would come from his heart.

"You revealed the man I was meant to be, Tessa, and he is here before you, still growing in the light...in *your* light." He threaded his fingers through hers and squeezed. "I won't be perfect. I will make missteps. But I will always strive and fight for *us*." With his other hand, he reached out and hesitated. "May I?"

Tears shining in her eyes, she nodded.

He placed his palm on her still-flat belly. "I will always fight for you and our child."

"And yourself, Julian."

"You deserve better than me, my darling Tessa."

She shook her head, the adamancy in her eyes enough to rival her sisters. "What I deserve or what you deserve doesn't matter. You are the man for me, Julian. The solution to our equation is simple. One and one makes *us*." Doubt flickered in her eyes. "But..."

"*But?*"

"How can I trust..."

"*Me?*"

"*This.* That you won't wake up in a week or a year and allow the fear to take over again?" She shook her head, fervent. "I cannot—*will not*—allow a fear of bad blood to touch our child."

A reasonable response, he understood with his mind. He hoped his heart had the correct answer.

"The fact that you love me, Tessa, has shown me something. I need to love myself to be worthy of loving you. And that's all I want—to be worthy of you...to be worthy of our love. To prove myself worthy of it every day—and I shall. That is my solemn vow to you and our child."

He dropped to his knees before her and pressed his mouth to

her stomach, hoping he'd had the correct words in his heart. And yet, still more needed airing. He tipped his head back and met her eyes. "You freed me."

She lowered herself to join him on the floor. Their eyes on an even plane, she said, "You freed yourself."

A chuckle rumbled through his chest. "You're allowed to take due credit."

She smiled and ran her hand through his hair. "As are you. I might've shown you the path, but you've done the uphill work of treading it. I didn't solve or fix you. It's always been your work to make yourself whole."

"Ah, but there you're not entirely correct, my darling."

Her brow lifted in tolerant disbelief. "I'm not?"

"It's love, Tessa, that makes us whole, and that must be shared." He pulled her close. "I want you. I want our child. I want a dozen children—"

"Let's not get carried away," she cut in with a laugh.

"The more love, the merrier."

He cradled the nape of her neck and pulled her mouth to his. All the vows now and soon-to-be spoken demanding to be sealed with a kiss.

One and one makes us.

Within its simplicity lay its strength—the solid foundation for the rest of their days.

Some days would be perfect; others rotten.

But he and his darling Tessa would face them together.

EPILOGUE

NONSUCH CASTLE, FIVE YEARS LATER

*C*larissa's fifth annual birthday fête hadn't started as a children's pony race.

To Tessa's way of thinking that idea wasn't at all a safe or wise proposition given the ages of the participants ranged from three to four years old.

But she'd been assured by Julian, reassured by Rake and Gemma, then further reassured by Celia, that the children would be unharmed, as each child would have a parent supervising them for the duration of the race.

However, it wasn't the adults who convinced her to give over, but rather her daughter's pleading summer-blue eyes that perfectly matched her father's. "Mummy," said Clara, who had been named after her aunt. Her year-younger brother, James, excitedly hopped up and down at her side, game for anything that involved his sister. "Papa will be there. He would never let anything happen to me."

As their third child—a baby son by the name of Ian—bounced on Tessa's hip, she flicked a glance toward Julian, who gave a sure nod.

And that had done it.

She would never doubt or diminish the beautiful trust between Julian and their three children.

With a sigh that wasn't yet convinced of the wisdom of the venture, she'd relented and walked to a relatively secluded spot on the hillside as ponies and children were assembled.

"Sister," said Gabriel, angling close, his own boy, Andrew, settled onto his shoulders, while Celia tended their three-year-old daughter on her pony. Clio wasn't about to let her cousins race without her. "I would've thought you could be relied upon to offer the voice of reason."

Tessa laughed. She knew her brother's game. "So you wouldn't have to be the one to tell your wife and daughter *no?*"

Gabriel shifted uncomfortably, but didn't deny it.

"This is what comes of marrying the horse-mad," she said with a long-resigned sigh. Like her brother's, her gaze was fastened upon the wrangling of ponies and children in the distance. "One begets horse-mad children."

Gabriel shook his head. "There truly is no cure for it, is there?"

"Merely acceptance, I'm afraid."

Gabriel grunted, looking disinclined to further conversation as he concentrated all his mental faculties on the continued well-being of his firstborn child.

It was the sort of high-summer day that dazzled, all the colors in the world more vivid than usual—the yellow of the sun...the blue of the sky...the green of the grass...

And how right it was, for today was Clarissa's birthday, no longer a dark day of grief, but a sunny day of celebration when all their family and friends, and local villagers, too, gathered at Nonsuch Castle for an afternoon and evening of fun, games, food, and pony rides.

Tessa nuzzled her face into Ian's baby-soft neck. "Leave it to that lot to turn pony rides into a horse race."

Ian blew a juicy raspberry of agreement and reached his

pudgy hand out in the direction of his sister and brother. Only a few more months now before this little chap was on two feet and dogging their every step.

"Shall we judge the finish line?" she asked, her feet already on the move. She flicked a nod of farewell toward Gabriel and entered the flow of the fête, which, a few hours in, already had the relaxed, settled feel of a good party.

She greeted one and all in a manner befitting marchioness, hostess, and friend, just a few of her many roles in this life she'd formed with Julian. She even remained part owner of The Archangel, which was still the most exclusive gaming hell in London. Somehow, the notoriety and undeniable, dangerous magnetism of Blaze Jagger had only amplified its preeminence.

But none of those roles held a candle to the two always topmost on her mind—those of wife and mother.

This life with Julian was all she'd hoped it could be—and more.

There was so much she hadn't known to hope for on that long-ago day when she'd spoken her first I-love-you to him. The incomparable joy of their wedding day...the exhausted joy of the birth of their first child and somehow, improbably, that exact same surge of joy with each child after...the joy of their life together as mother and father...as husband and wife...as friends and lovers.

"Mama!" came the shout.

Tessa's hand flew to her forehead, and she squinted in the direction Clara's voice had come from. Her parental mind worked a quick calculation of tone and timbre. No wobble...So, not teary. No fractiousness...So, not exhausted to pieces. No fear...So, no injury.

She could hear the shout for what it was and relaxed.

Her child's shout of pure happiness.

Perched comfortably atop her beloved pony, Sir Galahad, Clara waved ecstatically, and a baby giggle of delight bubbled up from Ian, who returned the wave with a wild abandon that surpassed his sister's. Tessa's heart expanded another increment. Perhaps she and Julian *should* try for that dozen...

She cupped a hand to her mouth and called out, "I'll judge the race."

From her place at the finish line, she watched the competitors assemble, but she couldn't say exactly who the competitors were. The children on their ponies—or the parents. To a one, their eyes held the glint of competitive anticipation—from Julian with his deceptively amiable smile to Rake and Gemma who were very obviously imparting racing wisdom to their respective three- and four-year-old sons, Charles and Daniel, to Celia whose daughter Clio listened attentively to every word her mother spoke into her ear.

Oh dear, it truly would be a race.

In the absence of a starting gun, she held up an arm. "Competitors to your places," she called.

A crowd composed of Nonsuch's servants, local villagers, friends, and family assembled to the sides of the "race" course, which was but thirty or so yards long. She spotted Eloise and her Mr. Lancaster, as Tessa ever thought of them though they'd been a married couple for as long as she and Julian. They'd arrived with their baby daughter, along with Saskia and Viveca, who continued to reject all suitors and run their circulating library and publishing house with a success that continued to increase year upon year.

"No false starts," Rake shouted to the amusement of the crowd, though the stern expression on his face indicated he didn't see the humor.

Julian flashed a wink Tessa's way, which she caught, even from this distance.

And even from this distance, that wink from her husband still set her heart aflutter.

Next, her arm swept down and all the ponies were off to the races.

What followed on the Nonsuch racecourse was, perhaps, the slowest horse race of all time.

Though the surface battle was waged between the children and their mounts, who looked to be having the time of their lives as they coaxed their ponies forward with words of encouragement and promises of treats. But the fiercest battle was presently raging within the parents as they balanced the instinct to keep children recently on the other side of toddlerhood safe with the need to urge their children on to a win. After all, in any competition there had to be a winner and it might as well be oneself—a lesson one was never too young to learn.

It was the first instinct that won out as they kept the ponies to a walk.

A *brisk* walk.

But as all races came to an end, so did this one—eventually.

To the screaming delight of their children, it was Julian who ushered Clara and James to a tying win, the other ponies coming just a nose behind.

And if anyone protested the result, that was the story Tessa was sticking to. Knowing this lot, there would be plenty more races in the future.

"Home turf advantage," groused Rake, but with a smile tipping at the corners of his mouth.

Gemma laughed at her husband who was already spoiling for a rematch.

"Mama?" Clara was off her pony and tugging at Tessa's skirts.

Tessa lowered to a crouch, so she could meet her daughter's solemn eyes. "Yes, dearest?"

"Does a tie mean James and I are both second place?"

Julian's boisterous guffaw beat Tessa's. "She's been taking lessons from her aunts and uncles, it would seem," he said, as he, too, settled onto his haunches and gathered his family in his arms.

He'd never once wavered as husband and father, even in those rare moments when Tessa had felt a bit wobbly herself—childrearing wasn't for the faint of heart.

And that, her husband wasn't.

He was all heart—and safely tucked within that heart were the children and her.

And in those wobbly moments life was so adept at delivering unawares, there was no place she would rather be.

The End

ALSO BY SOFIE DARLING

All's Fair in Love and Racing

Odds on the Rake

The Duchess Gamble

Wager With a Siren

Shadows and Silk

Three Lessons in Seduction

Tempted by the Viscount

Her Midnight Sin

To Win a Wicked Lord

At the Pleasure of the Marquess

One Night His Lady

Nell and the Runaway Duke

ABOUT THE AUTHOR

Bestselling and award-winning author Sofie Darling's passion for historical romance began in middle school the moment she cracked open *Wuthering Heights* by Emily Bronte. An instant and enduring love affair was born.

Sofie spent much of her twenties raising two boys and reading every romance she could get her hands on. Once she realized she simply must write the books she loved, she finished her English degree and set pencil to paper. (Ticonderoga #2 is her quill of choice.)

When she's not writing heroes who make her swoon, Sofie enjoys a nice weekend hike, a visit to a crumbling medieval castle whenever she gets the chance, and a slightly codependent relationship with her beagle, Bosco. Visit her website.